Rogue Faction Part 2

Xander Weaver

Rogue Faction Part 2

Copyright © 2015 by Xander Weaver
ISBN 978-0-9904394-6-2 (eBook)
ISBN 978-0-9904394-5-5 (Trade Paperback)
www.XanderWeaver.com

Cover Design by Lee Roesner, Paradigm Graphic Design
Image sources by alexfiodorov/bigstockphoto.com and yuran-78/bigstockphoto.com

Release version: 1.0

—For my readers—

You share your valuable time with me, and I'm grateful.
Every book is an adventure we take together, and I look
forward to taking many more.

Chapter 1

Natasha watched the deserted city streets pass through the window of the small four-wheel drive truck Cyrus *borrowed* for their escape from *The Cuban*. The old truck's heater was running at full blast, but still did little to stave off the cold of night. Thanks to their rapid departure, Natasha didn't even have time to grab her coat. She had taken her guitar, though. The base rested on the floor between her feet. The instrument's neck was clenched in her white-knuckled grip while she watched billows of her warm breath hang in the air of the dark cabin.

The guitar was a special keepsake that Natasha had come to treasure in recent years, despite complicated and conflicted feelings relating to its origin. After tonight, she knew the instrument would mark another such memory. The body of the guitar had taken a bullet at some point, and since it had literally been strapped to her side at the time, it was a reminder of how close she'd come to being killed.

Though they'd driven in silence since leaving the bar, Natasha found herself casting curious glances at Cyrus from the corner of her eye. There were so many questions—she didn't know where to begin. Somehow silence seemed like the better alternative; letting him remain focused on their escape seemed logical. They drove slowly through the city, obeying posted speed zones. She noticed how his eyes followed an ever vigilant rotation, scanning the road as well as their periphery while still keeping watch on the rear facing mirrors.

As they took a turn at yet another intersection, Natasha was puzzled by their new direction. "Why aren't we returning to the compound?" she finally asked.

"We have to make a stop first," Cyrus said. His eyes never left the road.

After traveling several additional blocks, Cyrus took a long look at her. She was surprised by the uncertainty in his eyes. "How are you holding up?"

She laughed at the absurdity of the question. It had been a long time since she'd been shot at. "Just like old times," she said, with a roll of her eyes.

He checked the road, then glanced back at her for another long second, but said nothing. In that quick look, she saw pain and disappointment painted across his face.

They'd been shot at once before, in the middle of a mess that Cyrus—she knew him as Jon, back then—had gotten them into. It was the trouble that led to him leaving school, and ultimately brought about the end of their relationship.

"I'm sorry," she said quietly. "I didn't mean it that way."

He shrugged. His eyes still followed their patterned scan of the side and rearview mirrors. "I understand. But, to be honest, it wasn't me they were shooting at this time."

"Wait—. You're saying they were after me?" she stammered. "Why would they be after me?"

She realized, for the first time, that they were headed for the International Airfield. Cyrus had just turned onto a wide strip of road, what constituted as a highway on the island nation, leading directly to Kapros' largest airport.

"I told you before. We really need to talk," Cyrus said quietly.

She pursed her lips and glared at him. It was a withering look that spoke a thousand words, and a sentiment that would've been more effective if he weren't focused on driving.

"No kidding, I was never supposed to see you again. Wasn't that how witness protection works? You were never allowed to see anyone from your old life? No calls; no email? Nothing?" she wanted to rage on but stopped herself, mostly because she wasn't sure she could rein her emotions back in once she released them.

He shot her a crooked grin with a quick glance. "Did you really think I could stay away?"

"No," she admitted. "I didn't. But when I didn't hear from you for a month, I got worried. And when one month turned into three—and three turned to six…" A tear dropped from the corner of her eye and she felt a new flash of anger, this time aimed at herself. She'd made an internal promise to never have this conversation.

Natasha swallowed hard before speaking again. When her voice once again filled the cabin, it was little more than a hoarse whisper. "After six months, I realized you were never coming back." Wiping tears from both cheeks, she kept her eyes forward, aimed at the dark, lonely highway.

Realizing she was now throttling the neck of her guitar, she loosened her grip. Taking a deep breath, she let it out in a slow, silent puff of warm vapor. When that didn't help, she followed it with another. Reliving this pain yet again had brought more anger than she would've guessed possible. It was one thing to have Cyrus leave three years earlier. At the time, it wasn't as though he'd had much choice. Witness relocation was his only option. Unfortunately, it had been an option that didn't include her. So, as with everything else in his life, she'd been left behind.

It was only later Natasha realized that his relocation wasn't what it seemed. It wasn't that she couldn't go with him. She came to find out that the U.S. Marshal Service had put the option on the table—Cyrus had simply never given her the choice. So her pain was two-fold; it was the loss of him coupled with the unanswered question of why he'd never offered to take her with him that had been so difficult to live with.

Even at the time, the rational part of her mind knew they were just kids. They were both in their freshman year of college. Neither knew what it was that they didn't know about the world. But she knew that she loved him. She loved him in a way she'd never experienced before, and it made him the single most important thing in her life. It wasn't a logical feeling, especially since they'd been together only eight months when the bullets started flying. All she knew was that if he had asked, she would've relocated with him without a thought for her own safety. Natasha would've walked away from everyone and everything she'd ever known, just to stay by his side.

She cast a tear-streaked look in his direction and hoped he wasn't able to see her in the shadows of the truck. The last thing she needed was for him to know that his presence still had such a powerful effect on her. Even back then, she'd been sure—absolutely certain—that he shared her feelings. But what she never understood, the question she thought would never be answered, was how or why he could leave in such a cold manner if he really had loved her as deeply.

Now, no matter how badly she wanted to ask that question, she couldn't bring herself to speak the words. It was the reason she'd worked so hard to avoid him since he turned up at her home.

"We need to talk about what happened back then," Cyrus said finally. "I don't expect you to forgive me, but I want you to understand."

He looked her in the eye. "I believe I owe you at least that much."

The truck passed through the front gates of the International Airfield and they followed the signs pointing to 'Departures'. Natasha saw their path and immediately shot him an accusing look.

"Don't worry," he said in a calming voice. "We're not going anywhere. I'm retrieving something."

They drove past a series of sliding glass doors and the wide, multi-lane road that allowed for easy unloading of passengers. Beyond all of that was another small, curbside stop for a bus line which ferried passengers all over the island; the bus line had its own terminal at the airport for regularly scheduled routes.

Pulling to the curb, Cyrus shifted the gear selector into 'park' and looked around carefully. Following his eyes, Natasha confirmed that they were alone. There were no flights leaving at this late hour and, though the airport was technically still open, it was virtually deserted. Still, Cyrus was looking around more carefully than she expected.

"What's wrong?" she asked.

The concern was etched on his face. After a few moments of silence, he looked her in the eye. His face was largely cloaked in shadows but that couldn't conceal the intensity of his eyes.

"A three man team tried hitting me on the train," he offered. "There were only two guys back at the bar." This mission had started on a train leaving Paris on its way to Hamburg. Cyrus had been teamed with Agent Gladd, working to identify the courier transporting prototype hardware to Natasha's father. Three highly skilled assassins had nearly derailed the mission before it had begun.

At first she didn't catch his meaning. Then it clicked. "You think there might be another gunman out there somewhere?"

He exhaled, a puff of vapor clouding the air as he considered the question. "I wasn't able to identify the team on the train. I don't know if they were independents or part of an organization. If they were independent, anything goes. Most likely they would've been hired for a one-off job. They could be working in any configuration. But if they were part of a larger outfit, they'd be more organized and there's likely to be another man out there."

Natasha felt her jaw drop. His analysis of their situation was shockingly clinical and succinct. ...And chilling.

"You've changed." The words shot from her mouth before she realized she'd said them aloud.

He nodded. "A lot's changed in the last three years. Just promise that you'll let me explain things. I'm not saying it'll make everything alright. I just think there are things that need to be said—things you deserve to hear."

"Alright," she agreed. The truth was, she wanted to know what was going on. The subject was clearly important to him—his persistence, and the events of the last hour, had proven as much.

"Get whatever it is you need so we can get back to the compound. I have a feeling we won't be safe until we're back behind those walls."

Cyrus nodded again. "Keep the engine running. If you see anything suspicious, just honk. I'll be through those doors." He pointed to a set of double sliding glass partitions a few yards down the sidewalk, marking the entrance of the small bus depot.

Chapter 2

Passing through the automatic doors, Cyrus was grateful there were no metal detectors. He was still armed with the semiautomatic he'd taken off one of the shooters at the bar, and he didn't want to leave it in the truck.

The bus station was deserted. There was a small section of rowed seating near the door. Maybe three dozen utilitarian plastic chairs were lined up, waiting for a surge of traffic that Cyrus doubted the station would see, even at rush hour on a holiday. There was a ticket counter along the wall to the right, complete with a short series of switch back paths marked by vertical poles linked by retractable bands. They formed an orderly approach to three ticket windows, only one of which had a light on, even though it was empty. The other two windows were blocked by drawn shades.

At the back of the room stood a series of seven-foot tall lockers of varied shapes, and split into different sizes. Renting a locker was a simple matter. Anyone could rent a locker by simply dropping a series of coins through a slot in the locker door and pulling the key from the lock.

Cyrus walked around one row and found what he was looking for. Locker 211 was on the bottom; three feet by three feet square. After confirming the door was undamaged, he stood up and went to the small emergency light on the rear wall. Standing on the tip of his toes, he could just reach the top edge of the small wall-mounted light box. Running his fingers through the dust atop the box, he felt the key right where it was supposed to be. At least his support team had made good on the fallback plan. He would have to thank Luke Reid for that.

A moment later he used the key and pulled open the door to locker 211. It was a relief to find a small, black backpack—yet again, right where it was supposed to be. Removing it, he closed the locker as quietly as possible. Kneeling, he unzipped one of the pack's side compartments and retrieved a mobile phone. Though the phone looked like an off-the-shelf smartphone, the device had a state-of-the-art satellite uplink, ideal for field use because it couldn't be traced across local phone networks.

Tapping out a number from memory, the call was answered after the first ring.

"United Global," the voice greeted.

"Authentication: oscar bravo seven foxtrot," Cyrus said without pretense. "Put me through to Stalking Horse."

There was a hesitation on the part of the operator that wasn't lost on Cyrus.

"Please hold," the operator responded after only a second's delay.

Stalking Horse was Boone's code name. With all that had happened, Cyrus was overdue to check in. It was to be expected with an operation of this nature, but it was time to confirm that the mission was still on track. There was a barely perceptible click in the line before he heard the phone being picked up on the other end.

"Please authenticate, Livewire," a female voice requested from the other end of the line. Cyrus was almost certain he was talking to the Red Queen. That prospect was troubling.

"You first," he countered.

"Sierra victor two four four," the voice grumbled. *"Please authenticate."*

"Oscar bravo seven foxtrot," he muttered through clenched teeth. "What the hell is going on over there, Monica? They were supposed to connect me to Boone."

He heard the Red Queen exhale a lung full of air and knew something was wrong. "Boone's team was attacked in transit. There were casualties. Most of the team was wiped out. Two members are still missing and unaccounted for—Boone and Agent Hobbs." The Red Queen, aka Monica Fichtner, called the shots for the Coalition. For better or worse, she was the boss. Boone was Cyrus's immediate supervisor. Boone had been his training officer when he joined the group; he was also head of Field Operations. Hobbs was one of the agents teamed with Boone on the latest operation.

His mind spinning, Cyrus struggled to reconcile the unexpected information with what had just happened to him. Of the two of them, maybe Natasha hadn't been the one targeted at the bar, after all. "What the hell happened? Just tell me what you know."

"Boone's team was heading to intercept his target, Professor Ragsdale, at the University of Paris. Apparently they were ambushed along the way and the team sustained casualties."

"Wait——. You're saying that Boone never staged Ragsdale's injuries? He didn't fake his hospitalization?" Cyrus couldn't make sense of what he was hearing. Based on what he'd been told by Voss, Ragsdale was in the hospital, which would indicate that everything had gone according to plan.

"He never had the chance. But it looks like whoever ambushed Agent Boone's team attacked Ragsdale the same night. Ragsdale was hospitalized in the end, but we have no idea if he will recover. His surgeons are not optimistic."

Cyrus clenched his eyes tight and tried to factor this new information into the larger picture. No matter how hard he worked the facts, he couldn't force them into a logical scenario. He had a puzzle with a bunch of pieces that suddenly didn't fit.

"To be honest," the Red Queen continued. "We didn't think you were still operational. After Agent Gladd's report of what happened on the train out of Paris, we've been operating under the assumption that you were eliminated prior to reaching the Voss compound.

"We had eyes on the compound's front gates for over thirty-six hours after the incident on the train. When you didn't show, and with what happened to Boone's team, it seemed very likely that you'd been ambushed, as well."

Grinding his teeth, Cyrus decided that it wasn't the time to explain his need to improvise following the attack on the train. The Red Queen's information meant that Boone had been missing for over a week. It was possible he'd gone dark in response to the ambush. Cyrus even considered it likely, since an attack on the team prior to reaching their objective indicated that someone at the Coalition had leaked their plan.

It all boiled down to a very simple situation. Boone was either dead or he'd dropped off the grid. Either way, Cyrus knew he was on his own. The rest of the plan was scrapped. It was up to him to find out what was going on. He was the only one in the position to discover who was behind his attack on the train. It stood to reason that the same party had attacked Boone's team. Cyrus knew he needed to gather intelligence. It was the only way things would start making sense.

With his current mission in shambles and no reliable support, everything that happened from this point would require improvisation. While that might have panicked some field agents, it didn't bother Cyrus in the least. He did his best work when flying by the seat of his pants.

"I'm sending an extraction team," the Red Queen said. "We're getting you out of there. As of last week, half of our field operatives have been wiped out. We'll reel you in before we lose you too."

"Negative," Cyrus said in a calm, clear voice. "I'm staying. It's the only way we'll get to the bottom of this."

"Excuse me?" the Red Queen somehow managed to sound indignant while still seeming surprised. "Damn it, Cyrus! You're coming in now, whether you like it or not."

"If I come in now our guys died for nothing. But if I stay, I can find out who's behind this. They must be after Voss's work. It's the only thing that makes sense. All of this started with Voss."

"If you stay, I'll end up with another missing agent," she insisted. "As long as you're alive this isn't over. Come in now.

You can lead the investigation from here. We will find out what's going on and who's behind it."

Cyrus wasn't going to be talked out of it. Interestingly, he was pretty sure she knew as much. "Look, your conscience is clean. You ordered me back—but I'm seeing this through." He was nearly certain that the Red Queen didn't have a conscience and wouldn't know what to do with it if she suddenly acquired one.

"I'll contact you again when I have this sorted out," Cyrus concluded and tapped a button ending the call.

His mind ran wild with the new information. It was hard to believe. Could Boone really be gone? He was commonly considered to be the best that the Coalition had to offer. That someone had gotten the drop on him was hard to conceive, let alone believe. He was a living legend in the trade.

As Cyrus rose to his feet, a tiny tingling at the base of his skull told him something else was wrong. His first thought was to check on Natasha. Unfortunately, that thought was counter to his training, and his base instincts. When he rounded the corner of the locker, he walked directly into a swinging combat baton.

Caught unprepared and off guard, it was all Cyrus could do to spin away as he saw the sleek, polymer baton head for the bridge of his nose. As he spun, he folded at the knees and let the weight of his body pull him from the path of the weapon. As it was, he still took a glancing blow, though it missed its intended target and mostly slid across the back corner of his skull before impacting the end of the lockers with a thunderous clang.

Cyrus had captured only the vague impression of his attacker before the room was reduced to a blur by his own dodge and subsequent impact with the floor. But he knew the attacker's position. He kicked out hard with one leg the moment he hit the floor. The impact of his knee on his attacker was instant and he heard a grunt from the man as he absorbed the blow. Cyrus didn't wait for a counter attack. He was pulling the auto from the back of his jeans even as he fought to clear his vision and acquire a target.

Though he hoped to take his attacker from his feet with the kick, Cyrus realized that hadn't been the case. As he brought his gun around to take aim, the attacker landed a jarring kick across Cyrus's arm, sending the gun flying. Even before Cyrus could fully turn to face his opponent, he was struck by a devastating blow to the face.

Still on the floor from his initial attempt to dodge the baton, Cyrus slumped backward from the punch. The impact made his eyes water, reducing the room and his attacker to blurry blobs in his field of vision. Knowing his compromised sight was a major detriment, however brief, Cyrus took immediate action. He rolled off his backpack, slipping his arms out of the straps as he went. Halfway through the roll, Cyrus brought the pack up as a shield. A fraction of a second later he heard the barking report of two gunshots and felt the pack jolt violently in his hands.

While he was maneuvering the pack into position, Cyrus rapidly blinked the tears from his eyes. He slipped his hand into one of the pack's outer compartments in search of a defensive weapon. The backpack bucked from the impact of a third fired round just as he wrapped his hand around the grip of a revolver.

Cyrus didn't hesitate in the slightest. He knew he was lucky to catch the first shots with the small backpack. With only a slight adjustment for trajectory, he pulled the revolver's trigger, still unseen inside the compartment of the backpack.

The attacker's third shot was followed a second later by the more muffled rounds as they exploded from inside the black, nylon bag in rapid succession. His butt still on the floor, Cyrus was backpedaling across the tile while triggering the weapon. He slipped into the cover behind the end of the lockers at about the same time he heard his attacker's body crash against another row of the small, steel vaults. Another muffled thud marked the man's collapse to the floor.

Slipping the pack's zipper back more fully, Cyrus pulled a .357 revolver from the bag and swung it to cover himself. The room seemed silent, but Cyrus couldn't be sure. The thunder of gunfire still rang in his ears. He wiped the last of the fogginess from his eyes and quickly regained his feet.

As he peered around the corner of the lockers, Cyrus found a man dressed in dark jeans, boots, and a dark coat. He was sprawled across the tile floor. His attacker had pale white skin. A glassy sheen had settled over his eyes. There was a sizable pool of blood already spreading around his torso. One of the man's hiking boots twitched, but Cyrus knew it was only a postmortem spasm. He'd seen it before. His attacker was dead.

Pulling the phone from a compartment inside the backpack, Cyrus snapped off three photos of the man's face. One from the front, and profile shots from each side. He also leveraged the man's right hand into a position that allowed him to get a clear shot of the pads of each finger. The phone's high-resolution camera was designed for detailed identification work and could capture the loops and whorls that were common to fingerprints. Unfortunately, Cyrus was limited to snapshot photos of the man's right hand since his right arm had fallen across his body when he dropped. The left hand lay in a pool of blood. Cyrus knew that attempting to snap photos of the prints on that hand would lead to an unusual crime scene, and detectives asking questions he didn't want asked.

It was only a matter of time before authorities responded. *The Cuban* was located on the other end of the island. After what happened earlier, the incident would be pulling in most of the regular police force. Still, someone who had no relation to the real 'law and order' on the island would soon show up to investigate reports of gunshots at the airport.

Cyrus grabbed his attacker's discarded gun and baton. It took him nearly a minute to locate the gun he'd lost at the start of the scuffle. Once he had everything, he stuffed it into the bag and threw the backpack over his shoulder. A quick check of the body confirmed what he already suspected; the man lacked any form of identification. Even his clothing was devoid of branding tags. He carried nothing that hinted at his nationality, let alone his employer. He was a professional. Aside from the weapons and a small wad of cash, there was nothing on him. Disappointed, Cyrus tucked the revolver close to his side and headed for the door.

At the curb, he found that Natasha not only had the engine running, but she'd taken a place behind the wheel. Judging by the relief in her eyes, she must've heard the gunshots. He was impressed with her resilience given the circumstances. All the same, they needed to get back to the compound before anything more could go wrong.

Just as Cyrus reached the passenger side of the borrowed 4x4, the distant sound of screeching tires drew his attention. His first thought was that the distant headlights belonged to airport security. But when the pair of headlights split into a pair of vehicles, Cyrus realized that neither had emergency lights and there were no sirens wailing. And while the cars could represent the cautious and furtive approach of law enforcement, a sinking feeling told him that the cars were more than likely backup belonging to the dead man waiting inside the station.

Chapter 3

Natasha was terrified after gunfire broke out inside the bus depot. But as frightening as the shots had been, it was the silence that followed that truly tore at her. She sat frozen, one hand on the door handle for what seemed like endless minutes, unsure what to do. There was movement behind the station's frosted windows but it had brought her no reassurance since she couldn't tell if it was Cyrus, or someone dangerous.

Finally deciding on a course of action, she slid behind the wheel of the vehicle. She would be ready no matter who emerged from the building. Thankfully, Cyrus stepped through the doors a few seconds later.

She let out the breath she'd been holding and saw pinpoints of light dotting her vision. She had no idea how long ago she'd stopped breathing, but the vapor cloud suddenly filled half the cab. Cyrus approached, but stopped short of getting into the truck. Knowing that time was short, she couldn't imagine what prompted the delay. When she cast a glance over her shoulder and spotted a pair of oncoming headlights, her stomach summersaulted. *That would be the Royal Police,* she reasoned. It had to be. Her father would deal with any problems with the authorities, but she just didn't know if they could survive the delay. The people who were after her had already proven their efficiency, particularly if Cyrus had met resistance inside the bus station.

The distant clatter of small explosions caught her attention. She shifted once more to look through the truck's rear window. The pair of oncoming vehicles were drawing closer. They were several hundred yards off, and she saw sparks flying from one of the cars.

Cyrus threw open the passenger side door and jumped into the seat. "Drive!" he bellowed. "They're shooting at us!"

The thought was as shocking as anything else that had happened so far, and she reacted instantly. Dropping the gear selector into 'drive', she smashed the accelerator to the floorboards. The old four-wheel-drive truck shot forward on spinning tires and left twin patches at a slanted angle across the pavement.

Throwing the wheel to the left, Natasha powered through the multi-lane curve that led away from the departure gates. She accelerated so quickly that the truck skidded sideways across all three lanes before she regained full control. Never once did she take her foot off the gas pedal.

Seconds later they had exited the confines of the airport. The narrow highway entrance ramp was design for traffic to enter at sedate speeds. When Natasha hit the end of it pushing eighty miles per hour, the old truck lifted fully from its suspension. That part had been graceful. Twenty yards later, gravity reasserted itself and the truck's body came crashing down once more to rest on the now overworked drivetrain.

"They're still coming," Cyrus confirmed with a look through the rear window. "Through no fault of your driving," he added with a crooked grin.

"I'm glad you're having fun," she muttered through clenched teeth, "but I'm not sure how long I can keep up this pace."

Cyrus was still looking out the window, presumably assessing their options. "I'm more worried about our ride than you driving. I wasn't anticipating a high-speed chase when I stole it."

"Stole it?" she smirked.

"Sorry, *borrowed*," he corrected.

In spite of herself, she laughed.

"Okay, we definitely have a problem," Cyrus said, after a brief silence.

They were thundering down the open, empty highway and Natasha had her foot to the floor. The tachometer was bordering the red line and, even if it weren't, the truck had nothing more to give.

"They're catching up fast," he confirmed. "Whatever they're driving, it's got a lot more on the top end."

"What do we do?" she asked. Her knuckles were already wrapped so tightly around the steering wheel that they'd long since gone albino white. She'd never driven so fast in her life.

"Working on it," Cyrus muttered. He was fishing around in the backpack he'd retrieved from the bus station.

The sudden rush of air flooded the cab and pulled her attention from the road. Cyrus had lowered the window on his side of the vehicle.

"Keep the hammer down," he said. "I'm gonna make them think twice about getting too close."

Without any hesitation, he shifted in his seat, leaned out the window, and opened fire on the pair of cars that were now a little over fifty yards off their back bumper. Natasha thought the bitter bite of the wind whipping through the windows was brutal, but somehow it failed to compare to the staggering thunder of gunshots as Cyrus fired savagely on their pursuers.

Reaching up, she adjusted the rearview mirror. It hadn't been aligned for her new position, riding low in the driver's seat. A smile crossed her face when she saw the pursuing headlights shimmy, then double their distance from her bumper. The trailing cars were at least a hundred yards off and the gap was increasing.

Cyrus pulled himself back inside. She heard the sound of his spent magazine hitting the floor, followed instantly by the telltale noise of a new load being slapped home.

Rolling up his window, Cyrus exhaled deeply. His teeth were chattering. "That bought us some breathing room, but they'll get their nerve back soon. I got a good look at their cars; a pair of late model BMW's. We won't lose them on the open road in this old bucket."

"I'm open to suggestions." She was all for making the getaway, but he was right. Unless both of the pursuing drivers were completely incompetent, they were at too much of a disadvantage.

"We play to our strength," Cyrus said with a satisfied smile.

Not understanding, she waited for him to elaborate.

"They have the advantage on the open road," Cyrus explained. "But we have four-wheel-drive and a high wheel clearance. We need to take them where they can't easily follow."

The smile returned to her face.

"You know the island better than me. Any ideas?" he asked.

She nodded in the darkness. "I know just the place. If you can keep them off us for another mile, there's an old quarry just off the highway."

Cyrus tapped the button on the passenger side door. "Sounds good to me." Leaning out the window, he opened fire once more.

Chapter 4

The mountains outside of Rivven Rock
2:05 am

They took the exit ramp at break-neck speed. Cyrus struggled not to be thrown against the dashboard, as Natasha brought the small truck to the end of a T-intersection a half-mile after leaving the highway. The stretch of road dead ended at the base of a fifteen-foot concrete retention wall. The road made a ninety degree turn at the foot of the wall before running parallel to it east and west. Natasha locked up the brakes and put the truck into a skid just in time to make the corner and turn right. The truck was still rocking on its suspension when her foot hammered the accelerator once more. All four wheels chirped on the pavement and they shot down what Natasha had explained to be the last stretch of paved road before reaching the perimeter of the abandoned quarry.

Cyrus's plan worked perfectly.

As soon as they went into a sideways skid at the intersection, Cyrus knew that their exposed broadside would make them easy prey for their charging attackers. To improve their chances of survival, Natasha had let the BMW's draw close as they approached the intersection. As anticipated, when Natasha locked up the brakes and spun the wheel, the shooters—perched in the passenger side windows of both BMW's—opened fire. Cyrus heard the dull thuds of several wild shots impacting the truck's body as it spun ninety degrees and turned broadside on the pavement. Fortunately the attack was short lived. No sooner had the gunmen opened fire when the drivers of both cars realized they were approaching an intersection, and a solid concrete wall. Both cars were moving much faster than the truck in a frantic effort to close the gap. Both drivers took evasive action— slamming their brakes before putting the cars into aggressive, uncontrolled slides.

The action had the effect that Cyrus hoped for. The sudden braking launched the unrestrained gunmen from their positions in the passenger side windows of each car and sent them hurtling out into the night like rockets of flesh.

The truck was a hundred yards away when Cyrus and Natasha heard one of the cars impact against the wall. Cyrus let out a victorious cheer, spinning in his seat in time to see an oily fireball light up the night. There was no hiding Natasha's satisfied smile, visible even in the dim glow of the instrument panel.

The sound of gunshots pulled Cyrus's attention back to the rear window. One BMW had managed the corner, but it had lost ground in the process. The car's gunner had been replaced by another who was opening up on them with abandon. But at such a distance, and over the hilly stretch of paved road, it would take a lucky shot to do any damage. Natasha had already expanded their lead to a quarter mile.

Suddenly the truck lurched. At first Cyrus thought one of the gunner's long shot rounds had scored a lucky hit. Then he turned forward to see that they'd left the paved road behind and entered the perimeter of the gravel pit.

"There's a fork coming up," Natasha said with some urgency. "Are we going up or down?"

She was referring to the gravel pit itself. They needed to decide if they wanted to take the fork to the left that led down a series of switchbacks and into the fathomless darkness below. The fork to the right led up a steep, washed-out, dirt and gravel slope.

"Up," Cyrus decided without hesitation. "Always up. Never let the enemy occupy the high ground."

With no time for debate, Natasha twisted the wheel to the right and feathered the gas. The truck tires threatened to break free in the loose scree as they started across the incline. Cyrus was prepared for this. While Natasha had been focused on the road and keeping them on course, he had already searched the unfamiliar dashboard of the 4x4. He reached over and tapped a button on the console, dropping the transmission into four-wheel-low. The differential locked into synchronized movement and prevented the tires from slipping independently of each other. All four tires bit into the loose gravel and pulled the truck up the slope without the least bit of effort.

As the top of the hill came into sight in the moonlight, Cyrus had a new idea. Actually, it was a new revision on his previously improvised plan, but the environment was ideal.

"Do you trust me?" he asked, shooting a serious look at Natasha.

She flashed a suspicious glance back, but quickly returned her eyes to the hill ahead. The long second it took for her to respond shocked Cyrus. Her delay wounded him more deeply than he might've expected. He was asking a question about their current situation, but they both knew there were more far reaching implications when it came to her reply.

The truck shimmied and shook as it hopped over the rutted incline and continued a slow ascent of the slope. She glanced back, looking him directly in the eyes. "I never stopped," she said in a quiet, husky voice. Another rut in the path slammed them both violently against their seat belts and ended what might otherwise have been a thoughtful moment.

"Ouch," she gasped and struggled to correct the trajectory of the slow moving truck.

"After you crest the hill," Cyrus explained, "go on for another half mile. If I pull this off, it'll all be over. But if you see headlights coming your way, shift into four-wheel-high and hit the gas. Don't worry about me, and for God's sake don't stop till you get home."

"What do you plan to—"

She never got the chance to finish the question. Cyrus reached up and disabled the cab's dome light. He grabbed his pack, shoved the door open, and stepped out of the moving vehicle.

The truck wasn't moving very quickly as it struggled to climb the washed-out road. Still, Cyrus was glad when Natasha kept driving. The door slammed shut behind him and the truck bounced and crawled higher up the incline.

Cyrus threw himself into the tall, wild grass lining the rocky wash. He rolled over just in time to see the truck's brake lights flash before cresting the hill. The engine revved as it once more found stable ground; then he could hear the sound of the vehicle moving off into the distance.

As soon as the clattering of the truck disappeared, Cyrus heard what he was expecting. The BMW was maybe eighty yards behind, climbing the hill at a much slower pace. As it came closer, he could hear the sounds of the tires scraping and spinning as they broke traction and once more gained purchase. The car's undercarriage was constantly smashing against the rugged ground as the tires dropped into washed out furrows, each time nearly beaching the vehicle. Whether through luck or pure determination, somehow the BMW continued to manage the ascent.

The car's glacial progress gave Cyrus more than enough time to prepare. Safe in the seclusion of the tall grass, not ten feet from the side of the road, he sorted through the contents of the backpack. He double checked the 15 round load in his semi auto, then slid a spare magazine into his back pocket. Then, with a whimsical smile, he pulled a small, tennis-ball-sized hand grenade from the bag. With time to spare, he even stopped to zip the backpack closed once more, though he left it in the weeds.

Finally, the grinding and scraping sounds told him that the BMW was nearing his position. Cyrus crawled through the grass on his belly until there was only a foot of concealment protecting him. Taking a deep breath, he readied the pistol in his right hand and the grenade in his left. Holding the grenade's spoon with two fingers, he pulled the pin with his teeth. The pin fell from his mouth and disappeared into the grass while his eyes remained fixed on the road beyond the weeds.

The BMW's undercarriage suddenly made a crashing sound that was far more dramatic than anything that had come before it.

When the sound was followed by the wild and useless spinning of wheels, Cyrus grinned. He knew the car had just hit the same rut that had nearly knocked the wind out of Natasha and himself.

Stepping from the tall grass, Cyrus saw the silhouettes of three men in the car; two were in the front seats and one was in the back. Almost comically, all three men were looking at each other. They seemed to be arguing. His gun was already up, and Cyrus opened fire. The front and back passenger side windows disintegrated in rapid succession as Cyrus hammered away at the would-be assassins. The man in the back went down fast since he was alone and unprotected. Likewise, the man in the front passenger seat was swiftly ventilated. But the passenger had been a giant of a man, and his girth blocked many of the rounds fired at the car's driver.

The driver had already lived longer than Cyrus had intended. If he couldn't take the man out in the next second or two, the man might yet get his hands on a weapon and become a threat. Stepping to his right, Cyrus tried to get a better angle on the man through the windshield. His timing was fortunate. Cyrus stepped aside just as the passenger side door was eviscerated with a burst of automatic fire from inside the car.

Cyrus pumped the last of his rounds through the windshield. The gun's action locked open, leaving it useless. He was certain he'd scored solid hits on the driver because the windshield and driver-side-window were splattered with blood. Still, he didn't want to see what would happen on the off chance that anyone inside the car could still pull a trigger or aim a gun. With a quick toss, Cyrus hooked the grenade through the window and into the car's back seat. Without looking back, he ducked into the weeds and rolled downhill for cover.

Seconds later the car exploded in a fiery wreck. The detonation paled in comparison to the car that had impacted against the concrete barrier only a mile away, but results were no less lethal. The car had been turned into a ton of burning shrapnel.

One good thing came from the explosion. The fire provided ample light and made it easy for Cyrus to find his backpack before making the hike up the slope to be reunited with Natasha.

Chapter 5

After being confined to his room and dropping into bed from exhaustion, Cyrus expected to spend the night examining all that had happened and reevaluating everything he now knew. But in short order fatigue had set in. His body began to stiffen as new bruises formed around earlier injuries. Still, he was happy to be back inside the walls of the compound. More importantly, he was relieved to have Natasha back in the safe embrace of the facility walls. Not that he was being allowed to see her; once she'd finished tending to his immediate medical needs, security had seen to that.

Phoning from the road, Natasha had a security detail stationed at the gate and ready to escort them inside. They had returned from the mountains sometime shortly after 3:00 am. The call had caught everyone off guard because, at that point, as far as security was concerned, Natasha was still safe and sound in her quarters. The fact that she was off gallivanting around the countryside was extremely unexpected.

For their part, the security detail was on the ball. When Natasha called in, they were already aware of the shootout at *The Cuban*—they simply had no idea that a member of the Voss family had been involved. Cyrus was impressed to learn that Dargo's team constantly monitored the island's emergency radio frequencies. Dargo ran a tight ship with a team that was thorough, if not terribly friendly.

Upon their arrival, Cyrus and Natasha were hustled through the front gates under the watchful eye of a half-dozen armed guards. Voss met them in the common area of the building's first floor. There, he listened patiently as Natasha explained all that had happened. Cyrus, for his part, only contributed to the tale when he was directly questioned. He could see that Voss was deeply concerned, but he was waiting to see how Voss reacted to the night's events before he committed more information than was minimally required.

Cyrus knew he had reached a tipping point in the mission. With personal objectives that didn't necessarily align with those handed down by the Coalition, he knew he was walking a proverbial tightrope. Natasha was the only thing that mattered to him. He would do whatever it took to protect her. Cyrus had used his position and the resources of the Coalition to gain access to the compound, but once he was through the door, Coalition objectives had become secondary. Voss's actions following the evening's events would dictate Cyrus's actions from that point on.

To Cyrus's surprise, Voss didn't rush to a reaction of any kind. First and foremost he was a relieved father, happy to have his eldest daughter back safe and sound. But beyond that, he'd chosen to defer additional conversation until the morning.

Voss explained that he wanted to confer with Dargo, who was still away and dealing with matters in the United States. Though not present, Dargo had insisted Cyrus be confined to quarters and placed under guard until his return. Given the circumstances, Voss had been inclined to agree with the request. However happy Voss was to have his daughter back, he found it curious that Cyrus was so *capable*, as he put it, of dealing with such extreme circumstances.

Before Cyrus was escorted to his quarters, Natasha noticed the thick patch of blood that had saturated the lower portion of Cyrus's shirt in the short time it had taken to discuss things with Voss. Reluctantly, Cyrus revealed new damage to his earlier gunshot wound. Nearly all of the stitches had been torn loose on both the front and back of his abdomen.

Seeing this, Natasha looked aghast. Cyrus tried to shrug it off, content to return to his room for some much needed rest. But the blood loss wasn't something to be taken lightly; the sutures required immediate attention. Thus, Voss, Cyrus, Natasha, and a small contingent of security personnel shuffled off to the infirmary.

Voss watched with quiet patience while Natasha cleaned, re-stitched, and re-dressed Cyrus's wounds. She also administered another dose of antibiotics via an injection after cleaning out the more serious of his new abrasions.

All the while, Voss watched without a word. Cyrus could see the man was contemplating all that he witnessed. But Cyrus had no idea what conclusions were being drawn from what Voss saw. When it came right down to it, Cyrus knew just two things mattered at that moment. First, that he was ultimately powerless in his current situation. Voss would either let him stay or kick him out. There was a slight chance, however minimal, that Voss would have Dargo go to work on him and try to get a more complete explanation of his reasons for being there. But the more he considered that last option, Cyrus didn't think it likely. He'd looked into the eyes of some truly evil men over the last three years, yet when he looked at Voss, he didn't see anything resembling the hard-hearted monsters he'd worked against or with, in the past.

The second thing Cyrus knew was that he was just too tired to care anymore. The night had put him through the wringer and he was cashed. While accustomed to the fall his body suffered following an adrenaline dump like the one that had fueled him so far, he was feeling wiped out in a new and unique way. So when the security detail accompanied him to his room, he simply didn't care. Not even when two armed guards remained to stand station inside his bedroom door. It was just another worry among many at that point as he began to slip into unconsciousness.

When the doorbell chimed, Cyrus opened his eyes and tried to pull himself up on the bed. He was immediately greeted by every ache and pain from the night before, though they now seemed magnified. Looking down at himself, he realized he hadn't moved since collapsing on the bed hours earlier. He still wore the same clothes.

He was more exhausted than he could ever recall being. It was a fatigue that seemed deeply settled in his bones, and he wanted nothing more than to sleep for another dozen hours.

One of the guards flanking the door tapped the panel on the wall. The doors whisked open and Voss walked in looking rested and refreshed. When he looked at Cyrus, he grinned and shook his head with a chuckle.

"You look like you've had a rough night," Voss said with surprising levity.

Cyrus rolled his head slowly on his shoulders. The stretch resulted in several audible pops from his upper vertebrae. "Believe it or not, I've had worse," he said with a shy grin.

Voss's gaze was penetrating as he studied Cyrus. He stood silent for several long seconds as if considering his words, or perhaps making an important decision. Cyrus felt as if the man was weighing him in some way.

"I suspect that's not far from the truth," Voss said at last.

Cyrus could tell from Voss's penetrating stare that he wasn't going to be able to attribute last night's escape to blind luck. He'd feared as much. The concern had been among his last thoughts before passing out the night before.

There was also a very good chance that Voss's security guys had used the time to take a deeper look into the events of the previous night. While they wouldn't know for certain everything that had happened, once they started checking, there was a pretty obvious trail of carnage and destruction that could serve as testimony.

"I think it's time you and I had a talk," Voss said. "Why don't you get cleaned up and get yourself some breakfast. Once you're ready, security will bring you to my office."

Cyrus only nodded. A serious conversation was overdue. And though it went against mission objectives, it was now unavoidable. Sliding to the edge of the bed, Cyrus noticed that his arms were darkened with dirt and grime. He smelled of gunpowder and burnt *whoknowswhat*. He needed a shower. A little breakfast wouldn't hurt, either.

Chapter 6

Pushing a slice of banana across her plate, Anna glanced at her sister. It was just the two of them, sitting at the same long table they'd used for dinner the night before. The innocent look on Natasha's face made Anna smile as she considered all that had happened since their last meal together. And, while Anna had missed out on all of the previous night's drama, Natasha had reluctantly brought her up to speed when she appeared at her bedroom door sometime after 3:00 am.

Natasha looked pale and exhausted when Anna found her at her bedroom door. So wiped out, both mentally and physically, that Anna had to guide her sister by the arm to bed. After several minutes of not-so-gentle prodding, Natasha relented and was willing to spill what she knew of what had occurred. The tale had taken over an hour.

They sat at the foot of Natasha's bed, talking in the dim light cast by her nightstand lamp. To Anna, it sounded like something out of a Hollywood action movie. But looking at her sister left no doubt as to the veracity of all that she described. Near the end of the story, when Natasha had broken down in tears, Anna at first mistakenly thought her sister had finally succumbed to the stress of the life threatening events.

Finally choking back the tears and catching her breath, Natasha explained that it wasn't the dark journey with Cyrus that was weighing on her. She finally admitted to having known Cyrus long ago, well before this had come to fruition. They'd gone to school together.

"We were…" Natasha paused, searching for the right words. *"Together."*

Anna shook her head, at first unclear regarding Natasha's meaning. Then shock spread across her face. "Wait—you mean *together*, together?"

Natasha responded with only a simple nod.

"But you were all serious about a guy named Jon." She didn't understand. "What was his name…Jonny Webb!"

Offering a slight smile, Natasha leaned closer and spoke more softly. "That's what I mean," she said. "Back when I knew him, his name wasn't Cyrus—it was Jonny."

Her brow crinkled; Anna sat back and stared at her sister for several long seconds. "Very funny," she said finally. But the look Natasha offered made it clear that absolutely no levity was part of her explanation.

"What the hell is going on around here?" Anna huffed.

"That's what I want to know."

"Wait a minute," Anna said, her voice sharp. "This doesn't make any sense. You and Jonny broke up after he got into trouble writing something for the school paper. You told me he went into witness protection."

Natasha offered a shrug. "That's exactly what happened," she said. "And that was the last I saw or heard of *Jonny* until *Cyrus* showed up here in the infirmary with a bullet hole in him."

"That's messed up." It was a weak retort, but what more could Anna really offer?

"That's nothing," Natasha went on. "You didn't see what happened last night. These guys started shooting and everyone just...lost their minds."

"Can you blame them?"

"No. Everyone, except Jonny—err, Cyrus. Dammit—I don't even know what to call him!"

"I don't understand."

"I mean there were guns going off *everywhere*. People were getting shot down left and right. People were scattering for cover—there must've been a hundred of them, all rushing the exit at the same time. But Cyrus grabbed me and pulled me behind the stage. *Then he went after the guys shooting at us.*"

"You must be remembering it wrong. It's understandable, with everything happening so fast."

Natasha shook her head. "I remember it perfectly, mostly because it was so strange. He should've been terrified, but he wasn't the least bit scared. He even told me what to do...he had me create a distraction. I didn't know what he was going to do—I just did what he said. The next thing I know he went after the gunman with a drumstick!

"A few gunshots later and it was over. He killed two armed men while everyone was either running or hiding."

Anna thought about what she'd been told. After a few moments, she had what she considered to be a credible list of explanations.

"The way I see it," she offered. "Either you're crazy and have it all wrong, or your ex-boyfriend isn't the same guy he was a few years ago. But either way," Anna continued, throwing her arms around her sister's neck. "I'm just happy you made it home safe."

When Cyrus walked up to the dining room table, both Natasha's and Anna's eyes rose to greet him. Anna couldn't help herself. She let out an excited squeal and launched herself from her seat. She circled the table in a flash, threw her arms around Cyrus, and pulled him into a crushing hug.

"Thank you for keeping my sister safe," she said with a childish laugh that could only come from a desperately relieved younger sibling. "It's taken me twenty years to train her just right. I don't think I could handle it if I had to start from scratch with a new one!"

Natasha laughed and shook her head. The two security guards escorting Cyrus simply watched the display, unsure how best to respond.

"It was my pleasure," Cyrus said. His eyes swam from the crushing hug but it was only Natasha who noticed.

"Okay," Natasha said, as she carefully tried to pull her sister off of Cyrus's beaten and battered form. "Nothing says thank you like a plate and a fork. Why don't you get him what he needs so he can eat with us?"

Anna laughed and gently elbowed her sister. "You just want him all for yourself," she chided.

"Hardly!" Natasha blanched. "I'm more concerned about the gunshot wound you just crushed under the weight of your *happiness*. If those stitches break again, I'm not sure I can fix them."

43

Anna's hand leapt to her mouth and her eyes bulged as she realized that she'd just hurt Cyrus with her affectionate display. Cyrus only laughed.

"No harm done, really," he smiled. "Though breakfast would really hit the spot. Where *do* I find a plate?"

Natasha shook her head. "Have a seat. I'll take care of it."

She disappeared through a doorway in the far wall.

Anna pulled out a chair beside the one Natasha had used. "Here," she said with a sly grin. "I have a feeling you two have a lot to talk about."

Cyrus lowered himself gently into the seat. His movements were slow and precise. Since her sister wasn't prone to exaggeration, it was likely the events of the previous night had been even more harrowing than she'd described.

Stepping up behind Cyrus in the chair, Anna kissed him gently on the top of his head. "Thank you for bringing her home safely," she said quietly. "I don't know what I would've done if something happened to her."

Wiping a tear from the corner of her eye, Anna left the room without another word.

———

Natasha returned with a plate stacked high with pancakes, and another, smaller plate piled with bacon. Someone from the kitchen staff followed with a place setting and a tall glass of orange juice.

"Just the way you like them," Natasha said.

Cyrus watched as breakfast was spread out before him. He found himself at a loss for words. It was the personal touches that were most impressive. The pancakes had been poured with blueberries mixed into the batter and the OJ was thick with pulp… just the way he liked. His gaze was focused intensely on Natasha as she settled into the chair beside him.

She looked him in the eyes and gave a knowing grin. Not sure what to say, all he could do was stare back.

Finally Natasha glanced at the pair of guards standing station at the edge of the room. "Give us the room, would you guys?" she asked with a comforting smile.

"Sorry, ma'am," one of the guards responded in a thick German accent. "Our orders are explicit. We must never let him out of our sight."

"Are we really going to go through this again?" she asked with a roll of her eyes. "Look, I would consider it a personal favor."

The guard just shrugged. There was nothing he could do.

The other guard, however, leaned over and whispered something to his partner. They engaged in a quiet, but spirited back-and-forth talk before arriving at a decision.

"Alright," the first guard decided. "As long as he stays in this room. I'll stand over there," he nodded at the far end of the open common area. The far wall was at least forty feet away, beyond the entertainment area and just short of the elevator. "Wagner will take-up position beyond the door to the kitchen. As long as your guest doesn't attempt to leave the room without us, I see no harm."

Wagner had apparently campaigned on their behalf, in favor of giving them some privacy. Cyrus remembered Wagner, the guard stationed at his bedroom door. Wagner grinned and shot Natasha a friendly wink when the first guard wasn't looking.

"Thank you for your understanding," Natasha said with a smile that lit up the room.

Once both guards left, Cyrus felt more comfortable.

"Is it always that difficult to get some privacy around here," he asked.

"They don't trust you," she said frankly. "Can you blame them? They don't even know half the crazy shit you managed last night. If they did, I guarantee they wouldn't leave the room. In fact, I'd wager that you'd be confined to your room."

Offering a grin, Cyrus took a bite of bacon. "I guess I had that coming."

"No," she said more softly as she slipped her hand into his. "I should've started by saying thank you. I don't understand what happened last night, but I do know it would've ended differently if it wasn't for you."

He offered a resigned smile. "But you have questions," he concluded.

"A whole ton of them."

They were now seated very close together speaking softly in tones only slightly louder than a whisper.

"I know it's hard to believe, but that's the main reason I'm here," Cyrus explained. "Things didn't end right between us and I've always regretted not being able to explain that properly."

Running her hands through her hair, Natasha settled back in her chair and stared off into space for a few moments. "That's only one of my questions, but it's a big one," she began. "So let's start there. The last time I saw you was back at school. You were being taken into witness protection and you said I couldn't go along. But I found out later that you never asked them to include me."

Cyrus sat quietly for a minute and watched her. Finally, he leaned toward her and said quietly, "Would you have come if I asked?"

Her eyebrows shot up in response. "Would I—? That's not the point! The point is, not only did you *not ask*, but now I'm not even sure you went into the protection program in the first place."

Rubbing his temples with the tips of his fingers, Cyrus searched for the right place to begin. It was true that it was his own stubborn drive that had landed him in trouble in the first place. He'd joined the school newspaper at the start of his freshman year and found that it dovetailed nicely with his love of writing. Things quickly got out of control, however, when he began a series of investigative stories focusing on campus related issues. His stories quickly made a splash, and it wasn't long before he was working harder to come up with bigger and bolder topics.

That went on for several months until he found the story that caused all the trouble. Over the course of one weekend, three students were found dead on campus. The oddity, the horror, the mystery—everything caught Cyrus's attention, and he launched an investigation. The following weekend, thirteen students were arrested on various felony assault charges. That turned out to be eight times the normal average for any given *semester*.

A number of the violent assault cases contained extremely unusual details. In one case, it was reported that the aggressor had literally torn the door from a locked car before beating the driver into a coma. In another case, the perpetrator had gone on a rampage at a local restaurant, throwing tables around as if they were empty cardboard boxes. The arresting officers reported hitting the suspect with at least four taser blasts before subduing *her*.

At that point, Cyrus didn't need a bloodhound to know that something was going on. He started digging, asking questions, and following the clues wherever they led.

But Cyrus, then known by his birth name of Jonny Webb, uncovered more of a story than he'd bargained for. He soon found the source of the unexplained deaths and unusual violent outburst. A group of students were utilizing the university's chemistry lab after hours to prototype a powerful new designer drug.

Cyrus also learned that the enterprising students working on the drug had already found themselves sponsors in the form of an east coast mafia outfit. Once the stakes surrounding the story began to escalate, the editor of the school paper panicked and contacted the local authorities. Unfortunately, the support Cyrus's editor sought was already on the payroll of the project's sponsors, and Cyrus's covert investigation was no longer secret. His editor was killed before Cyrus was even aware that the gang was onto him.

After that, Cyrus had gone underground hoping to stay alive long enough to publish his story and bring the operation out of the shadows and into the light of day. His most pressing problem was that he didn't know who he could trust. The local police were obviously corrupt. He considered going to the FBI, but given the reach of the mafia, Cyrus had no idea if he would be safe asking for help at a federal level.

With all of his evidence gathered, and the story ready to publish, Cyrus realized that utilizing the school paper was no longer an option. Using the school press would only endanger more lives. With that in mind, he had to decide between taking the story to one of the major papers, or simply publishing it online. Either way, it was guaranteed to gain traction since he had all of the evidence necessary to substantiate his claims.

But before he could make a decision and publish the story, Cyrus was confronted by Greg Boone, an operative with an agency Cyrus had never heard of before. Boone explained the 'hows' and 'whys' of the *real* situation Cyrus had landed himself in. Namely that, once the story was out, he would never be safe. In spite of what the authorities would tell him, they would never capture everyone behind an operation of such magnitude.

And while Boone made some fair points, Cyrus had seen through his smoke screen. He knew that Boone had other reasons for wanting him to keep the story a secret. Cyrus refused to discuss the matter further until Boone told him the actual reason that his agency, the Coalition, was taking an interest in the case.

Boone had been taken aback by Cyrus's ability to see through his veiled, if accurate, deception. And though it went against all of his mission objectives, Boone leveled with Cyrus. The truth was that the substance the student chemists had developed as a recreational drug actually had greater potential if its development path were *altered*. Several characteristics of the drug indicated that it could be useful in certain military and paramilitary capacities.

Boone's truthfulness captured Cyrus's attention and Cyrus managed to keep his new friend talking. In the process, Boone explained a good deal more than he likely intended. By the end of the conversation, Cyrus had a plan to use himself as bait and trap the principal perpetrators behind the development of the designer drug. It was a plan that would result in the Coalition taking the new drug off the street, once and for all.

The operation had worked, and Boone's people arrested a large part of the mafia organization behind the drug in the process. As Cyrus's plan had dictated, the drug was stopped before it reached wide scale distribution. But there were two problems: The first was that it was impossible to be sure they had eliminated *every* threat to Cyrus's life. The value of the drug as a narcotic was high but its value as a black-market weapon was nearly priceless; and, second, Cyrus's intimate knowledge of the drug—its history and its origin—was ultimately a major national security problem. The formula was going to be modified and repurposed, and Cyrus knew enough to believe that it would also be more than dangerous.

While the offer of witness protection had been legitimately placed on the table, Cyrus knew that it would mean leaving behind everyone he'd ever known. But doing so would at least protect his friends as much as it protected himself. As such, it was worth considering. He discussed the matter with Natasha, though it was against procedures outlined by Federal Marshals.

Soon after, Agent Boone came to Cyrus with an even more interesting offer that held all of the benefits of witness protection but included something personally appealing, as well. Boone offered Cyrus a place in the Coalition. He'd been impressed, not only with Cyrus's investigative skills and attention to detail, but also with his ability to remain calm while under extreme pressure. Boone explained that both attributes were extremely rare commodities in a person, and highly valued in a field operative. Boone believed that Cyrus had what was required to be one of the agencies very best operatives.

So, with two options on the table, and lacking any option number three, Jonny Webb ceased to exist and Cyrus Cooper was born.

His one great regret was the girl he'd left behind. But fate was a strange and twisted creature. And to his surprise, Cyrus found his path once again crossing with that of his lost love.

Cyrus now took advantage of his limited time alone with Natasha to explain. He made an effort to keep his personal feelings out of it as they would only add fuel to an already emotionally-charged inferno. And though he skirted the topic, implying as much but never actually saying the words, leaving her behind truly had been the toughest, most painful experience of his life.

It was all just the long way of answering a simple question that wasn't simple at all. Why hadn't he asked her to go with him? In his heart, he simply wanted better for her. She was a bright, beautiful, intelligent woman, and he knew she would make her mark on the world. Life lived in hiding was no problem for him, but she deserved better. Then he joined up with the Coalition and there was no turning back. Deep-cover infiltration work wasn't the least bit conducive to a long term relationship.

It was a heavy conversation to have over breakfast. Cyrus took the opportunity to tell her all of the things that he'd come to believe he would never have a chance to express face-to-face. The chance to talk to her—to hold her hand and look into her eyes— it was his entire reason for forcing his way into the operation. For him, it had always been about her. In fact, he realized for the first time, his decision to join the Coalition had been about her, as well. He knew he would go nuts thinking about her if he couldn't sufficiently occupy his mind. At least the work he was doing with the Coalition was fulfilling; he believed he was making the world safer for her and people like her.

Still, it had been three years. Every day of which he'd thought about her. And nearly every day he'd fought the urge to look for her. Just to see where she was, what she was doing, or how she was getting along—it was an ever-present temptation. But it was an itch he'd never scratched. Not until this mission crossed his desk. But at that point, he realized he would do whatever was necessary just to see her again.

Cyrus took the opportunity to tell her all of these things. It felt good to get them off his chest, yet left behind a feeling of even more guilt for relieving his burden on her. In the end, his return had shown him something he had never even considered; his departure had been equally difficult for her.

Chapter 7

The pair of security guards escorted Cyrus into Voss's office. The space was expansive, easily forty feet wide and nearly thirty deep. Given the amount of floor space, there was surprisingly little furniture. A wide, dark mahogany desk sat centered against the back wall and facing the center of the room. A pair of comfortable armchairs sat before the desk. The walls to the left and right were covered with floor-to-ceiling bookcases that were filled, end-to-end, with hard backed volumes. A massive, oval conference table took up most of the space to Cyrus's immediate right, while the space on his left was entirely empty. That area seemed out of place, strangely unused, as if waiting for some piece of furniture or equipment to fill it.

Looking slowly around the room, Cyrus took it all in. They were on the fourth floor; it was the floor that held Voss's lab as well as his office. It was, in theory, the part of the building holding the secrets sought by the Coalition. He'd been ordered to infiltrate Voss's lab—an idea that almost seemed laughable now, when Cyrus considered it. After all that had happened, he'd finally made it into Voss's inner sanctum, and he could honestly care less about his prior mission objectives.

Cyrus regretted leaving Natasha all those years ago. But looking back, nothing had turned out as he expected. Even she hadn't turned into the person he'd anticipated. Though the idea was egocentric, he was afraid that his leaving had somehow done her more harm than good. When he'd left, the sky was the limit for her—she was limited only by the blockades of her imagination. She was a free spirit; she painted, sang, played guitar, and wrote poetry.

Without exception, she was the single brightest person he'd ever met. While he did well in school and never had trouble with grades, it was entirely thanks to his eidetic memory. It allowed him to coast through classes with little effort. Academics came with ease. That had never been the case for Natasha. She had no genetic crutch to fall back on, nothing to make her studies easy. Every grade she'd gotten was hard earned. Every course she took, she'd learned rather than absorbed. It was something he admired without exception. Math, science, art—she was brilliant. Maybe talent had just as much to do with it. But all of those gifts, combined with a warm heart and a lust for life unlike anyone he'd ever met, made Natasha extraordinary.

Of course, it didn't hurt that she was simply the most gorgeous girl he'd ever seen. He'd been infatuated with her from the moment he'd first laid eyes on her. But it hadn't been until they'd spoken for the first time that he'd truly fallen for her.

Pushing his thoughts aside, Cyrus walked further into the office. Voss was seated behind his desk. He looked up and smiled; his tired, kindly eyes showed fatigue. There was a click from an unseen button somewhere behind the desk and the wall behind Voss began to change. Cyrus had been so distracted by his own concerns that he hadn't noticed the back wall of the office was a floor-to-ceiling window overlooking an expansive laboratory in the next room.

But now, the lab beyond quickly disappeared as the glass became a pale, opaque white blocking his view into the inner sanctum. Voss had triggered the transformation via remote control. It was a shame. Cyrus really wanted a better look at the lab and chastised himself for being distracted at such an inopportune time.

There was a door in the left corner of the wall. It was made of glass as well. While there was no visible lock, Cyrus had no doubt that there was some sort of security to prevent unauthorized access. Actually, he was surprised that Voss had invited him into his office in the first place. It almost seemed a leap of faith from a man so security conscious, or paranoid.

"Thank you, gentlemen," Voss said to the guards. "That will be all."

Both men looked at Voss with apprehension. One of them, the one Cyrus knew as Wagner, seemed on the verge of protesting, but must've thought better of it.

"Sorry, sir," the other guard said, filling the awkward silence. "Dargo was very specific. We must keep Mr. Cooper under observation at all times."

Voss tipped his head slightly to the side and arched his eyebrows. He didn't say a word; he only looked at the two men as if to remind them who, exactly, was in charge.

Wagner tapped his counterpart on the shoulder. "Come on," he said. "We'll wait outside."

The other guard took a long look at Voss, then a longer look at his own shoes. Finally, he turned and followed Wagner through the door.

Voss, who hadn't moved a muscle the entire time, finally let a broad grin spread across his face. "Sometimes they forget who actually signs their paychecks," he said on his way across the large room.

Stepping up to Cyrus, Voss extended a hand. Not knowing what this was about, Cyrus shook it.

"I think that you and I are overdue for a talk," Voss said. He motioned for Cyrus to follow him back to the desk. Voss took a seat in one of the two armchairs in front of his desk and pointed Cyrus to the other.

Dropping into the seat, Cyrus watched Voss for any hint of what was on the man's mind. There was no doubt he had questions about what had happened the previous night. Voss would've questioned Natasha first, but she hadn't mentioned such a conversation. The mission had already strayed so far from the original objective that Cyrus was actually inclined to level with Voss, at least to some degree, if necessary. The fact that his Coalition support teams had been attacked, combined with Boone being MIA, meant that all previous plans were now out the window. Added to that was the growing sense of unease that the Coalition—perhaps the Red Queen specifically—wasn't being honest about the assignment. It was all making Cyrus increasingly uncomfortable.

"Trust is a valued commodity," Voss said, as if reading Cyrus's mind. "It's been my experience that in this world, it's also far too difficult to come by."

Not sure how to respond, Cyrus simply waited him out.

"I'm sure you've noticed the high level of security protecting my home and family," Voss went on. "I extended you a significant degree of trust by allowing you to recover in our infirmary."

Cyrus responded with only a nod.

"I believe you repaid that trust last night when you saved my daughter's life. Words can't express what that means to me."

The more he thought about the previous night, the more Cyrus was coming to question the intended target of the hit team. It was natural to assume they were after Natasha, given all of the security surrounding the Voss family. But the moves against Boone and the attempt Cyrus had repelled at the bus terminal now gave him doubts. Could he been have the target all along?

Voss took a deep breath. It seemed he was using the pause to search for the proper words before continuing. Cyrus sensed that whatever the man had to say next was difficult for him to voice.

"The events of last night call certain facts into question," Voss said at last. "Foremost among them are your intentions here. Put simply, the skills…the abilities you demonstrated last night…weren't those of a wayward university student."

The implication was clear, but since no question had been asked Cyrus was reluctant to fill the silence. Still, he felt he owed the man something. He responded with a simple nod of understanding. In it was the implication that Voss should continue.

"All of this leaves me with a dilemma. While I don't know exactly who you are, I feel confident that you are *not* a threat to my family. At the same time, however, I'm equally as certain that you are not who or what you claim."

After another pregnant pause, Cyrus once more offered only a slow tip of his head. He debated what he could and could not—*should or should not*—disclose.

Voss took even longer considering his next statement. When he finally did speak, he seemed to have come to a decision; his tone was fortified with greater conviction.

"So while I believe that you are not being entirely honest, I have to admit that I, too, have not been entirely forthcoming with you."

The statement put Cyrus's senses on full alert. He didn't know what was about to happen, but he was certain that some sort of hammer was about to fall. Given the circumstances, he had no choice but to hunker down and hope that he didn't end up being the nail.

"In the interest of putting all of our cards out on the table, as it were," Voss explained, "I will level with you. After that, you'll have the choice of whether or not to do the same with me."

Cyrus closed his eyes and considered Voss's choice of words. In spite of himself, he found himself genuinely liking the man. He seemed very direct and sincere. It made Cyrus want to trust him, which wasn't something that came easily. He had never experienced these feelings while working an undercover operation. Then again, this wasn't like other ops. He wasn't infiltrating a drug lord's stronghold or working his way up the ladder to get access to an arms dealer. Voss wasn't a criminal; he was a scientist. He was a father, and from all that Cyrus had seen, a good man.

"Sometimes the truth is overrated," Cyrus warned, speaking for the first time.

Voss sat back in his chair and considered this. Perhaps he was thinking about the warning in Cyrus's eyes more than the words themselves. Either way, he sat silently for several long seconds.

"I specialize in memory related research," Voss said simply. "Of course that's not the technical name for it, but you take my meaning. Anyway, as I explained earlier, I'm developing a procedure that will aid in the treatment of numerous cognitive disorders. Alzheimer's disease is a very good example.

"The present stage of my research focuses on recording memories—literally archiving them for later playback. This includes everything that a subject has seen or done during a given period of time."

Unable to hide his fascination, Cyrus found himself leaning forward in his seat. "What type of capture are we talking about? Is it like having a video camera running behind a person's eyes?"

With a grin, Voss shook his head. "It's far more immersive. We're capturing everything about the subject's experience—sight, sound, taste, and smell. Even the emotions experienced. Everything but the sense of touch," he admitted.

"Why not touch?"

Voss's face scrunched at the question, looking like he had tasted something unpleasant. "It's important to realize that the mind is entirely separate from the brain, though many wrongly consider them to be one and the same. But the mind is intangible whereas the brain is a tangible, physical organ. And though they are very different, they're also directly connected. What the mind realizes, the brain acts upon.

"So, say the subject of the recording experiences an injury. The experience of that pain response is recorded along with all of the related sensory input, and passed along to whoever retrieves those memories. The retrieval subject would *literally* experience the pain of the injury, though without the related physical disfigurement."

Cyrus sat back and considered the implications.

"You're saying that if the subject experienced a significant enough trauma…say, a heart attack—" Cyrus began.

"It could very well trigger a heart attack in anyone who replayed the experience," Voss confirmed. "There are some exceedingly dangerous aspects to this technology, I'll admit."

So pain could be inflicted without any telltale signs of bodily harm. Plus, the mind could be tricked into triggering a deadly physical response—like a heart attack.

Cyrus shivered. That was only scratching the surface of what more deviously creative minds might achieve using the tool. His imagination reeled with the implications. There were countless new and interesting ways the technology could and would be weaponized. On a lighter note, an errant thought crossed his mind. He realized how the technology would also be exploited for frivolous purposes, such as sexual gratification. It never failed; the two forces that ultimately brought the best and worst out of people were sex and violence.

"As a result," Voss explained, "touch was the first of the senses to be purposefully removed from the project. It held the greatest dangers."

"And the most potential for abuse," Cyrus offered.

This brought a knowing nod from Voss. Cyrus knew he understood exactly what he'd been thinking.

"But it's important that you understand how the technology works," Voss went on.

This caught Cyrus off guard.

How the technology works?

"Wait a minute," Cyrus sputtered. "Are you saying you have this stuff working, now? That it's not just a theory, or an idea?"

Voss grinned. "Of course. The components you delivered from Professor Ragsdale simply allowed me to augment and accelerate the memory restoration process. But I have a working prototype. It's simply a matter of fine-tuning the settings and optimizing the necessary chemical portion of the procedure.

"It's particularly important that you understand the chemical component," Voss said with emphasis.

With that simple statement, Cyrus became uneasy. He was certain Voss was referring to something specific. And as much as he wanted to rush things along, he let the scientist continue at his own pace.

"As I said before," Voss went on, "the mind is an intangible entity while the brain is malleable and tangible. Think of the brain as a computer hard drive; the mind is the software that resides on that hard drive. Are you with me?"

Cyrus offered a cautious nod. He had the sneaking suspicion that he was going to be the hard drive in this metaphor. Was this the experiment he had agreed to when he said he would allow Voss to test his photographic memory? If so, it sounded more invasive than he'd originally expected. Not to mention the fact that he couldn't let Voss, or anyone else, near his thoughts and memories. They contained far too much sensitive information. It would be a catastrophic breach. There was no question; he couldn't allow such an experiment to take place.

"So if the mind constitutes the sum of all the information that a brain contains, as well as other intangibles that make us who we are, the trick becomes accessing only a portion of what the mind contains. It's not practical to capture the full contents of what reside in the mind. The mind is more than memories; it's also made up of emotions and beliefs. Its dozens of other details that, when combined, make us individuals. As a whole, there's simply too much information for anyone to integrate into their own cognitive construct.

"One person, essentially having the full life experiences of two individuals in their head? That's a one-way ticket to a straitjacket. I'm sure you would agree?"

"Yeah. I could see how that's a big problem. Most people can barely keep track of their own lives, let alone multiple lives—multiple personalities."

"Right," Voss laughed. "So I developed a drug—a drug cocktail, actually. It acts as a marker of sorts. It serves as a chemical bookmark in the subject's brain, designating the neurological locations of all new memories formed from that point forward."

Scratching his jaw, Cyrus sat back and considered the simplicity of the solution. "Sure," he said. "You're essentially tagging the person's new memories. But doesn't that mean every memory from that point on is also flagged? In perpetuity? Don't you sort of have the same problem as before—essentially gathering too much data over time?"

Voss's eyes gleamed in response to the question. "There are no flies on you, are there?" he laughed. "You're exactly right. That's why the tag breaks down, essentially degrading into a benign protein compound after twenty-four hours.

"Twenty-four hours after the tag is put in place, unless it's reinforced with another dose of the drug, the tag dissipates and the bookmarked memories are no longer retrievable."

Shifting in his chair, Cyrus took a fresh look at the man before him. Putting all preconceived notions aside, he regarded Voss anew. There was a kindness in his eyes and an unmistakable gleam that shone when he spoke about his work. But there was also a hint of something more. If he didn't know better, Cyrus guessed the man was feeling guilty about something.

"That twenty-four hour period," Cyrus said, "wouldn't have any correlation to the daily antibiotic injections I've been receiving, would it?"

When Voss's gaze dropped away for the first time, Cyrus realized his guess was right on the mark.

He'd been tagged.

Likely tagged when he'd first entered the compound.

Letting the silence between them drift on, Cyrus considered the implications of what Voss had done. Exposure to his memories represented a serious breach of security. Voss was now a threat to his safety as well as a danger to the Coalition. If Voss was allowed to retrieve everything Cyrus had thought about since arriving at the compound, Cyrus knew his mission was likely to be compromised. Not only his thoughts, but also every memory he'd experienced since his arrival would be laid bare for Voss's perusal.

The consequences were almost too much to consider.

"When you arrived here," Voss said finally, "I considered tagging you to be a wise security precaution. I couldn't turn you out into the street—certainly not when your life was in danger. But my first priority is to protect my family."

"And your work," Cyrus added in a dry, unsympathetic tone.

A look of pain crossed Voss's visage. He shook his head slowly. "My work is nothing when compared to the safety of my family. When it comes to the two, there is no competition."

He took a long pause, apparently giving his next words great consideration before continuing. "I lost my wife many years ago. It caused me great pain. At the time, I was overly consumed by my work...it is a mistake I'll never make again. Family *always* comes first."

"I know about the loss of your wife," Cyrus said, his words softening again.

Voss's surprise was plainly evident on his face. "What do you know about that?"

"To be honest, I have more questions than answers," Cyrus admitted. "I guess you'll soon see for yourself, if you intend to use your procedure on me."

The piercing look Voss offered at Cyrus's mention of his wife quickly withered. His eyes once more sought the floor. "That's why I wanted to speak with you in private," he said in a soft voice. "Given the events of the last day in particular, I must admit I've developed a certain respect for you. I was never entirely comfortable tagging you without your knowledge. I find myself unable to complete the procedure after what you did for my daughter."

Cyrus was glad Voss was still looking away because he was unable to mask his surprise. He was left momentarily speechless. Voss was proving to be worthy of his respect, after all.

They sat in silence for longer than either would have preferred; neither seemed to know what to say or do next.

"Your procedure," Cyrus began. "You're telling me you can actually transplant my memories of the last week and place them

64

into your mind, complete with everything that I've thought, tasted, seen, and heard?"

Voss nodded.

"What about the *memories* I've experienced over the last week? For example, memories I've recalled from years in the past. Would those be transplanted?"

"Of course," Voss confirmed, matter-of-factly.

Hanging his head, Cyrus slowly rubbed at the corners of his eyes. This wasn't ideal under the best of circumstances. What he had in mind had the potential to rocket his investigation forward…or cause it to blow up in his face with shocking efficiency. It would all depend on Voss.

Being that the circumstances around Cyrus's mission had changed since his arrival at the compound, with Voss's technology no longer the objective, Cyrus had new concerns. There had been an attempt on his life, one on Natasha's, and Boone was now missing. Boone was either dead or he'd gone dark, dropping off the grid and hiding out in response to the attack on his team. Either way, that end of the operation had gone sideways, and finding out why was now imperative. Cyrus knew two things with certainty. First, everything happening now was centered around Voss's work. Second, whoever was behind the attacks had professional resources who wouldn't stop until they accomplished their objective.

"I need your help," Cyrus said finally. "But I know I won't get your full cooperation unless I have your trust. The only realistic chance I have to gain that, as far as I can tell, is if I let you complete the procedure."

The series of expressions that crossed Voss's face were everything Cyrus would've expected given the situation. Voss opened his mouth to speak more than once, only to stop before uttering a single word. He was clearly puzzled, concerned, and likely more than a little surprised.

"I have the strong sense that I can take you at your word," Cyrus explained. "So I need a promise on a very specific agreement. If I consent to this, it is critical that no one other than you *ever* be allowed to play back my memories. Secondly, the recording must be destroyed once you've reviewed it."

Voss seemed puzzled by the fervor with which Cyrus insisted upon his points. Still, he willingly agreed.

"There's more," Cyrus continued. "For reasons that will become clear once this is done, you can never speak of my cooperation in this procedure to anyone—ever."

"I can respect your need for privacy," Voss offered by way of reassurance.

Cyrus shook his head. "This isn't a matter of privacy," Cyrus warned. "This is a matter of safety and security. *Yours and mine.* If anyone ever learns of this, both of our lives will be forfeit."

The explanation clearly troubled Voss.

"I'm not being dramatic," Cyrus clarified. "You need to fully understand what you're getting yourself into. You're right, I'm not who I claim to be. But we've reached the point where I need your help to keep you and your family safe, and this is the only way I can convince you of my intentions."

Voss stared at Cyrus, clearly unsure how to respond.

"Honestly," Cyrus explained. "I'm here to help. But things have spun out of control and I can't sort this out on my own—certainly not with the level of security you have running around here. So I need your help. This is the only way to make that happen."

"Well, it seems you've left me with no choice in the matter," Voss said at last. "Curiosity alone compels me to see the procedure through."

With a grimace, Cyrus sat back once more. He ran his hand through his hair and considered how to explain the last part of his problem.

"I need to warn you," Cyrus said. "If this procedure works the way you say, you're going to experience some things that aren't going to be easy for you...*on a personal level*. I...,"

Floundering, Cyrus really didn't know what to say. He felt like he should give Voss some kind of heads-up in regards to his past relationship with Natasha. Particularly if his technology was about to expose the man to the feelings Cyrus had for her—not to mention their past intimate experiences. Seeing her again had brought back a torrent of memories and emotions, some of which were explicit enough to thoroughly traumatize the girl's father.

And that was nothing compared to what Cyrus had dug up relating to the death of Voss's wife. In researching the case, he'd studied the murder of Eleanor Voss in explicit detail—more detail than an already grieving husband would ever want, or need, to revisit.

The one saving grace had been Cyrus's knowledge of the Coalition. To a large degree, he had compartmentalized his thoughts of the organization since the start of the operation. Part of that was simply his need to stay focused, but largely it was the result of prudent planning. He knew the sort of research Voss was conducting, and one of his potential approaches involved volunteering as a research subject. His photographic memory had the potential to make him a valued test case and one Voss was likely to be interested in. So, aside from a few phone numbers and contact protocols, Cyrus didn't think he'd be exposing much of the Coalition's sensitive information. Besides, if Voss kept his end of the bargain, those secrets wouldn't matter.

"I mean they won't be easy for you to deal with as a father and a husband," Cyrus concluded.

Voss's face blanched. "What exactly does that mean?"

"It means that reading minds is a noble endeavor, but you're going to find that it's messy business." Cyrus didn't like being cagey, but he knew that nothing he could say would fully prepare Voss for what he was about to experience.

"Why don't you talk with Natasha before the procedure," Cyrus suggested as an afterthought. "Explain to her what you're about to do and see what she has to say."

Voss looked anything but comfortable at the thought.

"What is it?" Cyrus asked.

"She won't be happy," Voss admitted. "She doesn't know the tagging solution was added to the antibiotic injection she's been administering."

Cyrus smirked. "All the more reason for the two of you to talk."

Chapter 8

The Voss Compound
12:08 pm

Cyrus was still in his room lying on the bed when one of the guards let Natasha though the door. She crossed the room quickly and stood over him.

"You have to believe me," she began. "I had no idea he was using the tag on you."

Based on the troubled, near frantic look on her face, he had no doubt that was the absolute truth. Plus, Voss had been very specific about that particular detail. "It's okay." He pulled himself into a sitting position. "I understand."

"I don't think you do!" she insisted.

Turning to the pair of guards at the door, Natasha cast a stare that could've withered a stone statue. Thankfully, Wagner was once more on duty. He raised a placating hand in an effort to ward of the verbal attack that was sure to follow.

Motioning to his counterpart, Wagner pointed to the hallway. The other guard looked confused. "Don't ask," Wagner muttered, as they crossed the threshold and left Natasha and Cyrus alone.

"Neat trick," Cyrus grinned. "You've got them trained. I think they're afraid of you."

"This isn't funny," she snapped. "Father said he isn't making you go through with this, but you've agreed to the procedure anyway. You clearly don't understand how the process works."

Swallowing a deep sigh, Cyrus asked her to have a seat. She was reluctant, clearly wired with far too much anxious energy to sit. But he insisted, and she finally acquiesced.

"Thanks to all the security here, I haven't been able to explain what's going on. Things really have changed since we were in school."

"No kidding," she growled; her tone was increasing in anger. "Starting with your name?"

He knew that the barbed comment was only the tip of the proverbial iceberg.

"Were you ever actually *in* witness protection?"

He shrugged. It should've been a yes or no answer, but the truth was more complicated. "I was headed that direction," he explained. "Until I realized the FBI would never be able to clean up the entire mess. I would always be looking over my shoulder. With that in mind, I took a different path. It wasn't really witness protection. That's a defensive strategy. I met some people who helped me become a lot more proactive. We approached the situation more offensively."

She shook her head. "What does that mean?"

He met her eye with a purposeful stare. "It means, rather than wait for them to come after me, I chose to go after them."

Judging by the look she returned, she still didn't understand.

"Before I went into protection, I was approached by someone. He represented a branch of federal law enforcement that specialized in working between legal lines. Someone in their group had been monitoring my case. He saw the situation I was in and how I'd gotten there. The day before I was supposed to meet with U.S. Marshals for relocation, I met with representatives from that group and came to a different arrangement. Rather than going into hiding, the group agreed to use its resources and help me solve my problem. In return, I had to help them solve a problem their organization was dealing with. In a lot of ways the problems were intertwined.

"Anyway, a long story short, Cyrus Cooper was born that day. Instead of living in some obscure corner of the United States— always looking over my shoulder—I ended up with a job that lets me do good and keep people from getting into the sort of trouble I'd gotten myself into."

Even as he was explaining it, Cyrus realized his words sounded similar to the recruitment speech Boone had given him back at the very beginning. At the time, it seemed like an easy choice. He had an opportunity to stop bad people from doing horrible things. But recent events were forcing him to reevaluate his situation. The borderlines between right and wrong—good and bad—were now blurrier than he'd ever believed possible. For the first time since taking a position with the Coalition, he could see himself leaving their ranks. Once he realized that he wasn't being told the full story, or provided all necessary information, the doubts surrounding his work began to weigh heavily on him.

"I don't question that you did what you had to," she said quietly. "I just wish things had turned out differently."

He felt the sadness in his own tired smile. "I do, too. More than you'll ever know. But you really can't let your father complete the procedure. Just let the tag expire; drop the subject."

He held her hand and offered a smile, but she wouldn't look him in the eye.

"He'll know who you are. He'll know everything you've said, done, and thought since you arrived here."

"I understand," he said softly.

"I don't think you do," she insisted. "I don't know about you, but seeing you again has brought back some powerful feelings…and some amazing memories."

He smiled. "Are you saying you still have feelings for me?"

Natasha's eyebrows arched and her jaw trembled as she stammered a response. "Pay attention!" she bellowed; socking him in the shoulder, she offered him a glare. "I'm talking about some…*vivid, personal memories!* Unless you're a coldhearted bastard, you've been experiencing those old feelings, too."

A grin spread across Cyrus's face. He was happy to hear she'd also been recollecting the old days. Though it wasn't the point of her lecture, she still harbored some of the feelings she'd once had for him, and that brought a sense of hope and excitement that he hadn't experienced in a long time.

Still, the point she was making was valid. Unfortunately, it was one he'd already considered. The personal discomfort of the situation was simply outweighed by the danger of their present circumstances.

"We're talking about *my father*," she reminded him.

Trying hard to wipe the satisfied smile from his face, Cyrus did his best to explain. "I'm sorry. I know what you're worried about, and you're right. But, at this point, we don't have a choice. Your father has this place so saturated with security that I can't operate freely. I need access and autonomy in order to sort out who tried to kill you, me…even Gretchen. Someone's after your father's work and I can't find out who's behind it if there's no trust."

"You think you'll earn my father's trust by going through with the procedure?"

"I hope to," Cyrus admitted. "I don't see any other way. Call him whatever you want—security conscious, maybe paranoid? I can't operate if I have to hide who I am and why I'm here. We're beyond that now."

She gnashed her teeth, as her eyes bore into him. "I'm not sure I know who you are anymore. And I certainly don't know why you're here."

Natasha pushed herself off the bed and stalked across the room. At first Cyrus thought she was heading for the door…and maybe she was. But she altered course, perhaps thinking twice before leaving. She paced the far end of the room aggressively; white knuckled fists were clenched at her sides.

Tempted to say something, Cyrus decided it was better to let her vent for the moment. He sat silently at the end of the bed and watched her stalk back and forth. In time, her rapid march slowed, becoming less charged.

Finally she calmed, stopping her long march only a few feet away. Her gaze met his. There was no mistaking the pain in her eyes. He realized that, not only was all of this a shock to her, but it was emotionally devastating as well.

"Why *are* you here?" she asked. Tears had already formed in the corners of her eyes. Though none had yet fallen, they weren't far off.

Sliding from the bed, Cyrus crossed to her in a single step. He pulled her into his arms. The moment her face pressed against his shoulder, he felt her shudder. Her tears broke free in earnest.

"I came for you," he whispered. "My group was going to send someone to monitor your father's work. I made sure I was the one who was sent," he explained. "But I don't give a damn about the assignment. I took it because it meant being here, with you, right now."

He felt her arms wrap around his waist, and he held her tight...listening with both relief and guilt to the quiet sound of her sobs.

Chapter 9

The Voss Compound
12:52 pm

His wrists were secured with Velcro. Any restraint made him uncomfortable, but Voss explained that they would be extracting more than a week's worth of information from his mind. It was more raw data than had been attempted to date, and he wasn't sure what sort of physical reactions Cyrus's body might have under those conditions. The restraints were there to keep him from hurting himself during the short procedure.

Per Cyrus's request, Natasha was on hand to observe. Aside from her and Voss, the lab was empty. Cyrus sat in an elaborate looking, semi-reclined chair. It looked like the sort of thing one would see in a dentist's office…or a futuristic execution chamber. The chair had plush, comfortable padding but there were wrist and ankle restraints secured to its underlying steel frame. A small, wheeled, stainless steel cart sat beside a short stool located off to one side.

"As I said, this is a very simple procedure," Voss explained. He opened a small, metal case that was about the size of a shoebox. Inside was a custom cut foam liner cradling a pair of sleek goggles with opaque lenses. Taking them out, Voss placed them gently on the cart.

"The goggles send a signal pulse into your eyes. It's a sort of negotiation, at which time the software driving the system calibrates itself and makes hundreds of adjustments specific to your optical and neurological parameters. Each subject is different, so this calibration takes place every time the system is used. We're essentially using the optic nerves as conduits for communication with the brain, so precise calibration is critical.

"The calibration pulse lasts only a fraction of a second. The subject doesn't even perceive the pulse. After that, all of the data is transmitted out of the brain along the optic nerves. The goggles receive the signal and translate it into a data stream that the computer can understand. The wire attached to the goggles transmits the data to a two hundred and fifty terabyte flash cluster where the data is captured," he continued. "Though we will be pulling more than a week's worth of experiences from your mind, the entire transfer process will take less than thirty seconds."

Cyrus's jaw dropped. "Thirty seconds? And you'll have everything that I've tasted, smelled, and thought in the last week?"

Voss smiled proudly. "Yes. The technology is only in its infancy. In time, I'll be able to extend the shelf life of the tagging solution as well as reduce the requirements of the hardware capturing the raw data. But none of that matters today. Per our agreement, I'll be purging your imprint as soon as I've personally reviewed it."

Cyrus glanced at Natasha who was standing silently off to the side. She still looked profoundly uncomfortable with the arrangement. He couldn't blame her. But then it was next to impossible for him to properly explain why all of this was necessary. It all came down to his need to convince her father, with one hundred percent conviction, that he could be trusted.

"Are you sure I can't talk you out of this?" Natasha asked in a dry husky voice.

"Sorry," he said softly. "It's the only way."

"What about you?" she asked, putting her father on the spot.

"You've both made it very clear that I will experience things that I will not find agreeable," Voss said with great patience. "I'm willing to accept that. The truth is, this is exactly the sort of moral issue this technology will face when it goes into practical use. In that regard, perhaps this is an ideal experiment on multiple levels."

Cyrus smiled, offering his own nonverbal agreement. But from Natasha's look, he could see she would never be convinced. It really wasn't fair. This procedure was a major intrusion of her privacy, as well as his. She simply had no idea how much more Cyrus was risking with his participation. His circumstances were unprecedented. While he didn't know what the Coalition would do if his participation came to light, he knew that the organization would act swiftly and decisively to mitigate any threat to its personnel, or its well-kept secrets. That fact represented a very real danger to Voss's life, and perhaps Cyrus's as well.

Voss pulled a small data cable from the top of the metal cart. It wasn't much thicker than a thread of yarn. He plugged the end of the line into a small port on the side of the goggles before slipping the eyewear over Cyrus's head.

"Is that comfortable?" Voss asked.

"Just fine," Cyrus confirmed.

"Alright then," the older man said with a weary smile. He looked to Natasha and she lowered the room's overhead lights.

Voss retrieved a small, handheld tablet computer from a shelf under the wheeled cart and began tapping on the screen.

Voss began: "In five…four…three…two…one."

A blinding white strobe pulsed from the goggle lenses, completely obliterating Cyrus's vision. But as quickly as the light pulses had begun, they ended just as abruptly.

"Holy shit! What the hell was that?" Cyrus bellowed.

"That was the download," Voss said in a matter-of-fact tone. He was already removing the goggles from Cyrus's face.

Blinking rapidly, Cyrus still saw nothing but the blinding wash from the white light. He fought the panic for several seconds, hoping his vision would return quickly. When it didn't, his concern reached its apex. "Doc, something's wrong. I can't see a Goddamn thing!"

Cyrus felt a hand on his shoulder. "Don't worry," Voss said reassuringly in his ear. "Your vision will return in about a minute's time. We've just transmitted an incredible amount of data across your optic nerves. Since they aren't used to the experience, it takes a few moments for your brain to compensate for what just happened."

Choking back a wave of fear he had never experienced, Cyrus held his breath and waited. But when he felt Natasha's hand slip into his own, a warmth rushed through his body and the panic suddenly disappeared.

"I'm right here," she whispered.

She held his hand for another minute before the room began to shift back into focus. The ball of white light that had consumed everything in his eye-line began to dissolve. The contents of the room, in full living color, began to materialize at the periphery of his vision. The ball of white faded until it was a pin-sized dot before him, then finally disappearing entirely.

Seeing the smile on his face, Natasha moved to release him from the hand and foot restraints.

The first thing he noticed was the pinched look of concern on Voss's face. He was tapping on the screen of the handheld computer and examining the contents of the display.

"What's wrong?" Cyrus asked. "It didn't work?"

Voss looked up, confusion clear in his eyes. "No…it worked," he said in a hollow voice. "I'm just not sure how it worked."

Cyrus waited for nearly a minute for Voss to continue, but the man just stared at the screen in his hands. Just when Cyrus thought Voss wasn't going to clarify, he finally spoke.

"The transmission period was surprisingly brief," Voss explained. "It should've taken thirty seconds—maybe a little more—to move that volume of data across your optic nerves."

Rubbing the last of the fuzzy, washed-out, white halo from his eyes, Cyrus stared at Voss. "That didn't feel like thirty seconds."

Voss shook his head and turned the screen for Cyrus to see. It was a meaningless gesture since all he saw was a screen riddled with numbers and half-a-dozen small graphs.

"2.101 seconds," Voss mumbled. "I've never seen anything like it. And the transfer is complete…in a fraction of the time it should've taken."

Not sure how to interpret that information, Cyrus rubbed his eyes once more. *At least that explained the headache*, he reasoned.

Chapter 10

Much of the remaining afternoon afforded Cyrus some rest and relaxation. It was time he gladly shared with Natasha. They sat in the building's common area on the first floor and watched movies on the flat screen television. Although he was grateful for the down time, Cyrus also found it troubling. Voss had gone ahead with the memory restoration process less than a half hour after Cyrus and Natasha had vacated the lab. Since that time, neither had seen or heard from the scientist. Cyrus wasn't sure what to make of the man's absence, and it was all he could do to keep from grilling Natasha for more information about the restoration process.

What little he knew about the memory retrieval procedure was that, while it wasn't as fast as the download process, it took only a matter of minutes to upload the data for review. The viewer accepted the upload using the same pair of goggles. The data, likewise, was transmitted to the brain along the optic nerves. But restored memories were flagged in a way that Natasha had difficulty describing. She said it was the mental equivalent of watching a video that had a two-inch thick red border around the edge of every single scene. It was a way for the person playing host to the restored memories to discern the transplanted experiences from their own without confusion or disorientation. It was complicated, she explained, but without it, the restoration process would've been impossible.

So what did it mean when Voss had disappeared for the remainder of the afternoon? The implications concerned Cyrus deeply.

Natasha, for her part, seemed at ease for the first time since his arrival. Apparently their impromptu airing of concerns had brought about a positive and cathartic calm. Still, Cyrus found himself waiting for the other figurative shoe to drop.

That's just what happened when he saw Wagner. The guard at the far end of the wide room put his hand to his earpiece and tipped his head in concentration. He spoke quietly into the cuff of his sleeve for a moment, then approached Cyrus and Natasha where they lay reclined and nuzzled in the corner of the L-shaped sofa.

"Excuse me," Wagner said. "Doctor Voss would like to see Mister Cooper in his office at his earliest convenience."

Earliest convenience? Cyrus thought. He didn't know what to make of the request after the man's afternoon spent in mysterious seclusion.

Chapter 11

Somewhere over the Atlantic
9:31 pm (Isle of Kapros; local time)

Sitting at the window of the Gulfstream G450, Dargo stared silently into the darkness beyond. An endless expanse of ocean passed by far below the expensive executive jet, but he couldn't see it thanks to the late hour. Even at its cruising speed of Mach .8 the cabin was deceptively quiet. The aircraft was a virtual duplicate of the one belonging to the Voss family, only this one belonged to King August Casper Borden, ruler of the Isle of Kapros, the sovereign country the Voss family called home.

From what Dargo had been told, Voss had provided the specifications for his plane and its outfitting upon the King's request. Now that he sat in the aircraft's cabin, he realized that the King's aircraft was duplicated in every regard, right down to the color of the leather used on the seating, as well as the seat arrangement within the cabin. The only obvious difference was the color scheme used on the jet's fuselage and, of course, the designated tail number. When Borden found something he liked, he didn't believe in half measures.

Gretchen had taken Voss's jet to the United States. When her security detail ran into trouble, Doctor Voss had secured a favor from King Borden, and borrowed the King's personal jet for Dargo's emergency flight to the U.S. Until he'd stepped on board, Dargo had written news of the duplicate jet off as nothing more than a fanciful rumor. Given the situation, Dargo had a newfound respect for the King's excesses, his generosity, and the respect he had for Doctor Voss. After all, it would be these qualities which moved him to cross the Atlantic in record time.

Though Dargo knew the jet's price tag was more money than he would earn in his entire life, he understood why Voss considered the aircraft a good investment. It was one of the select few business class private jets with the range necessary to cross the Atlantic Ocean without stopping to refuel. And since Anna Voss traveled the world competing in professional tennis tournaments, the ability to do so with a minimum of layovers made Dargo's job of protecting her that much easier. Perhaps the aircraft's capabilities also made it an ideal choice for King Borden.

He was on the return leg of his trip and his body was desperate for sleep, but Dargo found it difficult to quiet his active mind. The attack on Gretchen and her detail still wasn't sitting well with him; some unseen part of what happened was causing him unrelenting anxiety.

Gretchen's security detail had been decimated—six men lost in the operation. It was more than enough to rankle anyone's nerves. But it was Gretchen's survival that was ultimately setting off warning bells in his mind, Dargo realized.

Anna Voss's change of heart and decision to participate in a charity tennis tournament had resulted in Gretchen's last minute flight to the United States. There, her security detail had been attacked, while Gretchen herself was left entirely unharmed. Lee Fairfax, the man she had flown out to meet, had been murdered, presumably prior to her arrival. But why? Only the security team had been harmed. What was the assassin's objective?

She had described the receptionist who met them upon their arrival. The discarded wig, as well as the lack of the woman's corpse, were clear indications that she was responsible for the loss of the security team. And although Dargo found it troubling that one person—one woman—could dispatch six of his highly trained men, he knew it wasn't out of the question. Not if the woman was a highly skilled professional, which was clearly the case. But why had six armed bodyguards been killed only to leave Gretchen unharmed? It was the part of the puzzle that didn't fit.

While Dargo was en route to the United States aboard King Borden's jet, Gretchen was inflight and crossing the Atlantic in the opposite direction. A video conference link allowed Dargo to interview her before he reached the U.S. and before she'd landed on Kapros. Unfortunately, the details she provided had proven as fruitless as his efforts to collect evidence from the scene of the attack. In the end, he'd come away with absolutely nothing to help him understand who was behind the attack on his people.

Now on the return leg of his trip, Dargo was feeling more anxious than ever. His investigation was stalled until he could land on Kapros. He hoped that speaking with Gretchen face-to-face would prove more productive. She was his best hope of drawing understanding from the senseless attack.

Dargo couldn't fathom the point of the assassin's operation. The killer hadn't demanded anything of Gretchen. Even more perplexing, apparently Gretchen hadn't even been confronted by the assassin following the elimination of the security team.

It just doesn't track.

If he thought she was lying, Dargo would've had something to work with—some rationale to help him offer an appropriate and effective defense against whatever was coming next. But his complete lack of understanding hampered his response and left him at a distressing disadvantage.

There was just no logic to attacking Gretchen's security detail, only to leave her unharmed. The only thing the assassin had accomplished was to send him winging across the Atlantic to deal with the issue personally. It was a waste of—.

Dargo felt his blood run cold. His gaze darted violently around the jet's small cabin. Two of the men from his security team sat at the front of the cabin, their backs to the forward bulkhead just behind the cockpit. Both men were awake and alert. Each was belted into his seat and staring out the window into the endless black as if he could see the Atlantic far below.

Glancing over his right shoulder, Dargo saw three more of his team seated at the rear of the cabin. Nothing seemed out of order, and none of his men seemed the least bit anxious. There was only one man on the entire team who had a fear of flying. Dargo had been content to leave Talbet behind to oversee security at the compound.

Despite his overwhelming trust in his men, Dargo now had the nagging feeling that something wasn't right. There was only one logical reason for attacking Gretchen's team and leaving her unharmed: She'd been used as bait to pull him away from his duties back at the compound.

Releasing the buckle of his seatbelt, Dargo pulled himself upright. In a hunched position, he headed for the cockpit. He needed to radio the compound and sound the alert. While he didn't know what was about to happen, he was now certain that someone was planning to make a move against that installation.

No sooner had he stepped through the cockpit's narrow door then the jet lurched to the right. The starboard wing dropped as if the pilot had executed an evasive maneuver. Seeing the pilot's frenzied reaction, Dargo knew the violent move had surprised the flight deck crew as much as it had him.

Dargo's head crashed against the frame of the open door before he had a chance to brace himself. He turned quickly, wedging his broad shoulders in the narrow doorway and preparing to stave off another fierce shift from the aircraft. It was easy since he barely fit through the door in the first place.

"Jesus, Walker! What the hell was that?" the copilot squawked in an unprofessional, piercing voice.

"It wasn't me," the pilot bellowed as he fought the control stick. "I've been compensating for some kind of drift—it's been pulling us starboard for about a minute and a half. All of a sudden, it was like the wing just turned to…concrete."

Dargo could tell the jet was losing altitude fast. It was hard to make out the horizon through the windscreen, but the floor beneath his feet was pitched forward at a pronounced angle. Had he not jammed himself in the doorway, he would've been thrown into the cockpit and made a bad situation worse.

Glancing over the pilot's shoulder, Dargo realized the man was fighting some sort of invisible force that was dragging the jet to the right; like a large, unseen magnet. As a result, the pilot had the control stick pushed far to the left, feathering the control with minute and constant adjustments.

"We just lost the starboard turbine," the copilot croaked. "I'm shutting down fuel to that power plant."

"Damn it!" the pilot growled. He had the control stick pressed so far to the extreme left that it was banging against its stops. "I don't get it. It's like an elephant just climbed on our wing! I can't fully compensate. Radio our coordinates and declare an emergency. I can't keep us in the air."

The copilot reached for the instrument console to prepare the radio for the call, but Dargo reacted on instinct. He pulled a shoulder free from the doorframe and grabbed the copilot by the shoulder. "Nyet," he commanded.

The copilot shot a terrified look over his shoulder, evidently seeing the large Russian for the first time. "There's nothing we can do! We're going down, Sir!"

"Not a word over open airwaves," Dargo yelled over the cacophony of alarms sounding from the instrument clusters. "This is an attack. Using the radio will give away our position."

"In two minutes that's not going to matter," the pilot said. The absolute certainty of his warning rang out crystal clear in his voice.

"Understood," Dargo said. He had already pulled a satellite phone from an inner pocket of his jacket. Tapping two buttons, he waited for the line to connect. "I will call for help," he told the pilot. "You worry about putting us down in one piece."

"One piece?" the copilot quivered allowed. "There's no place to land for at least a hundred miles!"

Dargo was already on his way out of the cockpit. The pair of guards beyond the bulkhead grabbed him as soon as he appeared, offering him support as the cabin jolted beneath his feet. With the help of the men, Dargo flung himself into the first empty chair and cinched the safety belt tight. At last, he heard the click of the satellite phone making a connection to a secure line.

"This is Triad," the voice said.

"This is Graystone, declaring an emergency. Pull position from my GPS until you lose contact. The aircraft has suffered critical damage to the starboard wing and is losing altitude quickly," Dargo offered in a calm, clear voice.

"Roger that, Graystone," the voice responded from back at the compound. "We'll send all available help immediately."

"Negative," Dargo snapped in response. "I repeat, negative. Do *not* transmit an SOS on open frequencies. Find us help, but do so quietly."

The voice on the other end of the line took a moment to respond. "Ah, roger that, sir. We have a fix on your position and we're scrambling for a solution now."

"Also, be advised—I believe an attack on the compound is imminent. I have no specific details. Put every man on alert and lock everything down."

When a response was not immediately forthcoming, Dargo bellowed, "Do you understand?"

"Yes, sir," the voice confirmed. "Understood. I've already raised the alert inside the installation. We're on it, sir."

The aircraft dipped hard to the right once more and Dargo had to struggle to keep hold of the phone, as well as his most recent meal. Moments later, the vicious pitch was countered by the pilot, and the cabin rattled as the plane drew slowly closer to upright. Dargo felt his body weight fall from the safety restraint and drop back into the leather upholstered seat. He immediately cinched the seatbelt tighter.

"I must be clear," Dargo said into the phone. "The safety of the facility is priority one. No manpower can be diverted to aid or assist in our recovery. I have reliable information indicating that someone is about to move against the compound."

"Understood, sir," the voice from base confirmed. "We're tracking your location and circling the wagons here. Don't worry, sir. We can walk and chew gum at the same time. You get that plane down in one piece and we'll find a way to pick you up."

Walk and chew gum? Dargo rolled his eyes. It was obviously Mister Wagner's shift in the control room. The man was ex-special forces and prone to using idioms that confused the rest of the civilized world.

A painful screech blasted from overhead speakers as the pilot's voice filled the cabin. "This is Captain Walker Gilmour. As you may have noticed, we've got ourselves in a bit of pickle, folks. At this point, it sort of goes without saying, but I need everyone in their seats and buckled in good and tight.

"Best put those heads between your knees, too, folks. We're going down. Keep in mind that each seat is equipped with a flotation device so be sure to take that with you on your way to the exit."

The intercom cut out with another screech and Dargo was left shaking his head. *Pickle?* The pilot was another American and, as such, Dargo had no idea what a pickle had to do with their predicament.

Chapter 12

Voss was sitting at his desk, staring idly at the ballpoint pen in his hand. He'd been there in the dark for hours, awash in a turbulent sea of confusing thoughts and troubling emotions. The memory dump he'd recovered from Cyrus was the most ambitious of his experiments to date, and he rationalized, as a result, that it was also the reason it was the most complex. In spite of all of his research, he'd failed to consider how subjects might function on differing levels of complexity, or that sharing in their experiences might offer varying physical and mental challenges.

Voss was quick to understand that Cyrus's mind operated on a level beyond that of previous test subjects. The complex nature of his thought processing was overwhelming. For such an unassuming young man, it was second nature for him to consider the actions and motivations of everyone he encountered. It made Voss curious how Cyrus would score on a standardized IQ test;

he found the mental gymnastics constantly taking place in his mind astounding.

Following the memory restoration process, Voss had been entirely overwhelmed by the onslaught of information and emotion. Realizing immediately that it was too much to handle, he took a sedative. It was a crude, improvised attempt to slow the flood of data that his mind was struggling to integrate. Afterward, it had taken hours—and two additional doses of sedatives—before Voss felt he was gaining control of the turbulent onslaught on new sensory input. Finally, the newly assimilated information began to collate into memories he could access and understand.

One thing was certain—Cyrus Cooper wasn't like any of his prior test subjects. And for someone who never seemed overly concerned with what was happening around him, he maintained a shocking level of situational awareness at all times.

With time, Voss was able to sort through everything Cyrus had given him. What he learned left him at a loss for words, and unsure how to proceed from that point. Sitting alone in the darkness of his office, hours had passed before he finally felt able to discuss his concerns with Cyrus.

When Cyrus stepped into the office, he didn't seem surprised that the lights had been turned low. Voss took a sip from a bottle of water, hoping to find his voice. He found himself reluctant to meet the eyes of his guest and he knew that speaking with Cyrus would be an altogether greater challenge.

The memory transfer had already changed their relationship in some tangible way. It was a side effect that Voss didn't fully appreciate until that moment.

Cyrus was looking around the silent office. That the guards had left them alone wasn't lost on him. But then, precious little was lost on the young man. "Your security escort has been suspended," Voss said, finally meeting Cyrus's eyes. "Permanently."

The surprise on Cyrus's face was genuine, Voss was now certain of that. That moment brought new understanding to Voss. He now had unique insight, not only into the way Cyrus thought, but in his emotional responses as well. It was the sort of awareness he'd hoped his technology would provide and aid in treating mental illness. It was a welcomed relief that such tangible understanding really could result from his work. It didn't help him with Cyrus, but it was proof that his work had practical medical applications.

Pointing Cyrus to one of the chairs opposite his desk, Voss then pulled himself to his feet. He was still far more weary than expected. When he rounded the desk, it was a relief to slip into the chair beside Cyrus.

"We have a great deal to discuss," Voss said quietly. Even the sound of his own voice seemed thunderous in the silence of his office. The words rattled in his ears along with the sound of his own heartbeat. He wondered how long it would be before the headache subsided. It felt like it would go on indefinitely.

"I guessed as much," Cyrus admitted. "To be honest, I wasn't sure if you'd lock me up or kick me out once you were done with the memory transplant."

A grim smile played across Voss's face. He leaned back in the chair and eyed the ceiling. "That's interesting. I never considered it, but you're right. The procedure really is more like a transplant than anything else."

When Cyrus didn't respond, Voss remembered how the young man had an aversion filling a silence with his own thoughts. The insights he'd gleaned from the *transplant* were remarkable.

Choosing his words carefully, Voss studied Cyrus. "You're not who you appear to be."

"Few of us are," Cyrus countered philosophically.

That brought a chuckle. "True. But you, more than most."

"I can't deny it."

"Your reasons for being here aside, I'm concerned about what brought you in the first place."

Cyrus met his gaze with a penetrating stare. "I can't overstate this enough," he warned. "No one can ever know what I've shared with you. That knowledge would put you and your loved ones in exceedingly great danger. Myself included."

"That's where this procedure is helpful. I *fully* understand what you mean," Voss assured.

Glancing at the floor, Cyrus shook his head. He seemed resigned to the fact that there was no turning back now. "I hope you do."

"Your people, the Coalition…they pose a threat to my family."

"They want your technology," Cyrus said bluntly. "But more than anything, they're worried about what others would do with it. I'm sure you can see how it could be manipulated and made harmful."

Voss took a small sip of water from his bottle. "The same can be said for fire. Put to proper use, it warms us and lights our way. But if not properly managed it burns us; kills us."

A small smile crept across Cyrus's face. "Fair enough. As you know, your technology is why I was sent here. But I *chose to be here* for reasons of my own."

"You've come for my daughter." Voss said, trepidation lacing his words. But when Cyrus didn't look away under his withering glare, Voss felt satisfying confirmation of everything he already knew.

"I won't let anything happen to Natasha," Cyrus said flatly. The truth of the statement was reflected in his stare as fervently as it was in his mind. And it was true. He'd demonstrated as much since his arrival.

Voss closed his eyes and nodded. He took a few deep breaths and made an attempt to calm his frayed nerves before looking at Cyrus once more.

"It's me, isn't it?" Cyrus asked, his voice almost a whisper. He looked concerned. "You absorbed it all? Not just the memories but the emotions too?"

A tired smile touched the corners of Voss's lips as he offered the barest hint of a nod.

There was a long pause.

"And you disapprove?" Cyrus asked.

Voss stared down at the floor. He considered his response; he sat motionless for well over a minute. There was nothing he could say that seemed appropriate. For everything he now had swirling around inside his head, words weren't capable of expressing what he was experiencing. He'd just communicated with another person in a way that was beyond anything Homo sapiens had ever managed. Finding that communication to be only one directional was disconcerting. It meant he had to find words to express complex feelings, concerns, and thoughts verbally, which he wasn't sure was possible.

Finally, Voss reached out and placed his water bottle on the corner of the desk. There was a slight tremor in his hand; one that hadn't subsided since the event. He knew it made him look as weak on the outside as he felt inside.

"The procedure has shown me a great deal about you, Cyrus. But only three things matter right now. The first is that, regardless of what brought you here, you mean my family no harm. Second, whoever is attacking us, I think you're our best chance we have at stopping them. And third, you *are* a good man. You love my daughter, and you would die to protect her. I don't just believe this—*I know it.*"

Never breaking his gaze, Cyrus sat silently. Voss knew he was being given a chance to speak his mind. They both knew there was far more left unsaid. But for the moment, that was enough.

"I will speak with Dargo," Voss said. "You'll have access to his resources, and whatever else you need. You'll also have access to any part of this facility below the fourth floor. And your security escort has been reassigned."

Thinking better of it, Voss added, "I wouldn't expect Dargo to go out of his way to make you comfortable. As you requested, I won't be telling him why I've come to these decisions. While I'm confident he will comply with my wishes, I'm certain he won't do it happily—or without question."

Cyrus smiled. "I can live with that. I appreciate your support and your consideration."

Standing up, Cyrus took a long look at him. Voss knew what he saw. At that moment, he was more exhausted than he could ever recall feeling. Slouched in the chair, with shoulders slumped, Voss couldn't imagine the pain behind his eyes leaving him any time soon.

"There's more, isn't there?" Cyrus asked, seeming suddenly to decide against leaving the room.

Voss offered a slight dip of his head. A new level of defeat shadowed his countenance. "I need to know... No—I should say, I feel compelled to ask: What will you tell her about her father?"

There was no question in Voss's mind that Cyrus would understand what he was referring to. Though judging from his expression, he hadn't anticipated their conversation taking this particular turn.

Cyrus walked back to the chair, and sat. "As you already know, I only have suspicions."

"Yes, and as we both know, your instincts tend to serve you well in these matters. So I'll save you the trouble of checking for yourself. You have guessed correctly."

Lapsing into a long silence, it was some time before Voss finally met Cyrus's stare. "If you intend to tell her, I only ask that you allow me time to prepare for what will follow," he said quietly.

Voss felt the weight of Cyrus's penetrating gaze and realized the young man was sizing him up. If there was any levity to be found in the moment, it was the fact that his daughter's suitor was taking *his* measure of *her* father. The spark of admiration Voss held for him grew stronger as he realized, with some personal pride, that his daughter had chosen well.

Still, Voss was left to wonder exactly what Cyrus saw when he studied him. Voss was a man who had made his share of mistakes, but Cyrus knew nothing of those—No...that wasn't entirely true. He knew enough. He knew part of Voss's single greatest regret, but it wasn't the full story.

"It's not my place," Cyrus said at last. "I'm not here to intrude on family matters, not unless they compromise Natasha's safety."

With a silent sigh, Voss slowly closed his eyes. To his surprise, he found himself mouthing a silent prayer—something he hadn't done since he was a child.

After a minute had passed, Voss opened his eyes once more. They were moist, and he felt as though he'd been offered a reprieve of some kind. Fear and relief were now present in equal measures, where before there had only been fear.

"You must think it terribly unfair of me to keep such a secret," he said.

When Cyrus didn't respond, Voss continued, "Before Natasha was born her mother, Eleanor, and I, were going through a rough patch.

"It was entirely my fault, I'm afraid," he explained. "We'd been married for several years and were both working for the same company at that point. I'm sorry to say that I'd become entirely consumed with my work on Shadowlight, and our married life suffered."

Cyrus watched Voss as he spoke. There was no hint of judgment on his face.

"I was almost never home," Voss continued. "I worked day and night in the lab; often gone for days at a time. I was doing remarkable, cutting edge research," he said with a sad smile. "But it's funny how little that means in the grand scheme of things, when all is said and done.

"Eleanor was working, too. She was a corporate attorney for Onyx Gander, a position that had her traveling often. At the time, Dargo was also employed by Onyx. He was one of their security people—a bodyguard, really. All the top executives were assigned a security detail when traveling. It was an unfortunate fact of life back then. Not much has changed in that regard, I suppose.

"Anyway, fairly frequently when Eleanor traveled, Dargo was assigned to her detail."

"And they had an affair," Cyrus contributed for the first time.

Voss's eyes rose, filled with indecision. His head tipped slowly from side to side as he considered the statement. "I don't know," he said slowly. "To call it an affair threatens to cheapen it in some way. Eleanor wasn't like that, you see. Not the type to cheat or fool around.

"No," he said, as if his mind had drifted off to some long faded memory. "For her to have a relationship with Dargo there would have been something there. Not something cheap or tawdry."

Voss's focus quickly shifted back to the present and a sad smile crossed his face. "Once Eleanor became pregnant, it was as if the entire world around me came into focus for the first time in many years. I was happier than I'd ever been. The baby changed everything for us, mostly because it changed everything for me. I shifted my attention away from work and started spending all of my free time at home, getting ready for the baby—Natasha. In every way, it really was the best thing that ever happened to our marriage."

Voss realized Cyrus was sitting silently, hanging on every word.

"I know what you're thinking," he said with a disappointed shake of his head. "But I didn't find out about that until later. For Eleanor, it was enough to have me back in her life—and she was happy, too. Everything just clicked. And not long after Natasha was born, *we* became pregnant with Anna. Those were absolutely the happiest days of my life."

The bright rays of happiness shifted and a darkness appeared in Voss's disposition. "But sometimes the best of times can't be made to last," he said in a dry, husky voice. "Not long after Anna was born, Eleanor was taken from us."

"It was a car bomb," Cyrus said. "Right in the middle of downtown?"

Voss nodded silently. He sat for a long time before finding the words to continue. "It was never determined why she was killed. And I was never sure whether she'd been the intended target. Only one thing was certain—I would do *anything* to protect my family. So I left Onyx Gander. I cashed in my stock options and sold my rights to the company patents. I moved my family here. I built this place so no one could ever hurt us again."

Cyrus offered a nod of understanding. But then, Voss realized, what could he say to such an outpouring.

"But you have Dargo working for you now—a constant reminder of it all. Isn't that difficult for you?" Cyrus asked finally.

Voss grinned, but shook his head. "I didn't learn about Eleanor and Dargo until after Eleanor was taken from me. And at that point, I realized that it didn't change things at all. If anything, I owed them both for what had happened. If it hadn't been for Natasha, my life would've turned out very different, and it wouldn't have been nearly as rewarding.

"Dargo might be Natasha's father, but in my heart she'll always be my little girl. For that, I owe Dargo a debt I can never repay."

"So you let him work for you?"

"He's an unusual man," Voss admitted with a shrug. "But this arrangement is of *his* choosing. It allows him to watch over Natasha. He's watched her grow into a beautiful and strong young woman. He doesn't have good people skills, and I don't think he would know what to do with a family if he had one of his own. So this works best for everyone. He watches over both girls as if they were his, and I know without any doubt that they are as safe as humanly possible."

"Alright," Cyrus said with some degree of finality. "I think that actually makes sense to me. It's unconventional, but it works for you. But you know that you'll have to tell her the truth one day."

Taking a deep breath, Voss released it slowly. "True. It was easier to deal with that concern when she was young. As you say, the matter was so unconventional that I couldn't very well explain things until she was old enough to understand the circumstances involved. But now, that day has come, and I'm just biding my time until I can find the right words to explain things."

"Well…good luck with that," Cyrus said with a good natured laugh. "Maybe a memory transplant is the best approach," he chided, "because I don't know if you'll ever find the right words to fully explain this one. Not to someone with so much invested."

Voss smiled, but he knew Cyrus was right.

"All kidding aside," Cyrus said frankly. "It's a big deal, and she deserves to know. But it's not going to change the way she feels about you."

"I wish I knew that were true."

"You do," Cyrus said, tapping his index finger audibly on the side of his own skull. "You know for sure because I know for sure. There's not a doubt in my mind," he grinned.

Voss laughed, "Yes, you do offer *a unique perspective*."

The implications of Voss's phrase held several meanings, more than he might have intentionally voiced given the circumstances. But he could tell from Cyrus's expression that he understood his alternate meaning.

"I feel like I should apologize for the things you must've experienced," Cyrus said, searching for his own appropriate words. "But the truth is, the thoughts and memories that are probably troubling you the most are the ones I'll never apologize for. To anyone. Ever."

Voss burst out laughing. It was a tired, but sincere belly laugh. "Nor should you, my boy. Not ever. If anything, I'm the one who owes you an apology. The fact is, I never considered the breadth or scope of the experiences transferred. In this case it constitutes an egregious breach of your privacy—err, and that of my daughter's. And for that, I can never make amends. But I am truly sorry."

After a shake of his hand, Voss watched Cyrus leave the room. And as he made his way back to his desk, Voss's mind was already considering ways he might isolate the types of memories that were selected in the transfer process. As it turned out, the massive information transfer was a good start, but the process had yet to be perfected. He was suffering, both under the load of information he'd received, as well as the scope of the memories that were transplanted. The procedure would be far more effective if he could develop a way to further isolate selective memories and restrict the capture of additional sensory related data. Medical science was currently suffering from an information deficiency that made treating patients with cognitive disorders far too complicated. But if he couldn't better isolate the information targeted with his memory procedure, superfluous information might prove equally detrimental. If he'd learned anything from

Cyrus's download, it was that targeting certain memories would be critical to the future of his work.

Chapter 13

Cyrus stepped off the elevator and started down the hall. Shedding his security escort felt good; he had breathing room for the first time since entering the compound. There was a quickness to his step; he was anxious to find Natasha and update her on the conversation with Voss. He knew she was worried about fallout from the transplant procedure, and she had every right to be uncomfortable with it. Many of the exposed memories were deeply personal and they involved her.

No sooner had he tapped the doorbell on the control panel beside her bedroom door, and the doors shot open with a swish. Natasha was standing there staring him right in the eye. Her bare feet bobbed between flatfooted and tiptoed, and she practically dripped with nervous energy.

"Well?" she demanded instantly. "How bad was it?"

He shrugged, his stare noncommittal.

Her eyes bulged and her lips puckered. She looked like she might explode in anticipation. A moment later, she cast him with a more calculating expression that he didn't understand. She leaned out into the hallway and looked both ways.

"No security detail?" she grinned mischievously. She slinked up in front of him and slid her arms around his neck. "I'll take that as a good sign."

"A very good sign," he admitted, and kissed her tenderly. Her body drew more tightly against his. A moment later, he felt her pulling him into the room. *A very good sign*, he grinned and let her lead the way.

"Don't you even want to know what we talked about?" Cyrus asked, daring to tease just a little more.

"I'm pretty sure I don't," she whispered and bit gently at his lip, making it clear she intended to get her way.

Three rapid bangs sounded from somewhere nearby, just before the doors slid shut behind them.

"What was that?" Natasha whispered. Her eyes were wide and he could feel her pulse quicken further beneath his touch. Cyrus knew she recognized the sound of gunshots from their close call the night before.

Shit, he thought. His eyes flashed a quick circuit of the bedroom in search of anything that would be useful as a weapon. There wasn't much. The gunshots had come from somewhere upstairs. Either from Voss's office and lab on four, or the security center and guard's quarters on five.

Cyrus knew that if he were trying to sack the compound from the inside, he'd start with the security office. He wasn't familiar with the layout of level five.

"Where's the bag I brought back from the bus station locker?" Cyrus asked.

"Security took it as soon as we got back. I tried to keep it but—."

He squeezed her hand. "It's ok," he said softly.

Rifling through Natasha's art supplies, Cyrus found a pair of thick, wood handled paintbrushes. He took one for himself and gave the other to her.

"I'm going to find out what's happening," he said as he led her back to the door. "Anna's in her room?"

She nodded.

"Get her and bring her here," he explained. "I want you both in the hidden stairwell behind your closet. If I don't come for you in the next hour, take the tunnel and get out of here."

"We can't leave without my father."

"Take care of your sister. I'm going for your father right now, but you can't wait for us." He kissed her quickly before ducking through the door.

Cyrus stopped when he reached the balcony overlooking the common area three floors below. Another volley of gunshots sounded from above; it sounded more like small arms fire. He hit the elevator button and glanced over the railing. The first floor was deserted. Even the guard normally stationed at the front entrance was missing. The panel beside the front doors flashed a bright red security alert. Even from a distance, Cyrus could see it was displaying a security lockdown message.

He glanced back at the elevator. The lockdown explained why the elevator wasn't responding to his call. It also meant one of two things had happened. Either the facility had suffered an incursion, or their security had been infiltrated. Either way, some kind of enemy force was clearly inside the building. Their first order of business would be to dispatch the security staff.

Suddenly everything Cyrus had overheard about the attack on Gretchen made sense. No one could find logic in the assault at the time. The reason for the attack was now painfully obvious. Dargo had left the facility, taking half the remaining security force to deal with the assault on Gretchen. The entire attack had been a diversion intended to lead Dargo away from the compound. It was a ploy to weaken internal security.

Circling back to the emergency stairwell, Cyrus found the door sealed. The security system's electromagnetic locking mechanism had secured the stairwell, just as it had the elevator. He was effectively trapped on the third floor.

More gunshots sounded from above.

Being trapped was a mixed blessing. He was stuck and unarmed, but there were no hostiles on his level. It also meant Natasha and Anna wouldn't have trouble reaching the hidden stairwell through the access panel in Natasha's closet. Unfortunately, it left him unable to respond to the attack.

That was unacceptable.

Returning to the balcony, Cyrus took another look at the common room three floors below. The sofas arranged around the entertainment center were almost right beneath him. Aside from that, all he really saw was a lot of unforgiving stone tile. Undeterred, he stuck the wide, wood shaft of the paintbrush in his back pocket and climbed onto the stainless steel rail atop the pane of thick glass at the end of the balcony.

Stretching as far as possible, he still couldn't reach the floor above. He stood there, teetering like a clumsy tightrope walker on the round steel railing for what seemed like an eternity before finally committing to a desperate vertical jump. He would either reach a handhold on the floor above or go crashing to the lobby below.

From his perspective, the jump was executed in painfully slow motion. Even as his leap neared its apex, Cyrus wasn't sure it had what it took. But stretching his arms with everything he had, his fingers slipped over the right-angled edge of the balcony above at the exact moment he ran out of vertical life.

Struggling to keep his tenuous grip, Cyrus lifted his body weight using only the tips of his fingers. Slowly, he was able to extend his grip and slip the second knuckles of each finger over the ledge. Two more gunshots broke out nearby, and Cyrus held silent and steady. He could only hope that no one above had heard or seen him.

After about twenty seconds, he knew there wasn't any choice. He couldn't hold on much longer. The silence in the immediate area was enough to make him risk his next move.

Drawing himself up required great effort. Most of his strength was sapped while hanging silently by his fingers. The strength in his arms was fading fast.

Clenching his teeth and bearing down, he pulled harder, levering himself onto a tiny four inch ledge that extended beyond the glass and chrome railing at the end of the balcony.

Throwing a leg over the railing and huffing a sigh of relief, Cyrus dropped to the safety of the fourth floor. But that safety was short lived. He heard the sound of someone slamming themselves bodily against a door not far down the adjacent hallway. Without stopping to see who was coming, Cyrus ducked around the corner where the hallway opened onto the balcony.

A moment later, a guard stepped from the end of the hall. He had his gun raised and ready. For a fraction of a second, Cyrus struggled to designate him as either friend or foe. While it was clear that a rival force had infiltrated the building, possibly posing as guards, the sounds of weapon fire meant there were friendlies still in play.

When the guard turned, bringing his weapon to bear, Cyrus knew he wasn't facing an ally. It wasn't so much that the man was challenging him. Present circumstances dictated that loyal guards would have as much trouble deciphering Cyrus's intentions as he did theirs. It was the look in the man's eyes that told Cyrus he was an assailant. The guard had chosen to target him with clear and obvious intent. There was no indecision—a luxury afforded only to the attacking force at that moment.

The guard swung his gun laterally toward Cyrus who batted it away with a swift parry of his left hand. At the same time, Cyrus snatched the paintbrush from his back pocket using his right. Spinning the brush in a single fluid motion, he gathered both speed and inertia in his swing. He planted the blunted tip of the brush's handle solidly in his attacker's abdomen, just below the ribcage. To Cyrus's shock, his improvised weapon failed to penetrate flesh. Unfortunately, the tip of the brush met a rigid, solid surface that stopped his assault cold. Cyrus felt the shaft of the brush slip through his hand.

The gunman was wearing body armor.

The man cast his eyes down and saw the paintbrush for the first time. A grin spread across his face as he locked eyes with Cyrus. Still fighting with the man to keep the gun at a safe angle, Cyrus spun his opponent a hundred and eighty degrees and forced him backward until he was pinned against the steel railing.

"What are you laughing at?" Cyrus said through clenched teeth. He took a half step backward and then smashed his forehead into the man's nose. There was a sickening crunch of cartilage, and Cyrus felt the man's strength leave the arm fighting for control of the gun. Without wasting a second, Cyrus let go of the gun and shoved his left hand under his assailant's chin. At the same time, his right hand found the man's belt buckle. In one swift motion, he hoisted his attacker by the belt and sent him tipping backward over the railing.

The man disappeared in an instant. The crunch of shattering bones that followed was unmistakable. Cyrus didn't even take the time to look at his handiwork. He knew from the sound of the previous gunshots that more than one gunman was on the loose. His only regret was not relieving his opponent of his firearm before sending him to his death.

Snatching the paintbrush from the floor, Cyrus darted down the hall. *Body armor.* He wouldn't make the same mistake at his next encounter.

Stopping at the door to Voss's office, Cyrus considered his options. Voss was unquestionably the target of any operation. Whoever was behind the attack clearly wanted something from him. The surest way to ensure Voss's compliance was to leverage his daughters. The same theory had been floated by Monica Fichtner prior to Cyrus's infiltration of the compound. That was why Natasha and Anna were already safely out of harm's way, hiding in a part of the building that not even Voss knew existed.

Whoever was attacking the compound would need to approach Voss directly in order to get what they were after. With that in mind, Cyrus's plan was simple. He needed to get to Voss before his opponents could. Failing that, he would need to recover Voss at all costs.

Simple... Yeah, hardly.

Cyrus stood at the door to Voss's office armed with only the short shaft of wood that was a paintbrush handle. The sound of his heartbeat thundered in his ears, and his head was sore after using it as a blunt force weapon against the man on the balcony. A stabbing pain in his side reminded him that he was still suffering from a gunshot wound, and he was pretty sure he'd already torn some of his stitches for the umpteenth time. On top of it all, as soon as he walked through Voss's door he was likely to be shot full of holes.

A grim smile crossed his face. Natasha would be upset when she had to stitch him up once more. The idea brought a silent laugh, and the laugh brought a surge of pain. But when the pain sucked his breath away, Cyrus was left with an idea. As far as plans went, it wasn't genius, but it *might* do the trick.

A wounded target represented a much smaller threat. That might be something he could use to his advantage.

Sagging and clutching his side, Cyrus took a deep breath and tapped the button on the panel beside the door. As the doors whisked open, he crumpled against the frame and feigned a struggle to stay on his feet. Though he didn't make a show of it, as soon as the doors slid away, he'd taken the whole of the office in before stumbling and looking away. There were two men from the security team present, dressed in their traditional dark suits, just like the man he'd encountered in the hall. But Voss was nowhere to be seen.

"Don't move!" one of the guards ordered. He kept Cyrus covered from the middle of the room while the other man moved to intercept him.

"Seriously, kid," the second guard said as he advanced. "Take it easy. You don't have to die, too. We're just here for the family."

As the second guard came within arm's reach, Cyrus finally raised his drooped head and looked the man square in the eyes. His steely glare startled the man who stopped in his tracks. "Over my dead body," Cyrus growled. Standing suddenly upright from his stooped position, Cyrus closed the gap between them in two long steps. He batted his assailant's gun away and slammed the tip of the paintbrush down into the soft tissue where the man's neck met his shoulder. The handle of the brush plunged in, stopping only when Cyrus's closed fist impacted the man's collarbone. Blood sprayed from the gory wound as the guard's eyes bulged helplessly, his breath already gone; his life was soon to follow.

Staying in motion, Cyrus spun, keeping this collapsing opponent's form between him and the remaining gunman. Two shots rang out but caught the dying guard in the back. By that point, Cyrus had already stripped his human shield of his gun. As the bloody body fell to the floor, Cyrus came out firing.

The first two shots Cyrus fired caught the remaining gunman in the center of his chest and sent him staggering. Cyrus knew those wouldn't be kill shots—he was now aware the men wore body armor. Still, the shots were enough to keep his attacker from drawing a bead on him, and a fraction of a second later, Cyrus snapped off a third shot to the center of the man's face. The blood splatter on the back wall left no question as to the lethalness of the shot.

Twenty seconds later, Cyrus had relieved each of the gunmen of a pair of spare magazines. For the first time since taking up the paintbrush, he felt properly outfitted for the task at hand. Still, he needed to find Voss. It seemed like the two gunmen had been left behind to bar access to the lab beyond. Cyrus eyed the door on the back wall leading to Voss's private lab.

Tapping the button on the wall, Cyrus stepped aside as the doors whisked open. It was some relief when he wasn't immediately greeted by a hail of gunfire. Still, he wasn't feeling overly optimistic. Leaning only as far as was required, he peeked around the doorjamb, leading with the muzzle of his gun.

The lab was dimly lit. There were sterile lab counters covered with equipment, just as there had been when Voss performed the transplant procedure hours earlier. At first glance the lab appeared uninhabited. But that didn't make sense. Cyrus stood silently and listened. After a moment he heard the sound of fingers flying across a computer keyboard. They were distant and almost inaudible over the low hum of idling lab equipment.

Stepping into the room, Cyrus moved slowly and silently. He heard the doors slide shut behind him and strained for the sounds of distant keystrokes. They hadn't so much as paused, so there was no indication that his approach had been compromised.

Moving further into the room, Cyrus made his way along the edge of a massive walk-in freezer. When he reached the corner, he peered around the end. Twenty yards away, Voss sat on a tall stool before a computer terminal. He was entering commands into the computer at a rapid pace. A tall man in a dark suit stood beside him with the barrel of his gun pressed behind Voss's ear.

"You have to give me a few minutes. It takes time to decrypt the files," Voss was explaining to the man with the gun. "If I give you the data now it'll do you no good."

The man in the suit pushed harder with the gun, causing Voss to shudder in pain. "Don't test me. I know the difference between encrypting and decrypting. You're trying to encrypt the files before you copy them to the drive. If you mess with me, I swear you'll regret it!"

There was no response, only an involuntary whimper from Voss. A moment later, he began entering commands once more. "Alright—Alright! Just give me a minute. There is a lot of data. You said you want copies of everything," he said in a sad, placating tone.

"You'd better get it all. If you miss anything, you won't be the one to pay the price. If you miss even a single file it'll cost you one of your daughters."

Voss's keystrokes fell silent. Cyrus saw him try to turn and face the man in the suit, but with the gun pressed so rigidly against the corner of his skull it made the motion painfully impossible. "You leave them out of this!" he demanded, even as he squirmed in pain.

Cyrus didn't like the look of the situation. The guard had the gun pressed far too tightly against Voss's head. Taking the man out was a dicey proposition at best. Making matters worse, the guy wasn't smart enough to keep his finger off the trigger while corkscrewing the end of the weapon into Voss's flesh. It meant there was far too much of a chance that the weapon would go off even if Cyrus clipped him with a head shot from a distance. Hell, it would be a miracle if the guard didn't kill Voss by accident before he was done. It raised an important question. These guys were clearly just hired muscle, marionettes doing a job. *So who is pulling their strings?* Cyrus knew it would be the same person behind the attack on the train, the assault on the bar, the attack at the bus terminal, and certainly the same person responsible for what happened to Boone's team.

"Not going to happen," the gunman threatened in a cold tone. "My team's collecting them as we speak. You just finish up quick.

While you're at it, best give some thought to which one you like best. I have a feeling you'll have to make that choice real soon."

The tired gasp that escaped Voss told Cyrus just how terrified he was. "Why are you doing this?" Voss asked.

"It's just a job," the man answered flatly.

"Killing my security team and threatening my family is just a job? What have I ever done to you?"

"Nothing," the man grumbled. "Not a damn thing. This is just business—nothing more. I deliver you and your daughters, I get paid. Simple as that."

Cyrus had the man solidly in his sights when he cleared his throat, making himself known for the first time. The gunman shot an urgent glance over his shoulder but never moved the gun away from Voss's head. "Just a job?" Cyrus asked. "Who hired you?"

"Whoa!" the gunman roared. "Back off or I'll kill him!"

"Go ahead," Cyrus said with a carefree shrug. "I'm here on a job, same as you. But I don't need Voss in order to complete my mission."

The man's eyes narrowed as he took Cyrus in once again with new eyes. There was an odd look in his gaze and Cyrus wasn't sure how to read it. He knew the gunman was trying to read his intentions, as well. Being one of Dargo's security guards, of course he knew who Cyrus was. Still, Cyrus saw indecision in the man's eyes. It was as if he were trying to size Cyrus up but was entirely uncertain of what he was now seeing.

"Stand down," the gunman demanded. "I'll kill him!"

"Like I said," Cyrus reiterated. "That's not my concern. His daughters are safe. You can't touch them."

"Bullshit!"

"Do I look like I'm bluffing? Do what you want with Voss. Just keep in mind that when you're done, you still have to deal with me."

Voss spoke; hope appeared in his voice for the first time. "Is it true? They really are safe?"

"I give you my word," Cyrus said with gentle reassurance. He knew what would come next.

Even though Voss had his back to him, Cyrus could see a sense of ease overtake the man. His rigid, pained stature relaxed in a very visible way. A moment later, the clatter of keystrokes resumed at the computer terminal.

"Hey! What the bloody hell are you doing?" the gunman bellowed.

Undeterred, Voss's rapid assault on the keyboard continued. With a final, solid strike of the 'Enter' key, he finally lowered his hands to his lap. "You said you could tell what I was doing," Voss explained. "If that's true, you should know that I just wiped all of the data from your flash drive and executed a command to encrypt the entire database."

Voss turned his head and looked the gunman in the eye. "My girls are safe. You'll get *nothing* from me."

Everything had played out exactly as Cyrus anticipated. When Voss turned to face the gunman, it was proof that the guard was so stymied that he'd let the pressure of the gun sag from the side of Voss's head. So, too, had gone the man's concentration, and that was Cyrus's ultimate objective.

Cyrus squeezed the trigger, scoring a perfect headshot. The rogue guard's hands dropped, his gun clattering harmlessly to the floor. It was followed a full second later by his corpse after it bounced off the end of the counter and landed with a bloody thud.

———————

Turning on wobbly legs, Voss looked at the gruesome mess that was his attacker, and then at Cyrus. With a dry swallow he stepped away from the corpse.

"Are you alright?" Cyrus asked. He tried to draw the older man's gaze away from the blood.

Voss felt his hands trembling; they mirrored the sensation threatening to buckle his knees. "Yes. Fine," he responded in a gravelly voice. "Thanks to you."

Meeting Cyrus's eyes, Voss drew a measure of strength from his steady demeanor. Cyrus took Voss's arm and led him several paces away from the aftermath.

"You really secured the files?" Cyrus asked.

Voss offered a crisp nod. "As soon as you said the girls were safe, I encrypted everything with a 2048 bit triple AES cypher. It won't matter if they take the data now. It would be useless to them."

Cyrus grinned. "Well done."

Walking to the nearby table, Voss leaned against it to steady himself. He took several slow breaths and struggled to control his racing heart.

"Are you alright?" Cyrus asked once more. He circled Voss, examining him with clinical eyes.

When Voss didn't answer, Cyrus leaned across the table and looked at him more closely. "I didn't mean what I said," he explained. "I had no intention of letting him take you."

Voss grinned. He nodded, the amusing thought lifting his spirits. "Never a doubt," he chuckled from beneath arched eyebrows. Then he offered a glance at the corpse on the other side of the room. "Lucky for me, he fell for it."

The questioning expression from Cyrus told Voss that he needed to elaborate. "I suppose I've gained some insight into your mindset over the past twelve hours," Voss explained. "I knew your game even as you were maneuvering the bastard. You were afraid to pull the trigger while he had the gun to my head. You needed to distract him before you could risk making a move." He tapped his own temple. "I've learned a great deal about the way you think, Cyrus."

Gnashing his teeth, Cyrus looked away. "Then you know that I really needed to take him alive. He was my best chance at understanding what's going on here."

Voss started for the door leading to his office. Cyrus quickly moved to follow.

"I understand," Voss said over his shoulder as he walked. "For what it's worth, I'm glad you made the choice you did." He stopped suddenly and looked Cyrus square in the eyes, a flare of urgency sparking in his gaze. "Tell me—what you said about my girls—they truly are safe?"

Cyrus slapped the older man on the shoulder and offered a solemn nod. "Safe and sound. That part was true."

"Good." Voss stepped through the door and into his office. After making it less than two paces, he stopped suddenly upon seeing two more dead security guards. "My word!"

Cyrus tapped the release on the side of his gun and let the magazine drop to the floor. Pulling a spare from his back pocket, he slapped it into the grip and charged the action. "We need to be careful," he warned. "I don't know how many of the guards are against us."

Walking slowly through the room, Voss found himself at a loss for words. His workplace—his home, had become a killing field. All of this, after everything he'd done to protect his family.

He stepped around the congealing puddle of thick arterial blood that had spread across the floor, only to have his eyes fall squarely upon the next body. Squinting, Voss leaned over the dead man for a closer look. The soft bristles of an artist's paintbrush protruded from the corner of his collar at an oblique angle.

Voss's jaw waggled as he worked mechanically to find the words to match what he was thinking.

Cyrus saw this and shrugged. "I improvised."

Turning to Cyrus, Voss's jaw fell slack. He looked from Cyrus to the corpse with unblinking eyes and tried to fathom what kind of person saw an artistic tool as a weapon. Still, in spite of his shock, Voss couldn't argue with the end result. It dawned on him for the first time that, in order to save his life, Cyrus had to make it past multiple armed and well-trained aggressors.

In a flash, perhaps just in time, Voss's mind returned fully to the present. He was in very real danger of slipping into traumatic shock. "Dargo!" Voss declared, the sound of his own shout startling even himself.

Cyrus stepped toward Voss at the sound of the outburst. "Quiet," he shushed. "We don't know how many more of them are out there."

Pulling his hand away from his own mouth, Voss shook his head and quieted his voice. "Sorry. But right before these three came into my office I received a call from security. Dargo called in. His plane was going down. *He was crashing.*"

"Crashing?" Cyrus asked with a degree of skepticism. "Are you sure it wasn't part of a ploy?" He glanced at one of the fallen security guards.

"No," Voss said with confidence. "Dargo didn't want to declare an emergency over open radio frequencies. He was afraid it was part of a larger operation here. It seems he was correct."

Falling silent, Cyrus slowly paced the room. Voss watched, unsure what to say or do. He only knew that it was best not to interrupt. The young man's instincts had gotten them this far. He had confidence that the boy could see them through.

"I have to get to the communications room," Cyrus said at last. "Where is it?"

"Fifth floor," Voss said quietly. "One floor up. But do we stand a chance if Dargo's men are working against us?"

"It's not all of Dargo's men," Cyrus explained. "There must be some sort of rogue faction inside your security force. There's been gunfire. It means, whoever's behind this, they don't control the entire security team. Some of them are still on our side—if anyone's been left alive, that is."

Moving to Voss's desk, Cyrus rifled through its surface contents until he found a pen and a pad of paper. "Sketch me the layout of the fifth floor. I need to know what I'm walking into."

"It's ok," Voss said. "I can show you."

Cyrus shook his head and handed him the paper. "No way. If there's more of them, it'll be like walking into a buzz saw. You're staying here where it's safe."

Voss didn't understand, and Cyrus must've noticed as much.

"You and the girls were their mission objective," Cyrus explained. "While I don't know what they're up to, I know that keeping you safe is the key to stopping their plan. So you stay here. I'll hit the security office and see what I can learn."

Reluctantly, Voss accepted the orders and began sketching a simple drawing of the fifth floor's layout.

"Dargo left the building with a sizable portion of the security team," Cyrus thought aloud. "That reduced the number of guards on site to protect you and your family. The gunfire confirms that they weren't all compromised," he reasoned. "Do you know how many guards remained after Dargo and his team left?"

Voss stopped drawing and considered the question. It was frustrating because Dargo had explained these details specifically—Voss just hadn't been concerned enough to pay close attention. At the time he'd been more worried about getting Gretchen back and out of harm's way.

"I'm sorry," Voss said sadly. "I truly wish I had your memory."

He struggled to recall the brief conversation he'd had with Dargo only minutes before he left for the Royal Airfield. "Ten," Voss said finally, with confidence. "He left ten men on site."

"Ten?" Cyrus asked. "Jesus, doc. How many people do you employ?"

Voss offered a sad smile. "Apparently, not nearly enough."

––––––––––

His time with Voss had brought Cyrus multiple advantages. He was now armed for the first time, he'd gained insight into the potential numbers he was facing, and just before leaving, Voss had provided an emergency override code that would override the lock on any door or elevator in the building.

Using the master code, Cyrus entered the stairwell and headed for the fifth floor. He'd left Voss behind, hidden in an out-of-the-way cubby that held the compressor and motors for his lab's walk-in freezer. Cyrus was pretty sure that the corrupt guards were as hampered by the lockdown as he'd been without the override code. They didn't seem to have the ability to move from one floor to the next. That was a distinct advantage because it meant Voss should be safe since all threats on the fourth floor had already been eliminated. Still, with all that was happening, Cyrus couldn't be sure of anything. He'd stashed Voss in an attempt to play it safe.

The stairwell was deathly quiet as Cyrus moved slowly upward. The steps and the walls around him were made of poured concrete, so even the slightest sound was amplified and threatened to echo in the confines of the vertical space. Only the hum of the wall-mounted fluorescent lights offered a break in the silence.

Rounding the switchback halfway up the flight of stairs, Cyrus gained view of the fifth floor landing. He reached the platform with his finger on the trigger of his gun, only a hair away from releasing a round, but was relieved to find no one lying in wait. It made sense. With the lockdown in effect, no one should've had access to the stairway. Voss's overwhelming sense of paranoia had led him to install a personal override code. It was something the building's attackers wouldn't have anticipated. Cyrus's odds of catching the last of the opposing force were improving.

Reaching the door at the top of the stairs, Cyrus tapped Voss's override code into the security pad. But before he pressed the button to open the door, he noticed an option in the corner of the screen that he'd missed earlier. It was labeled simply, 'Camera'.

He tapped the button on the touch screen, changing the display. A live video feed of the fifth floor balcony filled three-quarters of the screen. It was the high-tech equivalent of a door's peephole, only the display offered greater detail, higher definition, and a wider field of view. It was interesting since the doors to the stairwell and those to the medical area were the only conventional swinging doors in the entire building so far. They seemed decidedly low-tech when compared to the rest of the well-fortified compound.

After studying the view outside the door for nearly thirty seconds, Cyrus decided his chances were as good as they were ever going to get. He tapped the lock release icon, pulled the door open on silent hinges, and stepped across the threshold with his gun ready.

He was standing alone on the platform. He backed against the wall and inched near the corner leading to a short hallway, listening. According to Voss's sketch, the corridor led from the elevators to the rest of the floor.

In the distance, Cyrus could hear a voice but he couldn't make out the words being stated. Hazarding a glance around the corner, he witnessed two supine forms. Each was a man lying awkwardly in a sizable pool of blood. This was the fate of the guards loyal to Voss. They didn't have a chance when members of their own team turned on them. Deep gouges in the walls and floor told of a firefight, and explained the sporadic gunshots he'd heard at the onset of all this. Though caught off guard, apparently the loyal among Dargo's men had managed to put up some sort of resistance, however futile.

Moving silently down the hall, Cyrus stopped at the body of the first guard. He laid two fingers against the man's jugular and uselessly hoped for a pulse. Without delay, he stepped to the next man. There, he found the same disappointing truth. Both men were dead and already cold. Cyrus was about to move on when something made him stop and reevaluate the body of the second fallen guard.

It took a moment to realize what his subconscious was suggesting. At first, all he saw was the suited body of a man lying awkwardly on the tile floor. He lay mostly on his back, with blood pooled around his left shoulder.

When he pushed the man fully onto his back, Cyrus knew what was out of place. The guard had taken three rounds, just left of center torso. Aside from that, there were no obvious signs of injury. Pressing his thumb against the right side of the chest, Cyrus confirmed what he'd already assumed. The guard was wearing body armor.

Ripping open the dead man's white, button-down shirt, Cyrus further confirmed the confusing fact. The shots to the chest had, in fact, penetrated his armor.

Rising to his feet, Cyrus strained to hear the voice speaking in the distance. It was still too far off to discern the words, but he was pretty sure the man spoke with a French accent.

Hitting the release on the side of his gun, Cyrus dropped the weapon's fully loaded magazine into his left hand. Examining the top round, he found the cause of the useless body armor. The slugs were coated in solid jackets of Teflon.

Armor piercing ammunition.

Suspicious, he searched the dead man. Retrieving an unused magazine from the guard's belt, he slid his thumb across the top of the magazine and dropped the first round into his hand. He held the bullet up to the light. The slug on this round was a hollow point and jacketed in copper. It was an off-the-shelf round that could be purchased at any sporting goods store.

Laying the loose round and the magazine on the dead man's chest, Cyrus regarded the body once more. He didn't need the ammo—he was already well armed with what he'd taken from the men in Voss's office.

Reaching the 'T' intersection at the end of the hall, Cyrus could go left or right. The security office was to the left but the voice he'd heard was coming from the right. More than that, a new, more prominent voice could also be heard speaking with a mild French accent, Cyrus could now make out the faint words of another man. Whoever he was, he hadn't offered much in response to the first Frenchman's babble; this second voice was strained and quieter.

Cyrus recognized the second voice.

Turning right, he headed for the voices. He passed several open doors along the way. One led to a kitchen, another to a small rec room. But as he drew near a wide opening in the wall on his right, Cyrus knew he'd found the voices. Glancing around the corner, he saw one of the guards seated on the floor with his back trussed up against a rack of free weights. Another of Dargo's men stood over him, thumping the end of a lightweight graphite baton against the palm of his hand.

The man on the floor was slumped forward, sagging against his bindings. It was obvious he no longer had the strength to sit upright. His chin drooped to his chest as blood and bile dripped from his mouth and down the saturated front of his filthy, white shirt.

The man with the baton still wore an immaculately pressed black suit—another of Dargo's men. This was clearly an interrogation, and the man with the baton was obviously enjoying his work far too much. He paced slowly back and forth before the bound and defeated man while swinging the baton through the air with dexterity and skill. "It is within your power to make all of this stop," the man commented as he paced slowly.

Now that Cyrus was near, the French accent of the guard was unmistakable. He'd seen the man around the building over the last day or two but he'd never interacted with him. Now that he thought about it, there were several guards with French accents.

Could there be a connection?

"Tell me about your communication with Dargo," the persecutor insisted. His voice was impatient; he bared his teeth as he pronounced each word with precision. He'd clearly been at this for some time.

"I told you," the seated man said in an exhausted slur. "He radioed an SOS. The plane was going down. I didn't get his position. We lost communication when we lost him on radar."

The interrogator turned suddenly, bringing the baton down on his charge with a lightning swing. The blow struck the seated man just below his right shoulder. The crisp snap that issued was more than just the impact of the weapon on flesh. Cyrus cringed. The bone in the seated man's right arm had just been destroyed.

The man on the floor tipped his head back and howled in agony. His face was drenched in sweat—the kind of perspiration the body secretes, not from exertion, but from times of extreme stress—in this case, torment.

He cocked his head back, banging it against the steel weight machine to which he had been bound. He gasped, each breath a struggle to pull fresh air into his lungs and fight back the pain.

His eyes rolled in their sockets as he teetered on the verge of unconsciousness.

The moment the man's head swung back for the first time, Cyrus recognized his face. The bound guard's name was Wagner. They'd spent a great deal of time together, while Cyrus convalesced, and in the time that followed. Wagner had shown him respect in that time, bending the rules and allowing him to steal private moments with Natasha.

Seeing Wagner treated this way was unacceptable. Cyrus fought against his better judgment and the urge to step around the corner with his gun blazing. A primal part of him wanted to cut down the sadistic interrogator where he stood.

Still, he could not. The gunshots would give away his position, and he needed to gather as much information as possible before he took the man out. Though it pained him, Cyrus waited.

Wagner sobbed, unable to control himself through what must've been staggering pain. The broken arm was just the latest of several savage injuries, Cyrus knew. "Just kill me," Wagner said through choked breaths.

The Frenchman knelt before him and laid the baton down at his side. He took a hand full of Wagner's hair in his fist and used it to pull his drooped head up before looking him in the eyes. "Tell me what I want to know and I will not kill you," the man growled. "Speak now and I will let you go. You can seek medical treatment as soon as my team has taken the Voss family and left the building."

Wagner looked back through swollen and bloodshot eyes. His breathing slowly came under control. He held the man's attention for nearly a minute but still said nothing.

"Just tell me what happened to Dargo," the interrogator insisted. "You managed to delete the recordings before we could pull you out of the communications room, but do not fool yourself. Fortier will recover the data. Once that happens, we will no longer have any use for you."

Cyrus did the math in his head. One hostile dead when he went over the railing, two more shot in Voss's office, plus one more in the lab. Add to that a pair of friendlies down in the hallway of the fifth floor, the interrogator, Wagner, and a man — Fortier—working to recover recordings in the radio room. That accounted for nine of the ten Dargo had left behind to protect the compound. It meant there was still one guard missing, and Cyrus couldn't be sure if he was friend or foe.

What were the chances that any of these men knew the name of the puppet master behind all of this? Whoever was organizing the operation against Voss was skilled enough to keep all information compartmentalized. He was a pro. And that meant that there was likely little more information that the Frenchman could give him.

Good enough.

Stepping around the corner, Cyrus raised his gun. "Hey, asshole," he growled.

The interrogator released Wagner's head and launched to his feet as he turned to face Cyrus. The Frenchman was well trained because he wasn't fully upright when he pulled his gun free from its holster. Cyrus saw recognition in the sadist's eyes in the half second it took for him to draw. There was a look of satisfaction there. He was excited by the prospect of shooting Cyrus.

To be fair, it might've been a little vindictive of Cyrus to even let the Frenchman think he had a shot at out-drawing him. Cyrus could've shot the man down a dozen times over before the man had either his balance in place or his gun anywhere near a targeting vector. But letting the sadist think he had a chance was about two things. First, it was an opportunity to see how the man reacted to his presence. In the fraction of a second it took for events to unfold, Cyrus didn't know what to make of the rapid series of expressions he saw play out across the gunman's face. Only that some of what he saw wasn't right. The gunman wasn't as surprised as he should've been—or maybe he recognized Cyrus as more of a threat than his cover allowed for.

But mostly, it was about letting the sick bastard know he'd come close to surviving—to winning—just not close enough.

Cyrus squeezed the trigger as he walked toward the man at a smooth, steady pace. Then he squeezed the trigger again and again.

The first round caught the Frenchman in the neck at the base of the spine. He was still spinning to face Cyrus, and drawing his sidearm while he did it. The shot landed exactly as intended, clipping the man's spine and shattering bones and nerves alike. The following two shots were ancillary, striking his torso a half second apart; both scored direct hits to the man's heart.

The interrogator's gun skidded across the floor and his body hit with a heavy thud three feet from where Wagner sat bound. The report from Cyrus's three shots shocked Wagner awake, returning him from the edge of unconsciousness. His eyes were wide and his head wobbled with a lack of coordination. He looked up in time to see Cyrus stop at the side of the fallen man with his gun still at the ready.

Cyrus looked at the crippled interrogator. He was alive and breathing, but he wouldn't be for long. Only the man's eyes moved in their sockets. Cyrus could tell that the he was trying to make sense of his sudden loss of bodily control. When the first bullet shattered his spine, he'd lost all sensory input from his extremities. He didn't know that his heart had been destroyed or that he had only seconds left to live.

Leaving the man to his fate, Cyrus knelt beside Wagner. Using the knife he'd confiscated earlier, he cut his bindings.

Wagner struggled to sit upright, clutching his right shoulder with his left hand. "My god," he mumbled. "Where did you come from?"

"Long story," Cyrus said with a sad smile. "Can you walk?"

A pained chuckle escaped Wagner's lips. "Not a chance," he groaned.

"Fair enough."

Cyrus retrieved the gun from his fallen foe and checked the magazine. It was fully loaded, as he expected, with armor piercing rounds. Taking it, and a spare magazine, he set both beside Wagner on the floor. He stood the extra magazine upright. Should he need it, Wager could singlehandedly eject the spent magazine and slip the gun down over the top of the spare. It was an improvised one-handed operation, but it would keep Wagner safe.

Doing a press check of the newly acquired gun, Cyrus confirmed there was a round in the chamber. "The safety's off," he said to Wagner as he handed the weapon to him.

Wagner had watched Cyrus's entire process with unblinking eyes. He accepted the gun but looked at him with a curious expression. "Given that a lot of thought, have you?" he asked grimly.

Cyrus shrugged. "I'm sorry, but I'll have to leave you here. By my math, there's still one man unaccounted for. I don't know if he's one of ours or one of theirs, but I need to sort that out before we can regroup."

Laying the gun in his lap, Wagner held up a hand. "Wait a second. What are you talking about? There's ten of us on station here."

Cyrus nodded. He ran a quick tally, explaining the trail of bodies that had led him to the fifth floor. "You said they have a man in the communications room. That makes nine. I need to collect him and then find our missing tenth man."

"Jesus," Wagner breathed. His eyes threatened to drift to some faraway place. After a moment, he took a deep breath and winced when he made a move to sit more upright. "Get me up. You'll need my help."

"Take it easy," Cyrus said. He helped the man shift to a slightly more comfortable position and then checked his pulse. It wasn't good but that was to be expected after everything he'd been through. He should've been lost to physical shock by now.

"Just stay here and keep yourself out of trouble," Cyrus said in a mild tone. "I'll take care of the rest. But when I'm done, we need to find out what happened to Dargo. Voss told me his plane crashed on the way back from the U.S."

"That part's covered," Wagner said with a pained smile. "I was able to make arrangements before they pulled me out of the booth."

"I don't understand," Cyrus admitted.

"Dargo called in from his sat-phone and said they were going down. He didn't want to make the call over an open frequency because he was afraid the attack on the jet might be part of a coordinated assault on us here."

Wagner shook his head, likely considering the call and all that had happened in the short time since. "I guess he was right. We just couldn't have guessed that it was part of an attack from operatives already on the inside—our own guys."

Cyrus offered a nod of understanding. He was with him so far.

"Anyway," Wagner continued, "Dargo had me sound the alert and put the facility on lockdown. That was priority one, as far as he was concerned. But after I lost contact with him, I had another idea. I was able to set it in motion before these bastards broke into the radio room.

"I knew we were already spread dangerously thin, men either lost on Gretchen's detail, or in the air with Dargo. And he was right about a coordinated attack. We just didn't expect it to come from the inside. We didn't have the resources to launch a rescue mission for the downed plane, given our situation."

"What's the plan?" Cyrus asked. He couldn't figure out how Wagner thought he could rescue survivors from the plane at that point.

"I contacted King Borden on a secure line. I didn't even have to explain much," Wagner admitted. "I just told him that we had a jet going down nearby and that we had a security breach. By that point, I had these sonsofbitches tearing at the radio room door."

Wagner was straining to tell the story through clenched teeth. Rage was clear in his eyes as he looked at the dead man only a few feet away. "So I gave Borden the last known coordinates. He said he would deal with it."

Cyrus still didn't understand. "What can the King of a small island nation do in this situation?"

"I can only guess," Wagner said. "But the King has a sizable personal security force and substantial resources. Kapros doesn't have its own military, but it does have rich mineral resources that have brought about partnerships with the world's leading nations. The country is not without assets. If anyone has the resources to recover the downed jet before it's too late, it's King August Borden."

"And he was willing do all of that with just a phone call?" Cyrus was skeptical.

Wagner's eyes rolled as he fought to remain conscious. "Did I mention that Borden is godfather to both Anna and Natasha?"

Cyrus grinned. That wasn't mentioned in any of the Coalition's files.

———

Cyrus was able to move with greater speed on his way to the security office. He'd committed Voss's crude map to memory and had confidence that at least one of the two unaccounted for security guards was in the process of recovering a recording of Dargo's distress call. Things were making more sense now, too. Wagner had been the one who put the facility on lockdown, a situation not ideal for the invading force since it restricted their ability to move freely throughout the building.

There was another advantage to the situation. If Cyrus could take the man in the radio room alive, he could gather additional intelligence. While he still believed that the operation had been tightly compartmentalized, restricting information was difficult. Operatives often knew more than they were supposed to; it was a hazard of the trade.

Moving silently down the last stretch of hallway, the pair of sliding doors leading to the security office and communications room came into view. If Wagner was right, Cyrus's target would be locked inside that room, struggling to recover deleted recordings. Still, Cyrus wasn't about to rush in blind.

Tapping Voss's code into the panel beside the door, Cyrus brought up the camera showing what was waiting for him beyond. It was a wide room with the main wall covered by dozens of LCD displays. They showed security feeds from all over the compound.

Unfortunately, the room was unmanned. That's when Cyrus felt the barrel of a gun touch the back of his head.

"Toss it," a voice from behind ordered.

The unseen figure also possessed a distinct French accent. It didn't take a detective to find commonality among the rogue portion of Dargo's force.

The gun fell from Cyrus's fingers. It hit the tile floor with a clatter, shattering the eerie silence. Very slowly, he raised his hands to near shoulder level. It was a calm, submissive gesture. The security feeds that were displayed across the walls of the office flashed through Cyrus's mind and he realized that his target had literally seen him coming.

It was a foolish mistake.

"You've been a busy boy," the Frenchman said. He kicked the gun away and stepped out of Cyrus's reach. "Turn around slowly."

Completing a slow rotation, Cyrus met the eye of the gunman. As with the others, he'd seen this man around the building. "You've been watching me?"

The gunman offered a nervous grin. The look told Cyrus that the sweat clinging to the man's face wasn't from exertion. He was feeling the strain of the situation. No…he looked closer at his eyes—the man was afraid. Obviously, the operation hadn't gone according to plan. But from the looks of this guy, the plan had diverged from any scenario his team was prepared to handle.

Cyrus took a certain amount of pride in that.

"You want out," Cyrus said, suddenly understanding the man. "You've watched everything that's happened and you want out, but you can't make it. You were locked in when Wagner put the building in lockdown."

The Frenchman's complete lack of response was all the confirmation Cyrus needed.

"Wow," he continued. "Wagner screwed you good. No wonder your buddy was working him over like that."

The gun pointed at Cyrus wobbled slightly as the Frenchman virtually throttled it in a white-knuckled grip. A slight tick caused the corner of his eye to twitch, and Cyrus knew his opponent was weighing his options.

"What has you more worried," Cyrus pressed. "Getting out of here in one piece, or dealing with your employer when you come back empty-handed?"

The twitch at the corner of the man's eye told Cyrus he was onto something.

"Someone must've found the magic number. Getting you to turn on the rest of your team? That couldn't come cheap."

When the gunman raised his second hand to steady a tremble that was becoming impossible to hide, Cyrus fought the urge to smile. The man was scared, but the failed mission wasn't his only problem. He had serious concerns about the person, or persons, who had put him and his friends up to this.

Now he just needed to learn what he could about the puppet master behind the Frenchmen's betrayal. A common thread had emerged over the course of the repeated attacks. And though Cyrus hadn't been able to contact Command to confirm his suspicions, everything he'd seen was reinforcing his gut feelings. Each attack had been separate and unique, conducted by a small team of hitters. On the train, it had been a three-person team. The operation at the bar was a larger, more concerted effort, but something about the series of events had Cyrus rethinking what had happened. He had originally thought the attack at the bar and the subsequent ambush at the airport bus terminal were orchestrated by the same, larger team. But upon reflection, he suspected the attacks were the work of separate hit squads, dispatched independently and sent after him, not Natasha. The way they operated, even the way they moved, had been entirely different.

And now he was dealing with a group of Frenchmen already embedded and working for Voss under Dargo's command. The Frenchmen had been loyal to Voss and Dargo at one time, and had turned on their employers. But why? Or, more importantly, why now? Dargo wasn't just security conscious—there was such a thing as borderline paranoia and Dargo lived well on the other side of that border. For these men to make it to the inside it would've required extensive preparation and a very long-term plan. Cyrus knew how those operations worked. He'd lived them. But nothing that had happened in any of the prior attacks displayed that required level of preparation. In fact, each attack seemed almost improvised. No one knew Cyrus and Natasha would be at the bar that night, and certainly not at the bus station lockers after trading bullets at the bar.

It was far more likely that the French portion of Dargo's team turning on the rest wasn't planned in advance. Their treachery was more likely the result of bribery or some kind of coercion. Long-term plants would've had a better plan and had a better understanding of the building's security systems.

The use of disparate mercenary teams against him told Cyrus something more. He wasn't dealing with an organization with personnel and resources. It was more likely that a single person— at most, a small group—was behind everything. What was lacked in manpower was made up for in willingness to throw money at the problem in the form of mercenary muscle.

"How much were you paid?" Cyrus asked. He was careful not to imply whether the payment came from a person or a group. With luck, the gunman would fill in that blank for him.

"Do you see the gun?" the man snarled. "It means I ask the questions!"

Cyrus shrugged. He wasn't the one holding the gun, but he was the calmer of the two…and he was certainly thinking more clearly. Despite the look of the situation, it meant he was the one in control, so long as he could keep talking and not get shot in the process.

"Fine. You have the gun, and you have questions. Ask away."

The Frenchman's brows arched at the idea but he didn't respond.

"You must have questions," Cyrus urged. "If I were in your place, I'd want to know if the person who put me up to this knew all of this would happen. I would wonder if I'd been intentionally put in this position. I'd be thinking *real long and hard* about what I was getting out of this and questioning whether it was worth it in the end."

"The money's good, don't worry about that," the gunman uttered through clamped teeth.

Cyrus shrugged and pointed with the thumb of his raised hand over his shoulder at the closed door to the security office. "I suppose the money's only gotten better, what with the rest of your guys not around to split it."

Rage flared in the gunman's eyes. He stomped forward, closing the distance between them. Jamming the gun in Cyrus's face, spittle flew from his lips as he bellowed, "I have you to thank for—"

He never had a chance to finish the thought. Cyrus batted the weapon from his face and delivered a tooth-shattering uppercut to the bottom of the gunman's jaw. The gun slipped freely from the man's hand, dropping into Cyrus's left, almost as if it had been intentionally handed off. The Frenchman staggered backward a single pace before dropping hard onto his butt. His eyes fluttered but his face was expressionless. Switching the gun to his right hand, Cyrus brought the grip down in a backhanded swing, cracking it across the side of the Frenchman's skull. The blow sent his unconscious body sliding two feet along the tile floor before stopping in a heap.

Sticking the gun down the back of his waistband, Cyrus retrieved his own weapon from the floor. The building had once more returned to complete and utter silence. The unconscious Frenchman lay face down on the floor with a short, crimson, skid mark leading to his broken jaw.

Chapter 14

With nine of the ten guards accounted for, it was the missing man who still concerned Cyrus. After binding the Frenchman hand and foot with sets of flex cuffs from the security office, Cyrus locked him in a utility closet and secured the door using Voss's master code. Using the restrictive access code was overkill as far as precautions went, but the evening had turned into a bloodbath and he needed to be certain that the night held no more surprises.

Armed with two handguns, several magazines, a spare set of flex cuffs, and Voss's master code, Cyrus made a meticulous room-by-room sweep of the building. He cleared the fifth floor without finding any surprises. Wagner remained in the weight room in sad physical shape but surprisingly good spirits. When Cyrus stopped to report the apprehension of the ninth man, it seemed to have a rejuvenating effect on Wagner. And though Wagner insisted that his injuries left him in no immediate danger, Cyrus wasn't buying into the story. Wagner was in bad shape and needed medical attention at the first opportunity. Unfortunately, unless Natasha had undergone extensive trauma training, Wagner would need the sort of help she couldn't provide.

Pushing the thought aside for the moment, Cyrus focused on his most immediate problem. He had to finish his sweep of the building and discover the fate of the missing tenth man. Wagner insisted he could wait that long. Cyrus hoped he was right. In any case, they didn't have much choice in the matter; until the building was secure, they were all still in danger.

Completing his sweep of the fourth floor, Cyrus retrieved Voss from the hiding place where he'd left him. Passing one of the guns to the reluctant old scientist, together they searched the third floor.

When that floor failed to yield their missing man, Cyrus opted to leave Voss with Natasha and Anna. After completing a sweep of the floor, Cyrus doubled back to Natasha's room. He guided Voss across the room and directed him to her walk-in closet.

"I don't understand," Voss mumbled, as he followed Cyrus to the back of the space.

Cyrus grinned but said nothing. Pushing on a section of the wood paneling, a portion of wall swung free. He stepped aside to reveal the waiting and anxious faces of Natasha and Anna.

The girls charged from their hiding place at the sight of Voss, throwing their arms around the haggard, exhausted man. Cyrus saw Voss was equally relieved to see them. But there was still work to be done. As Cyrus coaxed all three family members into the hiding place, he could hear Voss mumbling something about not knowing that the passage had even existed.

Anna and Voss disappeared into the darkness of the space beyond, but Natasha stopped just inside the small door. She put her hand on Cyrus's arm and looked deeply into his eyes. "Please, be careful," she said quietly. "I don't want to lose you again."

"Not a chance," he said with a wink.

Crouched on her knees, she leaned through the small door and kissed him. It was a kiss that instantly reminded him of everything they had once shared. As her arms slid around his neck, he lifted her through the hatch. He cradled her in his arms and sat back on the floor. She pulled him against her. The deeply passionate nature of her touch expressed feelings that neither had forgotten.

There was a sincere sense of disappointment when she slowly pulled away. They were sitting in the middle of the floor like a couple of teenagers. The thought made Cyrus smile. Looking into the depths of her eyes, he saw the same passionate, expressive person that he'd once known. It made him realize that, though time might have passed, things might not have changed as much as he'd feared.

Her voice cracked with her words. "Come back soon?" she asked with a tired smile.

"Count on it," he whispered.

Once she'd stepped back through the hole in the wall, Cyrus sealed the passage and took a look at the area. He made sure they'd left nothing to give away the hiding place. He should've had more confidence, knowing the building was in lockdown and that he was the only one able to move freely.

The search of the second floor was uneventful. It took time to search every nook and cranny of the kitchen and attached cafeteria, but Cyrus left no stone unturned. His examination of the medical suite proved equally uneventful, though he did stop to dry swallow three prescription strength ibuprofen before moving on. Though he was still moving with efficiency, he was feeling the effects of the recent physical abuse.

Clearing the first floor also went easily. Nothing seemed out of place until he reached the sub-levels. The first sub-level held the motor pool as well as an Olympic size swimming pool and a sauna. Opting to start with the motor pool, he walked to the dark garage.

The cavernous space was lit only by small, dim bulbs that were spaced evenly around the upper perimeter of the room. It was the same type of emergency lighting that lined the hallways of the underground levels. It did nothing to illuminate the garage. As much as Cyrus strained, the small bulbs didn't even reach the floor, let alone provide enough light for a thorough search.

Standing silently in the doorway of the garage, Cyrus listened for anything out of the ordinary. Left with no alternative, he decided to activate the overhead lights. He stepped into the room, but stood an arm's length away from the bank of light switches—and opposite the side from which someone would normally activate them. If someone was lying in wait, Cyrus knew he might survive the initial assault simply by not standing where expected.

With a slow, deep breath, Cyrus brought his gun up and to the ready. He started flipping the switches three at a time. Even as the halogen lights on the ceiling high above buzzed and began to flicker to life, Cyrus was stepping further from the switches, his eyes moving quickly across the wide room in search of a threat or a target.

But as sure as he'd been that a trap was waiting, no attack came. He stood silently and observed the contents of the room. The motor pool was a wide concrete expanse that occupied the majority of the basement level. The walls were poured cement to match the floor, the only difference being that the floor had a visible polish and sealed shine. There were half-a-dozen black Chevy Suburbans parked in a line facing a massive closed overhead door to the left. Beyond the overhead door, Cyrus knew there would be a short ramp leading to the surface where another, even more imposing retractable security door, was waiting. He'd seen the doors on the screens in the security office.

Moving slowly past the first Suburban, a row of long tool benches came into view. Beyond the six SUV's were a four-door BMW X5 SUV and a late model Porsche Cayenne four-wheel-drive. There was another Suburban up on a lift, apparently in the process of undergoing maintenance.

Walking past the second of the Suburbans, Cyrus stopped short. Stepping back between the first and second vehicle, he glanced at the floor to confirm what he'd seen from the corner of his eye. The tires of the second SUV were slashed. Oddly, the first vehicle was still in working order.

Moving on, Cyrus quickly confirmed his suspicion. The tires on the remaining four had been slashed as well. All but one of the trucks sat on deflated tires, their rims touching the concrete floor.

This was the French team's exit strategy, Cyrus reasoned. One vehicle had been left for exfiltration.

Moving on, he continued his search of the garage. Aside from the damaged 4x4's, he didn't find anything of further interest. But when he neared the wide window spanning the front of the shop manager's office, his eyes were instantly pulled to the set of feet protruding from behind the desk. Dark slacks and worn, but expensive shoes, that matched the rest of the security detail told Cyrus that he'd finally located the missing man.

Turning the knob on the office door, Cyrus pushed his way into the room. He kept his gun up and ready while he moved silently. The room was small but organized. Not surprising after seeing the rest of the shop. As he moved, Cyrus kept an eye on the feet belonging to the body on the floor beyond the desk. Finally, without wasting a second to overthink his situation, he stepped around the desk with his finger snug on the trigger and ready to fire.

But rather than a hostile attacker, Cyrus discovered an unconscious man who was bound hand and foot with thick zip ties. Stepping forward, he kept the man covered while he double-checked the bindings. They were intact. The restraints were cutting into the flesh of the man's wrists thanks to the awkward angle at which he lay. The ties had sliced into his skin, turning the wounds bloody from their bite. The purple bruises creeping away from the edges of the restraints spoke to how long the man had been bound.

Checking for a pulse, Cyrus was surprised to find him still alive. It took only a moment to cut the bindings. As they fell away, Cyrus wondered why the man had been bound using zip ties rather than flex cuffs. Maybe he'd been ambushed by his own men while making a check of the garage? Perhaps he'd even walked in on one of the guards and found him slashing the tires?

It was an interesting anomaly.

Laying the guard flat on his back, Cyrus carefully placed the man's arms out at his sides in hopes that it would allow better blood flow. He had no idea how long the man had been left trussed up on the floor, or why he was unconscious.

Standing, Cyrus looked around the office more carefully. A strange smell caught his attention, and not for the first time since entering the small office. At first, he'd written it off as one of the many odd chemical odors common to a garage. But this time the whiff had triggered recognition.

Checking the floor, Cyrus found the source of the odor. A small bottle of chloroform lay dumped and discarded under the shop manager's desk. Retrieving the bottle, he found it empty. A sticky residue on the floor marked where the contents had spilled before mostly evaporating. Searching the remainder of the floor, Cyrus found a chloroform drenched rag, the corner of which was sticking out from under the unconscious man's shoulder.

It was odd that the Frenchmen had no problems killing most of their comrades in the course of their operation, but this man had been drugged rather than murdered. What was different about him? Was he part of their escape plan?

Considering the disabled SUV's, Cyrus reasoned that he might be looking at the first casualty of the night's operation. If this guard walked in on one of his own slashing tires, they would've needed to take him out of play in short order. But if it happened before they were ready with the remainder of their plan, it made sense to do it quietly. A gunshot fired too early would jeopardize the entire operation.

So they'd taken this guard down silently.

Still...

Cyrus looked at the gun he held in his right hand and the knife in his left. These guys didn't have a problem killing. So why not just knife the guard? Cut him down quietly? At least that way he wouldn't pose a danger to the rest of the operation.

Plus, the use of chloroform hinted that certain steps had been taken to secure this guard while keeping him alive. Was there some unrealized part of the plan he was missing? An intention to hang the attack on a single guard? Was this man supposed to be the scapegoat?

No matter how Cyrus did the math, things weren't adding up.

A groan from the far side of the desk pulled him from his thoughts. Cyrus looked over the corner of the desk as the guard struggled to pull himself up and onto his elbows. His eyes rolled as he fought the effects of the drug for control of his body.

"Are you alright?" Cyrus asked.

The guard recoiled, his head snapping around to meet Cyrus's stare. He looked at Cyrus for a moment as if trying to understand his words. Then slowly, as if in great pain, he nodded.

Finally, after a few deep breaths the guard pulled himself into a seated position. His eyes were glassy, and he trembled. Normally Cyrus would've guessed it was due to a head wound but he had examined the man while he was unconscious. There was no swelling to indicate such an injury. Still, he'd been drugged; that was more than enough. An overdose of chloroform could paralyze respiratory functions and kill even a healthy person, so depending on how large of a dose he'd been given, any number of things could be wrong.

Cyrus offered the guard a hand and pulled him from the floor. No sooner had the man put weight on his feet then his knees threatened to buckle. Cyrus saw his eyes go wide in response. The guard spun quickly and vomited across the wall beside the desk.

Stepping into the garage, Cyrus retrieved some clean rags from a shelf over a nearby bench. He tossed one to the guard but said nothing. There was nothing to say in such a situation. The poor guy just needed some time to let the effects pass.

Chapter 15

The Voss Compound
2:25 am

After escorting the last guard to the infirmary, Cyrus returned to the third floor where he retrieved Natasha, Anna, and Doctor Voss from their hiding place. He explained what had happened and how he discovered the last missing guard, whose name turned out to be Talbet.

Cyrus took Voss and a wheeled gurney up to five and retrieved Wagner. Upon delivering him to medical, Natasha assessed his condition and confirmed that his injuries were beyond her ability to efficiently treat. They needed to get him to the island's central hospital as soon as possible. His life would soon depend on it.

Lacking better options, Cyrus would need to take Wagner himself. Now that things were under control inside the building, Voss firmly believed that he and his daughters would be safe in his absence. They would lock down the building once more, after Cyrus left with Wagner. Voss would even go so far as to replace all existing access codes, preventing anyone outside from getting in even if a corrupt member of the security detail had provided codes.

The family would be safe inside the building while Cyrus saw to Wagner, Voss assured. Cyrus wasn't entirely convinced. The calculating side of his mind warned that leaving the Voss family unguarded threatened to undermine all that he was trying to protect.

Still, in the end he didn't have a choice. Wagner needed medical help, and according to Natasha's evaluation, he needed it soon. Though he was stoically downplaying his discomfort, Natasha explained that Wagner's injuries would prove mortal if not treated immediately.

Cyrus loaded Wagner into the rear passenger seat of the only remaining Suburban four-wheel-drive. Getting the large man off the gurney proved challenging. In the transition, Cyrus noticed a tradeoff taking place. Talbet was looking better by the minute while Wagner seemed more lethargic and less responsive.

They needed to hurry.

Sliding behind the wheel of the 4x4, Cyrus tapped the mobile connection on the steering wheel. One ring came from the vehicle's built-in speakers before Natasha answered.

"We're all set," Cyrus said into the speakerphone as Talbet climbed into the front passenger seat.

"Opening inner door now," Natasha announced.

The massive, louvered steel, overhead door began retracting into the ceiling. Cyrus started the ignition and shifted into gear. They passed beneath the still opening door and began to climb the short concrete ramp leading to the surface. The ramp was part of a short tunnel that twisted ninety degrees in a slow, ascending bend. Just before rounding the corner, Cyrus saw the door behind them was already drawing closed. The headlights added to the bright sodium vapor floods that shone down from above as they approached a second massive door at the top end of the ramp.

"Ready when you are," Cyrus said.

"Lower door secure," Natasha confirmed. "Opening outer door now."

As soon as the second door reached the appropriate height, Cyrus pulled into the small plaza that filled the distance between the building and the perimeter wall.

The cold, steady rhythm of a driving winter rain greeted them the moment they exited the tunnel. Cyrus activated the windshield wipers and scanned the grounds for any sign of danger.

"Bugger," Talbet mumbled. "I'm going to get soaked!"

As they pulled up to the front gate, Cyrus looked at Talbet. "All set?"

The man squinted through the window and into the downpour. Cyrus could see the driving rain clearly in the beams of the vehicle's headlamps, as well as in the lights that sat high on the perimeter wall.

"Ready when you are," Natasha said from the dashboard speaker.

"Yeah," Talbet grumbled. "I'm on it." He slid the gun from the holster on his hip, took a deep breath, and stepped from the vehicle into the freezing rain.

Cyrus watched Talbet move to the side of the service door to the right of the massive gates. There, he checked a digital display. It showed camera positions outside of the wall. "Still look good out there?" Cyrus asked Natasha.

"All clear. But it looks cold. I'm glad I'm not out in that."

"Yeah, I think Talbet's having second thoughts," Cyrus grinned.

He looked up at the rearview mirror and his smile vanished. Wagner sat slumped at an awkward angle, appearing worse with every glance.

"Hang in there, buddy," Cyrus confided. "We're in the home stretch. Sure you're up for this?"

"Wouldn't miss it for the world," Wagner muttered in a dry voice that betrayed his weariness. "I'm seeing this through."

The massive gates had one security flaw that Cyrus could immediately see. Under normal circumstances, for the short time the gates were open the plaza had to be manned by security personnel, armed and ready to defend the facility. But at the moment, they didn't have the numbers necessary to repel an incursion, if such an attack occurred. Cyrus needed to leave the compound, so he used the only resource at hand—Talbet.

Natasha's voice returned to the line. "Talbet reports we're set. Here we go."

A moment later, the front gates began to separate. Once again, Cyrus waited only long enough for the large four-wheel-drive to gain clearance before powering through the gap.

"We're clear," he instantly relayed to Natasha.

"Closing outer gates now," she responded.

Cyrus braked and scanned the street around them with suspicious eyes. Voss's compound was located in the heart of Kapros's capital city. Although it was the tallest building for a block in either direction, the perimeter wall stood shoulder-to-shoulder with dozens of other squat, modern office buildings. The double lane street fronting the property was lined on either side by wide sidewalk. At this time of night and in a driving rain,

Cyrus would've expected it to be deserted. But Wagner had explained otherwise. There were many twenty-four-hour businesses in the area, so even in the middle of the night there was always some amount of foot traffic. Cyrus immediately saw that was a fact, as his gaze caught a few people out and about.

Talbet had left the wall to make a visual sweep of the outside before opening the gates. Once the SUV reached the street he stood station, watching the gates to ensure no one slipped through before they locked once more. Natasha was able to see as much from her vantage point in the security office, but Cyrus wanted eyes on the gate—and a gun—just to be sure. He knew firsthand how security measures—cameras specifically—could be subverted.

Cyrus's eyes swept the surrounding street while waiting for Talbet to complete his portion of their exit plan. Cyrus knew that all of this was overkill, but then again, they had just repelled a corrupt force from within Voss's own security detail. There was no such thing as being too careful.

Scanning the curb on the opposite side, Cyrus's focus snapped to a figure standing in the shadows two dozen yards down the street. He was beneath a wide eave but he'd been standing absolutely still. It made his form difficult to distinguish against the dim background and heavy rain. Squinting, Cyrus strained to discern what it was that had drawn his interest.

The man moved slightly. An orange bloom brought a sliver of definition to his features. It wasn't enough for Cyrus to identify the man as he searched for defining characteristics. He was smoking a cigarette, which accounted for the less than helpful blossom of light each time he took a drag.

Cyrus leaned closer to the steering wheel, his senses on full alert. But when he leaned forward, his face fell into the shine of a nearby streetlight as it spilled across the dashboard. The man on the street could now see he was being watched. If he were just an innocent passerby, it would mean nothing. If he were surveilling the place, he would know that he'd been made.

To Cyrus's surprise, the man took two steps forward. That brought him within the same wash of street light that illuminated the windscreen of the SUV. The bill of the man's baseball cap shadowed his features, and Cyrus could still see nothing.

The figure was looking right at him.

Glancing at the rearview mirror, Cyrus wondered where Talbet was. It felt like time was standing still. Talbet was approaching the vehicle. He must've missed the man across the street because he seemed more concerned with the rain as he approached the passenger-side door.

The man on the street took another step toward the SUV and pulled the cap from his head. He ran a hand through his short, drenched hair and turned his face to better catch the light. Cyrus felt the breath catch in his throat. The figure looked directly at him, and a relieved smile spread across his face. The man held up a small scrap of cardboard with black lettering on it. He flashed it for only a second, but it was enough. A satisfied chuckle escaped Cyrus just as Talbet yanked open the door and hauled himself into the seat.

"Turn the heat up, Goddammit," Talbet snarled.

The man across the street glanced at the ground, quickly drew the cap back over his head, and pulled it low over his eyes. He stepped back into the shadows and resumed his position, seemingly focused on smoking his cigarette. Cyrus read the implication clearly. *Keep quiet and don't say a word.*

Still, it didn't stop his satisfied grin. He shifted the transmission into 'drive' and accelerated down the flooded street. Not only was Boone alive and well, he was on the island.

Chapter 16

Pointing the vehicle east, Cyrus chose to rely on visual prompts from the navigation system and muted its audio instructions. Casper General Hospital was located on the opposite side of the small city. The facility took its name from the reigning king's grandfather who had started the medical facility generations earlier. The hospital still sat at the midpoint of a mountainous ridge that overlooked the city from its extreme outskirts. With the passage of time, the city grew and prospered. So, too, did the hospital, expanding until it had become as much a modern medical facility as any in the world.

Even at midday, the drive wouldn't have taken long. Given the late hour, the streets were nearly devoid of traffic. Cyrus knew they would make good time; after looking in the rearview mirror that fact came as a relief. Wagner sat slouched, and even in the dim light of the truck's cabin Cyrus could see he was growing increasingly pale.

"Hanging in there?" Cyrus asked. He didn't expect much of a reply. Wagner wasn't a complainer. Cyrus was more interested in how long it took the man to respond, plus the quality of his voice when he did.

"Never better," he replied in a tired rasp. "You guys wanna stop for coffee? I'm buying."

Cyrus grinned. At least he maintained a sense of humor. That alone could make the difference in a bad situation.

Talbet had been looking over his shoulder, eyeing Wagner when he replied. After taking a long look at the man, he turned once more and faced forward. He shot a glance at Cyrus that told of his concern. For the moment, all they could do was get Wagner to the hospital as quickly as possible. He was already on borrowed time.

"It's been a long day," Cyrus commented in a conversational tone. He'd directed the statement at Talbet. "How're you holding up?" He shot a look at Talbet and wasn't surprised to see him looking fairly ragged himself.

The question brought a wry grunt in response. "I've had better days."

When Cyrus failed to contribute more to the discussion, it took only a moment for Talbet to continue.

"You can bet I'll be looking for a new job after this fiasco," he admitted. "Although I guess it's hard to say what'll happen next—with Dargo gone and all."

When Talbet stopped speaking, he became distracted. He ran his hands through his hair nervously, then sat with them bound into tight fists in his lap. "Where the hell did I go wrong?"

"It's alright," Cyrus offered. "You can work that out with Dargo when he gets back."

Cyrus felt the burn of Talbet's sidelong glance as he made the left hand turn at the next intersection. He would've known the man was staring him down even if he hadn't been eyeing him in his peripheral vision.

"What are you talking about? Dargo's plane went down over the Atlantic," Talbet said. Judging by his tone, it sounded like he was stating the fact for himself to believe as much as Cyrus.

Cyrus offered the man a brief, curious look, then made a right hand turn without showing additional reaction to the statement. "Huh. I never said anything about Dargo's plane going down."

He continued to drive calmly down the dark, empty city street.

Shifting nervously in his seat, Talbet glared at Cyrus. "Must've been the Doctor—or one of the girls."

Cyrus glanced at the man for two full seconds. Finally, he shook his head once and returned his eyes to the road. "Nope." He said it in the same conversational tone. "Wasn't them either."

While the tension coming from the passenger seat was palpable, Cyrus continued to drive in a relaxed manner. He kept both hands on the wheel. Neither gripped the wheel too tightly, and he was certain his lack of concern was now driving Talbet crazy.

"That doesn't make sense," Talbet stammered. "Someone said something...*how else would I know?*"

Tipping his head from side to side, Cyrus pondered the idea. "Yeah...that's the question, isn't it?" His eyes remained on the road. He betrayed no apprehension for the man in the seat beside him. "As far as I can tell, there's only one way you could know."

Cyrus glanced at Talbet and offered a look that implied the answer was obvious. When Cyrus heard a distinctive metallic click, he looked down to find a gun resting in the shadows of

Talbet's lap. He was impressed. He hadn't seen him move for the weapon.

"You tricked me," Talbet admitted. "Dargo isn't on his way back. He's history." He shook his head in irritation and muttered to himself. "*How could I be so stupid.*"

Cyrus noticed it wasn't so much a question as a statement. His anger at his lack of intelligence was good, considering he had made more than one mistake. If he was disappointed with himself now, things were about to get worse.

"Hey, take it easy with that thing." Raising his right hand, Cyrus held it up as if the motion would be enough to ward off a bullet.

"Hands on the wheel," Talbet hissed. "No sudden moves, and keep your damn hands on the wheel."

Cyrus complied without a word, though his eyes now moved more frequently between the road and the armed man beside him.

"So how did you know Dargo's plane went down?" Cyrus asked. "You put a bomb on board!" he realized. "But how did you know when to trigger it?"

"Hardly! No. No bomb," Talbet chuckled. "Nothing so crude. It was an additive mixed with the fuel."

Stealing a sideways glance, Cyrus took a long look at Talbet. Cyrus's lack of understanding was clear on his face.

Talbet offered a shrug. "The science of it is beyond me," he admitted. "Cutting edge stuff, I'm told. It mixes with the fuel. After a certain amount of time, the pressure—or the oxygenation—something finally activates it. The chemical composition of the fuel changes and suddenly, poof! Jet fuel is jet fuel no longer. The plane simply falls from the sky!"

A burning pain flared in Cyrus's gut. Talbet's description of the technology was painfully familiar. He'd read about something similar in the not-so-recent past. But as his mind started to sort through its catalog of memories with near photographic detail, Cyrus reminded himself that it wasn't the time for that specific concern. He had to deal with Talbet before moving on to the next problem. His eyes shifted to the rearview mirror and found Wagner slumped and unconscious in the back seat. The slight rise and fall of his chin where it rested on his chest was the only indication that he still lived. The visage reminded Cyrus that he had a whole series of problems to deal with, and that Talbet had only added one more to the list.

"Sounds like high-tech overkill to me," Cyrus grumbled. "It's an overly elaborate plan to kill a guy you see every day. What did you have against Dargo?"

"Dargo? It was nothing personal. He always treated me well. He was actually a good man. It was just business."

Offering a contemptuous look, Cyrus grunted, "Business? Someone hired you to kill *Dargo*?"

Talbet's only reply was a sour expression.

"I don't suppose you're willing to tell me who hired you to do it? Or why?" Cyrus urged, attempting a good-natured grin. He didn't let the fact that Talbet was armed hamper the upbeat nature of his conversational tone. In fact, other than letting his eyes fall once on the man's gun, Cyrus hadn't done much to acknowledge the weapon, or that any danger was imminent.

His expression shifting, Talbet turned slightly in his seat, partly to get a better look at Cyrus and partly to give his weapon a better angle. "He said you were a handful," he chuckled, shaking his head. "That was an understatement. You're not very intimidated by the gun, are you?"

Cyrus took a long look at Talbet before returning his eyes to the road. They were on a long, flat stretch; if he wanted to make a move against Talbet, his opportunity would arrive with the next turn. But Cyrus didn't want to disarm him. The goal was to keep him talking. The real challenge was the relatively short drive to the city hospital, and how long it had taken Talbet to make his move. Cyrus was working against the clock to make the necessary headway in the time he had left. There was no doubt that Talbet didn't want them to reach the hospital, so the clock was running down fast. Cyrus didn't know what would happen when it ran out.

"Talk or don't," Cyrus said with a disinterested shake of his head. He kept his eyes on the road in an attempt to sell the ploy. "I really don't care. But I think you're being used. I don't see the point of going through all that trouble just to kill Dargo. You were close to him. He trusted you. If everything that happened was just a setup to take him out, you could've done that twenty different times on any given day."

Talbet sputtered, nearly choking on his derisive chortle. "You're right about that much. I could've finished Dargo anytime, anywhere. But that wasn't the point."

Cyrus glanced at the man but said nothing. It was the sort of look that said, *if you say so*. And when Talbet continued, Cyrus knew he'd played him properly.

"The Doc is the target," Talbet explained. "He's working on something my employer wants. I was just about to get it, too, when you showed up. You put the entire plan in a tailspin. You got Dargo all paranoid and looking over his shoulder. He started double checking *everything*. He didn't trust you at all."

Cyrus kept his eyes on the road and his hands at ten and two on the wheel.

"You threw off the timing of the entire operation," Talbet complained. "Then my contact reaches out and tells me to be real careful around you. He said to play it nice because you might actually catch on."

With a laugh, Talbet admitted, "It didn't make sense. I told him you were just some delivery kid who got beat up trying to get something to the Doc. But my guy said that was the problem—you didn't get beat up on the way to the compound. And he said you killed three of his hired guns along the way. Not bad for a delivery boy."

Cyrus fought the urge to glare at Talbet. Indifference seemed to be the key to keeping him talking but the self-centered fool was hard to tolerate. Plus, Cyrus suspected Talbet was using the opportunity to work things through in his mind. The man wasn't exactly sure what was happening, and his confusion had made him edgy. The rest of his team was dead, and he was now on his own.

That part of the night was still bothering Cyrus. Talbet didn't seem all that put off about his team being wiped out in the course of their failed operation. Then there was the slashed tires on the trucks in the motor pool.

Cyrus looked at Talbet. His eyes settled on the man, taking him in again as if for the first time. The moment wasn't lost on Talbet. He raised the gun, placing it in Cyrus's eye line. "Don't even think about it, kid."

159

"You were in the garage slashing the tires on the SUV's when the facility went on lockdown," Cyrus concluded. "You got stuck down there when the doors sealed, and you couldn't get out. When you realized your guys messed things up, you bound *yourself* with zip ties and faked the whole—"

"I wouldn't say that I faked it," Talbet interrupted. "For things to go that pear shaped, it occurred to me that you might actually be as good as my guy said. And if the rest of my team was down, I knew I couldn't complete the operation on my own. So yes, I did bind myself with the ties, but I knew that wouldn't be good enough so I used the chloroform, too."

Cyrus shot the man a grin. "No kidding? You dosed yourself—just to sell the lie?"

Talbet shrugged. He scratched a nonexistent itch behind his ear, never taking his eyes off Cyrus. He was clearly hesitant to continue. "If you were as sharp as I'd been told, I knew half measures wouldn't sell it. It was that or shoot myself. But at that point, you might hear the gunshot and…well, who's actually willing to shoot themselves to cover a lie? That crap only works in the movies."

Cyrus grinned and took a quick look at Talbet. "Well, I have to admit you don't half-ass it. Drugging yourself is what I call going the distance."

"Going the distance…" Talbet mumbled. "I almost killed myself with that *shit*. Did you know it's dangerous if you breathe too much of it? Well, hell! One whiff of that stuff and down I went. But I must've knocked the rag off the desk when I dropped because I kept breathing it. If you hadn't come along when you did, I would've offed myself and never been the wiser."

Cyrus laughed. Not a chuckle, but an outright laugh at the idea. It would've been fitting. "I think that's what you call karma."

"Karma?" Talbet's expression showed he didn't understand the implication.

Cyrus shrugged. "You slashed the tires on all but one of the four-wheel drives," he said as if it explained everything.

"So?"

Cyrus took a long look at him, but said nothing until his eyes returned to the road. "You were planning to leave there with Voss and his girls. That means you, them, and the rest of your team would never fit into a single truck. Obviously, you weren't planning on bringing your team along at the end of the op."

Sitting silently for a moment, Cyrus gave Talbet time to respond. When he didn't, Cyrus continued.

"So what kind of unfortunate fate awaited your friends? Were they going to die of acute lead poisoning, or did you have something more creative in store?"

When Talbet didn't react, Cyrus stole a look at him. He didn't appear well. While he'd been planning to bushwhack his confederates, the idea clearly didn't sit well with him.

"It wasn't your idea, was it?" Cyrus quietly urged. "Did your employer put you up to that, too? You weren't just getting greedy, were you? Your boss wanted you to tie up loose ends. Even if that included your own guys?"

If it weren't for his need to keep the gun leveled at Cyrus, there was a good chance that Talbet wouldn't have been able to look at him. Cyrus could tell as much—it was written on his face.

"What did he offer you," Cyrus urged. He kept his voice quiet and comforting, as if he were speaking to a small, frightened child. "What could be worth all of the bloodshed?"

A long silence stretched between the two men, and Cyrus started to become nervous. He didn't know if Talbet was about to break down and start sobbing, or snap and start shooting.

"People do stupid things for money," Talbet uttered in a dry cracking voice, at last.

Cyrus nodded. "Who put you up to this? Tell me who's behind this and I'll put an end to it."

Talbet had lowered the gun at some point; not putting it away, but resting it on the console between the two seats. The barrel was still pointed directly at Cyrus, and in a position that didn't offer him any defensive options.

"Not a chance," Talbet said. His voice was drawing on some steely reserve that was still very threatening. "I know how this works. My contact was a cutout. Giving him to you won't do you any good—it'll just get me killed."

"Tell me what I need to know. I can fix this," Cyrus pushed.

"Putting you in a body bag is the only way to fix this," Talbet concluded.

"Then putting you in an interrogation room is my only option," Cyrus countered. He turned to Talbet with a fire in his eyes. "I've asked nice. Make me ask again and I won't be so kind."

A wide grin spanned Talbet's face. He raised the gun, placing it in Cyrus's eye line once more. "I'm the one with the gun, kid. Don't forget that."

The enamored gleam in Talbet's eyes suddenly lost its fire. He heard the clicking of a pistol hammer as the barrel of a .357 revolver was place against the back of his neck. "Huh. Mine's bigger than yours," croaked a gravelly voice from the back seat.

Cyrus saw the cocky look vanish from Talbet's face. His eyes went big and round; Wagner had caught him completely off guard.

"Pass the gun to my friend, nice and easy," Wagner ordered.

Talbet hesitated for a moment, unsure what to do. For a second, Cyrus thought he might actually do as instructed. But when a coldness passed over Talbet's eyes, it was obvious he'd decided to go the other way.

"I still have the winning hand," Talbet countered. "Drop your gun or I'll kill the kid, right here and now."

"Come on," Cyrus needled. "How stupid are you? *You would shoot the guy who's driving the car?* Wait a minute—it's all becoming clear now. I see why you were picked to head this operation. There's not a lot of free thinking going on between your ears, is there?"

Talbet raised the gun, pointing in squarely in Cyrus's face. Cyrus looked down the barrel of the gun, making a show of sizing it up. But his expressed level of concern was on par with what you would expect from someone having a breadstick pointed at his nose.

Cyrus reached across his body with his left hand and stuck the tip of his index finger into the muzzle. Holding it there, he turned back to the road and continued driving as if his finger in the bore had neutralized the weapon.

In his peripheral vision, he could see Talbet's incredulous expression. The man was thunderstruck. He didn't know how to respond to the cartoonish action.

"I didn't know who you were or what you'd done when I found you in the garage," Cyrus explained. His eyes remained on the road; his finger still stuck in the barrel of the gun. "But I had you figured before we left the compound. Why do you think I couldn't leave you behind? Do you really think I needed your help driving Wagner to the ER? Do you think I would've left the family unguarded if you were on the level?"

Talbet didn't respond.

"While I was sweeping the facility, I noticed a few interesting facts. Not the least of which was how all of the crooked guards were armed with armor piercing ammunition." Cyrus stole an accusing glance at Talbet. "Every single one of them," he clarified.

"But every other guard was packing standard issue hollow points," he continued. His eyes shifted to settle on the gun that was pointed at him. "You might as well have been holding a sign that said you were with the other turncoats."

As Cyrus watched, Talbet's eyes moved to the handgun and then shifted to the grip where the magazine was housed. "That's right," Cyrus confirmed. "I checked it. While I was at it, I switched your ammo for some training blanks I found in the weapons locker. All of the bang—none of the bullet.

"Did you think I'd let you sit beside me with a loaded weapon?"

For a moment it looked like Talbet was going to test the theory and pull the trigger. Wagner intervened, persuading him that the effort would be foolish when he applied greater pressure to the gun still buried in his neck.

Working visibly to swallow his pride, Talbet's eyes finally dropped. He lowered the gun and handed it to Cyrus. It was just in time, too. Turning the corner, Cyrus entered the hospital parking lot. One more turn and they were about a hundred yards from the doors to the emergency room. Cyrus spun the newly acquired weapon around in his hand and clubbed Talbet across the head with it. With a sickening smash, he collapsed against the passenger side window.

Startled by the sudden violent strike, Wagner sagged backward in his seat. He glared at Cyrus in the darkness as they pulled into the well-lit portico outside the emergency room entrance. "What was that for?" Wagner grunted.

Glancing into the rearview mirror, Cyrus met the man's eyes. "The sonofabitch nearly shot me," Cyrus grumbled in frustration.

"Yeah? So? He only had blanks. What's the worst that could happen?"

Cyrus shook his head. "I never thought to check his gun," he admitted. "Let alone swap out the ammunition."

For all of his pain and injuries, a new pallor whitewashed Wagner's face. He glared at Cyrus's eyes in the rearview mirror; his jaw moved with the stammer of silent words, his voice clearly failing him.

"Plus, *he really hurt my finger,*" Cyrus added with a grin. He shook his hand in the air as he worked the circulation back into the tip. Without another word, he popped the release on his door and slid out in search of a wheelchair to haul Wagner inside.

Chapter 17

Blinking the sleep from his eyes, the ceiling above him came into view. Cyrus was immediately struck by the dozens of aches and pains that had settled into his body while he slept. The events of the last several days had taken their toll. He never suffered them as strongly as he did in his first waking hour. After the events of the previous night, he'd crashed out hard.

The room's lighting was designed to simulate daylight, which was a neat trick first thing in the morning. Since the building was a compound and each of the massive bedrooms had been designed without windows looking out into the world, the rooms were equipped with recessed lights that simulated the ambient light from traditional windows. It allowed the Voss family to live in the underground bunker-like conditions without suffering the negative effects commonly associated with such a situation.

It seemed Voss truly had thought of everything.

Rolling onto his side, Cyrus was surprised to find Natasha missing. She'd been waiting in his room when he returned from

Casper General Hospital, what seemed like only a few short hours earlier. In fact, after speaking with Voss and shackling Talbet, pushing him into a secure utility closet for safe keeping, Cyrus had returned to his room to find Natasha asleep in his bed.

It was a relief for him on multiple levels. First, it was a sign that she hadn't been unduly traumatized by the events of the last several days. Second, because by all accounts she seemed content to put their past behind them, if only for the time being. That was particularly satisfying for Cyrus. The last week had served to remind him just how much guilt he felt for the way he'd left things when he left school and ultimately ended up working for the Coalition. And lastly, her presence shattered any doubt as to whether they would still connect the way they had before everything had fallen apart.

They'd spent hours making love, wrapped in each other's arms talking about everything, and nothing at all. Every emotion he carried for her remained alive and well. It was mirrored, a fire buried—but still burning—and evident in the woman he loved.

Still, he was surprised and disappointed to find her missing after such a night so long overdue. Though, to be fair, this was her home and currently a disaster area. Voss's security detail had been decimated and the facility was a shambles in the most literal sense.

It was a moment before Cyrus noticed that a mobile phone had been left on the pillow beside him—Natasha's pillow. Rolling onto his elbow, he grabbed the device and activated the touchscreen display. The photo app had been left running; an image of Natasha filled the screen. She'd used the phone's front facing camera to snap several shots of herself, recreating a similar situation from their past. The first photo was a tight frame of her face, her blond hair a mess and covering the right half. What was visible of the left half was telling: her eyes burned bright, charged with excitement, a playful, sexy grin tugged at the corner of her mouth. Swiping the screen to the next photo, Cyrus found a wider framed shot. One where she'd pulled the hair back from her face. She clutched a bed sheet low against her breasts as she smiled into the camera lens. Her bare shoulders hinted at so much more. In the last shot, there was no bed sheet but she'd turned away from the camera slightly and blocked a portion of the frame with an outstretched hand making for a provocative, though well staged and disappointingly PG-13 photo.

All together, the three images were a recreation of three photos she'd left for him years earlier after a night they'd shared in her dorm room. Similarly, she had left early that morning, abandoning him in her bed. She was off to attend an early class, something Cyrus had been careful to avoid while planning his schedule. Before she had left, and while he slept, she'd shot three images with an old Polaroid instant camera and left the photos on the pillow beside him. She was taking a photography course at the time, so the photos had been both intimate and charming. Now, her attempt to recreate such a moment from their highlight reel struck him much more deeply. He flipped back to the first image and stared at it for a long while, considering their past and wondering where their future would take them. He didn't know what was in store for them, but he wouldn't let her slip through his fingers a second time.

Chapter 18

Sitting at the end of the long dining table, Dargo was glad to be back. Even the hardboiled, ex-Spetsnaz soldier had softened just enough to consider the compound his home. Following the crash of the private jet and the subsequent rescue of him and his team, he was relieved to return. Though he had feared the worst in his absence, he found the story of all that had happened difficult to fathom. Not only the mutiny perpetrated by members of his trusted team, but that it had been the newcomer, Cyrus, who had protected the Voss family.

In spite of all that he'd been told, Dargo still didn't trust the young man. It was clear that he'd made a believer of Voss, but the events of the previous twenty-four hours—in truth, the past several days—only proved that he wasn't who he originally claimed to be. Still, it was clear that Voss now considered the young man beyond reproach. On one hand, Dargo could understand Voss's rationale, attributing it to foolish sentiment following the trauma of what had clearly been an extremely trying ordeal. But on the other, Dargo knew that Voss lacked his field experience and situational awareness. He was blind to the potential dangers the young man still represented.

Sitting at the end of the table, Dargo found himself awestruck as the Voss family sat at positions around the table. Each was contributing what they knew of the events from the previous night. Voss sat opposite Dargo at the head of the table, with Natasha to his left and Anna to his right. It seemed that none of them had a clear understanding of everything that had happened. Still, one theme ran consistent through each tale. Had it not been for Cyrus, the night would have come to a decidedly different conclusion.

There was no question Dargo was as suspicious of Cyrus as ever. His actions and capabilities belayed the circumstances that had supposedly brought him to their doorstep. It was a fact that was now conveniently overlooked by Voss. Though, as Voss had hinted, there was more to the story—details better discussed in private.

Dargo eyed Gretchen who sat quietly at his left. She had arrived back on the island well ahead of him, returning on Voss's jet. While Dargo was on his way to the United States, primed to deal with the security nightmare that had been at the core of her trip, she had been airborne and heading in the opposite direction. Once back on the island, Dargo ordered her to book a room at a nearby hotel under an anonymous name. At the time, he didn't yet understand what had happened or who was after her, but he considered it prudent to keep her away from the Voss family until he had things sorted out. Accordingly, he'd sent three of his men to the hotel to watch over her. He now realized he'd been lucky to send the correct three men. Had he chosen differently, she might not be alive.

But the Gulfstream G450 had been a miracle. Dargo's insistence on outfitting the aircraft with a pair of eight-foot inflatable life rafts and flotation vests had proven a wise precaution. Though he'd never expected the jet to make an emergency water landing, the transport had most definitely been outfitted properly and prepared for any worst case scenario. And, thankfully, when King Borden purchased a duplicate of Voss's jet, he duplicated it right down to those same safety measures.

Dargo had never been so happy for a wealthy man's lack of originality. It had literally saved their lives.

Still, Dargo didn't understand the cause of the crash. The plane had lost altitude so quickly that there'd been no time to gather the necessary intelligence. The fact that any of them survived at all was a testament to the skill of the flight crew. They'd given their lives while making a heroic attempt to bring the craft down with a minimum of damage.

The actual impact was still a blur. Though he'd been strapped into a seat, loose debris had stuck Dargo in the head. His first memory was of retching sea water as he clung to the outside of an inflated life raft. Moments later, two of his security detail struggled to pull him onboard.

The second raft was lost in the plane's wreckage as it slipped beneath the rolling waves. Once Dargo was pulled into the inflatable, they managed to locate two more members of the team. The remaining members of his force were lost. To his surprise, one of his men explained that it had been Dargo who pulled the inflatable raft from the crushed wreckage of the jet's tail section only seconds before it slipped from sight beneath the waves. Though he had no recollection of those events, apparently he'd pulled the ripcord and inflated the raft in time to give each of the survivors the buoyancy needed to stay afloat in the rough ocean until help arrived.

The pilot and copilot were killed on impact. It was another portion of the crash Dargo couldn't recall; one the surviving members of his detail had been seated with his back to the forward bulkhead when the plane impacted. He explained that the cockpit was crushed and twisted like an empty beer can, only inches from where they'd been seated. And, despite their heroic effort, the flight crew never stood a chance.

One of Dargo's last memories was of his abbreviated conversation with Wagner back at base over the encrypted sat-phone. He'd given Wagner the same instructions he'd provided the pilot and copilot. No SOS calls over any open frequency. While he didn't know what treachery had befallen their aircraft, he had no doubt that it was thanks to careful design. He wouldn't let a radio transmission alert the responsible party of their success. Even then, Dargo had realized what was happening to the aircraft was only one part of a multi-pronged attack against the Voss compound.

It had been Wagner's experience and resourcefulness that had truly saved the lives of the crash victims. In the few minutes prior to the assault on the Voss compound, Wagner had taken initiative and contacted Saul Grae, the head of King August Borden's personal security detail. With only moments to spare, he'd sounded the alarm. Grae lost contact with Wagner immediately after, but by that point he had the last known coordinates of the downed aircraft and had scrambled two rescue helicopters and a naval cutter to the scene. It turned out that the jet had been less than two hundred miles from Kapros when it went down. It was one of several odd circumstances to which Dargo knew they owed their lives.

Conversation around the table rattled on, even though Dargo had been lost in his own thoughts for a time. But when Cyrus walked into the room, every voice at the table suddenly fell silent. With a suspicious eye, Dargo evaluated the young man as if seeing him for the first time. After everything that had happened following their last encounter, Dargo knew that some of his suspicions about him had proven true. Cyrus wasn't who he claimed and his reason for being here wasn't what he said. At the same time, there was no denying that they all owed him a considerable debt. Whatever his goals or motivations, he'd done them all a great service.

"I'm sorry to interrupt," Cyrus said with an uncomfortable smile. He looked around the room, clearly not sure what to make of the sudden silence.

Voss rose instantly from his seat and greeted Cyrus, first with a handshake and then with a fatherly hug. "Not at all, my boy!" the man laughed. "Join us, please."

What the hell? Dargo's hands dropped into his lap as he watched the events unfold with renewed suspicion. Voss was a functioning introvert. Dargo couldn't understand how he could welcome the relative newcomer with actual open arms…even after all that had happened.

Prior to sitting down at the table, Voss had only enough time for a few words with Dargo. They'd been interrupted by the appearance of Gretchen, Anna, and Natasha. Voss only explained, rather succinctly, that Cyrus was to be treated as one of their own from now on. And though Dargo urged Voss to reconsider his unwavering acceptance of the virtual stranger, Voss insisted that much had changed and that Cyrus was no longer a stranger to him.

The juxtaposition flummoxed Dargo. It was true that the young man had saved their lives, but even as he watched Voss exchange words with Cyrus, he could see that some sort of deeper connection had formed between them.

The grating scrape of a chair across the tile floor broke the low murmur of voices, and Dargo saw Natasha smiling. "I saved you a spot," she said to Cyrus in a soft, warm voice.

When Cyrus dropped into the chair beside her, Dargo saw the couple's eyes meet. There was a shared smile, an unmistakable spark of a connection. Dargo felt his teeth grinding as he sat silently and stared. It was another unexpected turn of events. When he'd left, Natasha was hard pressed to remain in the same room with the boy. She'd been reluctant even to treat his injuries while Gretchen was away.

Still, as he watched, Dargo saw that Natasha's view of Cyrus—like her father's—had shifted dramatically in his absence. It made him wonder even more about all that had happened in the short time he'd been away.

Natasha looked more healthy and alive than she had in years, Dargo decided. There was a color in her cheeks and a light in her eyes that he hadn't seen since...

Dargo's eyes narrowed and his pulse quickened. *It wasn't possible*, he reasoned. But once the thought formed in his mind, he couldn't believe he hadn't seized on it sooner. His fists clenched so tightly in his lap that his knuckles popped audibly in response. Slowly, he released his breath and struggled for another explanation. There was none.

Three years prior, Natasha had been attending school in the United States. She was dating an American who Dargo hadn't cared for much at the time. Unfortunately, there wasn't anything he could do about it and, for the first time, he realized that he actually suffered from fatherly instincts after all. After decades of watching over Natasha and pretending for himself and the rest of world that he was nothing more than her protector, he realized that he truly had a daughter.

Fighting his baser instincts, Dargo had willed himself not to interfere with Natasha's budding romance. Yet, all the while, he had two young guards attending the university and keeping a surreptitious eye on his daughter. He hoped that Natasha's silly teenage romance would go up in flames as was typical of so many. But as he learned through daily reports, not only was that not the case, but Natasha was spending more and more time with her new boyfriend.

In hindsight, Dargo realized he should've followed his instincts. But just when he thought he would have to make the hard choice and intervene, events at the school had exploded. Reports from his undercover security agents were confusing and contradictory, but things had quickly come to a head. The next thing Dargo knew, Natasha's boyfriend was in the custody of the American FBI.

At that point Dargo took a personal interest in the situation. At Voss's request, he flew to the United States to manage the matter. But by that point Natasha's boyfriend had been placed into protective custody. Even though Dargo leveraged all of his professional resources, he hadn't been able to learn anything more about the situation.

The boyfriend's name had been Jonny Webb, Dargo now recalled. He had considered it strange, even at the time, how all information relating to Webb suddenly led to a dead end. It was as if the boy had been swallowed by a black hole, ceasing to exist entirely. But he wasn't the only one shocked by the disappearance. Webb had disappeared from Natasha's life just as abruptly; there one day and gone the next, seemingly never to return.

But as Dargo watched Natasha and Cyrus from across the table, he realized that Jon Webb had returned after all. He had a new name and he was now part of an entirely new set of problems that, this time around, involved the entire family. The realization explained Natasha's utter vitriol toward Cyrus upon his arrival. Unfortunately, it also accounted for her paradoxical and sudden acceptance of his return.

One resounding question kept fighting its way to the forefront of Dargo's mind. What had Cyrus done to ingratiate himself so fully into the hearts and minds of both Voss and Natasha? In the case of Natasha, apparently he'd saved her twice in the past forty-eight hours—though Dargo still didn't know the full details of those events. But even with all the heroics, the acceptance Cyrus was being shown was in excess of anything Dargo had ever seen from the brilliant, introverted Doc. Certainly not since his wife's passing. The only thing that could explain Voss's unyielding acceptance would be—

For the second time, Dargo felt his breath catch in his throat and his teeth gnash. This time his focus narrowed on his friend at the opposite end of the long table.

Voss had used the 'device' on Cyrus Cooper. It was the only explanation.

Chapter 19

Wearing the coat of a dead man, Cyrus walked through the city park. Though he looked like any one of the other two dozen denizen enjoying the area's carefully manicured grounds on the autumn morning, his eyes were in constant motion. He'd taken precautions in the unlikely event of a tail, but vigilance was second nature. He'd even left the compound via Natasha and Anna's secret backdoor. After all that had happened, he couldn't be too careful.

Satisfied, he found a quiet area that he had mostly to himself. Unslinging the pack from his shoulder, Cyrus took a seat on a park bench and placed the bag at his feet. After a quick scan of his surroundings, he fished a mobile phone from the pocket of his dark, fleece lined jacket and placed it on the bench at his side. The jacket was a posthumous gift from one of the rogue guards on Voss's security detail. It had occurred to Cyrus, with some amusement while preparing to leave the compound, that he wasn't at all prepared for the cold fall weather of the region.

Having arrived at the stronghold without his luggage, and after spending the better part of the last two weeks stuck in the infirmary, he wasn't equipped with outdoor gear appropriate for the callous weather.

Ever the pragmatist, the solution quickly resolved itself. Following the group's breakfast that morning, Dargo's first order of business had been to scour the living quarters belonging to the traitorous members of his team. Cyrus wished he'd had the opportunity to do as much before Dargo returned to the facility, but time had not been on his side. Just the same, Cyrus took the opportunity to find the apparel he required amidst the off duty gear belonging to Dargo's dead agents. Once Dargo had searched the articles in question, he was content to turn them over to Cyrus.

Cyrus recalled the bitter scowl in Dargo's stare before he left the compound via the previously unknown exit. He was clearly not satisfied with Voss's decision to allow Cyrus autonomy. The frustration was no doubt compounded by the realization that the facility Dargo worked so hard to secure not only had a hidden access point, but a hidden stairwell that allowed access to every level of the building.

While he could understand the man's frustration, it wasn't his concern. Cyrus's goal was to divine who was after Voss's technology and find a way to stop them. In order to properly investigate, it was necessary to consider everyone a suspect. And the head of Voss's security team had, until recently, been at the top of his list of potential perpetrators. Dargo had the training and experience required for such an undertaking, which also meant he likely had the contacts needed for such an operation. But the sabotage of Dargo's jet went a long way toward removing him from the list. Unless he had compatriots who were using the plane crash to eliminate Dargo as a loose end. Cyrus didn't believe in ruling anything out.

But that line of thinking really didn't track anymore. First, there was the way Dargo looked at the Voss family. It was lost on everyone around him, but Cyrus had noticed. The man looked at the Voss's as if they were part of his own clan—family. And, secondly, to some degree they were. Voss had confided as much to Cyrus and eliminated his need to confirm his nagging suspicion for himself. Dargo was in fact Natasha's biological father, not Voss. A fact that both men appeared to have made peace with many years ago, since Dargo had begun in Voss's employ when Voss separated from Onyx Gander and began working for himself.

Though he couldn't begin to guess at the dynamic at play between Dargo and the Voss family, it was clear that Dargo harbored deep feelings for them. It was a solid dedication. He'd worked for two decades as head of security for the family and turned their home into a literal fortress.

All of this moved Dargo to the bottom of the suspect list, but it didn't remove him from it. No one was ever removed from the suspect list, as far as Cyrus was concerned. To do so would require an absolute faith in the available intelligence. Cyrus didn't believe in anything absolute. He'd learned early on that the key to solving any mystery, often the key to his very survival, was never to put absolute faith in anyone or anything. It was necessary to question every piece of intelligence accumulated, and question everyone's motives at every turn.

It was no wonder there was such a high mortality rate in his line of work. If the job didn't get you killed, emotional and psychological burnout stood a good chance of doing it in the end. For the first time in his three years with the Coalition, Cyrus knew that he wouldn't be able to do this job indefinitely.

He didn't see how anyone could. But, then again, Boone had. He'd survived decades doing this kind of work and was still alive and kicking. Boone was considered an anomaly, believed among many to be the very best in the game. But recent events had proven that even Boone was not infallible. Cyrus knew he'd saved his mentor's ass on their last operation. The way he saw it, it was the least he could do. Boone taught him everything he knew. Some operations went south. Some fell apart in unique and spectacular ways. But the disappointing truth was that Boone's ops had been a mess as of late, and Cyrus was covering for him. It was something he did without reservation, but now he did so with a heavy heart. He knew Boone's last operation to detain Professor Richard Ragsdale had suffered heavy casualties. Most of Boone's team had been lost. If that had happened because Cyrus wasn't there to cover for him, then those deaths were on his hands. Boone was his friend and mentor, but once this mission was over they needed to talk about all that had happened.

Unzipping the backpack at his feet, Cyrus removed a small, thin laptop and a USB thumb drive. He plugged the drive into the computer and started the machine. The laptop booted from a special, read-only operating system that was burned into the tamperproof thumb drive. When the prompt appeared on screen, he swiped his thumb across the invisible sensor hidden at the end of the USB drive and the machine continued to boot. The thumb drive was coded to work with only his biometrics. It was also designed to boot any computer while keeping the computer's memory independent of all other attached devices or operating systems. The process essentially turned any computer into a secure terminal that was accessible only by Cyrus. Since the thumb drive was read-only, it could not be altered or compromised. It also meant he couldn't save data directly to the device. He would need to either download to a separate USB device, or save any data to an encrypted cloud storage location.

With a few keystrokes, Cyrus tethered the laptop's Wi-Fi card to the cellphone and used it as an uplink to the internet. From there he launched a script that tunneled his connection through a series of random high-speed proxy servers housed at locations across the globe. The last step in the process called for a VPN connection that would link him to the Coalition network via a secure, encrypted tunnel and allow access to the central database. But something was wrong. The VPN connection failed.

With a few more keystrokes, he brought up the debug log and searched for the stage of the complicated process where things had broken down. He expected the failure to occur where his connection was relayed randomly through waypoints across the planet. It was the logical point of failure, though it didn't happen often. Unfortunately, he found that his request for a secure connection to the Coalition network had simply been *denied*.

Dammit.

He grabbed the phone off the bench and tapped out a phone number from memory. It was the Red Queen's private number; a hotline of sorts that connected her office to those of several high-ranking government officials. It would be nearly 4:40 am, eastern time in the United States, which meant the call would likely be routed to her mobile. When the phone was answer by a gravelly voice after only two rings, Cyrus knew he'd awakened his boss.

"Monica Fichtner," her voice cracked.

"Monica, it's Cyrus," he said simply. "I need—"

"Mister Cooper?" she mumbled. "How did you get this number?"

"It's the sort of thing you pay me to do," he reminded her.

"Actually," she snarled. "You're paid to follow orders. Since your orders were to return to Command, you'd better have a damn good reason for calling my emergency line at..." her voice disappeared for a moment. "Jesus, Cyrus. It's not even 5 am!"

"I wouldn't be bothering you at all, but someone's disabled my remote access. Since that sort of thing only happens with orders from on high, I'm talking to you."

Cyrus kept his tone firm and calm, even if the Red Queen sounded as if she were on the verge of blowing her stack. He knew that ranting and making demands would accomplish nothing. But she was management, and it was a common misconception among all levels of management that threats and demands were what got things done.

With a deep and exasperated sigh, it was a moment before Monica continued. Apparently she was trying to take the high road. "Your mission has been scrubbed, Cyrus. *Come home.*"

Cyrus didn't respond. He was unprepared for a fair and measured response from his superior. He'd expected her to either restore his network access or assert her authority and demand his immediate return to base. Once her voice took on a more reasonable cadence, he wasn't sure how to respond.

"Agent Boone's team has been wiped out," Monica continued. "Every last one of them. I received a call only a few hours ago. A burned out four-wheel-drive was fished from a shoal of the Seine river. Some sort of high temperature incendiary was used to destroy the bodies so we're not sure we can recover any usable DNA, but judging from the contents of the vehicle and the general descriptors of the two corpses, we're sure we've recovered the remains of Agent Boone and Agent Hobbs."

Leaning back on the bench, the implications of the Red Queen's statement struck Cyrus like a lightning bolt. The Coalition didn't know Boone was alive. He'd gone to a great deal of trouble to fake his death. Either that, or someone had done a terrible job of identifying the bodies. That didn't seem likely, even under rushed conditions.

"Cyrus? Are you there?" Monica asked.

"You said you can't do a DNA match on the bodies?" he asked in a quiet, dry voice.

"I'm told it's unlikely. Whatever accelerant or incendiary was used on the vehicle's interior didn't leave much to test. There are skeletal remains, but it's likely that the fire burned too hot for too long. The chances of uncovering usable biological matter are slim."

That's how Boone would operate; no doubt about it.

"So what was found in the vehicle that made it possible to identify the victims?"

"Well, as you know, neither man was caring his real identification. But a portion of Hobbs's cover ID was found in the vehicle. And—," she hesitated, which was unusual coming from a woman of such robotic countenance. "Two pins were clearly visible in the remains of one of the victims. They were part of a past reconstructive operation on the victim's knee and ankle. In one case, the serial number was plainly visible and identified the deceased as Agent Hobbs."

Cyrus was shocked. If what she said was accurate, it meant that Boone hadn't just faked his death, he'd used Hobbs's body to do it. The callousness of the idea sent a chill down his spine. Still, from a strategic perspective, it was brilliant.

"What about the other body?" Cyrus asked. He was legitimately afraid to ask.

"Less conclusive, I'm afraid," Monica admitted. "But no less convincing. The damaged remains of Mister Boone's Zippo lighter were recovered in close proximity to the other body. There was also remodeling consistent with breaks to three ribs he broke on a mission two years ago." She was silent for a long moment. "It was Boone," she said, sadly.

Silence stretched as Cyrus considered the information. He knew for a fact that Boone was alive. He'd seen him only a dozen hours earlier on the street outside the Voss compound. And while he didn't know what was going on, Boone was obviously lying low. But he had provided a contact number; Cyrus had already decided that would be his next call.

"You need to come in now," Monica reiterated. The tone of her voice indicated she had once more reprised her role as the Red Queen. "We don't know what's going on out there, but someone has declared it open season on Coalition operatives. We've taken massive casualties. You need to get back here before you're counted among them."

Cyrus grinned. This was the boss he was accustomed to dealing with. She said she was worried about him, but she was really more interested in saving face and limiting further damage to operations under her command.

"Your concern for my wellbeing notwithstanding," he said flatly. "I'm in the middle of this, and pulling me out now won't solve the problem."

"Dammit, Cyrus—"

"Don't interrupt," he interrupted while trying to keep a smile from showing through in his voice. "I'm the only asset you still have operational. Give me the resources I need and I'll find out who's behind this. Hell, I'll bring their head back in a box. We've lost too many good men. Someone has to answer for this."

"I will not lose another agent," the Red Queen literally snarled. "Request denied! Get your ass back here before you get yourself killed!"

"I think you should reconsider," Cyrus urged. His voice was confident and placid, as if speaking with a petulant child. "I'm not just talking about getting a leg up in this mess. I'm not stopping until I have the person responsible for all of it. If I pull it off, you save face and look like the hero. If I fail? What's one more dead agent on top of the mess you've already got?"

Cyrus had heard many different euphemisms regarding poking an angry bear. At that moment, every single one of them seemed appropriate. No words escaped the Red Queen, but Cyrus could hear her enraged breath as it tumbled across the distant phone's microphone. In his three years at the Coalition, this was the most emotion he'd ever seen, or heard, the woman express. She sounded like a ravenous dog preparing to devour the telephone.

It was a classic good and bad news situation, Cyrus realized. The bad news was that he wasn't going to get his remote network access restored. Hell, he might not even have a job if he made it through the mission alive. But the good news outweighed the bad. He'd called the Red Queen on her top-secret personal line and woke her only to deliver news that had driven her into a frothy rage. Sure, his good news/bad news scale was a little off-kilter, but he was satisfied with the way it was balancing out.

"You okay there, boss?" Cyrus asked when the breathing from the other end of the line began to dissipate. It had only lasted for seconds but in his mind it felt like an eternity.

"You *will be* on the next plane back to the U.S." Her demand was simple and unambiguous. She made no threats; she offered no room for argument. The moment she finished the statement, Cyrus realized that the line had gone dead.

Setting the phone aside, Cyrus considered the conversation. It hadn't started how he expected, but it had somehow managed to surpass his expectations before reaching a conclusion. He didn't for a moment believe the Red Queen had any real concern for his safety. She was in "cover my ass mode" and thereby trying to limit damage to her own career while dealing with whatever mess had been made.

For his part, Cyrus no longer cared about the original mission goals. Voss's technology was brilliant and potentially dangerous in the wrong hands. But Cyrus was more concerned with the current threats to the Voss family, as well as to the agents of his own organization. Whoever was orchestrating the attacks was brutal and efficient, but they had somehow managed to devastate a force of experienced field operatives. Voss and his family remained safe in their stronghold and Voss's work remained secure and unmolested.

Cyrus intended to keep it that way.

Tapping another number into the phone, the line was answered after a single ring.

"Authenticate," the voice on the other end demanded simply.

"Don't tell Scotty," Cyrus responded without a second thought.

There was an audible chuckle from the other end of the line. "Scotty doesn't know," the voice responded. Following a brief pause, the laughter burst over the line. "You can't take anything seriously, can you, kid?" Boone said.

They had used the improvised authentication system in the past. It was unique in that there was no predefined challenge or reply. The brief exchange was responsible for expressing the conditions under any circumstances. In this case, Cyrus's instant reference to an old movie he'd once forced Boone to watch was proof enough that Cyrus was intact and not under duress. If he had been forced to make the call, he might have referenced a different film, book, or shared experience. It wouldn't matter, so long as it instantly conveyed the present circumstances in a way that only the two of them would understand.

"We've got a lot of good people dead," Cyrus said with great sincerity. "I call that serious."

"You're right about that," Boone remarked, his voice shifting to a tone that was all business. "Still, it's good to hear your voice. I can't tell you how relieved I was to see your face in that truck."

"You caught me off guard," Cyrus admitted. "I heard the rest of your team was wiped out and you were missing."

"Missing and hopefully soon to be presumed dead. I left the burned out husk of an SUV behind with a body that, once crispy enough, should be taken for mine."

"They found it," Cyrus confirmed. "And it looks like they're falling for it. I just heard about it a minute ago, in fact."

"No kidding?"

There was relief in Boone's voice.

"No disrespect, kid, but I'm surprised Monica decided to keep you in the field. I would've put money on her calling everyone back and circling the wagons. It's more like her to cover her own ass."

"Huh," Cyrus grunted. "That does seem more her style. Let's just say she's not entirely happy with me at the moment and leave it at that. But what about you? I'm not the one playing dead. What the hell are you up to?"

It was Boone's turn to grunt. "It's complicated. Can we meet or do Voss's security boys have you on lockdown?"

"Actually, I've managed to cut my own parole. How about tonight? I'll text you later with the location. I have a few things I need to deal with in the meantime."

Boone took a half second too long to respond. "Heh—yeah, that works. I'm not going anywhere."

"Are you alright?"

"Me? Sure, just fine. Why?"

Cyrus had to think. He felt like something was wrong, but he couldn't put his finger on the odd gut sensation. "I don't know. You just don't seem yourself. You're not hurt? Can you make it till tonight?"

"Absolutely, no problem. I'm in good shape. A little banged up from a couple of close calls along the way. It's just...you know, this one's been rough. I've lost too many damn people on this go round."

Cyrus knew how he felt. It was as if a dark cloud had been following the mission since the beginning. There was a stifling sense of foreboding that had permeated nearly every aspect of the mission.

Still, it was worth it all for even the remote opportunity of rekindling his relationship with Natasha. The mission may have turned into a human meat grinder, but he would gladly suffer his personal hardships again for the opportunity to be near her. That was the one aspect of the mission that was going according to plan. And, he realized with an uncomfortable roiling in his gut, she was also the one part of his mission that had nothing to do with the Coalition. To date, every part of the operation that had been compromised had been specific to the original set of outlined objectives.

Cyrus considered the twisted logic as he slipped the laptop into the backpack once more. He said goodbye to Boone and set out across the park. His eyes remained in constant motion, searching for any sign of surveillance. It seemed that, for once, he was actually alone. He couldn't help wondering if that would still be the case if he'd left the compound through the front gates.

Chapter 20

Charlie Greene sat at the edge of her bed. With her legs draped over the side, her feet were touching the cold, hardwood floor. She stared at the cell phone in her hand and struggled to decide if the belligerent call she'd just received was real or imagined. Her eyes moved slowly back and forth between the digital clock on her nightstand and the now dark and silent phone. The sun wasn't even up and her boss had already called, ranting almost incoherently about security protocols.

Security had always been of the utmost importance as far as Charlie was concerned. She wasn't an operative, but she managed the logistics for every agent the Coalition had in the field and every operation underway. Her job might not offer the 'cloak and dagger' sex appeal of field ops, but without her department field agents simply couldn't do their jobs. While some believed her department and staff to be little more than pencil-pushing computer jockeys, she knew they played a pivotal role in one of the country's most effective—though secret—law enforcement organizations.

So why had the Red Queen phoned before the crack of dawn to chastise her?

A smile spread across Charlie's face. *The Red Queen.* She'd heard the name used in reference to Monica Fichtner before. Only now did she fully understand the apt significance of the moniker. Since taking over as head of logistics, Charlie had only limited exposure to the Coalition's Chief Officer. Her opinion to date was that Monica was aloof, but cordial. Of course, the day had yet to begin and she'd already seen a new side of the woman in charge.

When the phone in her hand chimed, the shrill sound caught her off guard. She fumbled with the phone, finally snatching it from midair a moment before it hit the floor. The caller ID displayed text she'd never seen before. Rather than showing the calling number or even the customary *number not available* message, the display showed all zeros. After the earful she'd received with the last call, it was with more than a little trepidation that Charlie activated the line.

"Hello?" she asked. The callow sheepishness of her own voice instantly frustrated her. She was made of sterner stuff. "Hello?" she asked once more, this time louder and with greater conviction.

"Charlie?" A voice asked. "Charlie, its Cyrus Cooper. I'm sorry to call so early."

A sigh escaped Charlie's lips and she smiled. Not only had she been holding her breath, but she was desperately afraid that the Red Queen would call back to continue her tirade. The fact that it was Cyrus was a relief. The fact that it was *anyone* other than the Red Queen was a relief.

"Cyrus? Is everything alright?" They had never spoken outside of the office. In fact, they'd only ever met face-to-face the day of the Brainstorm Session. She recalled meeting him in the hallway prior to the meeting, and running into him once more later that afternoon. She also recalled feeling like a foolish teenager when she gave him her private mobile number, saying that he should call if he ever got into a bind and couldn't reach help at the office. Even though she had regretted the clumsy overture the moment they'd separated, she was also powerless to undo her juvenile mistake. She never expected him to call. Certainly not now, with all that was happening.

"Alright?" Cyrus asked as if he were trying to decide that for himself. "Yes and no. Ah, the truth is…I'm not sure."

"I've heard a little about what's happened out there," she said in an attempt to coax him along. "Do you need me to call someone for you?"

"No, nothing like that. I actually need your help. But it's something I can't really talk about on a company phone."

At first Charlie didn't understand the implication. She was about to ask when the fog of her mind cleared and his subtext suddenly became clear. Her eyes went wide. "Oh, God," she stammered. "I don't think I'm the person you want to be talking with. I'm terrified just driving on the freeway—I can't—"

"Whoa—slow down, Charlie." Cyrus's voice was calm and reassuring. "I'm not calling about anything dangerous. I would never put you in that position."

Taking a deep breath, she felt her racing heart begin to calm. She was prone to overreacting in extreme situations. Still, it was an unorthodox situation and she knew that something wasn't right.

"That's a relief," she admitted. "I'm obviously not suited for the kind of work you do. I'm only talking on the phone and I feel panicked."

Cyrus laughed. His amusement was well-timed and broke the tension. He started to say something but stopped short.

"You know what? I shouldn't have called at all," Cyrus decided. "I'll find another way to sort this out. I'm sorry I woke you for nothing."

"Wait!" The word escaped her mouth before her mind had an opportunity to process it. "You might as well tell me the problem while I have you on the line. If I can help, I will. Besides, you didn't wake me. I was already up."

"No kidding?" Cyrus went silent for a moment and Charlie guessed he was double-checking the time. "What is it, going on 5 am there? You're up already? What are you, some kind of masochist?"

"Only today," she smiled. "I had a 4 am wake-up call from the Red Queen. She was furious! I've never heard her so angry."

As she said the words, an errant thought crossed her mind. She recalled hearing somewhere that Cyrus had been the one to christen the boss with the fitting moniker. She was about to ask him about it when he interrupted her train of thought.

"She called you at home at 4 am?" He sounded stunned.

"She was in a tizzy about remote network access rights. She wanted to know who could login, and from where."

Charlie considered the one-sided conversation once more. "You know, she actually didn't ask many questions. She mostly just ranted. It was like she was blowing off steam or something."

When she was met with only silence from the other end of the line, she decided to continue.

"So enough about my problems. Tell me about yours."

"I think you just had a taste of my problems, actually," Cyrus admitted. "Monica must've called you as soon as she got off the line with me."

"I don't understand. What's going on?"

Cyrus took a long, deep breath. She could tell he was deciding what he could, or maybe what he *should* say.

"You can trust me," Charlie urged.

"It's not that," Cyrus said quietly. "It's just like you said before, this is a little heavy. I think you'd sleep better not knowing anything about it."

It took Charlie a second to consider his words. The truth was that she was embarrassed by her earlier reaction, just as she'd been by the sound of her own voice when she answered the phone. "Tell me what's going on, Cyrus. I want to help."

"You may change your mind, Charlie. But I appreciate your willingness to listen, just the same."

Cyrus took a moment to collect his thoughts before he began his explanation.

"I don't know what you know about my current operation. I've been working undercover at an R&D compound off the coast of Norway. It's the mission we discussed in the Brainstorm Session before I left."

"Okay," she said. "I recall the high level details—vaguely. My department arranged transit for you, and Agent Boone's team. I thought you were heading to Paris?"

"That's right. Well, the mission has been a shambles. Agent Gladd and I were ambushed on the train between Paris and

Hamburg. We dealt with the issue but it turned out that was only the start of our problems. Boone's team was hit while moving to intercept an asset soon after that, at the University of Paris."

Suddenly, all of the hushed conversations she'd been hearing around the seventh and eighth floors made more sense. There was trouble in the field, and the 'powers that be' were struggling to deal with the situation.

So why wasn't my department looped in?

"Cyrus, are you saying we lost men in the field?"

"Yes."

"In Paris?"

"Yes."

She was momentarily frozen, her mouth agape. "Wouldn't standard protocol involve sending in some sort of backup?"

"Absolutely. Without question."

A chill ran down Charlie's spine. She felt the hand that was supporting the phone beside her face quiver, and took a deep breath to steady herself. "Cyrus? No one ever sent in a backup team." Her voice was so quiet and weak that she almost couldn't recognize it as her own.

"You're sure?" he asked matter-of-factly.

"Positive," she confirmed. "My team would've been involved. Even if local resources were utilized, we would've organized transportation, housing, weapons, ammunition—the usual. I'm telling you, *there was nothing*. Why would that be?"

"That's a good question."

"You don't sound entirely surprised," she realized it just as quickly as she stated the obvious.

"No," Cyrus said. "I guess I'm not. Something strange is going on. I'm just having trouble sorting out exactly what *it* is."

"What do you need from me?"

"To be honest? VPN access. I've been locked out. The Red Queen claims she's done it so I'll pack up and come home. But I'm not entirely convinced that's her motivation."

"That's actually funny." Charlie grinned. "Because the only coherent part of my early morning ass-chewing was her directive to have remote access restricted to the continental United States."

"*No kidding?*" Cyrus drawled slowly. "So whatever she's worried about, it's important enough to restrict field access to the company network? You're saying points inside the U.S. are still fair game?"

Charlie could practically hear the gears working in his mind.

"What's going on, Cyrus?"

"I'm not sure," he mumbled. "But I think I just got a lot closer to figuring it out."

There was a brief silence on the line, and she knew they were both considering the situation from new perspectives. She had the sinking feeling that Cyrus's call was about to come in direct conflict with her standing orders. Thinking further, she reminded herself that she lived a very different life—safe and secure behind a desk. Cyrus had a lot more to worry about. He hadn't come right out and said it, but that he was calling her at all should've made something clear. Lives were on the line.

"Did the Red Queen say anything about locking me out of the network specifically?" Cyrus asked.

"No. In fact, I didn't know you'd lost access until you mentioned it just now. She must've submitted the work order after I left for the day. It never crossed my desk. I would remember something like that."

The line went silent again.

"You need me to reactivate your access, don't you?" she asked with more than a little apprehension.

"No," Cyrus answered immediately. "Absolutely not. I'm not clear on what's happening, but if you did something like that, it would certainly be bad for you. It's not worth it."

"Well," she reasoned. "Correct me if I'm wrong, but if Monica's going to such great lengths to lock you out, there must be something she doesn't want you to see."

"It could be nothing, or it could be the answer to everything," Cyrus reasoned. She could tell he was working out the problem as he spoke. "Whatever it is, it's going to be buried in that black hole we call a database."

"Sorry, there's nothing I can do about that."

"I'll tell you what," Cyrus said with a sudden burst of enthusiasm. "There might be something you can do that won't land you in any trouble…but it still helps me get the information I need. Do you remember a system wide bug we had about a year back? Some kind of glitch hit the system and suddenly no one could login?"

"Yes!" Charlie laughed. "You would've thought the place was going to burn to the ground. With the flick of a switch, everyone was locked out of their computers, network wide."

"I talked with one of the guys in IT right after the glitch. He said they'd done a system update and it had rolled back everyone's logins by several weeks. Everyone was locked out— but anyone who could remember the password they used three weeks earlier could regain normal access to the system."

Charlie recalled the chaos that had ensued from the simple bug that surfaced when their central security software was updated. It was amusing and chilling at the same time. It was also a paradox of security in that situation. Since network security was of paramount importance to the Coalition, every network user's password changed automatically on a weekly basis. For the staff, it was a hassle because it meant that every week they needed to memorize a new password. But from a security standpoint, it was ideal because it meant that even if someone's login rights were compromised, the access permissions would become obsolete in relatively short order.

It was a further trait of the security system that each newly generated password would not be allowed to match, or be algorithmically similar to, the account's previous password. So, in maintaining security, the system was required to maintain a log of each account's password history. As such, the system was aware of not only each account holder's current login, but every past login as well.

"I know what you're thinking," Charlie reasoned. "But I don't see how rolling the system back to an old set of logins gets you the access you need."

"If you can roll the logins of all accounts back to April first of this year, I'll have everything I need."

"I don't see how," she reasoned. "You'll still be locked out due to your geographic location. Depending on the work order Monica submitted, your account is likely disabled altogether. That won't change, even if the passwords are rolled back. I would still need to reactivate your account."

"Not a problem," Cyrus said. She could practically feel his confidence through the phone line. "I won't be logging in using my account."

A knowing smile spread across her face, and Charlie was tempted to ask if he was planning to do what she suspected. Then she thought better of it. Some things were better left unmentioned; for her future career, if nothing else. Considering his comment, her mind flashed back to a startling demonstration of his eidetic memory at their last meeting. At some point in time, Cyrus had likely glimpsed the Red Queen's login. It was a safe bet that it had happened on or before April first.

Charlie's mind was already working through a way to bend the system to her bidding. Rolling back all of the logins would draw a great deal of attention. Particularly since steps had been taken to ensure such a thing could never happen again. But she had an idea how she might manipulate the authentication database in a way that would leave all of the existing passwords active while simultaneously resurrecting the logins from April first. Such a maneuver wouldn't trip any security warnings because it wouldn't even constitute a database intrusion. The system would simply be reconstituting historical data to recover from a minor corruption. Such an operation wasn't even uncommon for a database.

"One more problem," Charlie said. "You still won't have access from outside U.S. borders. The geographic restrictions will still be in place."

"That's not a problem," Cyrus said without worry. "If the Red Queen ever left the office and spent time in the real world, she'd realize the geographic restrictions are the easiest to circumvent."

They had a plan in place. It was both possible and low risk. Cyrus would once more have access to the Coalition network, and with it, a chance to get to the bottom of recent events. Charlie had a relatively simple task to perform that offered her virtually no risk.

At the same time, she knew she was really going out on a limb for a man she barely knew. The thought should've made her sick with tension; in fact, she was surprised when it didn't. Giving it more consideration, she knew the reason why. While she could never be sure who was in the right—the Red Queen or Cyrus—something was certainly going on inside the Coalition. And if the Paris operation had gone as far astray as Cyrus claimed, then there was no possible excuse for not sending a backup team. Validating Cyrus's account of events was a simple matter of checking into the Paris operation. If men had been lost, she would move ahead with the plan. But if Cyrus was leveraging her, she would take what she knew directly to the Red Queen. Still, in her heart and in her head, she already knew that everything Cyrus had told her was true. Further confirmation would simply settle her conscience.

Chapter 21

Sitting at a small table at the very back of the coffee shop, Cyrus had spent hours trudging through the Coalition's central database. Once he logged in as Monica Fichtner, he had access to files and reports that he didn't even know existed. Budgets, contact lists, performance evaluations, meeting notes, appointment schedules—it was amazing. It was like being given the keys to every nook and cranny of the Coalition. Except in this case, he'd stolen those keys.

The hard part was knowing where to start. Thinking of the bomb that had killed Voss's wife, Cyrus figured that was as good a place as any. It was one of the several discrepancies that had surfaced since the start of the case. It was also one of the most glaring since it offered a number of contradictions.

The gist, or summary report, Cyrus was given prior to taking the case, had clearly stated that Eleanor Voss was killed in a car bombing and that there had never been a definitive conclusion as to whether she or her husband had been the intended target. The reports stated that the bomb used was a conventional fragmentation device that had done extreme damage to the victim and the interior of the vehicle, while doing little or no damage to the surrounding parked cars. But in his brief conversation with Voss, he had described the bomb as heinous and barbaric. Voss said the bomb had clearly been designed to send a message. And while it was true that any man who had lost his wife to such a violent act might describe the tragedy in such a way, it was the look Cyrus had seen in his eyes as he described the bombing that made him suspect that there was much more to the story. Enough so, that twenty years later, Voss still seemed haunted by the memory of what he'd witnessed in the bomb wreckage. The point wasn't conclusive, but instinct made Cyrus suspect there was more he had yet to hear regarding the story.

It turned out he was right. The Coalition database contained detailed records of the bombing. Once Cyrus took a wider view of the case, it was clear the Coalition had conducted an extensive investigation of Voss's employer at the time, Onyx Gander, GmbH. Digging deeper, he was surprised to discover that what the Coalition had on Onyx wasn't all after-the-fact, supporting research. He found logs, phone records, wire taps, clones of computer hard drives, and thousands of pages of transcripts pertaining to the surveillance of Onyx Gander corporate facilities and its highest ranking employees. The records dated back more than a year before Eleanor Voss's death.

The implication was clear. Voss's old employer had something—or was up to something—the Coalition was interested in. Furthermore, at that point in time the Coalition was still a fledgling organization. Their charter had been signed only a few years earlier. The organization's budget and staff was a tiny fraction of what it was today. The Coalition putting so many resources into a single operation back then was reckless. It was the equivalent to a rookie poker player with a short stack of chips—and not so much as bus fare in his wallet—going all in on a single hand at a high stakes Vegas table. Whatever the Coalition was after, they wanted it in a big way.

But it was the discrepancy with the bomb that made Cyrus certain he was on the right track. While his case report had been limited and superficial regarding information about the bomb, the Coalition database contained the grisly details of the incident. The bombing wasn't at all what he'd been led to believe. In fact, the only portion that seemed accurate was that none of the surrounding cars were damaged when the bomb detonated.

Eleanor Voss had just entered her car, a late model Cadillac. It was parked in the underground garage of Onyx Gander's corporate headquarters in Munich, Germany. When she turned the ignition key, the bomb detonated. But rather than an explosive payload, the bomb consisted of several small charges, each containing a high potency hydrochloric acid compound. The charges were arrayed in positions surrounding the driver's seat, apparently in locations discrete enough to avoid detection by anything less than a thorough search of the vehicle. Upon detonation, small explosive charges acted as the delivery method, dousing both front seats in the fast-acting corrosive compound.

Eleanor Voss's skin had literally melted from her bones in a matter of seconds. It would've been a horrific and painful way to die, but it would've been quick. Analysts believed that seconds after the charges fired to disperse the acid, a secondary charge fired. This explosive was substantially more powerful and would've ended Eleanor's life instantly. Clearly Voss was right.

The bomb was less about killing Eleanor and more about sending a message. It remained unclear who the intended victim had been. If it was Rutger Voss, the message was received loud and clear. He subsequently quit Onyx Gander and severed all ties with the company. Soon after, he'd arrived on the Isle of Kapros and created his own personal stronghold with Dargo guarding the gates.

But as far as Cyrus was concerned, questions remained. The most important of which, was why he had been provided with wildly inaccurate information in regards to the bomb that killed Voss's wife. Cyrus didn't see how hiding the information could be relevant, or suppressing the details necessary. It seemed as though someone had gone out of their way to sanitize the information given to him. But then why alter the facts of the case if they had no bearing on the present day...?

Unless they did...and he just hadn't discovered the correlation yet.

Additionally, what was the Coalition's interest in Onyx Gander, or Rutger and Eleanor Voss twenty years ago? The database contained a veritable treasure trove of raw intelligence that was two decades old. Still, he found nothing to spark the agencies interest in any of the involved parties.

And now the Red Queen was pushing him to abandon the mission. Was she really concerned with his well-being? Or was she worried he might be onto something more than he was sent in to accomplish? A lot of good agents were dead. But as far as he was concerned, that was just an argument for him staying in the field. If he pulled out now they'd all have died for nothing.

There wasn't much making sense at the moment. Rather than accumulating answers, he was uncovering more questions.

Sitting back in his chair, Cyrus arched his back and stretched his arms. He went to take a sip from his coffee cup but found it empty. The work had taken hours and he wanted to stretch his legs. His eyes wandered the shop. Patrons had rotated in and out many times while he'd been sitting there. He didn't like sitting in one spot for so long, but he knew he wasn't done yet. He'd only scratched the surface of records pertaining to this case. He was fortunate enough to talk Charlie into opening up his network access and, while he didn't have reason to believe he might lose access, he was sure the answers were buried somewhere in the confines of the company's vast database. He had to gather what information he could and logoff as soon as possible. It was only a matter of time before whoever was behind all of this made another move against them.

Cyrus was considering returning to the counter for another black coffee when his eyes fell on the muted, flat panel television hung on the far wall. There was a news program running footage of a burned out SUV as it was dragged from a river. The bright morning sunlight shone in the background and a cameraman had to keep shifting his position in order to keep his shot clear of the glare. The sun hung low, half-cresting the horizon and back-lighting the scene. But when the footage headlines popped up on screen to describe the events being depicted, Cyrus squinted to read them.

At first, he was certain he'd read the headline wrong. Or, maybe the news network had made a mistake. But the flash of sun that momentarily blinded the camera meant there could be no mistake. With a tap of his keyboard, Cyrus loaded a web browser. He did a quick search to locate the news report via the headline from the television. He found a series of web pages showing not only the same footage he was seeing on TV, but several eyewitness accounts as well. He read the reports one after the other, waiting for some discrepancy, some conflict with the headline from the newscast. All of the sources were reporting the same basic facts. The burned out SUV had been pulled from the Seine River, just before the lochs at the Île de Puteaux. The four-wheel-drive had no plates and there were two bodies inside. Both had suffered gunshot wounds to the head.

Flipping to a new webpage, Cyrus loaded a map of the Seine River. Zooming out on the map, he located the Île de Puteaux, as well as the dam. He panned up river, scrolling across the map. A few seconds later, he came to Île des Vannes. It was another discrepancy. The Red Queen had told him that the bodies of Hobbs and Boone were found just north of des Vannes Island. But that wasn't possible since he'd just seen video footage of the vehicle being discovered some five and a half miles downriver in the early morning hours.

Closing the lid of the laptop, Cyrus looked around the shop once more. He suddenly felt very exposed. It was time to get moving. Pulling out his phone, he tapped out a text message and hit 'send'.

> **The Cuban. 9 pm?**

A reply came back seconds later.

> **See you then.**

Chapter 22

When Cyrus stepped through the door of *The Cuban*, not much had changed since his last visit. There was no live band tonight, and the crowd was substantially smaller. If anything, the bar was closer to its ideal capacity. He estimated, maybe seventy-five patrons were spread throughout the place. The stage along the back wall had been removed and replaced with three pool tables. What had been standing-room-only accommodations was now an open area occupied by dozens of small, round tables, nearly all of which were occupied by couples or small clustered groups. The same beaten and abused jukebox played in the corner. At least, Cyrus assumed it was the same. The place had been so jam-packed on his last visit that he'd never actually seen the jukebox. Unless the machine had caught a stray bullet last time, the sturdy, old clunker looked like it might run forever.

Stepping up to the bar, Cyrus was glad for the breathing room. He climbed atop a stool near the front entrance. The wall behind the bar was lined with dozens of bottles of every shape and color. More importantly, behind the bottles was a wide, five-foot high mirror that extended the entire length of the counter. Such mirrors were common to bars because they made establishments look larger, plus they made the collection of liquor bottles stacked before the mirror look more impressive. None of that mattered to Cyrus. He preferred sitting at the bar because it meant that from one spot he could see virtually every square inch of the place, even while keeping his back to it.

"What'll you have, honey?" the short brunette asked from behind the bar. Bright, alert eyes complimented her friendly smile. She was wearing a black tank top that was at least two sizes too small, and did little to conceal what was either the masterwork of a plastic surgeon, or a lucky seven when it came to rolling the genetic dice. *The Cuban* was stenciled in washed-out lettering across what was left of her intentionally threadbare top.

"A Modello, if you have it," Cyrus requested.

She gave him a wink before turning and heading in the opposite direction. "Coming up!" she called over her shoulder.

It was a cool night, but Cyrus had opted to leave his coat back at the compound. The night had proven unseasonably warm, at least relatively speaking. With the temperature in the mid-fifties, he'd simply pulled a flannel shirt over a T-shirt and exited the compound via the same secret rear escape route he'd used on his first visit to *The Cuban*.

Slipping the phone from his hip pocket, Cyrus typed out a quick message and hit send.

>How long are you going to stand in the corner? You're creeping everyone out, old man.

Looking squarely into the mirror for the first time, Cyrus saw Boone step fully into the light. He was shaking his head and wore a grin. He slapped Cyrus on the back and slid onto the stool to his right.

"How'd you see me?" Boone asked. "Even the bouncer didn't see me come in."

"The bouncer doesn't know you like I do." Cyrus grinned. He reached out and shook Boone's hand. "It's good to see you. I've been worried."

Boone's appearance was disheveled. His face was drawn and emaciated. There were dark bags under his eyes and he looked both mentally and physically exhausted. Contradicting this, his clothes were clean, his hair free from oil, and he didn't suffer from any undue body odor, so Cyrus was confident his friend had found some place comfortable and safe to hole up. Even if he wasn't getting rest, at least he wasn't freezing in an alley somewhere. Not that Cyrus would've expected anything less. Boone knew what he was doing. Still, from the strained look on his face, Cyrus could see his mentor had been through the wringer.

"You've been worried? Jesus, kid—I've been more worried about you. Before things went all to hell, I received a report about you and Gladd getting attacked on the train outside Paris. Gladd reported in after you reached Hamburg. He said you would be completing the remainder of your trip through an alternative route, but our spotter outside Voss's facility said you never arrived."

Cyrus offered an understanding nod. "Oh, I arrived alright—well, more or less. Just way behind schedule. Some improvisation was involved. You know how it goes. I'm surprised you were that concerned."

"I wouldn't have been—under normal conditions. But shortly after you were attacked, my team was hit. We never had the chance to pick up Ragsdale. We were hit before we could take him into custody, like we planned."

"I heard that, about a week after the fact," Cyrus admitted. He didn't know what to say. Somehow a sad shake of his head didn't seem like enough given the losses Boone's team had suffered.

"The plan was to take Ragsdale into custody and fake his injury and hospitalization," Cyrus said. "But someone hit your team, then took Ragsdale out *for real?*"

That brought only a grim nod from Boone.

"But why?"

Boone was silent for a long moment before finally shrugging. "I have no idea. And I wasn't in a situation to sort it out. Hobbs and I were the only ones to make it out. I lost the entire team. We went dark in hopes of losing the obvious bulls-eye painted on our backs. I was hoping to regroup and sort things out but…things just went from bad to worse after that."

A different bartender arrived and set a beer bottle on the coaster in front of Cyrus. She was tall, a few years older than the last girl, and her hair was long and blonde. "One Modello," she said with a smile. "How are you boys doing tonight?"

"Great," Cyrus said with a grin. He slid a ten across the counter to her. "How about you?"

The woman laughed. "Just happy to be alive," she smiled. She slid the money back in his direction. "Drinks are on me tonight," she said with a shake of her head. "I'd say it's the least I can do."

In spite of himself, the best Cyrus could offer was a questioning look that must've bordered on a scowl.

She offered him a conspiratorial wink and leaned across the counter. "I might not know your name, honey, but I remember you just the same. You're the reason I still have this bar, and a way to support my mother. Hell, if it weren't for you, Josie down there wouldn't have a job and half the people in this place probably wouldn't have their lives."

While Cyrus recognized the bartender from his first visit to *The Cuban*, he hadn't expected anyone to recognize him. Not after everything that had happened.

Cyrus smiled. "This is your place? You own the bar?"

She grinned and offered a proud nod. "I'm Lucy," she said and shook his hand. Then she took a loving look at the surrounding bar. "Yeah, she ain't much, but she's my pride and joy. Does your friend here know what you did the other night?"

Boone had been watching the conversation with mirth in his eyes. While Cyrus had been caught off guard by the conversation, Boone was entirely unprepared.

"Ah, no. He's been out of town. To be honest, I'm surprised you recognized me. A lot happened that night. How did you know I was involved?"

Lucy pointed to a camera lens recessed into the dark crown molding behind the bar. With the low light and the way the camera had been camouflaged, someone had to know it was there in order to have any chance of spotting it. "I've got a dozen of them mounted all around this place. The night those guys started shooting, I got the whole thing recorded in gory high definition. If I didn't know for a fact that it really happened, I would've bet it was some kind of crazy Hollywood stunt."

Cyrus shook his head. "I wish that had been the case."

He wanted to let the subject drop. He didn't care for the attention. But one question was nagging at him. "It really was a bad scene, Lucy. I'm glad to see the violence didn't turn people off coming here."

The pained expression on Lucy's face was certainly that of a business owner. "No kidding," she admitted. "I had the same worry. I was afraid the authorities would shut me down—or that people would be too afraid to come back after what happened."

"What happened with the authorities?" Boone asked, speaking for the first time.

Lucy shrugged. "Damned if I know. There were cops in and out of here for two days, asking questions, digging bullets out of the walls, the whole nine yards. It was just like you see on TV. I was sure I'd be shut down. Or lose my liquor license—you know, something. The police chief was leaning on me and threatening the whole works!"

Cyrus waited for Lucy to continue, but she'd concluded the story—at least in her mind.

"So what happened?" Boone finally insisted.

"I don't know," Lucy said at last. "The chief was on me something fierce, making all kinds of threats. The next day he comes back and tells me that the investigation is closed and that I'm free to reopen whenever I see fit!"

Cyrus could read the confusion on Boone's face. "Just like that?" he asked.

Lucy nodded.

Cyrus understood. Voss had said he would do something about the bar. He'd obviously spoken with King Borden and the matter had been swept under the rug. Not that he expected Voss to own up to it.

Cyrus knew that Lucy would benefit from the peace of mind that came from understanding what had happened to suddenly right her problems, but at the same time he didn't want to add to a story that was sure to be making its way around the bar, and would continue to for years to come.

"At least folks aren't afraid of the place," Cyrus said in hopes of moving the subject along.

"Ain't that the truth," Lucy blustered. "Once the trouble with the authorities went away, that was the next worry that cost me sleep. But it turns out, what they say is true: there's no such thing as bad press. People I've never seen before started coming in just to check us out. I guess it was inevitable. We were all over the paper and the news for days. People love a good train wreck. Between you and me, since we've reopened, revenue is actually up 44%!"

Cyrus laughed. There was no doubt Lucy was a 'dyed in the wool' entrepreneur. "Will you get back to having live music?" he asked.

A wide smile spread across her face. "Will we ever! Hell, yes—and I can't wait. I have some equipment to replace—and a stage to rebuild before we're ready for that, but it's at the top of my list.

"I really hope Natasha's willing to come back and play again. She really fills the house like nobody's business. I'm not kidding, we're talking standing room only, every time!"

Cyrus felt his jaw drop. He'd been under the impression that Natasha was making her debut appearance on stage that night. "No kidding?" he asked. "How often does she play here?"

The smile disappeared from Lucy's face and she shook her head. "It's hard to say. Its real hit and miss with that girl. I never know for sure if or when she'll show. The girl's a hell of a talent—but I get the sense that playing is largely therapeutic for her. She comes and plays when she wants. I might see her once a month, or I might not see her for three.

"She's a damn pretty girl with a whole truckload of skill," Lucy continued. "But she's odd, too. She won't let me pay her, and while every live act I've ever put on that stage would sell their baby sisters into slavery for a recording deal, she's never once been willing to talk with one of the bigwigs we get passing through."

Lucy thanked Cyrus once more and finally went on with her nightly business. But before she left, she made sure to reiterate the fact that their drinks were taken care of. Cyrus guessed that Lucy didn't realize he knew Natasha, which was just as well.

"The crazy lady behind the bar sure has a lot of nice things to say about your girl," Boone said after a few short minutes of silence. They'd both been nursing their beers and pondering personal thoughts.

Taking one more pull from his beer bottle, Cyrus cast a sideways glance at Boone. "My girl?"

Boone's lips stretched in a knowing grin. "Come on, you really think I didn't know why you wanted this assignment—why you *had* to have this operation? Hell, we dropped three cases in your lap. You solved one of them while sitting right there at the table, then delegated the other one to an outside agency so fast that no one could turn you down for this mission. You insinuated yourself into this operation right there on the spot. God only knows what you might've come up with if you'd had time to plan something prior to that meeting."

Cyrus said nothing. His eyes were making a mental study of his mentor. He knew he shouldn't be surprised that Boone was onto him. Boone had been the one to recruit him into the Coalition, after all. Of course Boone knew everything there was to know about him by now. His knowledge would certainly have extended to the woman he'd been dating at the time.

"Alright," Cyrus conceded. "You got me. But tell me how that was wrong in any way. The Coalition still needed someone inside Voss's compound, and I made that happen. I just happened to have a personal stake I wasn't willing to share with the group."

Boone's eyebrows arched as he considered Cyrus's logic. "That *personal stake* you're referring to could've worked against you just as easily as it worked for you," he reminded. "And we're talking about a connection to your prior life—your prior identity."

Boone continued, growing more animated as he went. "Furthermore, how'd you know she would keep your secret? You were showing up at her home—out of the blue—fully equipped with an entirely different name and a falsified personal history. How'd you know she would roll with that? Nobody's that good!"

Cyrus drained the last of his beer and pushed the bottle across the counter. He refused to meet Boone's eye. "I didn't know," he answered finally. "I had no idea."

Boone sputtered. An exasperated sigh was apparently all he could manage. He slammed his bottle down on the counter and stared at Cyrus. Everyone at the counter cast looks in their direction. Boone quickly realized the attention he'd garnered by losing his cool and responded with a sheepish look, silently mouthing the word "sorry" in the direction of the staring faces.

"What about you?" Cyrus countered after an awkward silence.

"*What about me?*"

"Don't give me that," he snarled. "You knew exactly what I was doing. You just admitted it. If what I was doing was so dangerous—and potentially detrimental, why did you let me do it?"

It was Boone's turn to take a long, appraising look at the situation. It seemed like forever before he finally spoke. "Because I trained you," Boone said quietly. "I trained you, and I've seen you do some of the damnedest things. I mean it, just *the damnedest.* I've literally watched you turn a failed operation into a successful mission more times than I care to admit.

"Why did I let you do it? Because on more than one occasion, you've made the impossible, *possible.* So when you have the bright idea of taking on a fake identity, and then knocking on the door of the fortress where your ex-girlfriend's father lives and works, who the hell am I to tell you that it can't be done?"

Boone's deadpan delivery was so convincing that Cyrus bought it. A great relief flooded him when a smile finally cracked Boone's stony countenance. A moment later, they both broke out laughing.

"Well, when you put it that way," Cyrus said quietly. "You can make anything sound like a foolish idea."

Boone laughed. He laughed harder than Cyrus had heard him laugh in a very long time. "Seriously, kid," he said as he tried to regain his breath. "I really don't know how you do it. You are, hands down, the best I ever trained. Without a doubt, the best agent we've got."

Cyrus shook his head. He waved at the distant bartender for another round of drinks. "First you're busting my balls, then you're giving me compliments. That tells me two things. The first is that I haven't had enough to drink."

Boone grinned and took the bait. "What's the second?"

"That you've recently suffered a concussion," he smiled.

It wasn't long before the conversation moved on to more serious matters. Cyrus felt a cold sensation in his gut before he changed the subject, but he forged ahead just the same.

"What happened on your side of things," he asked Boone. "Only you and Hobbs made it out alive?"

Boone took a deep breath and released it slowly. His eyes had dropped to the surface of the bar. He seemed to be staring somewhere deep inside the top of the countertop. Finally, his chin rose and he took a long pull from his beer.

"Hobbs was nearly my last mistake," Boone said cryptically. He took his time, as if considering how to explain something not easy to understand.

"I'm still not entirely sure what happened," he said at last. "As you know, I was taking a six-man team to collect Richard Ragsdale as part of *your* operation. It should've been a cakewalk. I figured I was easily taking twice the number of guys I needed. But after what happened on the Woo-jin Kang operation, I was making sure my bases were covered. It should've been enough. No one knew we were moving on the guy. No one knew we'd be there."

"So what happened?"

"I really don't know," Boone said with a sad shake of his head. "But we walked into a nightmare. We pulled onto the street outside Ragsdale's apartment and, before I knew it, we were taking automatic fire from every direction. It was a bloodbath."

"But you and Hobbs made it out," Cyrus persisted. "How?"

Boone shrugged. "I should've been asking myself that question. I didn't until it was almost too late. I watched my team get mowed down right there in front of me. I'm talking in the literal sense—these guys were just cut down by automatic crossfire. They never stood a chance. Hobbs was standing beside me at the time. We moved for cover behind one of the two armored SUV's we took. Everything happened so fast—the next thing I knew, we were in the truck and tearing ass to get out of there."

"Were you pursued?"

Boone offered a slow shake of his head. "No. That should've been another warning sign. I just didn't see it."

"What do you mean, *warning sign?*" Cyrus insisted. "What happened?"

"Hobbs drove us to a boathouse along the river. We knew we couldn't use our planned safe house. After what happened, we had every reason to think the rest of the mission was compromised."

Cyrus nodded. It was a safe bet.

"But as soon as we stepped out of the truck, Hobbs pulled his gun on me," Boone explained. "He was with *them*. He was behind what happened to the team. He must've been with the guys who tried to hit you on the train, too."

"Did you question Hobbs and find out what he knew?" That Boone had somehow gotten the upper hand on Hobbs seemed obvious since he was sitting there.

Another disappointed shake of the head came from Boone. "He took my gun. But once he did, he let his guard down, just like I trained him *not to*. So I made my move. It went smooth, too. I took him down quick. Unfortunately, I was in the process of restraining him when his partner showed up. We got into a shootout and both Hobbs and the other guy ended up dead."

Cyrus considered Boone's story. "So you set up the other guy to look like you when you burned the truck and dumped it in the river?"

Boone nodded. "If Hobbs was compromised, I didn't know who to trust. I didn't know if he was rogue or if he'd been a plant inside the company the entire time."

"So you went dark."

He nodded again. "So I went dark. I strapped both bodies in the truck and popped them both in the head. I figured it would keep the local authorities from looking too close. I found some kind of phosphorus accelerant in the truck of the guy who came to meet Hobbs, so I put it to use. I doused the inside of the truck with it, then I lit them up. I figured, since the SUV was armored, it would burn long and hot. Certainly hot enough to obscure any trace of their DNA. I even tossed my Zippo in to seal the deal."

Cyrus shook his head. He knew how much his friend cherished that lighter. Using it to sell the charade was the work of a desperate man.

"The real bitch of it was that I never got to interrogate Hobbs or his partner," Boone lamented.

"I wouldn't lose any sleep over that," Cyrus offered. "Odds are good that they were just one-off hires working on a compartmentalized, need-to-know basis. I'd wager they were just like the guys who tried to hit me on the train, or even here," he said looking around the bar. "Mercs, just hired to do a job. Disposable and clean as far as their employer was concerned."

Boone met Cyrus's eye and nodded slowly. "Makes sense," he reasoned. "You would be dealing with the same sort of thing on your end. You weren't able to take one of them alive?"

Taking a pull from his beer bottle, Cyrus offered a rueful chuckle. "I'll tell you this much. Whoever's behind this knows where to shop, because they're hiring some of the most hardcore, cut-throat bastards on the market. Not one of them has gone down easy. It makes it hard to get information when your opponent won't stop fighting until he's dead."

Cyrus had specifically declined to comment on the two rogue members of Dargo's team who were still locked away in the subbasement of the compound. He didn't have much faith that either man would know anything useful, and he didn't want to listen to Boone tell him that he needed to find out what they knew before Dargo did. As far as Cyrus was concerned, that part of the mission had come and gone. His priorities had changed. Not that he expected his mentor to understand that.

Boone huffed. "Well...at least we're still alive."

Cyrus smirked, then raised his bottle. Boone clinked his against Cyrus's, and they both took a drink.

It was almost a half hour and three drinks later before Boone broached the subject Cyrus was waiting for. He'd actually been eyeing the clock to see how long it would take.

"All of this trouble over Voss's work?" Boone said. "Is it even worth the effort?"

Slowly pulling the corner of the label back from the bottle in his hands, Cyrus considered the question. After a few moments, he cast a glance at Boone and gave a slight nod. "Our intel suggested he was in the early stages of his research. *We were wrong.*"

Boone leaned closer. "Are you kidding me? Has he started testing?" his voice was nearly a whisper.

"You could say that."

"Have you seen the data?"

This was the moment of truth. By telling Boone that he'd been tagged with the neurological agent upon his first entry into the compound, he would be putting himself and Doctor Voss in a potentially life-threatening situation. It was a virtual certainty that the Coalition brass wouldn't react well to the knowledge that one of their agents had experienced the memory recording procedure. It was impossible to tell how they might react, or the potential consequences—though time and experience had given him a fair amount of insight.

"Seen it? I've lived it," Cyrus bluntly admitted. "I was in bad shape when I arrived at the gates of Voss's compound. Worse shape than I expected, actually. I'd lost a lot of blood, and I had a serious infection. But that's essentially why they let me through the gates in the first place. I needed immediate medical care and I couldn't wait. So they let me in."

Boone watched Cyrus as he explained, but it was clear that he wasn't following.

"Shadowlight—Voss's memory recording protocol—stage one, is a neuropeptide tag that's injected into the bloodstream. It acts as a sort of marker, tagging the starting point for memory capture. I didn't realize it at the time, but when I was treated for the gunshot wound and the infection, I was also tagged."

A faraway look crossed Boone's eyes. He set his beer aside and leaned back on his stool. Cyrus could imagine all of the considerations that were flooding his mentor's mind at that moment. Not one of them was good.

Turning, Boone looked at Cyrus. A grave countenance had gripped him. "Tell me how it works."

"Parts of it are extremely complicated," Cyrus admitted. "The tagging agent was administered through a standard subcutaneous injection along with broad spectrum antibiotics, so we can be sure that the tag isn't something we can disable like a conventional bug or germ. But technically it's a neuropeptide, with a number of attributes that have more in common with a prion. It has the unique ability to cross the blood-to-brain barrier. That's rather unique, as I understand it. Neuropeptides and prions are both protein based, so it makes a lot of sense, actually. It's similar to the way Mad Cow Disease makes its way to the brain only, thankfully, this isn't fatal."

"It could be," Boone warned. "Depending on what Voss learns from your recording."

"Yeah," Cyrus said with a sigh. "I was blindsided in the truest sense of the word. But there's good news. The neurological recordings are monsters. World-class monsters. They require hardcore computing power to download and process before they can be played. So while the tagging agent can be easily replicated, the recording hardware is the barrier to entry. And right now, there's only one system in the world that can download and process the recordings."

"Let me guess," Boone said with a grunt. "It's safely locked away somewhere deep inside Voss's HQ."

Cyrus nodded. "For now that's a good thing."

"Have you thought about what Monica will do when she finds out you've been compromised? Wait—. Has Voss downloaded your recording yet?"

"Yeah, this morning. But it'll take at least forty-eight hours to process the data he captured," Cyrus lied. "It'll take at least that long for the computer to crunch the raw data."

"Well, that's something. It gives us time to figure things out."

"The way things are going, we've got a lot to figure out."

"You're telling me. We still don't know who's trying to kill us. That would be a great place to start."

They sat silently for a little while, both consumed with their own worries. But Cyrus had an agenda, a specific direction he needed this particular conversation to travel, and he needed to see it through before they were sidetracked.

"There's one more positive aspect to the tagging procedure," Cyrus clarified. "You can't just go and tag someone without them knowing. Well, they did it to me, but now I know what to look for.

"The first day I woke up after being tagged, I felt like hell. I didn't think too much of it since I had a small hole running straight through me, and an infection that was equally end to end. But it wasn't the normal fevered, infection kind of shitty feeling. Every muscle in my body hurt. It was like I'd been hit by a truck. Every joint in my body ached to the point where I didn't want to move.

"I wrote it all off as symptoms of a nasty infection. But once I found out Voss had used the tag on me, I started reading up on the little bits and pieces he'd told me. That's when it all made sense. In addition to the infection, I was displaying classic flu-like symptoms. It turns out that you can't just shoot a protein into the body's bloodstream. It'll be attacked as a foreign body and destroyed by the immune system. That's why a virus is used as a delivery vehicle. The neuropeptide compound is piggy-backed on top of some sort of viral agent—something the body can't destroy before the payload is delivered."

Rubbing his eyes, Boone raised a hand and tipped his head back in thought. Cyrus knew he needed a moment to consider everything that was flying at him. He would understand the generalities of the science as they were explained, but it was a lot of information to process.

When Boone spoke again, Cyrus knew he was reading his friend correctly. "Bearing in mind that I only understood half of what you just said, it does sound like good news—and maybe bad, depending on who's using it. With symptoms like that, anyone who's been tagged should stick out like a sore thumb," Boone reasoned.

Cyrus realized that he should feel guilty for fabricating many of Shadowlight's particulars, but strangely he didn't. The flu-like symptoms were a smokescreen. He just hoped he hadn't overplayed the details.

Chapter 23

The Cuban
11:29 pm

Making no effort to hide her amused smile, Lucy delivered another round of shots. She met Cyrus's eye and offered the barest hint of a nod. Without a word, she turned and headed for the far end of the bar. Boone watched the woman with curiosity but held his tongue until she was out of earshot.

"She's into you," he said with a rueful grin. "I swear to God, kid…every damn place you go… What is it? I sure don't get it."

Cyrus pulled one of the shot glasses in front of himself, and pushed the second over to Boone. They'd been drinking and catching up for some time, and while Cyrus was feeling no pain, he could see from the glazed pinch of his friend's eyes that Boone was way ahead of him in that regard. "It's all in your head," Cyrus said quietly before taking the shot glass and downing its contents in a single swallow.

"Bullshit," Boone slurred before downing his own shot. "Maybe you don't see it—or maybe you just don't want to. I think you put a part of yourself on a shelf when you left your girl all those years ago. That's why you had to come back now. You had to see if she still feels the same about you. I know you sure as hell feel the same way about her."

Unable to pull his eyes away from the surface of the counter before him, Cyrus considered his friend's words and wondered why the observation frustrated him so deeply. Boone was right, of course. But it was the fact that Boone knew about it at all that bothered him more than anything. It was a consequence of coming back now, when he was on the clock. He should've done it once he was done with the Coalition.

And with that alcohol-fogged thought, Cyrus realized for the first time what his subconscious had been trying to tell him since the start of the mission. Things just weren't right—the job just wasn't what it was supposed to be. He'd been lied to and manipulated by his superiors. They would say whatever was necessary to keep him in line. And while Boone might be right, that he was made for this type of work, doing it for the Coalition was becoming a problem. Cyrus simply didn't want to do the job if he couldn't trust the people he worked for—or with.

"What're you thinking?" Boone asked.

Popping from his slow epiphany, Cyrus raised his head. His eyes instantly moved to the mirror on the wall behind the bar and scanned the room to their backs. Such routines were muscle memory, or reflex. He really was hardwired for this kind of work. Interestingly, he'd also noticed that the more they drank, the less Boone was minding their surroundings. That wasn't like him. He was tired and worn. Even his hard won instincts had frayed with time and fatigue.

Catching Lucy's eye from her position at the far end of the counter, Cyrus signaled for another round. Sure, the booze dulled

Boone's instincts more than the stress and fatigue, but that was another thing that his one-time mentor would've previously admonished. A lot had changed with his friend over the course of the last several months. Cyrus had been away for most of that time, so maybe coming back and seeing Boone as he was only made it that much more obvious.

"Another round, boys?" Lucy asked.

Boone shook his head in a delayed response. "Not for me," he slurred.

Cyrus was watching Boone in the mirror's reflection and fought a mischievous smile when he saw his eyes wobbling with each shake. "Yeah," Cyrus said. "Why not?"

Lucy was watching Boone carefully. Clearly she didn't think he was alright. She shot Cyrus an, *are you sure?* glance. Cyrus nodded and gave her a quick wink. Shrugging, she departed to prepare another round of shots.

"I don't know where you're putting all this, kid." Boone leaned heavily on his elbows, putting the weight of his upper body on the bar to keep from teetering on his stool. A goofy sort of grin had spread across his face. It was an expression Cyrus had never seen before. For the first time since meeting Boone three years earlier, Cyrus wondered if this was what it looked like when Boone finally relaxed and decompressed.

The sight made him feel guilty for what he was doing to his friend. Still, he was doing what Boone taught him and following his gut. Things weren't adding up, and a voice in the back of Cyrus's mind was telling him things that the logical part of his mind—even his heart—wouldn't dare to examine.

Lucy placed the last pair of shots before them and then made herself scarce. Cyrus couldn't blame her. She was grateful for what he'd done to stop the gunman earlier in the week, and he was taking advantage of that by asking her to do something she couldn't understand. Still, all she had to do was serve the drinks. Adding a little something extra to Boone's was a small favor, but it was asking an awful lot.

"I'm surprised you're still here," Boone said without turning to Cyrus. "I figured Monica would've cut her losses by now and called you back to HQ. Too many dead agents with nothing to show for it. She's not the type to roll the dice and keep you in the field."

"You must've suspected I was still operational. You came here looking for me," Cyrus said, avoiding the point Boone was trying to make.

His friend looked at him. Boone's eyes were glazed but there was concern there. He licked his lips and took an unusually long time to organize his thoughts. "She ordered you back, didn't she."

Cyrus found it amusing that he hadn't asked a question. It was a statement. Boone knew him that well. Cyrus shrugged and refused to meet his eye.

"Well...that's why I'm here," Boone said simply.

"Even though you went through the trouble of faking your death?"

"All the better, actually. That way I could keep an eye on you—well, Voss's place, with no one really watching out for me. No one ever sees a dead man coming."

Cyrus smiled. *Yeah, fair point.*

"Besides, I didn't figure you'd pull the ripcord on this one, even if you were ordered home. This one's personal for you. That's never a good thing."

"Personal or not," Cyrus countered. "If we pull the plug now, we'll have lost a lot of good people with nothing to show for it. If I don't see this through, we may never know who's behind this."

Boone sat silently, taking a long look at his young contemporary. "That's one of your character flaws...one that I respect most," he admitted. "But it'll be the one that gets you killed."

Chapter 24

Boone woke up face down in a puddle of his own drool. Even as he blinked the sleep and grime from his eyes, he knew something was wrong. He propped himself up on an elbow and the room around him spun like a violent tilt-a-whirl. The contents of his stomach first churned and then quickly began to roil as his body threatened to expel everything where he lay.

Jesus.

He settled for rolling onto his back and letting the room spin unseen beyond closed eyes. He sensed the unpleasantly soft mattress and the bed's hideous, threadbare duvet beneath him. Not only was he fully clothed, but the bed was still fully made. He swallowed hard and made another half-hearted and failed attempt to sit upright.

Last night was a blur...

Struggling to recall why he felt so horrible, Boone realized he had no memory of returning to the hotel room. In fact, the last thing he could recall was drinking with—

Oh…that sonofabitch…

Girding himself in preparation, Boone slid upright and sat at the foot of the queen-size bed. Spreading his knees wide, he fought for equilibrium in a spinning world. His sense of balance warred with his better judgment as he smashed his eyes shut and reminded himself that the room was, in fact, stationary. The thundering cacophony taking place inside his head was unlike any headache he could ever recall. There was a stabbing pain behind his eyes—a throbbing spike being twisted between his temples and in his ears—and then there was the intense searing sensation that ran from the base of his skull, down a neck so stiff he could scarcely turn his head.

Boone hadn't had so much to drink in a long time. Not since college, in fact. While he could vividly recall some world-class hangovers, none of them compared to this. He knew he'd more than overdone it, but somehow the consequences seemed out of proportion to his excess. Was he just getting too old to tie one on like he had back in the day? What would Cyrus look like in comparison? He had drunk every bit as much.

Cyrus…

His eyes flashed fully open and Boone became completely alert for the first time. He fought back the nausea and the stabbing pain that came from the small bit of light filtering through the drawn curtains at the far end of the room. He was alone. His gun and two spare magazines sat on the small, crooked table a few feet away. There was a short dresser made of cheap imitation wood along one wall beneath a large discolored mirror that was bolted to the wall, and the floor beneath his feet was as worn as the bed.

Looking down at his feet, Boone wiggled his stocking-clad toes and noticed for the first time that he'd been relieved of his boots. He winced. Even his feet hurt.

With his weapon secure and in clear view, plus Cyrus missing, Boone reasoned that he must have rented the room after their drinking marathon the night before. Still, he had no memory of it. In fact, he had no memory of leaving the bar. Maybe he was just too old for this kind of foolishness. He was, without a doubt, regretting it now. Still, it had been a relief to catch up with Cyrus while getting up to speed on his side of the case. He could recall that much, at least.

After a few additional minutes to steel himself, Boone finally made his way to the bathroom. He ran cold water into a sink so dingy that he wouldn't want to actually touch the faux porcelain basin with any part of his anatomy. When he finally leaned forward to splash water on his face, his body surprised him by relieving itself of his stomach's contents, without any warning at all.

Several minutes later, Boone finished sloshing water around the sink and making short work of his own mess. When he finally splashed cold water across his sweaty flesh, it felt better than he could've imagined. And while his stomach continued to buck and twist, he no longer considered it a danger. The nausea had been replaced by an acidic burn that he could feel all the way up the back of his throat, but at least the twisting and churning was coming under control.

Looking in the mirror, he was surprised at what he saw. Though he'd just rinsed his face, it was dappled in sweat once more. Dark, half-circles of pure exhaustion hung under his eyes, and he looked pale. Ghostly pale.

"Definitely not as young as I used to be," he mumbled, as he stumbled back to the bed. It was the only place to sit in the horrible little room.

Sitting once more on the end of the bed, Boone considered what little he could recall from the previous night. Cyrus said that Voss was further along on the project than they had anticipated. He wondered how that might factor into the grand scheme of things. Certainly the mission hadn't gone according to plan, but it wasn't as far afield as Cyrus believed, either. Though he didn't know it, Cyrus was only a component in a much larger plan.

Working the larger operation through his mind once more, Boone wondered how Cyrus would react if he knew what was really going on. He wouldn't approve, of that much he was certain. But what if he knew what was truly at stake? The kid was rational, if nothing else. A case could certainly be made...

Shaking his head, Boone pushed the thought from his mind. It would never work. No matter how well intentioned, mistakes had been made and there was no way to sugarcoat or justify what had happened two decades earlier. And since he couldn't change that, Boone knew he had no choice but to move forward. Collateral damage was always a risk. As long as Cyrus remained ignorant, he would remain a powerful asset.

Yet, the number one risk to the mission had always been Cyrus. Boone had known it from day one, but he'd kept the assessment to himself. If Cyrus knew the truth he wouldn't participate. And depending on how much he knew, he might actively oppose the operation altogether.

A chill ran down Boone's spine at the thought. His young protégé had a knack—a gift—for problem solving. There was a very good chance he might find out what was really going on, and if that happened, not even Boone knew how he might react.

Sitting there, Boone realized that his mind had wandered. He was finding it difficult to concentrate. His thoughts were haphazard and his body ached. He was experiencing pain in the most unusual of places. It was then he noticed he'd been scratching a patch of dry skin on his right shoulder. When he turned his head to look, a sharp pain lanced through his skull.

Grinding his teeth, he made his way back to the bathroom. Flipping the switch for the overhead light, the bulb flickered slowly before filling the room with a blinding yellow glow. The sudden burst of illumination carried a stabbing jolt of pain directly into his brain. The effect was so severe that it sucked the breath from his lungs.

Rolling back the short sleeve of his shirt, Boone examined his shoulder in the mirror. The patch of scaly skin was plainly visible, its texture entirely different from rest of his arm. At the center of the small section of dry skin was a tiny, circular bruise. Inside of that was a nearly microscopic red dot.

Boone stared at the image reflected in the mirror longer than would normally have been necessary thanks to his weakened condition. As the seconds ticked by, his mind flashed back to his conversation with Cyrus. Flu-like symptoms…a virus used as a delivery vehicle…neuropeptide tag…

Voss's memory tag…

Cyrus was on to him.

Chapter 25

Setting the acoustic guitar beside her on the bed, Natasha leaned forward and showed Cyrus how to adjust his fingering for the next chord. Cyrus held a guitar that was similar to her own, though hers was an antique that she was normally reluctant to take from its case. It had been given to her by her father on her sixteenth birthday, and had once belonged to rock legend, Buddy Holly.

"There, just like that," she said. She sat back on the bed and once more took up her own guitar to mirror the chord she was teaching Cyrus.

They'd been making slow progress, moving through the song as she instructed him. It was a bittersweet experience since they had shared Sunday mornings doing exactly the same thing, years earlier. And while the music came much more naturally to her these days, at the moment it felt more clumsy and challenging than ever. She was distracted by warm memories of past shared moments, and isolated by thoughts of the present and far too many words left unsaid.

Still, there was one thing that hadn't changed. Jonny—well, Cyrus—that much had changed—was a quick study. She needed only to show him each position on the guitar once, twice at most, and he had committed the mechanics of each chord to memory. It never took long to teach him a song. His vise-like grip on memories never ceased to amaze her. But for as quickly as he could learn a new song, he still had to play it repeatedly before gaining a truly natural appreciation for the flow of the rhythms. Until that time, he was like a robot executing a pre-programmed series of commands. It took time and repetition for him to gain an organic sense for any tune. Even then, he had no ability to improvise and play a more ad-hoc or free form version of any given piece.

It wasn't long before they completed the song's final notes. When Cyrus's eyes met hers and she saw his smile, she knew what he was thinking. She offered a slight nod and they both launched into their first complete pass of Nirvana's *All Apologies*, singing and playing in unison without any breaks.

By the time they finished, they were both laughing. Natasha knew Cyrus shared her pride in their accomplishment. It felt just like old times. It felt good in a way she had long forgotten. But once the laughing was through, they sat there in silence. They stared at each other over the tops of their guitars, sitting on Natasha's bed in a windowless room in the high security fortress that was her home.

Maybe the good old days weren't so easily revisited.

"I thought—." she stopped. The words were clumsy and more difficult than she expected them to be. "I thought you might come to my room when you got back last night."

Ah!

In her mind, she'd known exactly what she wanted to say. But when she opened her mouth and *that* tumbled out, she knew the rest of what she needed to express was only going to be more difficult. She stared down at the guitar cradled in her lap. It was a rarity for her not to meet his eyes, but she didn't know what to do or say next.

"I'm sorry about that," Cyrus said quietly. "I wanted to."

He stopped short, and she looked up. She sensed there was more. He was having trouble finding the words, as well. At least she wasn't alone in that.

"Things didn't go as well as I'd hoped with my friend," Cyrus continued. "I wasn't feeling very good about it, and I sort of just needed to be alone."

Natasha could see the truth of the statement in his eyes. They clouded with pain when he thought about the events of the previous night. She wanted to ask what happened, but it was a simple question that would never work. If he wanted to talk about it, he would. Pushing never helped. She could never get anything out of him until he was ready to talk, so she settled for asking, "Will things work themselves out?"

Cyrus shrugged. "I'll find out soon, I guess."

Whatever it was, she could see he didn't feel good about it. For as well as she knew him, she still couldn't grasp the emotion she was seeing on his face. He wasn't angry. If anything, he seemed troubled…or disappointed.

Not sure where to go from there, Natasha decided to drop the matter and move on to what was on her mind. It would either make things better or worse—she had no idea which. But she had questions that needed answers, and the longer Cyrus stayed near, the more she wanted him to remain a part of her life. She fought a nagging question specific to what had brought him back to her. It was time to get an answer.

"What do you know about Lamplighter?" Natasha asked bluntly.

When Cyrus's eyes met hers, she knew there was recognition there. More than that, she knew she'd struck a nerve. But he was slow to respond. She could see him weighing his response, deciding what to say or how to say it.

"I know you," Natasha said. "Don't weigh it—this isn't the time to hold back. If I mean anything to you, you need to tell me what you know. *This is important.*"

Taking a deep breath, Cyrus set the guitar aside. "I'll tell you what I know, but then you have to do the same. You may or may not know it, but it's a big deal—and just knowing that name could put you in a world of danger."

Choking on a breath, Natasha was afraid to respond. Afraid that her words would betray her need to understand, and her fear for what she might learn. She nodded her agreement, all the while entirely certain that those fears were plainly visible in her eyes.

"I'd never heard of Lamplighter before a couple of weeks ago," Cyrus explained. "Then a case file was dumped in my lap. Some pretty powerful people were getting a little nervous about the technology your father was developing, and they wanted to keep an eye on his progress. The problem was the level of security surrounding your father, his lab, and his work. While they knew what he was working on, they had no idea how far along he was, or how feasible the project was."

Blanching at what Cyrus was explaining, Natasha felt disgusted. "You're talking about spying on my father's work?"

Cyrus nodded. "But thanks to the fortress he'd built for himself and his family, no one could get access. No one knew the status of his work."

"So they sent you?" She couldn't believe what she was hearing. "That's why you're here—to spy on my father?"

Cyrus shook his head. He didn't speak for a long while, but his eyes never left hers. He never looked away from her accusing gaze, and didn't whither under her allegation.

"No," Cyrus said finally. "I'm not here to spy on your father. But I used him as an excuse to come."

Natasha heard herself grinding her teeth. She couldn't believe how her question had so quickly spiraled out of control. While she hadn't known what to expect, it wasn't this. And, she realized, none of this did anything to explain Lamplighter.

"Go on," she managed to shoot through her clamped jaw. She felt tears threaten at the edges of her eyes, but for the life of her, she couldn't tell if they were from rage or hurt from his newest betrayal. Either way, she promised herself that he would not see her tears fall.

"I took the assignment," Cyrus explained. "I took it because if I didn't, someone else would. And with the security in place here, there was a good chance that whoever tried to breach the building would've been caught. If that happened, someone was likely to get hurt. I couldn't let that happen to you or your family."

"So you came to spy on us so no one would get hurt? It had nothing to do with our history? You didn't think you could use it to walk right in the front door?"

"Are you kidding?" Cyrus laughed. "I was probably the last person on earth you wanted to see. If I came knocking on your door, there was zero chance you were going to invite me in. Tell me I'm wrong?"

Natasha looked away. She didn't know what she would've done under the circumstances, but while she would like to think she would've taken the high road, she was fairly certain she would've turned him away. There was, as she was now experiencing, simply too much pain involved in seeing him after he'd disappeared from her life.

"Let's go back to the part where you're a spy," she said instead. "When did that happen? Who are you working for?"

Cyrus smiled. "Witness relocation wasn't a good fit," he explained. "There was a solid chance that I wouldn't be safe, no matter where they put me. So we set up a sting. The idea was to net everyone after me, all in one shot. I figured, that way I could come home to you."

Unable to keep the shock from her face, Natasha was rendered speechless. She heard his words but couldn't reconcile them with the events that had taken place. Not only was all of this news to her, but he had also never come back to her.

"The operation went off according to plan, more or less," Cyrus explained. "Maybe it went a little too good, I guess. I helped roll up a major terrorist network. When it was done, I guess some folks were impressed because they offered me a job."

Rubbing her eyes, Natasha marveled at the unexpected turn the story had taken. "So you took a job—you became a spy, rather than come back to school with me?"

Cyrus looked away for the first time. It was the first moment of regret she'd seen from him since the start of the conversation. More than that, she could see the pain in his face, his eyes, in the whole of his being.

"It seems really dumb now," Cyrus said quietly. He was still unable to look at her. "In more ways than you know."

It was nearly a minute before he was ready to continue. "I can only tell you that I thought I was doing the right thing. I thought I was putting the greater good ahead of myself. I had a knack for the kind of work I was doing. It came really easy to me, and I was good at it. It seemed right at the time, being a part of something bigger and more important than myself. No matter how much it hurt me personally, I believed I was doing the right thing."

It was Natasha's turn to look away. As much as she wanted to blame Cyrus for leaving, especially when she now realized that he could've come back, now she wasn't so sure. She knew what she wanted. She knew only of her pain and the toll his leaving had taken on her life. That it was equally hard for him had never really made it to the forefront of her mind.

"But a spy?" she asked finally. "*Really?*"

Looking at her, a sad smile finally touched the corners of Cyrus's mouth. "Did I mention that I was really good at it?"

She laughed. In spite of herself, Natasha laughed.

What was done was done; there was no changing it now. But it didn't stop her from wondering how things might be different if only he'd stayed with her at school. Then she would've stayed and the entirety of their lives would have played out differently as a result.

Natasha settled for asking, "Do you like your job?"

What seemed like a simple inquiry appeared to be anything but. It was a yes or no question, but one Cyrus wasn't quick to answer. Surprisingly, he was giving the matter a great deal of thought.

Finally he shrugged. "Not so long ago, I would've said yes. Now? I'm not sure," he offered. "Ask me again sometime."

The reply was unexpected, and Natasha found his indecision disconcerting. She'd always known him to be decisive and confident in his decisions. It was a hint that the matter was more complicated than he was letting on.

"Anyway," Cyrus said in an effort to bring the conversation back on track. "Lamplighter? It started out as an errant reference in a gist. It was only ever referenced once, and even that citation wasn't explained."

Natasha's nose scrunched at the odd statement. "A *gist?*"

Cyrus grinned. "Yeah, sorry. A gist is what we call a shorthand briefing. They tend to be thick on the primary facts while being thin on peripheral supporting evidence. The idea is to provide a high level view of a case without requiring everyone to become fluent in the minutiae. Most of our cases start out with a gist. If the case looks promising, my group takes it up and we dig deeper."

Nodding, Natasha could at least grasp the general concept. It was a summary report of sorts—detailed in some regards but lacking in many others.

"And one of your reports had a reference to Lamplighter?"

"Exactly," he said. But by the faraway look in his eyes, she could tell he was reviewing what he could recall of that particular report. It would be a long shot under normal circumstances, but she realized they had the advantage of the Cyrus's amazing memory.

"It's odd," Cyrus said finally. "There was only ever that one reference, and only a tangential mention was ever made. Looking back, it almost seems like the reference was there by mistake. Like a word being overlooked in a redacted file."

"But you know more about Lamplighter now," Natasha urged. "I can tell by the way you're talking about it."

"That's true," he admitted. She saw a darkness cloud his eyes. "But…maybe it would be better if you tell me what you know first."

Natasha instantly felt her temper surge. "*Really*? You're *really* going to play games with me on this? After everything that's happened!"

Waiving a placating hand of surrender, Cyrus slid himself across the top of the bed. He took her hand in his and looked into her eyes. His sincerity shown through even before he had a chance to speak.

"It's not that," he said quietly. "I'm asking you to trust me. Things have become complicated. But I'm only concerned with your best interests. I need you to believe me—you're the reason I'm here. You're my number one concern."

Taking a deep breath, Natasha choked down her personal reservations. In spite of herself, she believed him. She knew there was a reason he wasn't yet sharing. Though she didn't know why, she believed he would eventually reveal everything he knew, given enough time.

"Alight," she said finally. "I'm sorry." After taking a few moments to choose where to begin, she decided how to properly frame her story.

"After you left, I stuck it out…I stayed in school for a while," she explained. "But I just wasn't happy. It was the last thing I wanted to do, but I ended up coming back here. It turned out to be the best thing I could do for my family. My father was working around the clock on a new project, and Anna had just begun training for professional competition. Gretchen had just come on board as her coach and trainer, and I ended up being her training partner. That actually brought us closer than we'd been since we were children.

"Still, as much as being home felt good, Father was working far too much. I didn't get much of his time. All of mine was spent with Anna and Gretchen—which was great—but there was still something missing. And for the first time in years, I found myself thinking about my mother."

Natasha looked away, just before mentioning her mother. She was plagued by a myriad of complex emotions specific to that subject. They were emotions she had locked away throughout her teenage years. Now, fast-forwarding to adulthood when she was forming complicated and deeply personal relationships of her own, she felt there was unsettled business with a woman she knew surprising little about. Added to all of that, more than a little guilt due to her own inability to face her feelings for the first two decades of her life.

"Anna was born a year and a month after me," Natasha continued. "But my mother died only six months after Anna was born."

Wiping a tear from the corner of her eye, she met Cyrus's gaze once more. "I never *knew* my mother," she explained. "I have no memory of her. She was gone before I turned two-years-old."

Cyrus squeezed her hand. It was a small effort but she felt her heart beat stronger at his silent gesture of support.

"Anyway, with her on my mind and Father not terribly accessible, I set out to learn more about her the only way I could. We don't have any extended family on either of my parent's sides. Or, at least if we do, they've never been a part of our lives. So that wasn't going to help. But then I remembered seeing some old stuff in storage. I came across it when we were reorganizing the subbasement and getting ready for Anna's training regimen."

Natasha fell silent again, taking nearly two minutes to decide how to explain what came next. Her mind was awash with the countless documents and files she'd found in storage. She wanted to explain what she'd discovered, but to do that she needed to focus on only those facts she thought were relevant.

"When I was born, my mother and father worked together," Natasha explained. "Mother had an office at the company headquarters, but she traveled a great deal. As a matter of convenience, she also kept a small office at home. After she became pregnant with me, she began working from her home office more and more frequently. She continued the routine after my birth."

Seeing Cyrus's brow furrow, Natasha realized that part of her story wasn't making sense to him, and stopped.

"You seem to have all of this on good authority," Cyrus offered. "Were you able to contact a family friend for the information?"

Natasha offered a smile that was positively beaming. "No," she shook her head. "Even better. I found her journal. She'd been meticulously maintaining it for nearly twenty-five years!"

While she expected a shared sense of excitement from Cyrus, what she saw on his face was something that moved between relief and concern.

"Ok, out with it," she said flatly. "*What's wrong?*"

At first it looked like Cyrus was going to play dumb and pretend he didn't know what she was asking. But that idea quickly passed, evidently because his look changed entirely to one of concern.

"I think that's fantastic," Cyrus said. "A journal like that could offer rare insights into the mother you never had a chance to know. I can't think of anyone who wouldn't give their right arm for that kind of discovery."

Natasha waited for the proverbial, *but.* "But?" she finally asked. She could tell he was making great efforts to properly phrase his next words…she just didn't know why.

"While I'm sure the journal offers some powerful insight into the mother you never knew, I'm afraid there might be portions of it that you might find upsetting—even disappointing, on a personal level."

Natasha's eyes narrowed on Cyrus in an accusatory manner. Once more, she felt her blood pressure rise.

"I'm just saying," Cyrus said, raising a pacifying hand. "She was your mother, but she was also a woman. It's easy to forget that our parents are human. When reading something like that, it's important to realize that you'll be reading about her greatest triumphs as well as her most horrible mistakes."

Exasperated and out of breath with frustration, Natasha wasn't sure how to respond. On the surface, everything Cyrus said made a great deal of sense. It was the sort of advice she would expect from a world class shrink, actually. But he wasn't a shrink. If anything, it sounded more like he'd already read the journal. And after everything she'd just learned about him, she couldn't help suspecting that he had. She didn't know how, but it was the only explanation.

"You know!" she accused, her glare cutting into him. "But how?"

Leaning away from Natasha, Cyrus seemed genuinely concerned. "Know what? Please, take it easy."

"This isn't funny, Jonn— err, Cyrus. You promised to be straight with me. You know what she did, don't you? You know what she wrote? Have you read the book?"

"No," Cyrus said flatly. "This is the first I've heard about the journal. But it could answer some important questions, especially if it explains more about Lamplighter. But first, you've got to give me a hint. What is it you think I know?"

Natasha took a moment to assess his body language. She believed him. She knew she wasn't being entirely rational. Just the same, he did know things that he shouldn't, or couldn't. Why not this?

"Her affair," she said so quietly that it was almost a statement to herself.

After taking a long look at her, Cyrus only nodded.

"And me," she concluded. Her eyes rested in her own lap. This was the closest she'd ever come to discussing the subject with anyone.

Releasing an audible sigh, Cyrus quietly cleared his throat. "So you know that Dargo is your father?" he asked in a voice just a quiet as hers.

When Natasha's eyes found his, she felt her own brimming with tears. But even at that point, she wasn't sure why. She'd been aware of the fact for more than two years. Even she didn't know why she was getting this choked up over it now. Maybe it was admitting the facts out loud. Maybe it was admitting the facts to someone she cared about.

"If you haven't read the book, how did you know?" she asked.

Cyrus shrugged, reluctant to speak.

"Let me guess," she accused. "It's a spy thing?"

He grinned. "No. It's a genetics thing. Earlobes, specifically. Your mother, father, and sister all have attached earlobes. You don't. Yours are free, just like Dargo's."

Natasha felt breathless. She had earned a double major in school, chemistry and biology, but the simple truth had never occurred to her. She understood the dominant and recessive genetic traits that Cyrus was referring to. Attached earlobes were the type that swept down and attached the ear evenly to the corner of the jaw. Alternatively, so-called 'free' earlobes described those that had a tab of skin protruding from the lower slope of the ear, right before it joined with the side of the face. Free lobes were a dominant trait while attached lobes were recessive. It meant that if either parent had free lobes, the child would have free lobes as well. Since both Eleanor and Rutger Voss had the recessive attached lobes while Natasha had the free lobes, it meant that her father had to be a man who had the dominant free earlobes.

The logic had been staring her in the face for the whole of her life. Natasha bit down frustration at her own inability to see the obvious. "That genetic trait only tells you that my father was not my father," she said somewhat clumsily. "How did you know it was Dargo?"

"That was easy," Cyrus smiled. "I've seen the way he looks at you. A father's pride is hard to disguise. That, and once you're looking for it, there is a distinct resemblance around your nose and the set of your eyes. But to be fair, that part *could* just be a spy thing."

Natasha laughed, self-consciously hiding her smile behind an upraised hand. It was a subconscious gesture she was prone to making when she was nervous or emotional. But as her eyes threatened to overrun with tears, she couldn't help but feel a certain amount of comfort at the thought.

"Oh," she gasped, suddenly becoming deathly serious. "You have to promise me—you can never tell my father about this. Dargo is like a brother to him. I can't imagine how he would handle something like this."

With a grin and a shake of his head, Cyrus leaned back on his hands and took a long look at Natasha. "You're something else, you know that?" he marveled. "I'd expect someone in your position to be upset with the situation or worried about what her father will say to *her* when he learns of something like this. But you're worried about Dargo?"

Natasha responded by rolling her eyes. "I'm not worried about my relationship with my father—not at all. I just don't know how he would react to this news. Dargo works here, but in many ways he's family."

Her smile brightened, the literal sense of what she'd just said striking home.

"I'll tell you what," Cyrus offered. "I won't say a word about this. As we've already established, this is really none of my business anyway. But as an interested and committed third party, can I make a suggestion?"

When she didn't object, he continued, "Worry less about how your father will deal with this news. While you've only recently learned of it, the secret's been out there for twenty years. That's more than enough time for a sharp guy like your dad to work things out for himself. Consider giving him the benefit of the doubt. There's a real chance that while you're worried about talking to him, he's worried about talking with you."

Since Cyrus was never one to offer unsolicited personal advice, she couldn't help feeling suspicious at his suggestion. "Are you trying to tell me something?"

He shook his head. "Only that we sometimes get caught up in problems and only see them from our own perspective. When you look at the same issue from another person's point of view, things can change in unexpected ways. Sometimes it's enough to solve an issue entirely."

Thinking about it that way, Natasha had to agree that it made a great deal of sense. It wasn't the sort of advice she would've received from him three years earlier, and she realized for the first time that more than just time had passed. Clearly a lot had happened to him in that time. He'd grown in ways she had yet to fully explore. But with that realization came another. For the first time, without reservation, she knew that she wanted to know Cyrus Cooper as well, or even better, than she had known Jonny Webb.

"Alright," Cyrus said. "Back to Lamplighter. Tell me what you know."

He felt like he'd dodged a bullet with Natasha's questions about her mother's affair with Dargo. While he knew a lot more than he'd admitted, it wasn't his place to share it. Plus, if she'd found Eleanor Voss's journal, there was a good chance she knew more about the affair than any living person on the planet—including Dargo. It had been Cyrus's experience that people were willing to commit thoughts and feelings to paper in ways they wouldn't share with friends or family. The experience could be therapeutic, even cathartic. And depending on what Eleanor Voss had recorded in that journal, it could hold the key to resolving a mission that had become complicated and dangerous.

"My mother was a corporate attorney for a company called Onyx Gander. She handled all types of legal cases for them, all over the world," Natasha explained. "My father worked for Onyx, too, but in a very different capacity."

"Your father was heavy into the scientific end of the business as I understand it," Cyrus said.

"Absolutely. Father didn't go to board meetings or deal with shareholders. In fact, for years it was all Mother could do to get him home from the lab most nights. That's what was so unusual about Lamplighter."

"I don't understand," Cyrus admitted. "What does any of that have to do with Lamplighter?"

"It's like you said, my parents worked for the same company but in entirely different areas. They weren't likely to interact. Lamplighter was the only project that directly involved both of them at the same time."

251

Moments of silence stretched as Cyrus considered the implications. His first exposure to the project code came from the reports describing the operation to infiltrate Voss's stronghold. It wasn't until the previous day when he had once more gained access to the Coalition computer network that he'd been able to retrieve that file and load the supporting resources. To his surprise, the core of what they'd originally told him had since been altered. The seemingly ancillary inclusion of the word 'Lamplighter' had been removed. Had it not been for his confidence in his own total recall, he would never have known it had been there in the first place.

He went further and searched the Coalition database while logged in with the Red Queen's credentials, digging for additional mentions of Lamplighter. There were none.

This made Cyrus all the more curious, since he was absolutely certain the term had once been included in a document he'd held in his hands a while ago. For it not to appear in a server wide search meant that whoever had purged it from the original information had also done a thorough cleansing of the Coalition's most secure database.

Thanks in no small part to a fortuitous typographical error in a command prompt, Cyrus found a hidden directory located in the primary root of the server. The hidden directory contained a single file, a symlink that, once activated, dropped his terminal session into an entirely different portion of the network. Since the server root was only available to select company personnel and was highly restricted, Cyrus couldn't understand the need for the additional security—let alone an entirely hidden part of the fileserver. Something new caught his eye. Not only was the symlink hidden, it was only accessible from the Red Queen's user account.

He'd found a hidden server that was her private domain.

The first thing Cyrus did was search for the term 'Lamplighter'. Where the primary Coalition server had been a barren wasteland for that search term, the secret server returned thousands of documents. There was far too much information for Cyrus to digest in his limited time online. But prior to logging off, he managed to learn a few valuable details. First, whatever Lamplighter was, it was directly tied to Onyx Gander. Second, Lamplighter had been in operation for years. Some of the records he'd found were audio and video surveillance feeds dating back over two decades. Lastly, numerous executives and scientists working for Onyx Gander were subjects of surveillance. Rutger and Eleanor Voss ranked prevalently among those most closely observed.

While Cyrus had hoped that the Coalition database would prove the key to understanding what Lamplighter was, he'd been buried under a deluge of information instead. Unfortunately, the longer he remained connected to the remote network, the greater his chances of being detected. In the end, he'd been forced to download as much as possible before disconnecting.

His new hope was that the contents of Eleanor Voss's diary would help fill in many of the blanks that were left after accessing the Red Queen's secret files.

"Wait a minute," Cyrus said. "I know that Lamplighter was a project or an experiment of some kind. It was conducted at Onyx Gander. And I'm pretty sure that, whatever it was, it dates back at least twenty-five years. But you're saying that whatever the project was necessitated involvement from both the science and legal teams at the same time?"

Natasha took a moment to consider the statement. "I'm not certain of the timeframe, but yeah. They were both working on it. My mother was involved with the project shortly before she died. She was working from home a lot at that point, like I said before. I was a baby, and she'd just become pregnant with Anna, that's why I found it odd. Whatever the project was, I got the impression it was a big deal for the company. They were pretty upset that my father was spending more and more of his time at home. I think they were pressuring him and my mother to come back to work."

"Wait a second," Cyrus said. He stopped Natasha before she could continue. "Your mother said all of this in the journal? She actually described the company as *pressuring* them? Did she use that word?"

"More or less," she admitted. "I don't have perfect recall like you."

Natasha slid from the end of the bed and disappeared through the door to the walk-in closet. She was gone for nearly a minute. When she returned she held a thick, battered, worn leather-bound book that was tied shut with two lengths of cotton cord.

Releasing the knot holding the book closed, Natasha quickly leafed through the pages. She scanned them with practiced ease, clearly well-versed in their contents. Finding the correct passage, she handed the book to Cyrus.

Accepting the journal, Cyrus felt more than a little reluctant— like he was treading on the family's private space. It was an odd sense because he'd done much worse, many times in the course of his work, and had never once felt conflicted about it. "Are you sure you don't mind?"

Natasha shrugged. "You might be onto something. If showing you this helps us figure out who keeps coming after us, I'm all for it. Plus," she said with an edge to her voice. "I like to think I can count on your discretion."

Cyrus grinned. *If you only knew…*

Crawling across the massive king-size bed, Cyrus dropped onto his back and laid his head on one of several pillows that were stacked against the headboard. He raised the book into the light and was just starting to read when the bed jolted and Natasha landed beside him, lodging herself under his right arm. She slid close and rested her head on his shoulder. With a relieved smile, he wrapped his arm around her and set about reading the journal.

Chapter 26

Standing at the door to Voss's office, Cyrus waited to be allowed access. After reading Eleanor Voss's personal journal that morning, he'd spent hours researching public as well as private databases. The results had proven both illuminating and troubling. They also left him with no choice but to involve Voss directly.

The double doors parted with a hiss, and Cyrus stepped into the expansive office without a moment's hesitation. He failed to hide the hitch in his step when his eyes fell upon Dargo standing opposite Voss at the desk. When he'd requested the meeting, Cyrus intended for them to speak privately. Dargo's presence was unwelcome, and when he took into account the unusually deep scowl on the chief of security's normally serious face, it became clear that he wasn't the only one with something to share.

As he approached Voss's desk, Cyrus struggled to surmise what Voss might have to say that required Dargo's presence. Then again, it could just as easily be Dargo who had a matter to discuss. His disposition seemed even more sour than usual. Either way, Cyrus reasoned, he was about to find out. Besides, whatever the two had cooked up for him, it would certainly pale in comparison to what he'd found.

"I'm sorry for being so vague," Cyrus began as he reached the front of Voss's desk. He'd called Voss from Natasha's room only fifteen minutes earlier, explaining only that it was crucial for them to speak in private. "But this is a delicate matter—exceedingly sensitive."

Voss shook his head slowly and waved to one of the two empty chairs opposite his desk. He had a cordial, if slight, smile on his face, but Cyrus had come to know him well enough to recognize that something had him rattled. "No problem," Voss said. There was an awkward crack in his voice. "A set of lab results have just come back, and I wanted to speak with you about them, anyway."

While Cyrus didn't know what lab results Voss was referring to, he decided against inquiring. He needed to keep the discussion on topic and knew it was about to become an uphill battle. He lowered himself into the chair, taking care not to pull on his freshly redressed stitches. They ached from a thorough antiseptic cleaning, and he was feeling more pain than usual.

Voss returned to his seat behind the desk and looked across the near empty surface at Cyrus. Cyrus could tell Voss was looking for a place to begin, but that wouldn't do. Given the nature of what Cyrus had come to discuss, they needed to get rid of Dargo first.

When Voss opened his mouth to speak, Cyrus held up a cautioning hand. "If it's all the same with you, Doc, it would be best if we spoke in private."

Cyrus's eyes shifted to Dargo, less than ten feet to his right. Dargo stood station with his hands clasped in front of his belt buckle, his eyes intently focused on Cyrus. If he took offense at the statement, Cyrus couldn't tell. Dargo seemed to be in a perpetual state of unease—perhaps distrust—whenever Cyrus was in the room. While that level of vigilance was ideal in a bodyguard, it was also apparent that Dargo had the emotional range of a ham sandwich.

"It's alright." Voss offered a forced smile. "Dargo is fully aware of everything that is happening and all that has already happened. You may speak freely in front of him."

Cyrus realized Voss was referring to the matter of Natasha's paternity and Dargo's less than kosher relationship with Eleanor Voss twenty years earlier. Unfortunately, that had little to do with the matter at hand.

"Even in regard to Lamplighter?" Cyrus asked.

There was a momentary twitch of confusion that crossed Voss's eyes. Cyrus watched as the man's face paled before him. Voss said nothing; in fact, he made no movement for nearly thirty seconds. When he finally did, it was only to blink twice before leaning back in his chair with a queasy look on his face. Then a new silence began.

Dargo's gaze shifted between Cyrus and Voss several times in the resulting communication void. From his expression, it was clear that he, too, was confused by Cyrus's question. Cyrus watched Dargo. It was also clear that the chief of security didn't seem entirely surprised by his boss's response to the question. If anything, Dargo seemed puzzled that Cyrus was asking about Lamplighter.

After what seemed like an eternity, Voss broke from his trance. He closed his eyes and took a long, slow breath. When his eyes reopened, they fell immediately on Dargo. While Cyrus was certain that Voss was about to order Dargo from the room, he turned out to be wrong.

"You'd better have a seat," Voss said to Dargo.

Slowly, Dargo moved to the chair beside Cyrus. By the set of his jaw, it was more than apparent he was doing so reluctantly.

"It's curious that you should mention Lamplighter," Voss said to Cyrus. His voice was quiet and small as he forced himself into an area of discussion that he clearly found unpleasant. "It's actually—" Voss's concentration drifted as a new thought must've crossed his mind. "Why do you ask me about this? What do you know about Lamplighter?"

Cyrus didn't like the shift he'd just seen in Voss's eyes. The man's discomfort had suddenly been replaced by suspicion. And after all that had happened, Cyrus didn't appreciate the implication.

"I know it's the reason that your wife was murdered," Cyrus said flatly.

Voss looked as if he'd just been slapped across the face. But rather than anger in his eyes, Cyrus saw pain…and then, confusion.

After another deep breath, Voss cleared his throat. When he spoke, his voice was quiet once more. "I don't know where you've gotten your information, Cyrus, but you're wrong. Eleanor was killed in a car bombing. It had nothing to do with Project Lamplighter."

While Voss seemed confused, even lost in regard to Cyrus's statement, Dargo's guard had been raised. He sat at the edge of his seat, looking ready to spring with even the slightest provocation.

Time to shake the hornet's nest.

"Approximately twenty years ago," Cyrus began, "you were employed by Onyx Gander, a multinational pharmaceutical conglomerate—among other things. At that same time, your wife, Eleanor Margaret Schroeder Voss, was also employed by Onyx as their lead patent attorney. You were employed by the company for a little over eight years prior to your resignation. Eleanor worked for the company for just over six, right up until the time of her death."

Judging by the furrow of Voss's brow, he didn't understand the point Cyrus was building toward. Still, he made no effort to interrupt, clearly interested in what he had to say.

"After Eleanor's death, you resigned from Onyx Gander," Cyrus continued. "The last project you worked on was referred to as Lamplighter."

Voss responded with a slow nod. But judging by his questing stare, he didn't see how the events were related. "All true," Voss said simply. "But what happened to my wife had nothing to do with Lamplighter. It couldn't. She had no involvement in it. In fact, when I left the company, we were still in the very early stages of development. There was no substantive, tangible IP. At best, we were years away from having something we could patent." By IP, Voss was referring to 'intellectual property', the point where the scientists with whom Rutger Voss worked would then finally begin to interface with the patent lawyers, a team headed by Eleanor Voss.

Voss shot a questing look to Dargo before once more resting his concerned eyes on Cyrus. "Why do you think Eleanor's death was related to the Lamplighter project?"

Pulling himself from the chair, Cyrus turned and began slowly pacing the room. Suddenly he felt less inclined to make his case to the troubled older man. He was still every bit as confident in the facts and his own conclusions, but he was quickly becoming regretful for the pain he was about to bring the man. It was suddenly clear that Voss really didn't know his wife's death was connected to Onyx, or his own involvement in the company.

But in the end, he really didn't have a choice. Lives were at stake. The only difference being that, this time they knew their lives were in danger.

Cyrus stopped walking and looked back at Voss from about fifteen feet away. "You and Eleanor were having trouble," Cyrus explained. "Just as you had earlier in your marriage, you'd become overly engrossed in your work. She wanted you at home—needed you at home, really. Desperately enough that you talked about it repeatedly."

Watching carefully, Cyrus saw Voss's confused glare slip into a faraway stare. Voss was experiencing his own memories of the events recorded in Eleanor Voss's journal. Cyrus hated to send him down this particular memory lane, but there was no avoiding it.

"She was worried," Cyrus continued. "Worried that your relationship was falling apart. Worried that you were losing the connection that you'd once shared.

"Still, you had a job, and she knew how important it was to you. She tried to make due. She threw herself into her own work as a way to cope. She hoped it would be a way to gain some perspective. But what she found was Ian, a man who she respected, and a man who made her feel safe."

Cyrus's eyes fell on Dargo as he referred to him by his given name, a name he'd never heard used. Dargo's penetrating stare never shifted, never wavered.

While Cyrus didn't have a particular affection for the coldhearted head of security, he couldn't help seeing the man in a different light after reading Eleanor's description of her relationship with him.

"She became pregnant with Natasha," Cyrus continued. "It was an experience that nearly crushed her," he said more quietly. Adding more of the woman's personal thoughts at this juncture only seemed appropriate given the two men he was speaking to.

"On one hand, Dargo had shown her sensitivity and caring, at a time when she was in desperate need of both. On the other, she held the deep conviction that she'd betrayed her husband in the most unforgivable way. And though she feared for the sanctity of her marriage before all of that, she suddenly found herself in a position of inescapable personal chaos.

"She realized she was sinking to a personal low, one from which she couldn't return. It made her decide on a course of action. Despite her own better judgment, she went to you," he said to Voss, "and told you she was pregnant with your baby. It was a lie she believed would cost her soul."

Standing still, Cyrus realized for the first time that both Voss and Dargo watched him with unparalleled focus. But neither had the countenance he'd expected. He had anticipated anger from Dargo and discomfort from Voss. Neither showed any sign of those reactions. Both sets of eyes followed him, intent on the tale he was telling, seeming engaged by the rare, if painful insight into a woman they'd both cared for.

"I'm sorry to be indelicate," Cyrus said softly. "And to open old wounds. *But this is important.* You'll see why soon."

Voss's sad eyes didn't even blink. He just offered the slightest bob of his head, a silent bid for him to continue.

"She knew she was doing something unforgivable," Cyrus went on. "Even though Dargo had given her his blessing on the matter, she still knew she'd broken his heart. At the same time, she was betraying her husband in a way that put even her affair to shame."

Cyrus recognized the negative connotations of his last statement. He quickly looked to Dargo and cringed inwardly. For his part, Dargo's expression hadn't changed in the least.

"Ah, anyway," Cyrus struggled to regain his train of thought. "For all her personal torment, Eleanor never expected what happened next."

Cyrus began pacing once more as he continued to speak. "To her relief, you were elated at the prospect of a child," he said to Voss. "She suddenly experienced a side of you that she didn't dream possible. You were happy and attentive, and best of all, as far as she was concerned, you were home every night.

"No matter how things had started, Eleanor realized that her marriage had been given a fresh start. And once Natasha was born, she was beside herself to find you were every bit the loving and nurturing father that she knew you could be.

"Not long after, she became pregnant with little Anna and everything she'd been unhappy about was gratefully a thing of the past. You were off to work in the morning and home every night like clockwork.

"When she became pregnant with Natasha, Eleanor scaled back her duties at the office, frequently working from home. But once Natasha was born, it was obvious that it was no longer an option. She found herself excited to be something she'd never expected—a stay-at-home mom."

Cyrus stopped mid-stride with his back to Voss and Dargo. He took a deep breath and steeled himself for the point of the entire story. Pausing a moment longer to gather one more calming breath, he turned.

"Your sudden shift in priorities left Onyx Gander with a major problem." Cyrus met Voss's gaze. "Principals of the company had made commitments in regard to a high priority project that had recently been given the green light: Project Lamplighter."

Cyrus knew that at least a portion of the implications were made clear with the last statement. Voss pushed his chair back from the desk and lowered his eyes to his lap. He seemed to whither physically at the revelation.

For his part, Dargo's stoic exterior seemed to crack for the first time. He was confused.

"They pressured you," Cyrus said. "Didn't they? Pressured you to come back to work, maybe even wanted you to step up progress? They didn't like it when you shifted your priorities to home."

Voss didn't say a word. But when he raised his head to look Cyrus in the eye, it was all the confirmation that was necessary in regards to the truth.

"Did they threaten you?" Cyrus asked.

Voss shook his head slowly. "Not overtly," he said. "But there was no subtlety when it came to applying pressure. When I cut back my hours, some of the board members became very upset."

"What happened?"

"They wouldn't let up," he shrugged. "After Anna was born, I realized it just wasn't worth it. I knew what was important. The company certainly wasn't what mattered to me. About a month after Anna was born, I tendered my resignation."

Voss sat there, staring into the distance for some time. Cyrus wasn't willing to break the silence. And since Dargo almost never spoke, there was little danger of him doing so.

"I don't understand," Voss said suddenly. His voice was more firm and full of conviction than it had ever been. The cast of his eyes made it clear that his focus had fully returned to the conversation. "State your feelings, Cyrus. How is this relevant to Eleanor's death?"

Cyrus sighed, knowing that Voss was not about to admit the facts. Either he wouldn't, or he just couldn't bring himself to do the math. "You know why, Doc. They killed Eleanor to motivate you to go back to work," Cyrus spoke, forgoing any effort to soften the blow.

The sheer absurdity of the logic left Voss's face contorted. Cyrus allowed him a few moments to find sense in the statement, but he could see by the twist of his face and the pinch of his eyes that there was none to be had. Deep down, Voss knew. It was as if he simply wanted someone to offer up a detailed explanation; an explanation for the nightmares and the guilt he constantly suffered wishing his wife was back by his side.

"The principals of Onyx Gander—" Cyrus laid out what he knew, "several members of the board of directors—had taken on funding from an outside entity. They'd made promises—big commitments to the project. When you shifted your focus to your personal life, a complete one-eighty from your normal routine, the board knew the company couldn't meet the goals set by their investor. They got nervous.

"When you resigned from the company, it meant that their problem was taken to an entirely new level. You were the project lead—the brains behind all of the work. Without you, not only could they not meet their deadlines, they were entirely unable to manage their commitment. Forget the deadline—the project was toast."

Shaking his head slowly, it was clear that Voss still wasn't convinced.

"The people behind the funding for Project Lamplighter were a very serious group who believed you could be manipulated into returning to work. Since your wife and children had swayed you from your work, it was believed that the death of your wife would shake you to the core. They calculated a ninety-six percent probability that, following the death of your wife, you would recede into the safety of your previously preferred world following a manageable period of mourning and subsequent depression. They believed that the death of Eleanor would lead you back to Lamplighter."

Sitting back in his chair, Voss suddenly looked a great deal older than he was. Dark bags had suddenly formed under his eyes, and his skin had taken on a pale, ash-like appearance.

"It's not possible," Voss muttered, his voice a hoarse whisper. "It can't be… How could…?"

He stammered, mostly to himself, as he processed the horrific revelation, and felt the weight of guilt descend.

Cyrus felt for him. He couldn't imagine the pain Voss had endured with the loss of his wife. Having just experienced the very best days of his life, only to have them shattered by tragedy. Voss was a brilliant man; on some level, he must have connected the dots on his own, Cyrus was sure of it. But being unable to admit it to himself or move on had resulted in a self-imposed exile on this island. Voss had taken extreme measures to protect his family, but he was now being forced to confront the facts.

The one thing that had always been an out, one question that had kept Voss from becoming mired in the possibility of his own work causing his wife's demise, was the fact that he'd never been certain whether the bomb had been intended for him or Eleanor. At the time of the bombing, Voss's car had been in the shop for over a week. He and Eleanor had been forced to share her car—him for work and her to run routine errands while at home with the children. With only one car between them, it meant that the bomb could've been intended for either Rutger or Eleanor.

Recalling Dargo's presence, Cyrus turned to the large Russian. He was staring at him so intently that Cyrus felt as if the man were trying to see inside of him.

"To know these things…" Dargo said in his halting, broken Russian accent. "You have found Eleanor's missing journal?"

Cyrus was surprised Dargo was aware of the journal, and cognizant enough to refer to it as missing. It implied he'd searched for it at some point.

"Yes."

The man scowled. "And you believe it is your business to read such a thing?"

Under normal circumstances, Cyrus would've responded smartly to such a loaded question. But given the subject matter and those involved, he thought better of it. He decided that this was one of the rare cases where complete honesty was the best recourse.

"I didn't make the decision," Cyrus said. "Natasha gave me the book because she thought it would help sort out what was really going on here. She believes it's worth considering that the recent attacks are related to what happened to her mother twenty years ago."

It was a rare opportunity for Cyrus to see shock on Dargo's normally granite-like face. The man sat stunned for a moment, then his lips moved silently, mouthing some sort of Russian phrase that Cyrus couldn't make out.

"My God," Dargo said at last. "Then Natasha knows?"

"That you're her biological father? Yes. She's read the book many times. She's been aware for some time."

Chapter 27

His elbows resting on the desk, Voss sat with his head cradled in upraised hands. With his pulse hammering in his ears, the room continued to spin. He felt faint, and a migraine—the likes of which he'd never experienced—had enveloped him. His mind swam as he struggled to rationalize the crazy things Cyrus had just told him. But while his logical mind rejected the statements as outlandish accusations, in his gut he recognized the truth.

"Onyx," Voss said. His voice was low and scratchy and cracked before he offered more than a few words. "Those people were my friends—my business partners. Tell me…how?"

"It's been twenty years," Cyrus asserted. "It's hard to say. But there's talk of an outside investor who put up money, then pressured the board of directors. Word is, it was someone who knew how to get things done. And they're willing to play dirty in order to get what they want."

"Who?" Dargo demanded. "Who has done this? Who is behind it?"

Dargo looked ready to fly from his seat, and Voss suspected he would. At the same time, Cyrus seemed equally indignant in regard to all that had happened. Still, Cyrus was doing a remarkable job of maintaining his calm.

Voss wondered how the boy's calm attitude would handle the latest test results. His eyes fell momentarily on the thin file folder sitting on his desk beside his open laptop. Cyrus had closer ties to Lamplighter than he knew.

Reaching down to the bag on the floor beside his chair, Cyrus pulled out a folder of his own. He handed it to Voss who quickly turned it around and flipped open the cover. Inside was an 8x10 color photo of man, perhaps in his mid-seventies. His face was thin and unnaturally tan. Still, the hue of his skin did little to hide the liver spots that freckled his complexion. Voss recognized him immediately. He'd aged dramatically since they'd last spoken, but two decades would do that to a person.

"Gerard Combs," Voss said without hesitation. "He's the President and CEO of Onyx Gander."

"He *was* the President and CEO," Cyrus corrected. "He retired less than a year after you collected your severance package and allowed Onyx to buy out every joint patent you held with them. After his retirement, he was replaced by Philip Traue."

"That can't be right," Voss interjected. "Traue was only a junior member of the board when I left. How could he, of all people, replace Combs so quickly?"

"I think you're asking the right question," Cyrus said flatly. "It doesn't add up. But when I looked at the financial histories of both men, certain irregularities made it fairly obvious that they were the ones working directly with the outside influence responsible for putting pressure on your project."

"What sort of irregularities?" Voss realized that his dizziness had passed; it had been replaced by pure outrage. Still, the analytical portion of his mind required substantiating facts.

"I'll provide you all of the documentation you require," Cyrus confirmed.

Voss shot a quick glance at Dargo. For the first time, he saw a look of respect directed at Cyrus. Apparently the young man's investigative prowess had earned him points.

"From there, you can deal with Onyx Gander any way you see fit," Cyrus continued. "I only ask that you let me settle things with their outside investor."

Voss felt an acidic burn in the pit of his stomach. He knew what they were really discussing, and wanted no part of it. Even after all that had happened, he couldn't bear to be involved in such matters. It went against everything he believed in. One look at Dargo and he knew that the matter was settled. His head of security had his own views—ones that wouldn't be swayed by his objections.

Resigning himself to confirming Cyrus's information before action was taken, Voss decided to let the matter drop. He would never talk Dargo out of looking into Onyx Gander. Not after this. And truthfully, nor did he want to. It was bloodshed he detested. There had already been far too much of that. But they had passed the tipping point; he knew such things were now well beyond his control.

"No," Dargo grunted and glared at Cyrus. "I require the name of this investor as well. If he is responsible, as you say, then it is my *responsibility*."

Voss wanted to object. He didn't want Dargo extending the scope of his vendetta. There'd been enough loss of life already. Nevertheless, he reasoned, there was still a threat to his family.

"This all relates to the attacks on my family and my home? All of this is about Lamplighter?" Voss asked. He was attempting to put the discussion back on track. He suspected he understood how the facts of the past were related to the present, but such things had yet to be discussed.

Cyrus shook his head. "No," he said simply. "This is about Shadowlight, your memory recording device. Someone is after it. They think that by taking either of your children they can motivate you to finish developing the technology for them, using your family as pawns. I'm sure you can see how it could be manipulated."

"*Perverted, you mean,*" Voss virtually growled.

"I thought the gunmen at *The Cuban* were part of an assassination team. Now I'm pretty sure I was only half right. I think they meant to kill me, but they had another objective. They also intended to capture Natasha and use her as leverage against you."

Leaning back in his chair, Voss took a long look at Cyrus. His mind ran through a battery of scenarios while calculating their odds. It just didn't seem possible to him. As a scientist, he had witnessed profound luck and coincidence that could not be explained, he couldn't see Cyrus's presence in his home as such an example.

"Are you sure that's all they want?" Voss asked. He had many questions, but they all boiled down to just that one.

"I had no idea Project Lamplighter continued after I left Onyx Gander," he continued. "At the time, I was given the impression that the effort would be scrapped without my participation. There would've been a time when that motivated me to stay onboard to see it through. But after losing Eleanor, I had two beautiful baby girls at home. They needed my full attention. And that's what they got.

"As you said, I cashed out. I sold my Onyx stock options, cashed in my 401K, I even allowed the company to buy out our jointly held patents. But I never knew Lamplighter continued after that. I hope you believe me."

The curious slant of Cyrus's eyes suddenly caused Voss to reevaluate everything he knew. "Lamplighter," Voss said quietly. "Isn't that why *you're* really here?"

Cyrus shook his head. His gaze shifted slowly from Voss to Dargo, before once more settling on Voss. "I'm here for Natasha. The people who sent me are interested in your technology, yes. But I took the assignment because I care about Natasha. This was my opportunity to make up for the mistakes of my past. That's all. I had no idea that these attempts to kidnap or kill her were on the way. If I'd known, I would've approached this entire situation very differently."

Voss pinched the base of his nose between two fingers, trying to control his throbbing headache. He searched for a delicate approach for his question, but there was none to be found.

"Are you saying that you really don't know who, or what you are?" Voss finally asked bluntly.

Leaning forward in his chair, Cyrus glared at Voss. For that matter, Voss had managed to fully capture Dargo's normally stoic gaze.

"Lamplighter," Voss said. He flipped open his file folder and pushed it across the desk to Cyrus. "The genetic signature is unmistakable," he explained. "While I can't explain how it came to be incorporated in your genome, the markers are conclusive evidence."

The nearly blank look on Cyrus's face convinced Voss that the young man really didn't understand. He took a moment to consider the project and all that he knew of it while he searched for a place to start.

Voss began, "As I have stated, Lamplighter was in preliminary stages when I left the company. I was told it was going to be mothballed if I left. Apparently that never happened because, at some point, the project was taken so far as to include human experimentation."

Voss rubbed the side of his head, still struggling to placate his migraine. "And you...you were obviously a test subject."

Shaking his head, Cyrus rose from his chair and began to pace the room. He was clearly agitated. "I don't know what you're talking about, Doc. No one's ever experimented on me. Well, not until you slipped me that mickey along with the antibiotic when I got *here*."

That confused Voss. "You're sure? You were never part of a drug trial of any kind? Were you ever grievously sick at a young age?"

Voss knew he'd hit a nerve when Cyrus stopped mid step. He looked at Voss, his normal affable demeanor fractured and replaced by genuine concern. "How young?" was all he asked.

The best answer Voss could offer was a shrug. "I have no way of knowing. I would've been off the project while you were still in diapers. But someone clearly continued my work. Why? What do you know? What happened?"

Cyrus continued to pace for a few minutes more. Voss knew he was considering the question. When Cyrus finally returned to his chair, his walk seemed almost zombie like. His motor skills were functional at only a basic, muscle memory level. He watched Cyrus drop into the chair and feared the young man had checked out all together.

"What is it?" Voss coaxed. "What do you know?"

In a snap, Cyrus returned to the present. Life flashed into his eyes once more and he stared at Voss. Shaking his head, he still seemed unsettled. "It's what I don't know that bothers me. I have no memories at all prior to my tenth birthday."

Even Dargo looked confused, possibly even concerned. "How is that possible?" he asked.

Cyrus shrugged. "I don't know," he admitted. "I guess I don't really know that I was ten years old. I had to be something, though; ten was their best guess. They didn't even know my name, so they made that up, too."

Cyrus went on to explain how he'd been found in the wreckage of a train derailment a little over twelve years earlier. It was later deduced that he was traveling alone because no parent or guardian was found among the casualties. He was discovered in the wreckage, and no one ever came forward to claim him. He'd landed in the American foster-care system, where he'd remained until he was able to legally emancipate himself at the age of sixteen. After that, he took a job and finished putting himself through school. Along the way, he earned a scholarship to Brown University, where he majored in literature. There, he met Natasha. It was also there that he became involved in journalism, and the investigative report that had spiraled out of control and eventually landed him in trouble with authorities.

Dargo glared at Cyrus. "That does not make sense. You are saying you have no memory of your youth prior to that train crash? How? How do you not remember? How, with a eidetic memory?"

While Dargo didn't believe Cyrus's tale, as far as Voss was concerned it made a lot of sense, at least when he factored in the telltale markers in his genome. But even those were different from what he might have expected. The project signature was missing. A specific RNA tag was part of every alteration Onyx Gander implemented, and that tag was missing from Cyrus's genetic profile.

He didn't know what to make of the discrepancy.

"How about dreams," Voss asked. "Any flashes of your life preceding the train crash? Perhaps in dreams or following periods of extreme exhaustion?"

Cyrus just shook his head. This was clearly a sensitive subject for the boy. And the fact that Voss hadn't experienced any memories of the time following the train wreck among those he had gained from the young man, meant he had either done a thorough job of compartmentalizing them, or that there were no memories to be experienced at all.

Voss directed Cyrus's attention to the page inside the open folder he had pushed to the edge of the desk. He realized that, to those not familiar with a genome map, it just looked like a series of narrow, splotchy colored bar graphs that lacked a background grid. But he wanted him to see one sequence in particular.

"I can't be certain what sort of modification was made to your genetic model," he explained. "But this sequence here," he pointed, "was something I worked on at the very start of the project. It isn't naturally occurring. It is part of a base modification we indented to implement on every test subject."

Cyrus glared at Voss. "Base modification?" he asked in a cold, impatient voice. "What the hell was—*is* Lamplighter?"

Voss contemplated the question. "It was an attempt to augment genetic traits," he explained. "We looked at a lot of things, early on. At the most basic level, we thought we could alter a left-handed or right-handed person and make them naturally ambidextrous. Or take someone with a keen sense of hearing or smell and augment that ability, perhaps even learn how to trigger that trait in others.

"Some people are born with an innate sense of balance or coordination, for example. What if we could locate the genes responsible for those attributes and turn them on in others? Sort of like flipping the switch on latent talents, only at a genetic level."

"Oh!" Voss felt his stomach drop with the sudden realization. "That must be what they did to you," he muttered, almost to himself. "It would explain so much…"

"Doc?"

Voss looked up to see Cyrus seated at the edge of his chair, leaning toward the desk.

"What was that?" Cyrus asked again.

His mind racing as things suddenly made sense, Voss quickly organized his thoughts. "Your memory dump," he explained. "In all my testing, I've never experienced anything like it. You really knocked me on my butt—the procedure gave me migraines! I've never had a response that came anywhere near what happened during your download.

"At first I thought it was due to the duration of the memory log. You were here for over a week and we—I—kept renewing your tag on a daily basis. It was the single largest transfer conducted to date. I assumed that was the cause of the discomfort, but something about that hasn't felt right to me.

"It was the quality of your memories that seemed off. But I disregarded the observation, attributing it to the fact your experiences involved Natasha and therefore amounted to a very awkward and unsettling experience for me. But even that never seemed like an adequate explanation," Voss concluded.

"I'm not following," Cyrus admitted.

Voss could tell by Dargo's countenance that he was equally lost in regard to the explanation.

"Your eidetic memory, Cyrus," Voss explained. "That's what was altered. I'm certain of it!"

Cyrus looked unconvinced.

"By the time we left, all we had accomplished was theoretical and involved only rudimentary computer models," Voss explained. The technology of the day was so primitive when compared to—." He realized he was starting to ramble.

"Ah, we really hadn't gotten past square one," Voss went on. "But the theory was sound and there was marvelous potential. Ultimately, several stages down the road, we did have a plan in place for human trials. The goal was to take a subject's already prominent trait and attempt to augment it via genetic manipulation. To supercharge the ability, if you will. Several stages further down the line, if all went well, we would attempt to replicate a dormant trait in another subject. So, in your case, example one would be to bolster your already impressive memory skills. Then, example two, would involve using you as a template to impart that same amplified memory trait into a host with normal cognitive abilities."

Voss marveled at his own realization. Not only had his work been developed beyond theory, he was now confident that a living example of his theory's success sat directly in front of him.

"So, which one am I," Cyrus asked, pulling Voss from his revelry.

Not understanding the question, Voss thought he must've missed something while distracted. "I'm sorry?"

"You're assuming I'm part of example number one," Cyrus explained. "What if I'm part of example two?"

And with that, Voss was seized by the reality that truly was sitting before him. The thrill of seeing his work brought to life was suddenly smothered by the realization that someone had done this to Cyrus, and not taken steps to guide him afterward. Cyrus's loss of childhood memory was most certainly the result of the procedure. It made perfect sense…it made it a part of the later phase of testing. But assuming Cyrus had volunteered for the experiment, someone should've been there to guide him, even study him, following the procedure. By all accounts, Cyrus's life had been derailed every bit as much as the train that had wrecked and forever destroyed his youth.

The more he considered it, the more confident Voss felt that Cyrus had lost his childhood memories as the result of the work he'd begun back at Onyx Gander. Perhaps even more troubling, someone had been actively using Lamplighter out in the real world.

The thought sickened him.

"Lamplighter," Voss said. The anger and indignation that had sparked in his voice surprised even himself. "Someone has hijacked my work. I need to know who. If they did it to you," he said to Cyrus, "Then it's been done to others. I must know who is responsible. They must be stopped. This is an experiment that was never intended to leave the lab!"

"I don't think you're the first person to think that," Cyrus said coldly. He reached into the bag at his side and removed another folder. He handed it to Voss without opening it.

Voss flipped the folder open to find a computer printout of an online story about a gas explosion that destroyed a large portion of a palatial mansion just outside of Munich, Germany.

"That happened last night," Cyrus explained. "They haven't announced the owner of the property yet, but I looked into it. The estate is owned by Philip Traue."

Voss felt himself deflate.

Dargo stood and retrieved the printout from the desk. He shook his head. "Tying up loose ends," he said simply.

For his part, Voss didn't even know where to go from here. He was painfully out of his element. It was a good thing Cyrus was not.

"There's more going on than I originally thought," Cyrus admitted. "But Onyx Gander seems to be the common thread. Someone just offed their CEO. I'd be willing to bet that their retired CEO is next on the hit list. He would've been in the thick of it, back when you left the company, so he would need to be eliminated. If there are answers, Gerard Combs is our chance to find them."

"I will collect Mister Combs and bring him back here," Dargo said with cold determination. "If he is going to suffer an accident, it should happen at my hands."

Cyrus smiled. "Good. I'm going after the mysterious outside investor who was putting pressure on Onyx Gander. I suspect that Onyx and our mysterious third party have maintained a working relationship all these years. I just need to visit an old friend and see if he can get me the information I need."

Voss didn't fully understand what he was seeing, but for the first time Dargo and Cyrus seemed to be working together—and to Dargo's satisfaction.

"Do you need anything from me?" Dargo asked, further impressing the new found détente on Voss.

"Actually," Cyrus grinned. "There might be one thing…"

Chapter 28

The armored Chevy Suburban pulled up to the curb outside *The Cuban* and the engine idled. The parking lot was less than half full. From the dim light spilling from the bar's open entrance, Cyrus could tell it was a slow night. That was just as well. While he needed a public place for his meeting, it would've been difficult to talk if the place was too rowdy.

This was the first time Cyrus had visited the bar when people were not congregating around the entrance, smoking and socializing. There were still nearly a dozen motorcycles parked at the curb nearest the entrance, and he could hear the dull murmur of muted music and voices emanating from inside.

"Everything alright, sir?" the driver of the SUV asked.

Sitting beside the driver, Cyrus nodded silently in response. He was surprised just how apprehensive he was about this meeting. Boone held the key to understanding what was happening, and why. And while he was reasonably certain he had things figured out, Cyrus needed to be absolutely certain before responding to the threat and eliminating it. Cyrus was certain that his friend would confirm his fears.

Cyrus took a long look at the man beside him. He was one of the few survivors on Dargo's security team. It occurred to him that he didn't even know the driver's name. But for the first time, he had confidence in Dargo's people. He should. The disloyal members of the team had been whittled away in a bloody purge. While Dargo had started out with an impressive array of highly qualified men, he'd lost many along the way. Then suffering betrayal from a subset of his squad, Dargo had taken a much closer look at those who remained. While Cyrus wasn't sure what sort of additional vetting process Dargo had used on the remainder of the staff, he had no doubt that it was both thorough and invasive—perhaps even painful. Although he didn't know the driver personally, or Dargo for that matter, Cyrus had renewed confidence in them both. Unusual, given the situation he was about to walk into. Even more unusual with what he knew—and what he suspected—walking into the meeting.

"Thanks for the ride," Cyrus said at last. He swung open the passenger side door. "I won't be long."

He wasted no time crossing the short stretch of pavement before passing through the open door to the bar.

Chapter 29

Standing in the shadows, far from the nearest streetlight, Dargo hadn't moved much in the last twenty minutes. The single exception to his motionless state had been to pull the collar of his dark, insulated coat up around his neck.

In the time he'd been standing there, he had seen a total of half-a-dozen men enter the bar, plus three women. Only one couple had left the bar while he watched. Traffic on the surrounding streets was virtually nonexistent. The few vehicles which passed by did so with clear intention and offered nothing to draw his attention.

At last he saw the armored four-wheel drive round the corner at the far end of the street. His eyes followed it as it rolled smoothly down the lane and cornered into the parking lot. It stopped before the curb, not far from the entrance to the bar.

It was good, Dargo reasoned. At least this much was going according to plan. His eyes wandered the parking area surrounding the SUV as he searched for anything out of place.

Finding nothing, his gaze followed an ever-advancing search pattern that started at the SUV. From there, it widened, spreading out to eventually encompass the entire surrounding parking area and then the surrounding streets as well. While he didn't know exactly what he was looking for, he was certain that he would know it when he found it.

Chapter 30

Cyrus sat at the bar watching the area around him in the massive mirror hanging behind the counter. In fact, he was sitting in the same seat he'd occupied during his last meeting with Boone. He sipped his beer sparingly. He had no real interest in the drink, it was enough to have it in his hands. His guard was fully raised, and he was more than a little on edge. The heightened sense of awareness was only natural, given what he'd done to Boone at their last encounter. He had no idea how the man would respond to the cocktail he'd slipped into his drink near the end of the night.

He was about to find out.

Following his shocking sit-down discussion with Voss and Dargo, Cyrus had left to clear his head. He'd walked into Voss's office with a straightforward idea of where things were going and a solid plan for the discussion that would take place there. True, he hadn't expected Dargo's presence, but he'd quickly realized it

286

would be useful to have Dargo on hand so he could gauge his reactions to what he had to say.

As he had suspected, neither man had been fully aware of the real motivation behind Eleanor Voss's murder. But once provided with supporting evidence, both had been willing to accept the reality. Readily accepting of the situation, actually. It was obvious that his information resolved many unanswered questions.

Cyrus had been struck by just how difficult the last two decades had been for both men, neither knowing, or wanting to address who had killed Eleanor, or why. Cyrus had a new found respect for Voss's xenophobic desire to hole up in a castle of concrete and glass, blocking out the outside world while protecting his family. Voss had no idea who was truly out to get them, or why.

For as well as the meeting had gone, it had been Voss who dropped a proverbial bomb on Cyrus at the end of their discussion. Cyrus didn't take Voss's explanation of the so-called "genetic markers" at face value, but he had been blindsided by the discovery. Cyrus was certain that he hadn't thought of his childhood since arriving on the island. Natasha was the only link between his current life and his past. She was also the only one who knew of his sketchy personal history or his displaced upbringing. All of which, she'd sworn she hadn't shared with anyone. And he believed her.

So at least for the time being, Cyrus didn't know what to make of the story Voss had told. If Voss's explanation of the genetic markers was true, maybe there was something more to his missing past than he'd ever suspected. He'd been found amidst the wreckage of a derailed train before he was even a teenager. He had no memory of the train, the accident, or even his life prior to waking up in the hospital following the accident. Doctors believed the physical and emotional trauma caused by the accident had resulted in his memory loss. And while the explanation had never fully satisfied Cyrus, lacking any other, he'd been forced to accept it.

But now? He wasn't willing to jump onboard with Voss's explanation, but he would look into it. Cyrus realized his suspicion for people's motives came too him naturally, but as he caught Boone's reflection in the mirror, he remembered he had more than enough reason to question everyone and everything around him.

Sliding onto the stool beside Cyrus, Boone didn't turn to look at him. He kept his gaze fixed directly ahead, evidently choosing to study him in the mirror's reflection first. Cyrus recognized the glaring, unblinking set of his eyes and knew Boone already had his ire up. Between that and the unnatural pallor of his skin, Cyrus was now certain the cocktail he'd slipped him at their last meeting had done the trick.

Boone was uncharacteristically quiet for a long time. Even when Lucy, the bartender, deposited a bottle of beer in front of him, he didn't offer a single word. Cyrus did see Boone's eyes fall on the beer bottle. He studied the bottle cap, still in place atop the bottle. Cyrus knew he would take it for what it was, a sign that the drink had not been tampered with. Cyrus made the request of Lucy when he first arrived, asking that the drinks she brought be delivered with their caps still in place. It was customary for the bartender to remove the cap for the customer so it went against her custom. Still, she'd willingly complied.

Cyrus knew that the gesture would first irritate Boone. But hopefully, given a little time, it might help put him at ease. It was a small gesture on Cyrus's part—one that he had mixed feelings about, but it was also one that he thought might eventually help move things along.

After leaving his sit-down with Voss and Dargo, Cyrus had walked outside for some fresh air. As soon as he stepped from the building's front door, the phone in his pocket had chimed with a text message from Boone. The message didn't say much, only that they needed to meet. By the timestamp, Cyrus saw that it was sent hours earlier. He'd only received it once he passed beyond the exterior wall of the building and reacquired a cell signal.

Still, Cyrus had been reluctant to respond to Boone too quickly. He knew well what his training officer wanted. In light of his conversation with Voss, Cyrus hadn't been in a hurry to speak with Boone. The new information was tough to assimilate. To that end, he opted not to respond to the text message.

Later that afternoon, Cyrus was with Natasha when one of the security guards delivered a written message. The guard explained that someone had called the main switchboard and asked simply that the message be delivered to Cyrus. The message, of course, was from Boone. He would've understood there was a chance that Cyrus wouldn't get his text message while inside the building, so he'd resorted to plan B. The message passed to him was even more succinct. It was just a phone number. Cyrus realized that Boone had foregone any pretenses of Cyrus's cover by sending the message. Had he still been operating inside the facility undercover, this would've been a major problem since he wasn't supposed to know anyone on the island, and no one was supposed to know he had taken refuge at the facility.

It was obvious to both of them that the rules of the game were quickly shifting.

Sitting at the bar with Boone, Cyrus was reluctant to be the first to speak. It had been nearly five minutes since Boone arrived. So far he hadn't spoken a word, and he had yet to look at him without use of the mirror.

"How are you feeling, Boone? You don't look so good." Cyrus turned on his stool and had a great view of his friend in profile. He could see the muscles under his jaw cording as he ground his teeth, likely chewing on a retort.

While he knew this would be one of the most serious conversations of his entire life, Cyrus couldn't help but needle the man. Part of him was rebelling against the gravity of his circumstance, daring to treat the issue with reckless abandon.

"I think you'd better tell me what you've done," Boone offered through clenched teeth, his eyes finally meeting with Cyrus's directly for the first time.

Cyrus's eyebrows rose in response as he feigned indignation. "What I did? Why don't we rewind about two decades? Then you can tell me *what you did*," Cyrus accused.

A rapid series of emotions fluttered across Boone's eyes. So quickly, in fact, that Cyrus couldn't effectively discern one from the next. But he looked like he was going to boil over as a result of whatever was on his mind. And then, all at once, the flutter passed and Boone's eyes went cold. He took a deep breath. When he exhaled, he seemed to deflate physically. After the rapid onset of whatever had flooded his mind, in the end, he only shook his head in sad resignation.

"Don't give me that," Boone said in a surprisingly quiet voice. "You know how this works. You've been there yourself. You've just gotten yourself involved in something that goes back to when you were in diapers."

"I've been there," Cyrus conceded. "But I still know the difference between right and wrong. This goes back twenty years. Jesus, Boone, when did you lose your moral compass? There are shades of gray, but killing an innocent woman just to motivate her husband? You thought that would get him back to work? There's no *shade* for that!"

Boone shook his head. Glancing at his beer, he finally popped the top and took a long pull from the bottle. "It's more black and white than you make it seem, Cyrus."

"Are you kidding me?" Cyrus sputtered. His indignation was threatening to get the best of him. "*You blew the woman up!* A mother of two—she had two babies at home, you sonofabitch! Hell, you didn't just kill her, you made a spectacle of it. That wasn't just some run of the mill IED, either; that was some twisted, horrific shit. Who comes up with something like that?"

Boone just shook his head.

"No," Cyrus insisted. "I'm serious. I want to know who came up with the idea."

Leveling a cold glare at him, Boone made it clear that he wouldn't be answering the question.

"That was the real point of Asheville, wasn't it?" Cyrus went on, undeterred. "I was sent in and told that Sutter was my primary objective—that bringing the bomber, Eartzie, was a secondary, but necessary requirement. But that wasn't the case. Eartzie was the primary objective all along. That's why Monica was so pissed when I fragged him. Even though I bagged Sutter…she wanted Eartzie."

Cyrus was referring to the undercover operation he'd worked only weeks earlier. After six months undercover with a well-connected arms dealer going by the name of Sutter, Cyrus had singlehandedly captured not only the man in charge but also his entire mercenary team. Sutter had been working with a prolific bomb maker known only as Eartzie, and preparing to launch a major new operation. Cyrus had used Eartzie's death as a diversion when he made his move against Sutter. The mission had been a success, but Eartzie's death never sat well with the Red Queen.

Boone offered nothing. He only stared at his beer bottle.

"Eartzie worked for the Coalition back in the day," Cyrus went on. "As a contractor. Way back in the beginning. Monica was running the show back then, too, wasn't she?

"You guys were using Eartzie for his *special talents* way back then. It's why you wanted me to bring him back alive. What's going on? Did you have another job for him? Was the thermobaric formula ever a priority? Or was the entire operation just cover for retrieving the nut-job bomb maker?"

Cyrus glared at Boone, but he didn't seem inclined to respond. Boone's disposition failed to give Cyrus any indication to help judge the accuracy of his claims. Boone was mindlessly massaging a small spot on his shoulder, however. Cyrus recognized the location. It was where he'd administered the injection after delivering Boone to the hotel room the night before.

Boone's lack of a verbal response was undermined by his irritation, both at knowing that Cyrus was on to him and that he'd utilized Voss's memory tag against him. Cyrus knew it, and Boone knew that he knew it.

"What is it you want from me?" Boone asked finally.

"The truth. I don't like being used as a pawn. I'm done being manipulated."

"You're letting your personal feelings interfere with—"

"Don't even go there," Cyrus warned. His voice was low and his tone calm, but the admonishment carried just as much threat. He met Boone's eyes and made a point of directing his glance toward the spot that Boone was still fingering on his shoulder.

His eyes tightening, Boone quickly pulled his hand away from the injection site. He looked away. When he opted to take a pull from the beer bottle, Cyrus knew that his so-called friend was trying to buy time to think.

"I can't believe you used that goddamn memory tag on me," Boone groused. He didn't bother to look Cyrus in the eye when he made the comment. "Where's the trust?"

"I've been asking myself the same question. It was bad enough when I thought the Red Queen was behind all this. All the lies and manipulation absolutely reek of her. But once I realized you were in on it with her, and you weren't being maneuvered like me, that's when I knew I was really in trouble." Cyrus had no problem looking at his one-time mentor.

The statement finally drew a questioning glance from Boone.

"Really?" Cyrus snarled, not even letting Boone respond. "You think I'm going to let you put this all on her? You're both in this up to your ears. The morning I spoke with Monica, she told me your body had turned up along with Hobbs in a burned out four-by-four. She said it had just been pulled out of the river. But when I saw video footage of the vehicle recovery on the news, the truck was being fished out of the drink a good four miles downriver from the location she'd given me.

"The only reason for the Red Queen to give me the wrong location was if you'd given it to her when you put the truck in the damn river. She didn't figure on the wreckage being pulled downstream before it was discovered. And I messed up her timing by talking to her when I did. She knew where you dumped the truck, and Hobbs's body, because you told her all about it. She just didn't figure on the current moving it before someone could discover the wreckage for real."

Cyrus took a drink from his beer bottle without ever taking his eyes off Boone. He knew from experience that maintained eye contact could be painfully disconcerting. Since he wanted to put Boone as far back on his heels as possible, he was pulling out all the stops.

"It was a slip up on Monica's part," Cyrus continued. "But not a show stopper because it wasn't conclusive proof of anything—only that you were in communication with the boss at a time when you'd supposedly gone dark. The real mistake was yours. You told me a hit squad took out your team just before you could pick up Ragsdale in Paris. But that wasn't accurate since you were the one who opened fire on your own team.

"You shot them down—men who trusted you with their lives. You betrayed them and killed them in the street. *How could you? Why would you?*"

Boone had somehow found the will to meet Cyrus's gaze somewhere amid the accusatory attack. But the look he offered was surprisingly neutral. He seemed neither troubled by the accusations, nor concerned with the consequences of his actions.

Not even hurt that his friend might suspect him of something horrible.

"That's an interesting assessment," Boone said in a dispassionate, impersonal tone. "Do you care to share the facts that support your conclusion?"

Boone was treating the conversation as if it were one of their Brainstorm Sessions back at Command. It was a similar situation in that Cyrus would be given a series of disparate facts and expected to find a scenario explaining the circumstances. Since a Brainstorm Session had led to his present assignment, Boone seemed to find humor in the approach.

With a roll of his eyes, Cyrus decided to play along. "First of all, there's the aforementioned SUV that was fished out of the river at a location other than the one given. Add to that the injuries to the two bodies inside the vehicle. One was supposed to be you. I don't know where or how you found a double, but it wouldn't be too difficult. You're a white male of average height and weight. You just needed to find a man the right age, put a bullet through his head, and drop him behind the wheel of the truck before dumping it. Throw in your prized Zippo for good measure and you have a story you can sell. The incendiary you used would go a long way toward hiding the real identity of your double. But it was Hobbs who gave you away."

The look on Boone's face made it clear he didn't understand.

"Basic forensics," Cyrus elaborated. "The gunshot wound to Hobbs's head was postmortem. Whoever shot him was just doing it to make it look like he'd been killed at the same time, and in the same way as the driver. But an examination of Hobbs's body showed he had suffered multiple gunshot wounds in the days prior to his death. Those wounds were never properly treated. He was also malnourished at the time of his death.

"In short, he was on the run. Had he been in hiding with you following the ambush that killed the rest of your team, you would've provided him more adequate medical attention. But he received no medical attention at all. Why, was the question that really bothered me. If you were with him, he would've received at least basic care…unless you weren't with him, as you claimed. But then the question became, why would you lie?

"You were behind the ambush of your own team. But Hobbs got away and that was a big problem for you. He knew you were a double agent. You didn't go dark because you were on the run—you dropped off the grid because you were hunting Hobbs. You had to get to him before he could blow the whistle on you," Cyrus concluded.

A tight smile appeared on Boone's face. It was obviously forced because it failed to reach his eyes. "There are at least a dozen other scenarios that can explain that combination of circumstances. It's a creative conclusion, I'll give you that. But it's hardly the only possible explanation."

"But it's not the conclusion you should be disputing," Cyrus said with a sad shake of his head. "It's the supporting facts."

The smile slipped from Boone's face. He had realized his mistake. He was acting like this was an exercise conducted around a boardroom table. One where the conclusion was the subject of debate, and the supporting evidence was always a matter of record. But in this real world situation, the circumstances were different. The conclusion wasn't nearly as damning as each piece of supporting evidence. Boone hadn't tried to dispute the evidence—a slip, Cyrus saw, because Boone already knew the supporting evidence to be factual, even though he was guessing at parts.

When Boone looked quickly away, Cyrus realized that all pretenses could finally be shed. Boone no longer had the opportunity to feign ignorance or claim to be a pawn in what was happening.

"Why don't you just spill it?" Cyrus persisted.

Boone touched the dry patch of skin on his shoulder once more. "Voss's procedure really works?" he asked in a quiet voice without looking at Cyrus.

"He wasn't at the early prototype stages like we believed," Cyrus said simply. "That's why he needed the imaging hardware from Ragsdale. Voss was actively testing the technology, even before I arrived onsite. Ragsdale's tech only made the process more efficient. It was already fully functional. Ragsdale provided a single set of glasses that expedited the uploading and downloading of the neural data."

"And you tagged me." Boone glared. "Do you have any idea what you've done?"

"I'm more concerned with what you've done. It was the only way to know for sure. I had to find out where you stood. But a lot has happened since last night. I've gotten access to the Red Queen's personal files now. I know what you did to the Voss family, and I know why."

"You *had* access," Boone corrected. "That's been rectified. And your new friend, Charlie, is currently in custody. You can imagine the deep, dark hole she'll disappear into. You really should've left this alone and done the job you were given."

Cyrus felt his stomach drop at the mention of Charlie. It meant Boone wasn't bluffing. He'd done everything he could to isolate her, given the volatility of what was going on. He had no idea how they'd tracked his access, let alone realized Charlie's involvement.

Boone must've read Cyrus's surprise because a knowing smile quickly spread across his face.

"Yeah," Boone grinned. "You weren't expecting Charlie to be collateral damage in your little database incursion, were you?"

Cyrus fought himself. He wanted to know more. How had his access been tracked? How was the trail followed back to Charlie? But by asking these questions, Cyrus would be showing concern that would detract from any leverage he currently held.

Boone smirked and shrugged. "You don't miss a trick, do you?" he muttered.

Dammit.

Cyrus didn't need to ask the questions—Boone knew him too well. He might as well be reading his mind. Boone was the one who taught him how to maintain control in situations exactly like this.

"Relax," Boone said with genuine mirth. "You didn't make a mistake; we cheated. I knew you would make a move to regain access. Since the Red—Monica," he laughed. "Since Monica shut down all intercontinental traffic into the company network, we knew you'd need to use a cutout.

"Monica wanted to put Echelon on alert and monitor every single call coming into the United States. But you and I know that system only gets triggered by specific keywords. Words you would avoid, so there was no point.

"Instead, I just had her tap the phone lines of every woman employed by the company. If you were going to break radio silence and look for help inside our walls, odds were that you would call up some *pretty young thing* you met around the office and ask her for help.

"I honestly never considered that it might be Charlie. You really do work fast."

For the first time since their discussion began, Cyrus found his jaw tightening as he fought his own irritation. Was he really that predicable? Did Boone truly know him that well? Were there aspects to his personality that even he wasn't aware of? He was so accustomed to examining others, looking for exploitable flaws...maybe he needed to take a closer look at himself.

"I hope you got a good look at whatever you needed to see," Boone mocked, "because you're never getting back into that system. Monica was pissed. I guarantee she's got things locked down tighter than ever before."

It was Cyrus's turn to grin. He couldn't even help himself.

"What?" Boone asked defensively.

"Everything I need is right here," he said. He tapped a finger on the side of his head for effect. "That's the beauty of an eidetic memory. What's been seen can't be unseen."

Boone shook his head and laughed. "Kid, if you only knew. If it wasn't for me, that memory of yours would've gotten you killed years ago."

Chapter 31

The Cuban
11:35 pm

His eyes narrowed. "What's that supposed to mean?" Cyrus asked.

Boone marveled at the twisted way the world worked. He'd always intended to have this conversation with Cyrus—felt he owed it to him, in fact. But never in his wildest dreams would he have guessed he would be explaining his own origins to the kid on the day that he had him killed.

There was a twisted, circular logic to it, he mused. The case that had originally linked him to Cyrus back at Brown University, was actually related to the death of Eleanor Voss years earlier, as well as the present operation that would soon put Rutger Voss firmly in the employ of the Coalition.

"Back when you were at Brown and got yourself all jammed up with the cartel over the story you were working on for the school paper...did you ever ask yourself why I was watching you at the time?"

Scrutinizing Cyrus as he sat back on his stool, Boone witnessed a shock that was impossible to hide. He could almost see the question spinning around in the young man's mind—'*Why I was watching you?*' It had always been implied that Boone inserted himself into the case after hearing of the trouble Cyrus was involved in. The truth was far different than Cyrus had been led to believe.

"I wasn't called in to deal with the case," Boone explained. "I was already there, watching you when the trouble started. I just used my position with the Coalition to get you out."

"Wait, back up," Cyrus demanded. "Why would you be there watching me?"

Taking a deep breath, Boone gave his reply some deliberate thought. He drained the remainder of his beer while he decided where to start. The problem wasn't coming clean after so many years. It was the understanding that everything he was about to explain would be wasted; that his promising young protégé wouldn't live to see the sunrise.

It was such a waste.

All the same, he knew that even if things had gone differently, he would still be sharing this story with Cyrus. The truth was that Cyrus had outmaneuvered him. Though Boone hated to admit it, he'd been blindsided when the kid dosed him with the memory tagging agent the night before. Even if he hadn't been willing to explain all of this to him now, it had become only a matter of time before Cyrus learned everything for himself. Voss's Shadowlight technology was about to make secrets obsolete. It was another reason the Coalition had to be the sole purveyor of the technology.

"You must've missed that portion of Monica's files," Boone grinned. "Everything began with Project Lamplighter almost…two decades ago."

"Right," Cyrus confirmed. "Lamplighter was a project conducted by Onyx Gander. They had an off-the-books—supposedly silent partner—footing the bill in exchange for the sole access to the resulting technology."

Boone was impressed. Cyrus already knew more than they'd anticipated. "Very good. But do you know what the project entailed? What the ultimate goal was?"

Cyrus raised a wobbling hand to indicate he wasn't certain. "Some kind of genetic mapping and manipulation, as I understand it. I haven't had a chance to read up on the terms or the technology yet. Highly technical stuff, from what I've seen so far."

Boone rocked back on his stool. He instantly realized he'd done a poor job of hiding his surprise. With a wave, he signaled the bartender for another beer and braced a steadying elbow against the counter. Dipping his head toward Cyrus, he spoke quietly and more conspiratorially. He knew Cyrus well. With everything Cyrus was admitting to, Boone was suspicious about the details the kid had chosen to hold back. He was certain Cyrus kept key information in reserve. He'd seen him use the tactic many times in the past, and with great effectiveness. Boone recalled it specifically because it was an impressive tactic—one he hadn't been taught.

"Your host, Doctor Voss," Boone explained, "was the project lead for Lamplighter. The objective, as you said, was to find the genetic traits that make one person unique in some extraordinary way, and then map those markers. From there, the study forked into diverging sub-projects. One focused on enhancing the subject's innate natural traits. The other branch's goal was to find a way to activate a previously dormant trait forming an ability in a neutral subject."

"Essentially transplanting naturally occurring traits. Identifying and mapping them in one person, then trying to activate those abilities in another," Cyrus confirmed.

"Exactly. But that's branch two. Don't forget about branch number one. Their goal was to augment, or supercharge a naturally occurring trait—essentially taking it to the next level."

Cyrus nodded, urging Boone to continue.

Boone couldn't help but wonder if he was telling Cyrus things he already knew.

"You were part of that project," Boone said. "Which branch—I was never sure—but you were definitely a part of it."

"Bullshit," Cyrus countered flatly. "You expect me to buy that? You can do better than that."

Lucy arrived with a pair of beer bottles. She placed one in front of each of them. Boone watched her closely. She looked like she was going to say something, perhaps make some kind of small talk. When she saw the seriousness of their expressions, she seemed to think better of it. She abandoned a damp rang on the counter and made a quick exit.

Boone fought the urge to smash the beer bottle in his grip. It frosted him that the kid had gotten the drop on him the night before. Both that Cyrus was onto him in the first place, and that he'd come prepared to dose him with the memory tag were infuriating. It meant Cyrus had carefully planned the events of the previous night. It also meant everything they'd talked about had been a manipulation. His own agent was using everything Boone had taught him, against him.

And he'd done a damn good job of it.

"Lamplighter continued after Voss left," Boone explained. "At first we didn't think it would be possible. But in time, we found someone to continue his work."

Boone slid off his stool and glanced over his shoulder. "I gotta hit the head. I trust you'll stick around for a bit?"

"I don't think I have a choice," Cyrus countered. "I've waited this long for answers, what's a couple more minutes?"

With a knowing grin, Boone headed across the room.

———

Cyrus watched Boone in the mirror's reflection until he disappeared around the corner at the end of the distant hallway. As soon as his former friend was out of sight, Cyrus slipped the phone from his pocket and tapped a number from memory. He glanced at the clock on the wall. With the time difference, for once the offset was working to his favor.

"Hello?" a young woman's voice answered.

"Jessica, its Cyrus. I only have a minute. Is your dad nearby?"

"Cyrus? Hey. Yeah, he's in the garage. What's wrong?"

"It's a long story. Could you put him on the phone real quick? And, do me a favor? Don't tell him it's me when you hand him the phone?"

"Ah, sure. Okay. One sec." There was a definite hesitation before her uncertain reply. It was to be expected. He was calling her out of the blue and acting dodgy.

The line was silent for what seemed like an eternity before a new voice picked up; this one was male.

"Hello?" the man asked, mirroring Jessica's uncertainty at the unorthodox phone call.

"Reid, its Cyrus. Please listen to what I have to say before you contact Command. It's better for everyone if you don't try to trace my call. Besides, it's entirely unnecessary since Boone is standing in the next room."

"Boone?" The surprise in Reid's voice was unmistakable. It confirmed what Cyrus already suspected. Boone hadn't faked his death to hide his scent in the field, Command obviously thought he'd died in the burned out SUV, too. Only the Red Queen knew differently.

"What's this about, Cyrus?"

"That's the question of the day," Cyrus muttered, mostly to himself. "For now it's just about Charlie Greene. Boone says you have her in custody?"

Letting out a low whistle, Reid chuckled. "Yeah. I gotta say, you worked fast with that one. You landed her in a load of trouble—and in record time! I've heard Monica go on some rants over the years, but what she said about you and Charlie? The Red Queen was as close to unhinged as I've ever seen her.

"I don't know how you talked Charlie into helping you, but Monica's going to bury her. Apparently she's already spoken with counsel. Charlie's being charged as an enemy combatant!"

"Slow down," Cyrus warned. "Monica hasn't talked counsel, I guarantee it. She wants Charlie in a deep, dark hole somewhere, and that's nothing compared to what she's been trying to do to me."

"*What the hell are you talking about?*"

"Look, Reid—I don't have much time. I've got to make this quick. Monica won't be following procedure when it comes to holding Charlie because she can't afford a paper trail. Look into it. You'll see what I mean.

"Monica's been running her own personal black ops through the Coalition for years—decades, according to what I've found. Charlie's not the enemy. I need you to keep her safe until I can finish what I've started. She did me a favor, and I can't have her caught up in this—not now."

"You realize that I know what you're doing?" Reid offered with clear amusement. "It's exactly what you were trained to do. You're trying to confuse and divide us long enough to complete your mission, *whatever the hell that is.*"

"This isn't a game, Reid!" Cyrus snapped, for the first time losing his cool. "You don't have to take my word for it. I have all the proof you'll need. The anal-retentive, sociopathic bitch kept everything well-documented. And thanks to Charlie, I've got the files. I'll tell you where to pick them up. You can make up your mind for yourself."

The line went silent for so long that Cyrus thought the call might've dropped. He was just about to say something when he heard Reid take a breath.

Throughout the entire conversation, Cyrus had been watching the hallway behind him in the mirror's reflection. Boone was due back at any moment. He needed to get Reid on board before that happened.

"Assuming what you say is true," Reid began, "and Monica is dirty, what makes you think I'm any better? Wouldn't she make it the first order of business to fill key posts with people loyal to her?"

A chill ran down Cyrus's back at the thought. While it explained everything he suspected about Boone, as well as everything Boone was confirming for him, he still felt sick at the personal betrayal.

"I know she did that for a fact," Cyrus explained. "I'm dealing with one of her minions right now. But I don't think you're one of them. First of all, she's been at this for a long time. Far longer than you've been on board. Secondly, you're far too proud of your time with the A.T.F. I don't believe you would sully your accomplishments there by participating in the sort of operations she's been running."

"Careful, kid, that sounded dangerously close to something like respect. You wouldn't want to ruin our relationship."

"Really? I thought we put all the animosity behind us. Are we back to that again?"

It rankled Cyrus; Reid was being petty. He was almost certain they'd finally gotten to the bottom of whatever grudge he had against him. If he was wrong about that, it meant he could've been wrong about his entire take on Reid.

When he heard the man's resigned sigh, Cyrus knew he might've been right in the first place. He was rushing the conversation, pushing hard to turn Reid faster than he ought to, especially given what was at stake. Cyrus's eyes once more nervously flicked in the mirror's reflection. Time was running out.

"You're right," Reid admitted. "I'm over that. I guess some habits are just hard to break. Plus, you have to keep in mind what I've been hearing about you from the powers that be. I've got to be honest, Cyrus...your proof had better be damn convincing or I'm going to tell Monica about all of this. And that means things are only going to be worse for you—and Charlie."

"The evidence speaks for itself. Just make sure you download it from an anonymous connection, someplace the company can't track. I guarantee Monica's watching everyone right now. That's why I called you through Jessica's phone.

"Be smart with this info. Keep quiet until you hear from me, but take steps to protect your family. And get Charlie someplace safe. I don't know what Monica's going to do before this is over."

Cyrus waited for Reid to grab a pen and paper, then gave him an FTP server address and login where he could download the files he'd posted. Cyrus recited the information from memory, having uploaded the files from a coffee shop at the other end of the city earlier that afternoon.

"Look, Reid—I gotta go. Just take a look at the files and make a decision for yourself. This information is toxic. She'll do anything to keep it from going wide.

"Watch out for you and yours, and spring Charlie. She was only doing the right thing. She doesn't deserve what the Red Queen is going to throw at her."

Without waiting for a reply, Cyrus tapped the disconnect button. He'd just finished slipping the device into his pocket when Boone rounded the corner at the end of the hall. He couldn't be sure, but it looked like Boone was in the process of pocketing his own phone.

It explains the lengthy trip to the bathroom. But who was he talking to?

———

Grabbing the bottle opener, Boone popped the top on his beer before passing the opener to Cyrus. In some ways it was still like old times, he noticed.

"I'll tell you what," Boone continued as if he'd never made the detour to the restroom. "That project was nothing but trouble from the very start. We hit a major setback when we lost Voss, but we recovered. We even got things back online and started making progress. There were half-a-dozen successful test subjects, and a new set of candidates were about to begin the next phase of the experiment. That's when things went pear-shaped again.

"Someone hit the lab we were using," Boone eyed Cyrus to make his point. "To this day we don't know who was behind it. But they triggered the containment failsafe and the lab was destroyed, along with all the data and the test subjects. It was a real shitstorm."

"Why are you telling me this?" Cyrus asked. "Get to the point."

"The point," Boone grinned, "is that after sorting through the rubble left once our own containment protocol torched the lab, I wasn't so sure everyone had died in the purge. We had the right number of bodies—more than enough, in fact. Enough to account for the intruding force and everyone on staff. But it never sat right with me.

"I started looking closer. It wasn't easy; the only bodies I could identify were staffers. We had their DNA on file, offsite. But the six test subjects were a different story. Everything we had on them was housed at the facility. We lost every piece of identifying information when the lab was sanitized."

Cyrus shrugged and looked at his beer. He sipped it casually. He was doing his best to appear disinterested, but Boone knew better.

"What's this have to do with me?" Cyrus asked.

"When I realized the test subjects might not have died at the lab, I started looking for them. All I had was very generic information such as age, sex, and race. But, in addition to that, they were each unique in some way. While I didn't know in what ways, it was enough for me to start doing broad searches. Eventually you appeared on my radar."

Cyrus cast Boone a piercing gaze. "You're saying you were watching me even before all the trouble with my story for the school paper?"

Boone nodded.

Cyrus shook his head. "Why? What's so special about me?"

A smile crossed Boone's face, in spite of himself. "You really have no idea, do you?"

Offering only a blank stare, Cyrus said nothing.

"You don't have a clue how easily all of this comes to you— how hard others have to work just to do the things that come naturally to you?"

Cyrus shook his head. "You're overthinking it, Boone. Everyone's good at something. The trick in life is finding what you excel at, then running with it. It doesn't mean I'm some kind of freak of genetics."

Boone laughed. Oddly, he could offer no counter argument. What could he say if the kid didn't believe the truth? In the end, it really didn't matter. In a few minutes, it would all be over for him.

"Look," Boone said. "I just wanted to explain what led me to watching you. I was there to step in and get you out of that jam because I was already surveilling you. The point is, I never told Monica that I believed you were one of the six missing test subjects. She's always believed they were dead; I never told her about my suspicions. I just wanted you to know."

Eyeing him doubtfully, Cyrus took his time asking the question that Boone knew was coming.

"Okay," Cyrus began. "Assuming that you believed I was one of your *missing six*, then why *wouldn't* you tell your boss about it? It's not like you to hold back important details."

Boone shrugged and bought himself a moment's reprieve as he took another drink. He didn't know the answer to the question until the moment he heard it asked. The realization hit him like a jolt of electricity. It was so obvious, yet somehow he'd never admitted it to himself.

"I guess there was just something about you," Boone said quietly. "I watched you at school, at work…your time with Natasha. You were just a kid, but you had it all figured out. Something about you, something…likable. I had a good idea what was waiting for you if I brought you back. Lamplighter would begin again. I guess it just didn't seem right.

"Then you went and got yourself jammed up with the students and the faculty conspiring to cook that designer drug. Rather than look the other way—or even call the authorities— you rolled up your sleeves and managed to discover who was behind it, and how the operation worked. That's when I knew you had a talent we could use.

"Suddenly it was a better idea to bring you into the Coalition as an operative, rather than a lab rat. That way I could stay close to you and see the extent of your talents."

Cyrus put the beer down and pushed it away. He didn't look at Boone when he spoke. Instead, he kept his eyes straight ahead and his voice cold and level. "I don't know why you took an interest in me," he said flatly. "I've obviously been manipulated from the very beginning. You make it sound like I should thank you for it… You know me better than that."

Boone felt Cyrus's cold gaze fall on him, and saw anger in the young man's eyes.

"I've been used and manipulated," Cyrus clarified. "But I'm done—with you, and the Coalition. I thought the work I've done was something to be proud of. When I got a look at Monica's hidden records, I realized that I was never more than a cog in a larger machine. She's been using the Coalition to conduct off-the-books operations that have nothing to do with national interests for years.

"She might be the one calling the shots, but those jobs didn't get done without you out in the field. So I'm asking you, from one professional to another, how many more are in on this? Is the entire company corrupt?"

Boone offered only a sad smile. He shook his head. "You know how this works," he said quietly. "You can't keep a secret like this if too many people are in on it."

"Then who?" Cyrus demanded.

Boone grinned. Did the kid think he'd be able to weed out what he considered to be corruption inside the Coalition? It wouldn't matter, he reasoned. Cyrus would be dead soon; there was no reason to be dishonest.

It's a shame.

"It's not corruption," Boone corrected. "We're patriots. We're just willing to do what needs to be done, even if no one knows it. Monica and I were doing this work for nearly two decades before you came along, and we'll be doing it long after you're gone. It's just the way it is, Cyrus."

"Patriots?" Cyrus said, nearly choking on the word. "Call it whatever you like, but you've been busy lining your pockets every step of the way. That's not patriotic, it's opportunistic."

Boone felt his heart seize as if caught in a vise. His eyes narrowed as he tried to read the expression on Cyrus's face.

"Wait," Cyrus countered. There was a fresh gleam in his eyes. "Don't tell me that she's been the only one lining her pockets this entire time?"

While the logical side of his mind told him that Cyrus was making a play to divide them, Boone read nothing less than sincerity in the kid's face. And while he didn't believe his words at face value, Cyrus made a convincing argument. One that held the potential to be true, at least. If it was, it meant Boone had allowed Monica to leverage him in a way he had never expected.

"Wow," Cyrus needled. "I guess I wasn't the only one to get played!"

Cyrus slid off his stool and took a long look at Boone; grabbing his beer bottle, he headed for the door.

Chapter 32

The Cuban
12:44 am

Nearing the door, Cyrus heard the obnoxious scrape of a barstool across the tile floor behind him. He knew Boone was following him. It was to be expected. He anticipated what was coming but pictured it happening in one of two possible ways.

Tipping back the beer bottle, Cyrus drained the last few drops just as he stepped over the threshold into the brisk night air. His ears virtually rang as they adjusted to the silence of the outdoors. The droning white noise of background conversation and music receded quickly into the background.

Glancing over his shoulder, he saw Boone only a few steps behind.

Here we go...

Three dozen yards away, a black SUV sat idling with its driver waiting. Their conversation inside had taken longer than expected. The man behind the wheel lowered the tinted window and looked at Cyrus, offering the slightest of nods before once more raising the window.

Cyrus knew it would take only seconds to cross the deserted traffic lane to the safety of the armored SUV. Whatever was coming would happen quickly. He shot a look over his shoulder once more and found Boone had stopped a few paces away. Oddly, he'd stepped to the side of the walkway. He hadn't followed him directly from the bar. If he had, he would've walked the same invisible path down the sidewalk. That he deviated from that path meant something.

A sniper it is, Cyrus concluded.

"You and Monica killed an innocent woman just to trick Voss into going back to work on your project," Cyrus called out to Boone. "Nothing you can say will ever justify that.

"Then you killed your entire field team to cover your need to drop off radar while you organized mercenary teams against the Voss family, and against me. Let Monica know I'll be coming for her. I won't let this stand."

Boone offered Cyrus a sad look, and then his eyes fell to his boots. "I know you won't," he said, seemingly speaking to his feet. "For what it's worth, I'm sorry it had to end this way."

Boone looked up, finally taking Cyrus straight in the eye. Cyrus saw pain in Boone's gaze, and he knew what was coming. When Boone's eye line shifted a few degrees to settle on a building in the distance, Cyrus knew the moment of truth had arrived.

Boone nodded to someone unseen.

Cyrus refused to take his eyes off of Boone's. He remained stock still, only raising the empty beer bottle. He held it upright in the palm of his hand, as if putting it on display.

After two long seconds—in which nothing happened— Boone looked at Cyrus with confusion registering on his face. He didn't understand what was happening—or, in this case, not happening.

The bottle in Cyrus's hand suddenly exploded. Boone stepped backward in surprise and stared at Cyrus.

Cyrus offered only a small smile.

Quickly regaining his composure, Boone reached inside his flannel shirt. He was going for a gun.

"I wouldn't do that," Cyrus warned, before Boone was halfway to the firearm. "If you produce a weapon, he's been cleared to drop you where you stand. If you leave it where it is, we can both walk away from this."

Even from thirty-feet away, Cyrus could see the penetrating stare from his former friend. He could also see the corded muscles of the man's lower jaw. He ground his teeth and sorted through his options.

There were none.

"You know you won't get far," Boone warned.

"That's funny," Cyrus grinned. He backed slowly toward the waiting SUV. "I was going to say the same thing to you. Tell the Red Queen what I said. It's over."

Cyrus circled to the far side of the four-wheel drive and slipped into the passenger seat. No sooner had the door closed then the 4x4 was pulling away from the curb. It wouldn't take Dargo long to break down the sniper rifle and meet them back at the compound. He just wondered what had become of the mercenary who had previously manned the weapon. While he didn't know much about Dargo, he had little doubt that he'd made short work of the hired gun.

Chapter 33

The rendezvous with Dargo had taken place in the safety of the Voss Compound's unground motor pool following the meet with Boone. Dargo asked surprisingly few questions given the circumstances. He simply reported dispatching a pair of hostiles who had taken up an offensive position on a distant rooftop; a spotter and a sniper. Then, per their plan, he'd commandeered their perch and waited for Cyrus and Boone to exit the bar.

Cyrus rode the elevator with Dargo to the first floor. There, Cyrus exited without a word, offering Dargo only a silent nod of thanks for his support. Dargo would take the elevator up to five. There, he would check in with the evening security detail before turning in for the night, or doing whatever it was that Dargo did in his down time. Cyrus knew Dargo planned to leave first thing in the morning to pay Gerard Combs, one-time head of Onyx Gander, an impromptu visit. Even hours before he was due to leave, Cyrus could read the grim determination in Dargo's normally stalwart eyes. He was glad he wouldn't be standing in Combs's shoes come tomorrow afternoon.

Stepping into the common area of the first floor, Cyrus was surprised to see Anna sitting by herself on the sofa. Only one lamp was on, adding to the muted ambient moon and city light spilling through the building's massive glass facade. But what struck him as most unusual was that she sat alone, without a book or a magazine; not even a television ran to entertain her. She simply sat and stared blankly at nothing with her legs folded beneath her and her hands in her lap.

"Anna?" Cyrus said quietly. "Are you alright?"

His voice seemed to jolt her from a trance in a way that the elevator chime apparently had not. He saw her eyes snap into focus as soon as her head turned toward him.

"My God," she muttered as she launched herself from the sofa. "You're alright!"

"Of course I'm alright. Why wouldn't I be?" Even as the words left his lips, he knew something wasn't right. Only Dargo knew of his meeting with Boone. He hadn't told Natasha, and he certainly hadn't told Anna. "What's going on?" He could already see confusion on Anna's face that mirrored his own.

"Tash got a call from the hospital," she explained. "They said you'd been in an accident—that you were hurt. What happened?"

"I don't know—I'm fine. There was no accident. Please, explain?"

Anna looked around the quiet, empty room as if ensuring they were alone. When she spoke once more, her voice was hushed, as if afraid someone might overhear. "The man who called, he said you were hurt and that you needed to see her. He said she had to come right away, but that she shouldn't tell anyone."

318

Cyrus's heart sank with the realization that Natasha was no longer in the building. "Wait a minute," Cyrus said, nearly cutting her off. "Why would she do that? She didn't go by herself, did she?"

Anna nodded. "The man said he was calling about Jon Webb—she said that no one on the island knows you by that name. She left as soon as she hung up the phone."

"But security wouldn't just let her—"

"She used the tunnel!"

Cyrus's mind flashed back to the moment at the bar when he saw Boone pocketing his phone as he returned from the bar's restroom. He felt a white-hot flash of anger. But it didn't make sense. At that point, Boone would've been certain that his sniper had him dead to rights. Why would he—?

There was a very physical pain, as if he'd been punched in the gut. *Of course.* Boone was moving on with his plan. If the sniper was able to remove him from the equation, Boone would need to act fast in order to get his hands on Natasha before she received word of his death. He'd used his inside knowledge of their prior relationship and Cyrus's former alter ego to draw her out. Once Boone had his hands on Natasha, he'd have what he needed to leverage Shadowlight and Voss into the hands of the Coalition.

No, Cyrus reminded himself, given what he'd learned upon accessing the Red Queen's files, Shadowlight wasn't destined for the hands of the Coalition. It was a part of whatever personal plans Monica and Boone had set up.

The hospital.

She would never make it that far. Boone would send her there, then intercept her along the way. After that, they could have gone anywhere.

"How long ago did she leave?"

Anna looked at her watch and took a moment to judge the interval. "It's been at least a half hour, maybe more. I've been waiting for her to call with news."

It was already too late.

"What's going on?" Anna demanded. Her eyes were red, rimmed with tears threatening to fall at any moment.

His mind running wild, Cyrus began processing one plan after another, discarding each as quickly as the idea formed. Boone's sniper hadn't gotten him outside the bar, which would present an obstacle for Boone. He would need to adjust his plans to compensate. But as long as he had Natasha, Boone knew he'd effectively immobilized Cyrus, as well as Voss—even Dargo, for that matter. None of them could move against him so long as he held one of Voss's girls.

It meant that maintaining control of Natasha would be Boone's top priority. That would mean getting off the island as soon as possible—unless he had something else in mind. And God only knew what that might be. Boone had always excelled at thinking outside the box.

"Did she take her mobile with her?" Cyrus asked.

Anna nodded. "Of course. She was going to call as soon as she knew what had happened to you."

Darting back to the elevator, Cyrus tapped the 'up' button to call for the car. "Come on," he said over his shoulder. "It's time to see how well you know your sister!"

Chapter 34

Millennium Beach,
2:04 am

The waves were crashing far off to the right as Cyrus made his way along the perimeter of the jagged volcanic rocks. They marked the extent of the freezing, finely-grained sand that constituted Kapros's second longest uninterrupted stretch of beach. He hugged the natural wall of stone on his left, sticking to the murky shadows cast by the half moon. With few clouds in the sky, light wasn't a problem. If anything it was a hindrance. Darker conditions would've simplified his approach.

Cyrus looked up at the wide, two-story structure above him. It was built on a pier that extended almost fifty yards out into the rolling sea surrounding the island. The pier was supported by fifty-foot tall concrete pilings. Atop the platform sat a wide building with every external wall made of transparent glass.

It was the island's world famous Museum of Modern Art. A somewhat modest two-story, fifty-five-thousand square-foot structure made all the more dramatic by its perch on the concrete and steel pier, positioned over the island's sweeping coastline.

The building's aesthetic allure added to the diverse and unparalleled sampling of art within its walls. It was an attraction that drew art aficionados from all over the world.

It was a dramatic location to hold a hostage, Cyrus thought. Boone certainly knew he was coming. Cyrus's only advantage was that he knew Boone didn't have the untapped resources of the Coalition behind him. He'd learned enough to understand that the games Boone and the Red Queen had been playing over the years only worked as long as they kept their true agenda quiet. If they could manipulate Coalition assets toward their own goals, all the better. But they could never outwardly utilize company assets without blowing their own cover.

That much had been confirmed on Cyrus's drive to the beach. He'd phoned Reid to see how matters had progressed with Charlie Greene. To his surprise, it had been Charlie who answered Reid's phone. She put him on speaker while Reid explained that the information Cyrus provided had proven accurate. Subsequently, Reid moved Charlie into protective custody. The real problem was that he didn't know how to proceed from there.

Cyrus put Reid into a holding pattern. With a little luck, he would make major progress on cleaning up the mess before sunrise. But if things went sideways, he provided Reid with a contingency plan. He also asked Reid to do whatever he could to make sure that Charlie was safe. If Reid hadn't heard from him in three days' time, then it was up to him to do what he wanted with the information Cyrus had uncovered. Reid could go after the Red Queen with everything he had, or he could bury the info and go back to work. Cyrus said that he wouldn't blame him one way or the other. The man had a family to consider and, as Cyrus further explained, if they hadn't heard from him in three days, it was solid proof that hitting Boone and the Red Queen head-on wasn't the smart solution.

Anna Voss had been instrumental in Cyrus locating Natasha in the first place. Under normal circumstances, Cyrus might've had the resources to locate her using more traditional means. But without the Coalition's support, not wanting to involve Dargo and not having time to involve local authorities, Anna was his best bet.

Cyrus had put her in front of Natasha's laptop and shown her the webpage that allowed users to locate lost or stolen cellphones. It had taken Anna all of five guesses to gain access to her sister's account. After that, Cyrus had a GPS fix on the phone's location—accurate within thirty feet.

Not bad for off-the-shelf, consumer grade technology.

Cyrus took Anna's phone with him when he left the compound. Since Boone knew the number of his mobile, there was a good chance that its calls and location were being monitored, anyway. But he could use the web browser built into Anna's phone to keep a real-time fix on Natasha's location.

As Cyrus looked at the two silhouettes visible through the glass wall of the distant building high above the beach, Cyrus finally had an answer to another question. He wasn't sure why Boone hadn't destroyed Natasha's phone. Of course he knew it could be used to find them, but Boone had picked a meeting point that was far too showy to be secure. He'd done it for a reason. Not only did he know that Cyrus would come, the phone had been an invitation.

Seeing movement in the shadows where one of the museum's support pylons met the beach, Cyrus spotted the first sign of trouble. Actually, he was surprised he hadn't encountered resistance earlier. Boone had posted perimeter guards after all.

Nearly twenty minutes later, Cyrus had completed his circuit of the pier. He worked his way from the water's edge, through the supporting pylons, and up the rocky slope to the corner of the building at ground level. Circling the front of the building, Cyrus moved to the north side before stopping short of the craggy ledge where the earth plunged back to the beach forty-feet below. By the time he'd completed his circuit of the facility, he'd eliminated four hostile parties without firing a shot or raising the alarm.

Jumping a protective railing thirty-feet from the cliff, Cyrus stepped carefully through the tall, dry field grass and made his way to the ledge. Peering over the edge, he could see the jagged mesh of rocks on the cliff-face below. They mirrored the ones he'd climbed through on the south side of the building, halfway through his circuit of the facility. He knew them to be every bit as life-threatening as they appeared.

To his left, the museum stretched out on to the specially designed pier. The pier reached out across the beach, through the surf, and into the rolling ocean beyond. While he needed to enter the building, Cyrus had to avoid the obvious use of the front door. If he were Boone, in spite of the perimeter guard, he would've booby-trapped the doors. At the very least, the doors would be rigged with a signal. And since the building was two stories tall, a roof-based incursion was out. There was no way to scale the glass face of the flat, two-story structure. All of this severely limited Cyrus's access points.

He eyed the distant railing of the gallery's observation platform. It began about thirty-feet out from the cliff's edge and ran for almost fifty yards before meeting with another expansive glass wall where the building extended beyond the breakers and over deeper water. At his feet, a forty-plus-foot drop to sharp rocks waiting to rend flesh from bone.

Eyeing the railing suspiciously, Cyrus sized it up as he would any opponent. The jump was his number one concern, but his handholds on the other side were a close second. He would only have one chance, and if he botched it, Natasha's fate wouldn't be much better than his own.

Opting against overthinking things, Cyrus backed up, pushing the tall scrub grass flat with each step of his hiking boots. He was creating a short, single use runway that would likely mean the difference between life and death.

Dammit! Overthinking it again...

When his backside touched the fence designed to keep spectators from getting too close to the edge of the cliff, Cyrus took two deep breaths, bent his knees, and pushed off with all his strength. His legs pumped down the narrow path, his feet moving nimbly across the uneven ground. His arms swung with measured precision and his lungs gorged with oxygen, only to expel it again with every fourth step. Then, reaching the uneven ledge, he flung himself into a dive with his hands pointed for the very top of the distant railing.

With his breath seized in silent desperation, Cyrus watched the jagged outlines of the cliff-face pass below his airborne body. Every crack, crevice, and jagged point of volcanic rock waited to embrace him if he fell even an inch short of his goal. But as Cyrus's gaze rose to meet his destination, and his hands prepared to seek purchase, he was shocked to see that while the distant handrail was drawing quickly closer, it was also moving up and away from his outstretched fingers.

Clamping his teeth, Cyrus put every ounce of his focus into a stretch. The laws of physics had conspired to pull the handrail beyond his reach, but he still held desperate hope for Plan B.

Before his mind could work through the basic physical responses necessary to stretch his form, he felt his finger bend upon impact with something. The fingernail of his second finger scraped, confirming what he was afraid had only been wishful thinking. Immediately, he snapped his right hand shut, wrapping it around a vertical baluster that supported the lookout perch's perimeter railing.

A moment later, Cyrus's left hand caught up to his right and found purchase on a similar vertical iron support. His forward momentum didn't impact as gracefully, however. His skull thudded hollowly, striking more of the upraised iron, before gravity took him fully into its grip, pulling his torso down and smashing his chest and chin against the concrete platform supporting the art gallery.

A tear rolled from the corner of his eye, but a proud smile spanned his jaw as Cyrus pulled himself up and over the railing. He deposited himself unceremoniously on the balcony with a quiet 'thud'.

Not even sparing the time to regain his breath, Cyrus moved across the viewing platform and over to the sliding glass door. Beyond it was the art gallery, itself. With a gentle tug, the door slid easily aside on its track. Either someone had forgotten to lock it, or simply hadn't considered it a security risk. After all, who would be foolish enough to come over the railing in such a way? All the same, he had his trusty set of lock picks standing by, just in case.

Stepping onto the parquet floor, Cyrus strained to pick up a sound of any kind. He slid the door closed behind him, but still heard nothing. The building was shut down for the night, lit only by service floods that had been carefully concealed in the acoustic ceiling tiles. There would be no random security guards; Boone would've seen to that. That left Cyrus only one thing more to consider as he moved silently through the murky shadows between floor displays. What was Boone doing? Why go through all of this trouble?

As he neared the edge of a series of interspersed, freestanding sculptures, Cyrus saw an open expanse of flooring was about to come fully into view. Just before he reached it, he slid beside a large boulder-like piece of stone that had several perfectly round orbs protruding from its surface. He didn't know what the art represented, but to him it was a solid bullet stop and the last reasonable vantage point before the opening on the display floor.

His gun gripped loosely in his right hand, Cyrus took a slow, silent glance around the edge of his hiding spot. Natasha sat on a divan. Her hands were folded in her lap and she looked very, very unhappy. The small, ornate, backless couch had been placed conspicuously in the center of a wide open section of space that looked almost like a dance floor set amid the sea of priceless art.

It was a trap if ever there was one. And Boone was nowhere to be seen. Similarly, there didn't seem to be anything to tether Natasha to her location which raised the next question. Why hadn't she made a run for it?

Yup, it's a trap. But does Boone know I'm here?

"I'm told this is an impressive collection," Boone's voice sounded from somewhere in the distance.

Question answered.

"But if you ask me, it's all a bunch of useless crap. What's the point of modern art, anyway? At least with the classics there's some perceived value. Even if I can't appreciate the beauty, I can recognize the talent—there's at least some sort of history to consider. But *modern* art? What gives this junk value? I just don't see it."

At the sound of Boone's voice, Natasha became alert—even more on edge. Her eyes moved erratically, searching the surrounding shadows. Her divan was lit from above by a pale, muted, white glow. The floor around her was open for about fifty-feet in every direction before exhibits of one type or another came into view, making it look as if she was surrounded by a forest of indistinct shapes and shadows.

Cyrus knew it was as bad idea to give away his position. Then again, if Boone knew he was here, Cyrus had already lost the upper hand. It didn't matter that the perimeter team was gone. So long as Boone had Natasha, he was holding all the cards.

But how did he have Natasha? Why was she sitting still and compliant on the sofa? Cyrus knew the woman to be anything but timid or demure. She was intelligent, with a fiery wit and a fierce temper. For her to sit by and remain compliant wasn't a good sign.

"You can put a man in class," Cyrus called out into the murky shadows. "But you can't put class in the man."

Since the source of Boone's voice was difficult to locate, Cyrus hoped his mentor might have the same trouble. It must not have worked.

Boone stepped from the shadow of a display at the perimeter of the empty floor, almost directly opposite of Cyrus. "Oh, give me a break," Boone barked. "I know you. You think this is a bunch of pretentious crap, too, and you've been thinking it since you walked through the damn door! Nice Spiderman impersonation, by the way."

Stepping from his own cover position, Cyrus raised his gun in a double-handed grip. He had a steady fix on Boone, keeping him locked squarely in the sights. Oddly, Boone didn't make a move for cover and didn't raise a weapon to defend himself. He did, however, glare at Cyrus across the open expanse of floor and raise a finger of one hand in warning.

"Don't jump the gun, kid." His voice was smooth and confident, even though he was looking down the barrel of a 9mm. There was a hundred-feet of open floor between them, with Natasha in the middle, but she was a good twelve degrees off axis and out of the current line of fire. Boone knew damn well he could make the shot.

"Be cool, Cyrus," Boone warned again. "Or your girl won't live to see the sun rise."

Taking a moment to study Boone, Cyrus was confused. He didn't have a gun in hand. It normally would've made Cyrus suspect a sniper but he'd already tried that trick once tonight. Plus, with the surrounding artwork and displays, and with the building's location out on a pier, a sniper was an impossibility. There was always a chance there was another shooter knocking around somewhere out in the displays just waiting to drop him. But as odd as it seemed, Cyrus didn't sense anyone was watching them. He felt strangely confident that it was just he and Boone.

And Natasha.

So why was she still sitting quietly?

Stepping further into the light, Cyrus maintained a sight picture on Boone. But when his adversary failed to make a move to counter him, Cyrus started a slow walk toward Natasha. He felt her eyes, as well as Boone's, on him with each step he took. Boone maintained his position while Natasha never moved an inch.

"What did you do to her?" Cyrus demanded, as he closed the distance on Natasha.

His voice quieted. "Did he hurt you?"

As he stepped closer, she lowered her gaze. A new set of tears began to roll silently from the corners of her eyes. It was clear she'd been crying for some time. "Are you alright?" Cyrus persisted.

Natasha nodded slowly. When he stepped near, she stood from the divan and launched herself into his arms. "You shouldn't have come," she whispered. "I'm so glad to see you!"

"It's okay," he said. "But you have to tell me what he's done. I know he's up to something—I just can't figure it out yet."

"I—I—" she stammered.

At first Cyrus thought she was afraid to tell him, but that wasn't like her. Whatever it was, she didn't know how to explain it. He didn't even know how to process that. What could drive her to speechlessness?

His eyes shot back to Boone who was walking slowly toward them. His gun was still trained on him. "Easy with that," Boone warned. He waved the gun away as he advanced, as if it would have any effect on Cyrus's decision to pull the trigger.

"That's far enough," Cyrus snapped. The hammer was already back on the weapon and what little slack there was out of the trigger was already taken up. It would take less than a twitch to fire off a round. "Not another step!"

Boone stopped mid-stride, then took a half-step back to find proper footing. This time he raised both hands in a gesture meant to ward off any action against him. In one of his upraised hands, Cyrus saw what looked like a small, cellular smartphone.

"Drop the device and step away," Cyrus commanded.

Boone smirked, then turned the handheld object so Cyrus could better see the display. It showed a series of numbers counting down by the second. "You don't want me to do that," Boone warned. "If I don't enter the proper code in—" he turned the device and read the display—"fourteen seconds, the micro-facet charge located beside her heart will detonate. It's not much to see, but the effects are irreversible."

Cyrus felt like he'd been sucker-punched. His eyes shot to Natasha. "Is that true?"

Her eyes closed. She nodded as a pair of tears decorated her cheekbones. "He injected me with something. I don't know what it was." Her finger settled on a point over her left breast indicating where the injection had taken place.

Cyrus lowered the gun. "Enter your code."

Boone smirked. "Say please."

Cyrus shot the man a look that explained his eagerness to tear his head off with his bare hands. Boone rolled his eyes, but quickly turned the device around and entered what sounded like a ten digit code.

"Before you get ahead of yourself," Boone quickly warned, "It's not the same code every time. And the code must be entered every three minutes or the charge detonates—so don't get any ideas." He turned the display once more and showed them that less than three minutes already remained on the clock.

"So you're just going to reset that thing every three minutes until Voss hands over his technology?" Cyrus asked. He didn't buy it, but he wasn't clear on Boone's long-term plan.

"Of course not," Boone said. "The three minute clock just ensures your compliance while we get the ground rules straight. Once I'm safely out of here—." He stopped, seeming to think better of the idea. "Make that safely off the island, you get the benefit of a forty-eight-hour clock. That means, as long as I enter the reset code every forty-eight hours, the love of your life over there gets to live another two days."

Cyrus's mind ran with the possibilities. Forty-eight hours; two days and nights gave them a realistic period of time in which to immobilize the explosive Boone injected into Natasha's chest. While he didn't know the right people to perform the procedure, it was a solid bet Voss would have the right contacts. The only trick would be keeping Voss's tech out of Boone's hands long enough to disable the charge.

"And this isn't about Shadowlight," Boone went on. "Sure, we can make use of his latest tech, too. Especially if it's as effective as you claim. But we're putting him back to work on Lamplighter. I think we both know it's a viable project with *substantial* untapped potential."

"You plan on working Voss long-term—and holding Natasha hostage the entire time?" Cyrus couldn't believe what he was hearing. It didn't sound like an idea that would come from Boone. It did, he reasoned, sound like the sort of the plan that would come from the Red Queen.

But when Boone shook his head, Cyrus was at a loss.

"Not just Voss," Boone clarified. "You'll be going back to work as well. Only this time, on a much shorter leash." A devious grin had spread across his face.

"You can't be serious!" It wasn't what Cyrus wanted to say— or do, for that matter. He wanted to shoot his old friend in the face and walk away from the entire mess. But he couldn't do either if he couldn't take Natasha with him.

"What can I say? You're a victim of your own effectiveness. If you weren't so damn good at the job, Monica wouldn't insist on keeping you around."

Cyrus shook his head. Realizing he'd been hamstrung, he holstered his weapon. "You realize all of this just proves my point." His eyes scanned the floor as his mind searched for a way out. "That bitch is certifiable. She's bat shit crazy!"

Boone laughed; a heartfelt, honest laugh for the first time since stepping from the shadows. "You don't have to tell me, kid. Imagine how I feel after working with her for twenty-five years. Just when I thought I'd seen it all, she hands me this." He held up the remote for Natasha's wireless leash.

"Oh," he muttered, and then quickly typed in a new access code.

"You're not inspiring a lot of confidence with that thing," Cyrus quipped. "Maybe you should give it to someone who's a little more *responsible*?"

Boone's smile disappeared when he concluded that Cyrus wasn't just making a crack. He was being serious. "What's that supposed to mean?"

With a shrug, Cyrus continued his slow pace of the open floor. "I mean, we never really talked about it, but you've been losing a step here and there for some time. You're not the man you used to be."

Natasha moved closer to Cyrus, and whispered, "Did he say twenty-five years? Is he part of the group who killed my mother?"

Unable to lie, the best he could offer her was a grim look. "Don't worry," he said quietly. "We'll get through this. Once that charge is out of your chest, he'll get what's coming to him. Just remember, forty-eight hours is a lot of time to work with."

"Wait a damn minute!" Boone called out. "Just what are you saying, kid? I should be put out to pasture? Is that what you're getting at?"

"No," Cyrus countered. "I just think that if you're going to be the one responsible for entering the code that extends Tash's life every two days, maybe you should consider switching to desk duty. With the kind of mistakes you've been making lately, you're going to get yourself killed. And you'll end up taking her with you.

"Don't get me wrong, in light of recent events I'm fine with that first part. But I don't want your negligence to cost Tash her life."

Cyrus met Boone's eye. It was clear that neither man was joking around. Boone was as steamed as Cyrus had ever seen him. He'd really struck a nerve. A far more sensitive one than he'd anticipated. Cyrus wondered how he could manipulate it to his advantage.

"Listen here, you little prick—" Boone bristled.

"Hold on. Just hold on," Cyrus interrupted. "If you're going to freak out, a man your age could blow a heart valve, or something. Why don't you enter Tash's code one more time, just to be safe. That way, if you keel over, she can use her last three minutes to watch you turn blue."

Boone's lips pulled into a tight line; the muscles of his jaw were drawn and corded, a purple vein pulsed across his forehead. There was a new, feral, out of control look about him. It was a side of his former mentor that Cyrus had never seen.

"Hey." Cyrus began walking slowly towards him, suddenly very concerned he actually might have a stroke or heart attack. "I'm just giving you a hard time, like old times," he said in a quiet, reassuring voice. If Boone dropped dead right there, they wouldn't have the two days they needed to disable the explosive charge.

When he saw Boone take a few slow, deep breaths, Cyrus knew Boone was pulling himself together. He suspected Boone really did have difficulty manipulating them in this brutal manner. He was angry because he was conflicted, Cyrus was almost certain of it. There was more to the pain he saw in his eyes than just the anger Cyrus had invoked. But even if Boone was regretful, nothing would change the position he'd put them in or the things he'd already done. Not only had he sent trained killers after them multiple times, Boone had done something unforgivable to the only woman Cyrus had ever loved.

"I know what you're thinking," Boone said at last. His complexion was returning to normal and he'd regained his composure.

"I'm not so far out to pasture that I don't know what you're planning," he continued. "You like that two day window of opportunity. You figure you can neutralize the micro-facet charge in that time."

Cyrus was disappointed Boone had called him on the idea, but it was the logical conclusion. Still, hearing Boone mention it sent a cold chill through his entire body. He was up to something.

"The thought had occurred to me," Cyrus admitted. "Now that you mention it."

"Does the word, micro-facet, ring any bells in that big brain of yours," Boone asked with a grin.

Thinking it through, Cyrus was sure that it didn't. He looked at Natasha but she shook her head to the negative.

"Maybe this will," Boone said. He punched a fresh reset code into the handheld and then tossed the device to Cyrus.

Natasha looked at Boone as if he was insane. Cyrus knew there was nothing he could do, even with the controller. Taking it away from Boone wasn't enough. It was still active and functional. Then again, if it were dropped and broken...he suddenly understood the reason for her shock. Boone's casual disregard for the device that represented her continued life was a sobering example of just who they were dealing with.

Cyrus looked at the small device and instantly recognized it. The understanding must've registered plainly across his face because Boone began to laugh.

"That's right," Boone said. "Your buddy, Eartzie, built this little beauty! And you know what that means!"

Natasha shot a questioning glance back and forth between Cyrus and Boone. "What's it mean?" she asked when neither of them elaborated.

Cyrus dropped slowly onto the short sofa. All of his will to fight was finally driven from him. He rolled the device over in his hand, trying to glean any sense of understanding. If there was a weak spot in the design, would he be smart enough to find it? If not him, then who? And once the device was gone, what did they have to work with? What sort of safeguards had the madman put in place?

"That's right, kid," Boone said quietly. The defeat in Cyrus's face finally seemed to be enough. "Now you understand what you're dealing with. There's no disarming this one. Ain't. Gonna. Happen."

"Damn it!" Natasha bellowed. "What aren't you telling me?" She glared at both Cyrus and Boone, now begging for any answer from either man.

Cyrus wanted to explain but he couldn't find the words. He didn't even know where to begin.

Boone explained in a calm and patient voice, "It's something special, cooked up by a very talented, and very twisted little man who knew more about bomb making than any other person on the planet.

"That tiny injection I put beside your heart? *There's absolutely no way to disarm it.* You don't even want to go near it. Not with an x-ray, an MRI—nothing. In fact, there's a fifty-fifty chance that the anti-surveillance countermeasures your old man's using at home will trigger it."

As Boone explained, the blood drained from Natasha's face. She looked at Cyrus, hoping for some sign that Boone was tormenting her. But he could offer no such hope.

"Oh, my God," she mumbled. She spun on a heel and stumbled a few paces away before dropping seat first onto the wood floor. She pulled her knees to her chest and began to sob silently.

Cyrus was caught between the desire to rip Boone's throat out, and the need to collapse beside Natasha and cradle her in his arms.

"I'll be needing this back," Boone said, pulling the device from Cyrus's fingers. "Best not let that clock run down too far, you know."

Boone walked a dozen paces away. This time he had trouble turning his back on Cyrus. "You know," he said, "I had my doubts about you back at the very start—back when I recruited you, I mean."

He paced slowly, eyeing Cyrus while he moved. "There was something special about you," he continued. "There was never any question about that. But I had a suspicion you were trying to play me from day one. I couldn't help wondering if you wanted into the Coalition just so you could write another one of your exposés. I have to admit, it would've made big news. And if anyone could've blown our cover, it was you."

Cyrus glared at his former friend. Now that he was feeling the full brunt of Boone's betrayal, he was very tempted to spread the truth. The thought had crossed his mind more than once. Exposing the Coalition would've made one hell of a story. Even back then, Cyrus knew it was a career making opportunity. But the truth was, he'd been won over by the caliber of work the organization was doing. It was ridiculous, in hindsight. Boone and the Red Queen had conned him from the very start.

Averting his eyes, Cyrus bit back the temptation to tell Boone just how close he'd come to splashing the Coalition's secrets across the front page of every newspaper. But the situation was already far too emotionally charged, and Boone was more unstable than Cyrus had ever seen him. It wasn't the right time to rub his face in the revelation.

Turning and walking across the open floor in the opposite direction, Boone's gaze was clear. Cyrus guessed he'd shaken off his thoughts of the past.

"It's really not all that bad," Boone explained. He looked at Natasha while he walked. "As long as your father and Cyrus play by the rules, you'll live to a ripe old age. You can have kids, grow old—still live a very full life.

"Well," he reconsidered. "I suppose the kid thing will be a little tricky. You won't be able to give birth at a modern medical facility."

Cyrus shot Boone a concerned glance. He grinned and placed his fist over his heart. "Can't have any of that medical technology getting too close, after all, or—." Boone opened his fist and made a popping sound.

Without even consciously realizing it, Cyrus was on his feet and striding across the floor. He was three feet away when he felt a warm hand on his forearm and was stopped in his tracks.

"No," Natasha whispered in a ghost of a voice. She pulled him close and slipped her arms around his neck. Her face was milky white, so devoid of color that it looked like flawless porcelain. When she pulled herself close, the only feeling on earth was the heat emanating from her body.

"Is what he said true?" she whispered in his ear.

Cyrus pulled back only far enough to see her eyes. Her face was dry of tears for the first time since he'd arrived. Her eyes were clear for the first time.

"Eartzie specialized in building bombs that couldn't be disabled," Cyrus said quietly. "I would make him disable it himself, but he's dead."

Cyrus felt a tear run down his own cheek. He'd been the one to kill the twisted little troll of a man. If he hadn't, then maybe... Still, he couldn't find the words to tell her that part.

"And you know who's behind this?" Natasha asked without pause. Her eyes were locked on his as she sought out a specific line of reasoning. He recognized she had an idea, something that hadn't occurred to him. She was testing the logic.

"Yeah," he said. "This asshat's my former best friend, if you can believe that. It's him and the dragon lady who put him up to it. I just wish I'd known before it came to this."

"And they're responsible for my mother?"

Cyrus was slow to respond with the slightest tip of his head. He found no words to accompany it.

"Then you can stop them?" she asked with a slow nod and a strange smile that he could only see in the depths of her eyes.

"As soon as we figure out how to disable this thing in your chest, I'm going to rip their heads off," he whispered through gnashed teeth.

Natasha smiled. It looked like a literal weight had been lifted from her soul. "As long as they never have a chance to hurt anyone, ever again. And as long as they *never* get near my sister."

Natasha wrapped her arms around Cyrus and squeezed him with every ounce of energy that she had left. She buried her face in his chest. He could feel smiling.

"Then it's going to be okay," she said in a muffled voice.

Letting go of Cyrus, Natasha turned around quickly and glared at the man who had done this to her. "So, Mister Boone," she said in a crisp, disciplinary voice. "You and I *must* have a talk about the way you've been treating me and mine."

Boone's eyes rose to meet the young woman; her change in demeanor had caught him off-guard. His eyes widened when he saw the semiautomatic held in her single, upraised hand. Cyrus's hand moved to the holster behind his back but he found it empty.

By then it was too late.

The gun in Natasha's hand barked and a spent shell casing clattered across the floor. Boone caught the round just below the collarbone. Natasha stepped forward, advancing on the shocked man at a smooth and deliberate pace. She fired twice more, the weapon's report echoing through the confines of the silent building. With each shot she adjusted her aim, tightening her pattern as the gun recoiled again and again.

The remote device fell from Boone's fingers as she neared. The hard plastic shell was still clattering from the bounce as she stepped within reach of the man. Leaning over his fallen body, she placed the muzzle of the weapon against his chest.

"Right about here, wouldn't you say?" she asked in a cold, dry voice that rang with finality.

Cyrus saw her place the muzzle over Boone's heart. He heard the muffled shot as she pulled the trigger one last time, sending a round into Boone's chest from point blank range.

Boone was still wide-eyed and slack-jawed as he stared at the ceiling through lifeless, unseeing eyes. Natasha had driven him back two full strides with a withering display of gunfire. A bloody pool was already spreading beneath his unmoving form.

The entire assault had taken seconds. For maybe the first time in his life, Cyrus had found himself paralyzed by what he was seeing.

Natasha turned and looked at Cyrus. A proud smile spanned her face. She glanced once at the gun in her hand and then casually, almost comically, tossed it aside.

"My God!" Cyrus sputtered. "Do you know what you've done?"

"Sure do," she said with a proud, bright-eyed nod. "They were using one tiny bomb to hold three people hostage. I can't allow that."

Cyrus grabbed the timer from the floor beside Boone's lifeless corpse and looked at the display. Only twelve seconds remained. He raised the screen for Natasha to see.

"I don't suppose there's a chance he was bluffing?" she hoped.

Cyrus knew that the look in his eye confirmed the worst.

"Don't worry," she said. "Better to go out like this. Living in constant fear isn't living at all. Besides, if you look on the bright side, you've only got one of these traitorous shits left to deal with."

"There's got to be something I can do," Cyrus muttered. But he knew he couldn't. His only recourse was to hold her tight. For once, that wasn't going to be enough. He held her in his arms. It was all he could do.

"Just look out for my family," she said softly. "That's all I ask."

Her body suffered a mild jerk, like a hiccup that happened without a sound. Her eyes pinched with what looked like mild discomfort and Cyrus felt her grow suddenly heavy in his arms.

"Guess it wasn't a bluff after all," she said in a tired voice.

Lowering them both to the floor, Cyrus cradled her in his arms. For the first time in his life, he felt truly defeated. He knew nothing could stop the inevitable.

He opened his mouth to speak, but no words would come. He tried again, but still nothing happened. His own eyes were filled with tears. A pain that was deeper than any he'd ever known had stolen his voice.

Natasha smiled and wiped the tears from one of his cheeks. "It's okay," she whispered in a fading, angelic voice. Cyrus knew these were her last moments, and she was actually comforting him.

She kissed him. One last slow, gentle kiss…served up with the smile that had won his heart a lifetime before. Her lips moved slowly, "You're the best thing that ever happened to me, Jonny. I love you more than you'll ever know."

And with that, she was gone. Her focus never shifted; her beautiful eyes never closed, but the light he'd loved in so many ways simply disappeared. A flame of grace, kindness and love that would burn no more.

Chapter 35

The cool night air bucked against Cyrus's face as he hoisted himself to the top of the five-foot high cinderblock wall. The drop on the inside was more significant, eight feet, but nothing to worry about. He adjusted the pack strapped to his back and took a long, deep breath. The crisp air was a relief, not nearly as cold as it had been on Kapros, but unseasonably pleasant for this time of year in the northeastern United States.

His fingers slid slowly across the marble finish applied to the walls paralleling both ends of the penthouse's wide patio. He'd approached through a service area that occupied the majority of the building's rooftop. It was separated from the patio and hidden by the eight-foot wall. Walking across the patio and stopping near the outer rail, Cyrus took a moment to appreciate the cityscape. The apartment had a breathtaking view of the skyline. With the city streets more than seventy floors below, the ever-present noises of a world in constant motion were easy to ignore.

Pulling a phone from his pocket, Cyrus moved silently through the moonlit night. He approached the pair of wide sliding glass doors that blocked his entry to the penthouse. The alarm system protecting the apartment was top of the line; there were motion and thermal sensors, plus compression pads built into the frames of each door. It was a system that would take considerable effort to crack…luckily, he didn't have to bother.

Dialing a number from memory, Cyrus placed a call. When the automated system answered, he entered a pair of 24-digit codes. After that, he waited only two seconds to hear a pair of soft audio chimes. The line disconnected automatically.

If his information was correct, the chimes indicated the remote override code was accepted by the penthouse's alarm system. It was funny, he mused. With all the money that went into adding features that provided top of the line security, so many of the people protected by such systems were often unable to manage them for themselves. Such foolishness led to a dizzying array of remote access options being built into the high-end systems. Those options that made it easier for the homeowner and the security company to coexist, but they greatly undermined the overall strength of the system.

Still, knowing something to be true wasn't the same as proving it. While it took Cyrus only seconds to defeat the conventional lock on the sliding glass door, he still held his breath as he pulled the handle and slid it open along its track. A distant chime sounded, the security system signaling that one of the external doors had been opened. But it wasn't an alarm. Waiting in silence for what seemed like endless seconds, Cyrus exhaled a sigh of relief when no additional alert was forthcoming. He pulled the door shut and lowered the pack from his back.

As his eyes adjusted to the apartment's darkness, Cyrus slowly drank in his surroundings. He was standing just off a handsomely appointed formal dining room with a long table that provided enough seating for twelve. A massive china cabinet was built into the far wall. Through its etched glass doors he could make out stacks of serving settings and flatware.

To his right was a sprawling kitchen, complete with modern, industrial grade appliances and a massive island countertop. It was an amusing setup, since Cyrus had it on good authority that the apartment's owner never cooked for herself. Still, the open sterile expanse of the kitchen was ideal for his needs. He deposited the backpack on the island and set about unpacking his gear.

It had been four days since he had delivered Natasha's body to her father at the family compound. It was, without question, the most agonizing experience of his life and only the second most heartbreaking. Watching her die in his arms would always be his single worst moment. He'd been powerless to save her. If there was ever an event to top that experience, he hoped the fates would be merciful enough not to let him survive it.

Voss had dealt with the loss in a way that only a man who had already suffered great loss could. He'd knelt over his oldest daughter and wept without saying a word. When he was done, he stood and exited the room without comment. Cyrus knew the man was crushed beyond comprehension. He could relate.

Dargo had suffered no such communication breakdown. He had demanded every detail of what had happened. It was only after a very thorough debrief that Cyrus was allowed to leave the compound. He'd decided he was done with the Coalition long before that night's disaster. It didn't matter that the operations

Monica and Boone had been running were entirely independent of the larger organization. Too much blood had been spilled, too many lies told…and too much life lost.

Though it was never actually expressed, Cyrus suspected that his release from the compound had hinged on his decision to leave the Coalition. He never asked because it didn't matter. He had only two more tasks to perform before he put every bit of that old life behind him.

The first led him to Monica Fichtner's penthouse apartment on the seventy-fifth floor of the Stillson Building. It was an incredible home. One look was enough to convince any rational person that she was living well beyond her means. The penthouse was valued at $3.2 million in the present market; it had been appraised for $2.9 million when she'd purchased it seven years earlier. The fact that the United States system of checks and balances so frequently excluded its highest level executives didn't surprise him, but it galled him just the same.

But while Monica Fichtner had found a position of power that was entirely free from outside oversight, Cyrus reasoned that it was not free from justice.

At least not tonight.

Bracing the last corner of the six-and-a-half-foot long, soft-sided box, the remaining pleats went instantly rigid. The rig was a larger version of the semi-rigid container he'd used on the train at the start of the Paris operation. Only this box was oblong, being only three feet wide, and it used an entirely different set of binary chemicals. At twenty-four inches deep, the box looked like a camper's version of a casket that was missing the lid. The sides were a flexible, collapsible plastic polymer that had been pulled tight across a few sturdy rails to construct a temporary box.

Keeping the lights off, Cyrus continued to work in darkness. He pushed the lightweight rig across the smooth stone tiles of the kitchen floor. He positioned it within a few feet of the island counter which contained a vegetable rinsing station. After retrieving a short section of flexible tube from his bag, he clamped one end over the water faucet nozzle and dropped the other end inside the oblong box on the floor.

He eyed the bottom of the box as cold water began to spread across it. This was an aspect of the job he'd never done for himself. The company had people who specialized in this sort of thing. Plus, under normal circumstances he would've drawn the line long before reaching this point. Generally speaking he didn't have the stomach for this kind of work. Tonight was a rare exception; tonight he had no moral qualms or objections about what was about to happen.

It was justified.

It was more than justified. In fact, there was a certain degree of poetic justice at play that rivaled even the practicality of the methods he was employing.

The water reached the proper level, filling one-third of the soft-sided box. Cyrus had just turned off the faucet when he heard the sound of movement in the penthouse's private elevator. He glanced at his watch. His target was right on time.

When the thin shadowed figure stepped from the elevator, she was accompanied by a pair of stout, hulking men in ill-fitting suit coats. The thin figure stepped further into the room, moving through shadows with practiced ease. Cyrus saw her head toward a series of light switches on the wall and decided to let her go.

The moment the lights of the entryway sparked to life, Cyrus stepped behind the pair of burly security guards with a Taser grasped firmly in each hand. He placed the metal prods of the devices against the neck of each man at exactly the same moment and triggered them without warning. Both men hit the floor before they were even aware they were under attack.

The snapping crackle of the Taser discharge caught Monica Fichtner by surprise. With a shriek, she spun to face Cyrus, her flats slipping on the smooth tile floor. As her arms pin-wheeled for balance, the small handbag slipped from her grasp and clattered across the floor.

Monica's wide-eyed speechlessness was rewarding, as far as Cyrus was concerned. He knew the woman would be too self-important to believe him a viable threat, even after all that had happened. Catching her so off-guard was a satisfying bonus.

She recovered her will more quickly than expected, however, and dove across the floor in the direction of her fallen purse. Of course she would be armed. It was her last line of defense, Cyrus reasoned.

There was a clatter as she dashed across the cold tile on her hands and knees. Her efforts were hindered by the narrow hem of her knee length skirt and the gripless soles of her thousand dollar shoes. Her fingers quickly wrapped around the small designer handbag. She tried to pull it closer to her body and retrieve her weapon only to discover that the bag was stuck to the floor.

Monica looked up from her supplicant position with wide, terrified eyes to see Cyrus standing with one boot on the strap of the handbag. She opened her mouth to protest but Cyrus simply hooked his heel through the inside of the strap and jerked his foot back. The purse sailed from her grip and soared to the far side of the room.

"How dare you!" Monica bellowed, finding her voice for the first time. "Do you have any idea what—."

Grabbing her by the lapels of her blazer, Cyrus hoisted the woman effortlessly to her feet. She let out a horrified whimper, but her countenance shifted instantly back to one of righteous indignation the moment he freed her and stepped back.

"I'll see that you burn for this!" she fumed. She was seething; her anger and fury was far beyond anything Cyrus had ever witnessed, even in the woman's most venomous fits.

She took a breath, winding up for what Cyrus knew would be the mother of all tirades. But he beat her to the punch. With the snap of his wrist, a three-foot long carbon fiber telescoping baton sprang to full length in his right hand. With a single, violent snap of the weapon, Cyrus landed a blow to the side of the woman's neck, just below the jaw and the base of her skull. The sound of her cervical vertebrae shattering was unmistakable. She dropped like a marionette with its strings chopped.

Cyrus didn't take a moment to admire his handiwork. He moved quickly to the unconscious security guards and bound them hand and foot with thick zip ties. He dragged each man to a spare bedroom down the hall and left them behind a closed door. His target was the Red Queen, not the poor saps charged with her protection.

When Cyrus returned, Monica was still in the same small heap on the entryway floor. While her body had been completely paralyzed by his devastating blow, her eyes were open and alert— filled with their own form of crippling fear. They tracked him as he walked back into the room.

Cyrus stood over Monica's body. He bent over and looked directly into her eyes. They were wide, unblinking, and streaming with tears. Still, he said nothing. He just watched her for several long moments, wondering if she had any idea what was coming next.

Without offering a word, Cyrus stood and circled her motionless form. He grabbed her by the back of the collar and dragged her across the foyer, through the family room, down the hall, and into the kitchen. He pulled her paralyzed body until it lay neatly beside the long box filled partially with water. He let go of her collar and heard her head strike the stone tile with a hollow 'thud'.

While he didn't take pleasure in what he was doing, Cyrus knew it to be the most practical means to an end. Plus, it was the only way that true justice would be served. People in Monica Fichtner's position never went to prison for their misdeeds. Too often, it was better for everyone involved if even the most heinous atrocities were covered up and tucked away. Covered up *for the greater good.* There was always some bureaucratic justification for it.

Not this time.

Cyrus pulled a pair of one-liter bottles from the backpack on the counter. He shook the first bottle violently for thirty seconds before setting it aside and repeating the procedure on the second. Circling the counter, he approached Monica's thin form. He still couldn't believe that it had come down to this. So much loss of life. So much damage had been done by two people.

After taking a few deep breaths to steel himself, Cyrus knelt and scooped Monica up in his arms. Her eyes followed him with unblinking horror until he raised her from the floor and her head tipped backward without support.

He carefully lowered her paralyzed form into the improvised vat of cold kitchen water in the middle of the room. As soon as her body was laid out, it became buoyant. Her head floated up and her eyes once more fell upon him. There was horrified recognition there; he knew it without any doubt. She was familiar with the disintegration rig. It was, after all, a Coalition invention.

Pushing the pair of liter bottles aside, Cyrus reached into the backpack once more and retrieved a full-face mask with an integrated re-breather. It looked like something out of a science fiction film with the pair of small flat discs mounted underneath the large facial lens. The twin filters scrubbed the air free of vapor-based toxins with absolute efficiency; all without requiring the use of bulky oxygen tanks.

Cyrus pulled the mask over his head and snugged the seal around the perimeter of his face. Moments later, he'd dumped the contents of the first liter bottle into the cold water vat, fully aware that Monica's eyes followed his every movement.

The real drama wouldn't take place until he added the second chemical. Once more, Cyrus considered how he was about to apply the solution while the woman was still alive. It was a grotesque and inhumane process; the chemical solution was designed to break down organic and inorganic matter alike, reducing it to a horrible primordial stew. That he was doing this to Monica while she still drew breath would've previously been beyond his comprehension.

Now…she had it coming. The files she'd kept hidden on the server were shocking and detailed. Monica had ordered the execution of Eleanor Voss, and Boone had carried it out in the form of a car bomb. Two decades earlier, the mad little bomber, Eartzie, had been contracted to turn that execution into a spectacle. A car bomb wasn't sufficient in Monica's mind. Therefore, Eartzie had rigged the inside of the passenger compartment with a number of preliminary charges. They were attached to acid packs, and they weren't design to kill Eleanor. They were engineered to disperse the corrosive chemical across the inside of the car. Eleanor was made to suffer while the acid melted the flesh from her body. The ten seconds she'd survived must have seemed like a lifetime of torment until, finally, the primary charge detonated, destroying the car and concluding Eleanor's suffering.

Paralyzed, Monica wouldn't feel a thing. No. She deserved much, much worse. She was ultimately responsible for Natasha's death, every bit as much as Boone had been. Just as she'd been responsible for the death of Natasha's mother, Boone's entire field team, and God knew how many others.

With a sad shake of his head, Cyrus added the second chemical to the bath. This was the catalyzing portion of the binary compound that would consume flesh and bone—even most metals and synthetic substances, rendering the entire contents of the disposable tub into an inert, water soluble solution that would ultimately wash down the drain of the kitchen sink using the small handheld pump that Cyrus kept in the bag.

As the contents of the box began to bubble and froth, Cyrus took a deep breath. His own respiration sounded alien through the mask.

He set aside the second empty bottle and stood slowly. Walking back to the sliding glass door where he'd made entry into the penthouse, he pushed the door aside and stepped out into the night. Once he reached the far end of the patio, he removed the re-breather. Then, sitting on the railing at the edge of the seventy-fifth floor, he looked out into the moonlit night.

Pulling the phone from his pocket, he loaded the email app. The message he'd prepared was already on screen. This was his second task of the night. He tapped 'send' on the message and completed his resignation. The Coalition was now a part of his past.

For the first time in a very long time, he felt free. A reasonable person would feel something after what he'd done in the next room—but Cyrus felt numb. Numb to the ruthlessness of his actions…not even a trace of satisfaction for bringing justice to the guilty. Too much had been lost along the way. There was only cold, dark numbness where his soul had once been.

Cyrus had absolutely no doubt that everything he'd done was entirely justified. It was necessary that Monica Fichtner's body never be found. She would be the ghost story that served to keep future Coalition directors in check. Her disappearance would do the agency more good than her incarceration ever could.

People fill the silence with their own worst fears and doubts, he reasoned. Well, he'd just given the powers-that-be a lot to think about…and even more to fear.

Cyrus Cooper will return in…

Halon-Seven

A Note from Xander Weaver:

Thank you for reading "Rogue Faction: Part 2." I hope you've had as much fun reading it as I've had writing it. If you did, you're encouraged to show your support by posting a review with your online retailer of choice. Those reviews make a big difference to new readers, and are a definite aid when it comes to spreading the word about my work. Just a brief statement explaining what it was that you enjoyed is all it takes.

Your time and effort are sincerely appreciated.

Thank you!

—Xander Weaver

Acknowledgments:

What goes into the creation of a novel? Well, every book starts with long hours spent at a desk. In fact, that's what most people imagine when they think about a writer…sitting in a dark room, hunched over a laptop, with the clatter of keystrokes filling the air. But that's only the start. Before one of my books actually finds its way to readers, other talented and generous folks have contributed to its creation. Each of these people helps bring a level of refinement and polish to the final draft that makes it something much better than it was. This is my chance to thank them for their efforts.

First, my thanks go to Amy Lignor for her work as Editor. This is our third novel together and her contributions, as always, are nothing short of outstanding. In addition to being an editor, Amy is also a renowned author. Her "Tallent & Lowery" series has been a smash hit that's filled with action, suspense, and well researched historical mystery.

Long before my book is sent to the editor, however, a group of daring beta readers offer comments, criticism, and feedback that is vital to my revision process. Their contributions cannot be overstated. Every book is a learning process, and these people helped me hone and sharpen this book while assisting me to grow as an author. That's a big deal—not only did they have an impact on this book, but their contributions and feedback helped in ways that will contribute to my future work. I'm fortunate to have their friendship and support. For example, Jamie Dresser put in a profound amount of time reading and rereading the drafts of both Part 1 and Part 2 for this release. Wayne Manke and Tom Nielsen read while keeping a keen eye on critical technical details.

Terri Manke read several drafts and contributed greatly to each. She also read a final proof searching for last minute typos. These people and their tireless efforts helped me refine what was, at times, an unwieldy project.

The cover design is once more thanks to Lee Roesner from Paradigm Graphic Design. Lee has the kind of talent and imagination that makes complicated design look easy. And his work speaks for itself. I love the final cover art.

Last, but never least, I want to thank my wife, Carrie. Her contributions to each book are beyond compare. She listens to all of my crazy ideas and tolerates my need to duck out in the middle of a conversation or meal to jot down notes for a new scene, chapter, or character. She's the first person to read everything that I write, contributing comments and notes that influence my books in ways no one will ever fully understand. She is my wife, she is my friend, and she is my greatest supporter.

Newsletter:

Want to hear about the latest book release, contests, and giveaways?

Join the newsletter:
XanderWeaver.com/newsletter

About the Author:

Thank you for reading, "Rogue Faction: Part 2." The conclusion of this installment takes some definite twists and turns that change the course of Cyrus's life. An interesting fact is that the next book, Halon-Seven (to be released as Book #4 in the series), was actually the first Cyrus Cooper book I ever wrote. In it, I created Cyrus and many of the supporting characters. And when they appeared on paper, I gave Cyrus a backstory that I was compelled to further explore. Dangerous Minds and Rogue Faction were the result of this need to better understand my cast, and invite readers into their world. In Halon-Seven, Cyrus is running from the Coalition and dealing with the loss of Natasha. So, for as dark as the end of this book might seem, its conclusions were preordained. While much of what I write takes on a life of its own and ends differently from what I originally intended, the conclusion of this tale was decided far before its first word was written.

As a lifetime fan of thrillers, as well as science fiction, I love the opportunity to blend both genres in order to create excitement and adventure that includes a sci-fi 'kick'. I write the type of stories I enjoy reading, and I hope my 'recipe' resonates with you as well.

If you would like to be notified of future book releases in advance, you can join my newsletter at www.XanderWeaver.com. Rest assured that your personal information will never be sold or traded.

While I'm working on the newest thrill ride, I frequently post updates to my Facebook (Weaver.Books) and Twitter

(@XanderWeaver) pages. Please follow the progress and join in the fun!

Other books by Xander Weaver:

Book One: *Dangerous Minds*

Book Two: *Rogue Faction Part 1*

For more information, please visit:

www.XanderWeaver.com

www.ingramcontent.com/pod-product-compliance
Lightning Source LLC
Chambersburg PA
CBHW020527020726
47494CB00006B/1659